Chaingang

Chaingang

Rex Miller

First e-reads publication 1999
www.e-reads.com
ISBN 1-58586-079-4

Other works by Rex Miller

also available in e-reads editions

Chaingang
Iceman
Stone Shadow
Slice
Profane Men
Frenzy
Slob
Frenzy
Butcher

Ten Percent of this book
is dedicated to
Richard Curtis Associates, Inc.

Table of Contents

Chaingang

1

Marion, Illinois
Marion Federal Penitentiary

WARNING!

To all personnel/Effective immediately/TFN:
The following rules shall be rigidly adhered to regarding the maintenance of the occupant of Cell 10, **MAX D SEG VIOLENT** Unit: NO PERSONNEL SHALL ENTER THIS CELL FOR ANY REASON AT ANY TIME UNLESS ACCOMPANIED BY ONE OF THE FOLLOWING SUPERVISORS:

1. Dr. Norman
2. Captain Lawler
3. Correctional Officer McCullough
4. Correctional Officer Brock
5. Lieutenant Lopez
6. Myself

ANY VIOLATION OF THIS POLICY SHALL RESULT IN THE IMMEDIATE TERMINATION OF ALL PERSONNEL INVOLVED IN SAID VIOLATION.

Warden Carol A. Dickett

CELL TEN, MAX D SEG VIOLENT UNIT
GENERAL PROCEDURES

1. DAILY FEEDING

a. Cell occupant shall be given food and water three times per day. (SEE D SEG MAINLINE SCHED.)

b. Food is placed on formed feeding tray. Liquid is poured in cup.

c. Open inbound side of feeding port.

d. Place tray with cup in port.

e. Close inbound side of feeding port.

f. Press TALK on intercom unit and announce, "MAINLINE."

g. Cell occupant should then approach outbound side of feeding port. IF OCCUPANT DOES NOT APPROACH, NOTIFY WARDEN DICKETT, DR. NORMAN, OR CAPTAIN LAWLER IMMEDIATELY. When cell occupant is observed approaching feeding port, proceed with next step.

h. Open outbound side of feeding port. Cell occupant should then remove tray with cup. IF OCCUPANT DOES NOT REMOVE TRAY WITH CUP, NOTIFY ONE OF ABOVE-NAMED INDIVIDUALS AFTER CLOSING OUTBOUND SIDE OF FEEDING PORT.

i. After occupant removes tray with cup, close outbound side of feeding port.

j. Observe occupant during meal period.

k. When occupant has finished meal, occupant should approach outbound side of feeding port with empty tray and cup. ANY UNUSUAL OCCURRENCE OR VARIATION OF ACTION BY OCCUPANT SHOULD BE REPORTED IMMEDIATELY. When cell occupant is observed approaching feeding port with empty tray and cup, open outbound side of feeding port. IF OCCUPANT DOES NOT PLACE TRAY WITH CUP IN PORT AND IMMEDIATELY MOVE AWAY FROM FEEDING PORT, ACTIVATE ALARM AND NOTIFY ONE OF THE ABOVE-NAMED INDIVIDUALS.

l. After occupant has placed tray with cup in

feeding port and moved away from feeding port, close outbound side of feeding port. AFTER DETERMINING VISUALLY THAT OUTBOUND SIDE OF PORT HAS FULLY CLOSED AND ENGAGED, AND THAT ONLY THE EMPTY TRAY AND CUP ARE INSIDE PORT, YOU MAY PROCEED WITH NEXT STEP.

m. Open inbound side of feeding port.

n. Remove tray with cup from port.

o. Close inbound side of feeding port, and after visually determining that inbound side of port has fully closed and engaged in auto-lock position, daily feeding may be considered accomplished.

2. DAILY TOILET PRIVILEGE

a. Cell occupant shall be allowed to utilize toilet two times per day. (SEE D SEG SCHED.) Activate five-minute timer.

b. Press TALK on intercom unit and announce, "STOOL."

c. Cell occupant should then approach toilet commode and assume seated position, clothing positioned for utilizing toilet.

d. After cell occupant is seated on toilet commode, open inbound side of feeding port.

e. Place twenty pieces of toilet tissue in feeding port. (USE ROLLS MARKED "MAX/VIOLENT UNIT" ONLY.)

f. Close inbound side of feeding port.

g. Observe cell occupant during toilet period.

h. If occupant finishes toilet and approaches feeding port, open outbound side of feeding port. Cell occupant should then remove toilet tissue. IF OCCUPANT DOES NOT REMOVE TOILET TISSUE, NOTIFY ONE OF ABOVE-NAMED INDIVIDUALS IMMEDIATELY.

i. If occupant does not finish toilet before timer goes off, press TALK on intercom unit and announce, "STOOL PERIOD OVER." Occupant should approach outbound side of feeding port. IF OCCUPANT DOES NOT APPROACH FEEDING PORT IMMEDIATELY, NOTIFY ABOVE-NAMED INDIVIDUALS.

j. When occupant has removed toilet tissue, close outbound side of feeding port.

k. Cell occupant should then return to toilet commode for completion of utilizing toilet.

l. Continue to observe cell occupant to determine visually that all pieces of toilet tissue have been placed in toilet commode, and that commode is flushed in normal manner.

m. After wiping self, cell occupant should assume standing position, clothing positioned for observation.

n. Press TALK on intercom unit and announce, "STOOL CHECK."

o. Cell occupant should bend over in position enabling observer to make visual determination that no toilet tissue or other objects have been placed in occupant's rectum.

p. IF OCCUPANT DOES NOT COMPLY WITH "STOOL CHECK" TO SATISFACTION OF OBSERVER, NOTIFY ONE OF THE ABOVE-NAMED INDIVIDUALS.

q. Following accomplishment of visual determination that no tissue or other objects have been placed in occupant's rectum, daily toilet privilege may be considered complete.

3. WEEKLY HYGIENE PERIOD

a. Cell occupant shall be allowed to brush teeth, floss, gargle, shave, and take warm-water shower one time each week. (SEE VIOLENT UNIT HYGIENE PROCEDURES.)

"Well, ladies and gentlemen," the man in the white coat said, "the twenty-four-page memorandum you've been provided gives you an idea of the special care and attention to detail that goes into the performing of your duties with relation to Cell Ten. We call it the Cell Ten Bible. It is imperative that you learn every word, forward and backward, and never deviate from a single procedure. Your life and the lives of your fellow officers will depend on it." His voice was well modulated, but sounded loud in the small enclosure.

"Only six persons are Cell Ten-cleared to act in the capacity of advisory personnel: Warden Dickett, Captain Lawler, Lieutenant Lopez, Officers Brock and McCullough, and myself." The doctor wore a Formica name tag next to his ID. Dr. Norman was something of a legend in what was referred to in-house as "the program."

"You ladies and gentlemen will never enter Cell Ten for any reason without one of us being present. You will never transport, attend to, or otherwise involve yourself with the occupant of this cell for any reason, such as weekly hygiene, exercise, or medical matters, without observing the strictures set forth in the Violent Unit Hygiene Procedures section, which means a minimum of two supervisory personnel must be present.

"Entering the cell—one supervisor at all times present. Transporting, exercising, or otherwise directly attending to the occupant—a minimum of two supervisors required. Get clear on that. Never deviate from it. Remember—when you are in the immediate presence of the occupant of this cell, you are potentially in extreme danger. Even when all shackles, cuffs, restraints, and lock boxes are in place. The occupant of Cell Ten is . . ." The doctor paused, took a deep breath, and said in an almost reverent tone, ". . . probably the most dangerous individual living. You must never underestimate the risk you are in when you have any direct contact with said occupant, however protected you may be.

"You have been chosen because you have special aptitudes for working around violent persons. You are probably no stranger to D Seg, Disciplinary Segregation. And you've doubtless heard rumors about who occupies Cell Ten. Put all of it out of your mind—everything you've heard. Nothing—no wild rumor, no piece of grapevine gossip—has prepared you for contact with such an individual as this.

"As you know from the documents you've signed and the agreements you've made, you have entered into a contract with your government. That contract forbids you to ever discuss any of the events you will see or hear in your duties—and you will want to tell someone about this. You must not. You must keep your own counsel.

"As officers involved in the Cell Ten Unit, you will begin to learn jargon, a unique vocabulary. The person who occupies Cell Ten is never an inmate, a prisoner, a convict, a con, a fish, or anything but 'occupant.' In your reports it is never 'and then he said,' or 'we fed the man in the cell.' It is 'and then the occupant said,' or 'we fed occupant.' Get used to that euphemism. We never identify occupant, refer to occupant's name, nor—when addressing commands—do we employ any slang name, nickname, or proper name of any kind.

"We never threaten occupant or speak harshly to occupant in any manner. One issues a direct command, when necessary. Should occupant not comply, one withholds appropriate privileges: food, for example, for a daily feeding infraction such as refusal to return tray and cup. Or withholding of toilet tissue, or even weekly hygienic ablution—or, in severe instances, we have the spectrum of physical acts of recourse ranging from drugs to sleep deprivation.

"Are there any questions so far? I'm sure you must have many. Yes?"

"I was reading the hygiene period regulations. I can understand how he—uh, how occupant can never be allowed to retain anything like a toothbrush or shaving gear. But wouldn't it be easier if he had a small plastic bowl and a soft washrag and soap so the occupant could keep himself cleaner and—"

"You must get used to the nomenclature, Officer. 'Wouldn't it be easier if *occupant* had a bowl and a soft washrag and soap so occupant could keep cleaner.' No 'he' or 'himself' please."

"Sorry."

"It takes time. And one hears such questions frequently. Let me give you a rather bizarre illustration to answer your question. Here is a rare survivor of a brush with Cell Ten." He passed a photograph of a guard with a black patch over one eye. "He liked to call occupant by name and take other familiarities while in the cell and during transport. Occupant managed to hide a tiny piece off a bar of soap. We keep it as a kind of training artifact." The doctor produced a small vial and held it up.

"Would anyone like to speculate what this is?"

"It looks like a fleshette made for a .22 handgun," one of the officers said.

"Excellent. It's a dart for a blowgun. The body of the dart is soap that occupant managed to anneal in some fashion, then carefully reshape, harden, and sharpen to the tiny, needlelike dart you see. Interestingly, the feathery material happens to be rodent hair. The machinelike precision of the craftsmanship is quite typical.

"We never found the blowgun itself. Some speculated that it was part of a drinking straw and that occupant swallowed it after shooting the correctional officer. The dart struck the man in the left eye. It had been dipped in feces. The eye became infected, and as you can see—or rather, as you can't see—he lost it." The doctor almost had a note of pride as he explained the way the incident had occurred.

"Occupant's many skills include a martial art of considerable obscurity, one fighting technique of which involves the control of an acute and focused halitosis. It is my belief that one of the occupant's methods of passing time during incarceration is to practice control of vital signs—respiration, heartbeat rate, and so on—and that this martial skill is honed even while wearing a facial restraint. I further contend that one of the ancillary benefits of this odd discipline is increased facility at expectoration. The dart was—in my opinion—expectorated." There were a couple of nervous giggles in the room, immediately stilled by his look.

"The halitosis technique is called 'breath of death.' Bizarre, to be sure.

Once you become better acquainted with the occupant of Cell Ten, I can assure you that you'll find nothing whatsoever humorous about the possibility of occupant spitting a feces-poisoned dart into your eye—from some eight feet away, I should add—or forcing a column of foul exhaled air into your face when you least expect it, blinding you perhaps for just the half second it takes to head-butt you to death, or sever one of your carotids with his teeth." He looked into each face for a moment. He was certain he had their attention.

"And now we come to the reason why we've chosen the Cell. Ten Observation Room for this initial meeting," He glanced at the thick gray curtain behind him.

"Let me tell you a story."

The room itself was unthreatening in appearance: brown steel door and steel-rimmed observation port, over which a heavy security curtain had been drawn. Dr. Norman stood in front of the curtain, facing the small room. The men and women stood uncomfortably close, and there was some of the awkwardness one feels in a crowded elevator as one waits for one's floor. Norman, whose disciplines were in the mental sciences, chose his settings with the greatest care.

"An infant, a male Caucasian baby, was found in the garbage dump outside Kansas City, Kansas. The baby, filthy, on the threshold of death, was rushed to a nearby emergency ward. The infant miraculously survived. It was placed into a local orphanage maintained by the state. It suffered neglect, however, and the child was one of several children surviving when the orphanage was investigated and subsequently closed down. The word 'surviving' is one we encounter repeatedly in this story.

"The baby boy became a textbook victim of the foster care system. There was a pattern of accidents, some reported and some not. Injuries. Abuse and neglect. Once again the boy was abandoned. Once again the boy survived.

"He was 'adopted,' if that is the correct word, by a woman who was in charge of several foster children. Later it was learned that she was a former prostitute with a history of alcoholism and child abuse, and it was while in her brutal hands that the little boy suffered his most traumatic exposure to various forms of sadism.

"Both the child's foster mother and the man who called himself the boy's stepfather kept their charges tied up much of the time. But this child had ways that apparently infuriated them. They kept him in a metal box with a few air holes in it, in a stifling, dark closet, and chained under their homemade bed. He was forced to remain motionless for long periods, usually in total darkness, and to lie in his own urine and fecal matter. When he made a sound he was savagely beaten.

"The man, a known sexual degenerate, began abusing the boy, who was forced to eat and drink from a dog dish, which was also kept under the bed." The atmosphere in the room had grown extremely oppressive. The correctional guards had become more apprehensive as the doctor spoke, and some of them could imagine body odor smells in the small observation room. Coughs sounded loud as gunshots. There was more movement as the men and women grew tired of standing, and the brown steel and beige concrete, compliments of that uninspired interior decorator—the federal prison system—was becoming increasingly threatening.

"A little dog was also tied there with the child, and the animal became the boy's only friend. As with the boy, whose name was Daniel, the dog was beaten and kicked when it made noise, and so both of these poor creatures learned to be obedient together. The punishment that was meant as humiliation, presumably, was a godsend. The child and the dog helped one another survive." The doctor had little need of notes. The occupant of Cell Ten had been his pet project for a long time, and he knew the man's history as he knew his own.

"One day when the child and his companion had been locked in the dark punishment closet, the boy could hear a fight—not unusual in this home. The man, whom the boy thought of as "The Snakeman" because of tattoos that he had, was giving the woman one of her frequent beatings.

"The man threatened to throw the dog out the window of the apartment house they were living in, and perhaps the boy as well. He said he was getting rid of the dog and the boy, and the boy heard him and believed him.

"The child snuck down into the basement of the building, where he had once seen acid stored, found the bottle—which proved to be hydrochloric acid—and poured it into the eyes of the man while he slept.

"The child is now nine years old, and once again he is institutionalized. He becomes the target for more abuse in the reform school—a natural victim, one might say. There are older boys, one bully in particular, who continue to make his life a nightmare.

"The child grows taller, bigger, stronger—and at age twelve he has the appearance of a full-grown man. He kills his tormentor, and that is the point where young Daniel Bunkowski is seriously imprisoned. There are two more killings in prison. He escapes. He runs loose—killing at random. Killing for pleasure. He becomes the worst serial killer in American history. Growing bigger and stronger all the time. When he was captured in the sixties, he'd become a giant, huge—over four hundred pounds and nearly six feet eight inches tall. He had the beer belly of a power lifter who has gone to fat, but with legs like cannon barrels.

"At age eighteen he weighed four hundred and fifteen pounds, had a twenty-two-inch neck, and wore a custom-made size 15EEEEE shoe. By that time he was also perhaps the most accomplished killer alive.

"From the time of his earliest reform school incarceration, he'd devoted himself to mastering countless martial techniques, learning all he could about small arms and demolition, toxicology, man-trapping, camouflage—virtually anything that related to what he considered to be 'the killing arts.'

"He was also a genius. His raw intelligence was such that it could not be accurately tested. His intelligence quotient was so high, it went off every chart—warped every graph. He was technically brilliant beyond measure.

"But his mind did not function in any previously observed manner. He was worse than an animal in some ways, superhuman in others. Clearly he was presentient. He'd developed the ability to sense impending danger. It is his greatest survival instinct. I contended then, as I do now, that he is that rare form of human being called a 'physical precognate.'

"I came across his case history because the government was looking for individuals who would be emotionally, as well as physically and mentally, suited to be trained for special work in the military—hazardous work involving sanctioned assassinations. We were at war in Southeast Asia at the time, and the work was of a most sensitive nature. To put it simply, the government wanted expendable killers. As distasteful as such a program was, it was necessary for our country's prosecution of the war effort.

"Daniel epitomized the sought-after profile: a proclivity for and incredible proficiency in killing, in tandem with prodigious raw intellect. His hatred for human beings was—and is—absolute. He had a built-in survival system that could withstand blast furnace heat, long periods of claustrophobic isolation, or whatever hardships might inflict themselves. On top of all this he had a defensive mechanism that forewarned him of danger. He was the ultimate killing unit.

"Teaching himself, learning from both his omnivorous reading and hands-on experience, he had already learned how to take lives, and had proved that—serially—he possessed a masterful talent, if that's the word, for committing acts of homicide. But the military would give him something of great value—the technology of combat, and all that went along with it. The government, from his perspective, could turn him into a professional killer.

"Through various drug-induced interview sessions using sodium Pentothal, Amytal, the paradyzines, tri-Kayandaminopropene, other experimental drugs then being tried, we were able to learn ways that such a man might be at least partially controlled. We were able to manipulate him to the extent that he could be inserted into situations where he might slake his thirst for killing and serve the U.S. government at the same time.

"Now—once again—through a complex set of circumstances that do not concern you, we have this human monster of our creation close at hand. Under lock, key, and every restraint at our disposal. Here!" He gestured behind him. It was very still in the room, save for the breathing of the audience listening to Dr. Norman's every word.

"Some of you have heard rumors of a killer who has taken a human life for every pound of his body weight . . . of a monster of murder and mutilation. You may think the stories of the killer who eats the hearts of his victims are the work of overactive imaginations. But the rumors you've heard don't begin to describe this living horror.

"You are growing tired of listening to me drone on, standing in this cramped observation room, hearing how dangerous the care and feeding of one convict is, and the extraordinary lengths we must go to for our mutual protection. You may wonder why your government feels that you have a need to know some of the terrible, damning things you've been learning today.

"I ask you now, as absurd as it may sound to each of you, to try as best you can to free your thoughts from malice." He licked his lips and smiled. "Think of this man with pity, if you can. Think of him kindly—as a fellow human—whose beastly childhood rendered him into something other than one of us. Think of him with respect, great respect always, and remember that whatever you send in his direction may indeed rebound. Treat him in your thoughts, as well as your deeds, as you would be treated were the roles reversed.

"Ladies and gentlemen, steel yourselves and see, for the first time, the occupant of Cell Ten: Daniel Edward Flowers Bunkowski." Norman opened the heavy, gray curtain, and the shock wave that engulfed the room was both audible and palpable as they looked down into the pit and met the tiny, black, marble-hard eyes of the massive heart-eater.

2

Waterton, Missouri

At first Mary Perkins thought it sounded like real trouble, a note of seriousness in her husband's warm, friendly tone as he conversed with someone on the telephone. She hadn't been paying attention to what Sam was saying—their phone often rang in the morning, and it was generally something urgent to do with his real estate business. Over the years she'd become used to it. Mary had been sitting at the kitchen table, sipping black coffee as she worked on her grocery coupons and shopping list. But she heard a mild curse and a sharp change in his voice and tilted her head, suddenly aware of what he was saying.

"I know . . . huh-uh . . . no. I promise you that's not going to happen, Bill . . . sure. I'd be concerned too." She knew it was Bill Pike on the other end of the line, having recognized his voice when he'd called and asked for Sam during what passed for breakfast in the Perkins house.

"No. That isn't the case at all. Here's the deal on that: J. T. Delmar of Southland Growers, John Merriweather, and Wilbur Ferrell are the main guys behind it, Bill. Ocie Upton and the Newcomb brothers are in it too—that's who Maysburg Produce Enterprises is, okay? You know as well as I do that John Merriweather isn't about to stand for something like that. John's daughter and his son-in-law are building about half a mile down from you all. You think John's missus is gonna let him put three hundred migrant workers in a camp right in back of their own daughter?" Mary smiled at her husband laughing into the phone mouthpiece, and he winked at her.

"Yeah. I don't doubt they *would* like to get a hundred and fifty thousand for that ground. They done preemerged it so many times, they cain't get *weeds* to make a crop on it, but that's all right. Let me promise you it's not happening. They're going to put it over yonder on some of the Newcomb boys' wooded acreage." He lapsed into Good Ol' Boy now and then out of habit. It went with your chamber of commerce membership if you did business in Waterton. "That's all right. I don't blame you . . . I'd have been worried, too. Okay, Bill, no problem. Talk to you later . . . Sure. 'Bye!" He hung up the kitchen wall phone and sat back down at the table, a funny look on his face.

"Small towns," he said, shaking his head. "They just kill me." He reached for his coffee.

"Don't drink that," she said, getting up and taking his cold cup to the sink, which was filled with dishes.

"That was Bill Pike. Get this: His sister called him. He didn't tell me that, but I know it had to be because Mary Beth works down at the welfare office. Anyway, she calls him and says the Mexicans are here. What Mexicans? he asks. The ones who are going to move out in *back of you!* That's what Mexicans, she says."

Mary poured out the cold ink, and gave him a fresh cup. "Mexicans?"

"At the welfare office to get food stamps, presumably. Anyway, they asked around and found out these were some of the work force Southland Growers brought in to help do the planting. There's six guys in it—calling themselves 'Maysburg Produce Enterprises.' I coulda had us a piece of it, but . . ." He shook his head and jumped over his own thought. He sipped coffee. She was used to his discursive conversations.

"Did you say there were *three hundred* migrant workers?"

"No. I mean—there will be, yeah. When they start putting the crops in. It's about eight hundred acres. It's that ground the Newcomb brothers own across the river." He meant in Kentucky. "They tried to get that ground in back of Bill, but they couldn't get city water or sewage. I didn't see any point in going into all that—it woulda only worried him more. He's about to have a fit. All he can think about are knife fights and robberies. He says, 'The property values will drop to nothin' overnight. But that won't matter none because we'll probably be killed in our sleep anyway.'" He smiled.

"Not all Mexican migrant workers are bad people, you know." Mary checked off the last item on her list.

"Yeah. I know. But you don't want a seventy-five-unit migrant camp being built next door to you." He went on explaining the intricacies of the deal to

Mary, who tried to feign interest. She adored her smart, successful husband. She'd loved him for so many years—they'd been childhood sweethearts. In many ways they had a dream marriage. Over the years the romance had done what it does in so many marriages, but with that exception, they had it all.

For the first years of marriage—the first decade—Mary had stayed on the Pill. They loved other people's kids but had chosen not to start their own family. For the last few years the precautions had been Sam's responsibility, on those ever-dwindling occasions when the matter came up, so to speak.

Even if their marriage had become a bit too platonic, it was a good, solid marriage. There was a wealth of love between them. Mary thought she was one of the lucky ones. She had that rarest of all rarities—a genuinely good man. They were just as hard to find as the cliché said.

She turned the pages of a mail-order catalog while he told her about his lunch date, which was to take place in neighboring Maysburg. It was with an out-of-towner named Sinclair who claimed to be looking for a land investment in the Waterton-Maysburg area. She listened to his enthusiasm with a degree of pleasure, since she knew how much it meant to him to see their little town prosper, as he told her what a good omen it was that all this speculating and entrepreneurial investing was taking place. As with many longtime marrieds, she also read his mind and knew—from nothing more than the pause in his monologue—that he thought she wasn't listening.

"I'm listening," she started to say. "Oh, hon! Look!"

"What?"

"You like this?" She showed him what appeared to be a very plain, dark woman's suit. To him it looked like every other plain, dark woman's suit he'd ever seen.

"Yeah. Mm-hmm. Very nice."

"What!" Her pretty face contorted incredulously. "You don't mean it. They think I'm going to pay a hundred and sixty-eight dollars for that?" He'd never seen a woman like her. She never spent a dime on clothes, even though they had plenty of discretionary bucks. Yet she looked like a fashion plate.

"That's not so bad. Not if it's a really good suit." He had no idea whether it was high or low, but if she liked it, he wanted to encourage her to get it. He loved his wife more than anything, and would have given her the world if it had been in his power to do so.

Material things meant nothing to Mary. She was such a content person. She liked being a housewife and taking care of him, or so Sam felt. She asked very little of life, enjoying people, nature, and their good health. He felt she was also a very spiritual person, but it was something she chose to keep within herself, a private and sweet core that made her what she was.

He tried to give her some money out of his wallet, but she wouldn't touch it. She could be hardheaded, too, but when she was, it was usually for the best.

He changed the subject and talked to her about fashions, which he knew interested her, because he suspected his business stuff was boring her. He knew how boring he could be, but he couldn't help himself. Sam was who he was.

The child of a couple they knew had asked him his age, and when he'd told the little boy he was in his early thirties, the kid had said, "God! I thought you were about fifty!" To the youngster fifty was obviously as old as anyone got. You turned fifty and you died. Everyone had laughed, but inside Sam knew that the boy had seen the emperor sans wardrobe. He often caught himself acting fiftyish.

In business it had been a blessing. Thinking fifty had paid for a lot of land for a street kid from a small town—a kid whose father hadn't handed him a dime. But he wondered now and then if Mary was terribly bored with their admittedly dull version of domestic bliss.

Life was funny. He looked over at his lovely wife. Her robe had fallen open slightly and he could see the swell of her breasts, and the unintentionally provocative pose as she sat with bare legs crossed, absorbed in her magazine. Her legs were as beautiful today as when she'd been a fifteen-year-old cheerleader. By anyone's standards she was an extremely attractive woman.

Any other healthy man married to this woman, sitting across from her and seeing her the way she looked at that moment, would have but one thought: he'd want to jump on her bones. Sam? He had fucking *land deals* running through his head. Life was nuts.

3

Maysburg, Tennessee

Sam had always wondered what Pagoda Village looked like on the inside, having passed it countless times, but he'd never had any reason to enter. Business and pleasure had brought him across the river from his hometown of Waterton often enough, but the local wisdom had it that their Chinese food was tasteless and overpriced—also it wasn't Chinese—and he was less than adventurous when it came to trying new restaurants.

What he'd always liked about it was the mock Oriental architecture. Had he not gravitated toward real estate, he'd have doubtless become an architect, draftsman, or at the very least, a contractor. Buildings intrigued him. His "edifice complex" was one of his standard business jokes.

Pagoda Village's main roof was composed of overlapping pantiles, and the dissymetrical ogee curves shimmered in the noonday sun—if one had an eye for such things. He took his dark glasses off, opened the door, and stepped into the dark interior.

It was typical for an out-of-the-way Maysburg eatery. The town was regionally famous for having forty restaurants, give or take, which seemed to exist only for tourists, persons whose taste buds had remained in embryo, and those couples who—for whatever reason—did not wish to be seen. They were usually dimly lit, chockablock with skimpy tables, plants, and gimmicky decor, and the food was, as a rule, undistinguished.

He felt very odd about this meeting with the man who had spoken with him first a week before, telling Sam he was coming to town for "another party who was interested in buying some rural land." Nobody who bought ground, no serious buyer, that is, ever spoke that way. The choice of words was awkward, making him think that the man—identifying himself as one Christopher Sinclair—was not being especially forthright. Sam Perkins had been polite, and dismissed the call soon thereafter.

A week later his secretary told him Christopher Sinclair was on the line. He wanted to "talk turkey." The party he represented had made up their mind what kind of package they wanted. There was "a lot of money in this deal" for Sam. But there were certain restrictions. It was all very sensitive and hush-hush. "Let's meet and I'll put my cards on the table," Sinclair had told him, suggesting an out-of-the-way place in Maysburg, across the river in neighboring Tennessee.

Everything about Christopher Sinclair was immediately reassuring. He looked like the prototype of a Nashville con artist: big, bulky—fat, in fact—with a dimply smile and a hearty hail-fellow-well-met air about him. Not the sort to be cooking up shady real estate deals in dark beaneries. Or perhaps just that very sort. Beautiful pink skin (the color of a baby's tush, he told Mary that night), glossy, unbitten nails, good suit, and a gorgeous head of snow white, wavy hair.

He could have passed for a southern Methodist preacher on his vacation, or an insurance man from Moline—with "Chartered Investment Consultant" on his business card—until he opened his mouth to speak. As soon as he introduced himself and they started schmoozing "for serious," all glad-hander images were quickly dispelled.

This Christopher Sinclair was one smart, tough cookie. He knew his real estate. And he smelled like Big Bucks.

"You recognize this ground?" he'd said, partially unfolding a copy of a land abstract. A circle was drawn across the squares and rectangles of property lines, a circle in red, smack dab in the middle of some of the best black-dirt cropland in all of North Waterton.

"Sure do."

"My party wants to buy it."

"I've got bad news," Sam said, smiling. "No way." He shook his head. "It's not available."

"Doesn't matter," the silver-haired stranger whispered. "We're going to buy it." He obviously hadn't understood.

"No. See this here." Sam gestured at the parcels of land that represented maybe four thousand acres between the river and East Waterworks Road. "These are some of the biggest farms in this part of the state. You've drawn a circle through the farms of maybe a dozen big landowners. They'd never part with any portion of that land in a million years."

"Ten."

"How's that?"

"Ten big landowners. Well, ten landowners. Some are fairly big. Some aren't. My party is well aware of who owns this chunk of ground."

"No. They'd never sell these parcels. Not a one of them." Sam had already begun to lose interest. He decided he'd see if he couldn't salvage something out of the luncheon date. "What did your party want the ground for—if you don't mind saying? I've got some mighty fine properties that would do just—"

"Hold it, Mr. Perkins." He cut him off immediately. "Don't try to sell me. We're way ahead of you. We know precisely what holdings you have, who you represent, the real estate you're peddling, and so forth. You don't get the picture yet. We want you. We want a piece of ground. We're going to have you take serious cash offers to the ten individuals whose names appear in this summary." He handed a thick sheaf of papers across the table. Sam was already shaking his head. The guy apparently couldn't understand English.

"You're wasting your time. You've drawn a circle that cuts off prime corners of Augie Grojean's riverfront property. That ground was part of a family dispute that took four years to settle in court. That family wouldn't sell that ground for all the money in the world. I mean—Russ Herkebauer? The Herkebauers are one of the oldest families in this county. Russell's brother owns the bank here, for God's sake. That's the Genneret Ranch you've got circled. Doyle Genneret could set fire to a wet elephant with hundred-dollar bills, Mr.—" he'd already started to forget the man's name—"Sinclair."

But within the next thirty seconds Sam Perkins knew that he'd misjudged Christopher Sinclair, and for the first time he began to believe in business miracles.

"I hear you, Mr. Perkins—Sam, if I may? Look here, podna." He unfolded the sheaf of papers. "All those elements have been investigated." He tapped the sheaf with a manicured nail. It was a blur of words about a fifteen-hundred-acre property twenty-five miles to the south. "The Grojean family has just about farmed out that ground by the river. They've got problems even making a crop on some of that ground. If they doubled their present production for the next fifty years, they couldn't touch what *this* piece of land produces annually. We own that. We'll trade it for the ground we want. The family will *fight* to sign the deal. Herkebauer would love nothing more than to take his wife and go to Florida and retire. He's holding on for his two sons. Here's the figure we'll give him, and—see—look at the payout mode. The boys will each get a settlement in managed T-bond accounts, big-time trust accounts. Mr. Herkebauer will think he's died and gone to Heaven."

Sinclair took him through the rest of the stack. Big money was behind this deal. And they'd done their homework.

"I'm not sure you need me, Mr. Sinclair."

"Chris, please."

"Chris. I mean—you've already got this all engineered."

"You know how it is, Sam. Some persons of means like to be circumspect. Careful. Keep everything nice and discreet. My party wants you to handle it because you're the known, local person to do it—you're friends with these men and women. Known most of them all your life, right?"

"Mm-hmm. That's true."

"And that's why you're getting cut in for a slice of the apple pie. We don't want a lot of talk and speculation about this—more than there's bound to be anyway. You know how everybody is all up in arms about foreign interests buying up 'hometown America.' And I think that goes for out-of-towners. Nobody wants people coming in and buying up three hundred acres when they don't know anything about the deal. Makes it all look suspicious. They'll get to wondering if somebody's gonna start burying toxic waste next door." He laughed heartily.

"Are they?"

"Just the reverse. My party is into ecology. We'll clean up, not dirty up. We're going to build the most fabulous thing anybody's ever heard of." His voice dropped even lower. A look of almost evangelical zeal crossed his face. Sam wondered if any of this was for real.

"Might I ask what that would be?"

"The largest ecological research and development center in America. Three hundred acres—now just farmland—that will be turned into the most beautiful man-made park in the United States. And the whole thing will be open to the public in time—like Disneyland or Epcot or Six Flags—a giant theme park dedicated to the science and art of preserving the environment. It's something you'll be proud to be a part of."

"Wow!" Sam tried to swallow. His throat was suddenly dry. "That's quite incredible." He didn't know what to say.

Christopher Sinclair went on at length about some of the work that would be done at the environmental research center, and it sounded like important work. Genuinely beneficial and in fact vital research into such problems as acid rain and the greenhouse effect.

"The project has the name ECOWORLD—at least so far. That may change between now and construction time. But because we don't want any of this to leak out between now and then, we're using a code word. When we call you—or if you call us—let's always refer to the project with this word." He showed Sam the title sheet on the thick summary. RAMPARTS.

"This is a great project. It looks like you'd want to promote it."

"And indeed we shall when the time is right. But remember—we're talking about millions of dollars being expended. Hundreds of jobs will be created. When this thing is turned over to a big agency and the PR guys start doing their thing—can you imagine what will happen to the land values?" He winked knowingly at Sam. "You of all people should be able to see the advantages of keeping this quiet for a while. And if you make a couple of extra bucks in some smart land speculation—" his big, fleshy shoulders went up "—so who's going to complain?"

"Hmm."

"You'll front the project for me, just as I'm fronting it for my party. I expect two things from you—discretion . . . and competency. In turn, I promise you that when you make one of these deals for us, and we tell you our check is in the mail, why, that check *will* be in the mail overnight. And that check will float. I promise you that, too. Okay?"

"Okay," he laughed. "It sounds good."

"It is good. It is golden, my new friend. You're in the real estate business, and we're funding you to buy up a bunch of it and put it all together for us, and keep it confidential and one hundred percent professional all the way. You do that—" he tilted his large, silver-maned head and grinned—and you'll never have to put together another deal. This can set you up for life, Sam."

"I hardly know what to say. It sounds too good to be true, you know?"

"I know. But here it is in black and white. Are you our man for this?"

"I'll do my best," Sam said.

"That's what we want. And we're going to make it the best, sweetest thing you've ever been a part of." He reached inside the breast pocket of his suit coat. "Let's start with the easy ones and work our way around to the toughies, okay?" Sam nodded. "Why don't you get Cullen Alberson on the telephone later this evening, and see if you can't get him to take this off our hands."

"Jesus!" He couldn't help saying it when he looked at the numbers on the cashier's check.

"We want *him* on our side, too," Christopher Sinclair said, sitting back with a look on his face that Sam would later recall as "industrial-strength smug."

The basics were laid out, and they parted company, Sam with the heavy-duty check and the thick sheaf of contracts in hand. Sinclair headed back out of town with Sam Perkins's promise.

He would have many occasions to chew over their conversation. Many things about the deal bothered him, shook him to his core if the truth be known, not the least of which was the awesome amount of money. He was certain he'd stepped into something that was way out of his league.

But the one thing that disturbed him the most was the "why" of it. Why would any party, Japanese, Arab, or extraterrestrial, spend major sums of cash to buy the edges of ten prime pieces of Missouri gumbo? They could buy ten times that amount of ground, better ground in reality, for a tenth of the prices they were going to pay.

The answers, some technical double-speak about "suitability for organic research" according to "soil data" made not a whit of sense. Mineral rights—that's what Sinclair's after, Sam figured at first—until he read the contracts with care and saw that in some cases they weren't even *buying* mineral rights!

Something was jarringly out of place, and though he couldn't isolate what it was, the deal was as unsettling as anything he'd ever been involved with. And that night when he went home after an afternoon of talking with Cullen Alberson, who almost fainted when he saw the size of the check for his "corner ground," he sat and stared for a long time at the title sheet on the summary given to him by the mysterious Mr. Sinclair.

Even the hokey cloak-and-daggerish code word nagged him like a note scrawled on the bathroom mirror in lipstick the color of blood.

The deal was obviously not what it was presented to be. Or perhaps Sam Perkins was suffering from a case of professional paranoia. He'd know a lot more when he found out whether that monster cashier's check was going to float or not. That kind of money had a way of speaking volumes to a man.

4

Marion, Illinois

"How sure are you of the security elements, Dr. Norman?" the stern, faraway voice asked.

"Completely, I assure you." Norman was writing as he conversed, being one of those individuals capable of more than one simultaneous act of logical reasoning. "Two hundred monitor units, that is to say assets, will be in the field." Translation: two hundred armed shooters. "As you know, we have all the technology at our disposal. The coverage on the subject will be total, around the clock, across the compass. Now that the implant has been perfected, there is no way the subject can escape."

"This bug thing—whatever the implant is—it can't suddenly malfunction? The battery can't die or whatever?"

"No." Norman stopped writing and looked at the phone in wonder. He was genuinely offended by idiocy. "The implant is guaranteed to outlast the life of the subject." He went on, seemingly oblivious to the joke he'd made. "It's a perfect opportunity for first-generation research."

"I suppose so. I understand the need for the school, but the idea of letting a killer loose and observing him under field conditions seems . . . I don't know . . ."

"Insane?"

"Right. Insane!"

"Sir, every revolutionary idea has appeared to be insane before it was proved. The first airplane, the first firearm, these things always seem implausible until they work. Look, if I may say so, what are the options? Our resources are not what they once were. The country is being swallowed by foreign interests. We've had to wage costly, terrible wars because of one or two madmen. Had we been able to call on expert assassination teams, we could have saved thousands of American lives. If we must sacrifice a few lives now, to save a great many—perhaps even change the destiny of our country—in the future, then that is a price we have little choice but to pay. Don't you agree?"

"In theory, one agrees. But in actual practice things go wrong. This could explode in our faces. Equipment malfunctions. Computers make errors. Human beings make mistakes. Things happen."

"All those things have been factored in. Just remember this, sir, we're dealing with an art or science that is relatively virgin territory. The subject gives us the chance to study a Bundy, a Green River Killer, a Gacey, a Son of Sam, and the Boston Strangler all wrapped up in one execution machine.

"The implant will function flawlessly. We can obtain instant recovery or—if need be—termination at any moment during the operational phase." Norman could hear the party on the outbound end of the distant connection attempt to voice another cautionary note, and the shielded long lines hissed in disgust.

"When are you planning to do the surgery?"

"Very soon. One more test with the Alpha Group II drug, and we'll bring in the brain implant team from Walter Reed."

"Umm."

"The new drug has been remarkable so far. In fact—" he couldn't help but smile—"there's a curious side effect on the subject. It almost renders him—dare I say it—normal for brief periods following the IVs!"

"Outstanding."

"Yes," the doctor agreed.

They'd come to him nearly a quarter century ago, when he'd been a young doctor with a brilliant future, and they'd challenged him to give them unstoppable killers. He'd put his career on the line for the mysterious agency USMACVSAUCOG, working with his phenomenal find—a subject unlike any other. Everything he'd worked for, every program he'd managed to put in place, had brought them to this point.

He countered a few more flimsy objections, helping another witless bureaucrat to rationalize the impossible and think the unthinkable: they were building a school for covert executions, and the central program would be the study of a mass murderer unchained and allowed to kill or—perhaps—be killed.

For all the man's unknowledgeable questions, he'd learned nothing of the doctor's real agenda, nor had he learned of the secret that would, in fact, control the subject when all else failed. These components would remain as guarded as the equipment that carried and secured their conversation: the OMEGASTAR mobile tracker, which was the electrolink between the COMSEC and NEWTON SECURE systems. These were Norman's trump cards.

"We're good to go," the man finally said, into the ultracomplex guts of the Omni DF *MEGA*plex *S*ecure *T*ranceiver *A*uto-lock locator *R*elay unit and movement-detection monitor. Diode detectors buzzed, freq-counters purred, high-gain preamped scanners searched, mag-field finders countersurveilled, feedback loops engaged, timesharing codes interfaced, spectrum analyzers pulsed, servomechanisms clicked, microcircuitry fed, diffused, flattened, bled into parallel bug-jammers that probed and pried and silently shrieked through subaudible white-noise generators and whose *battery would not die!*

He inserted a patient history form into his typewriter and typed up the brief notes on a subject always near and dear to his heart:

The following is SECRET AND SENSITIVE and is not to be disclosed, divulged, copied, or disseminated:

A prefrontal lobotomy is not indicated although patient cannot be controlled by drugs, due to field requirements. Patient is rendered submissive and potentially nonaggressive by IV admin. of ALPHA GROUP II. A locator implant (laser) is needed.

See attached X RAYS, LAB WORK, CULTURES, CHILDHOOD

PATIENT HISTORY, SPECIAL EQUIPMENT REPORT (on implant device)

CONFIDENTIAL AND PRIVILEGED INFORMATION
NOT FOR DISCLOSURE TO INMATE

FACILITY Marion

PATIENT'S D.O.B. estimate 1950

PATIENT'S NAME Bunkowski, Daniel Edward Flowers

REGISTER NUMBER none/ see rider

RACE Cauc.

SEX	HEIGHT	WEIGHT	C.O.H.
M	6' 7 1/2"	475	Brn

FACIAL SCARS OR DEFORMITIES see GSW diagram for adult head wounds

BODILY SCARS OR DEFORMITIES see childhood burns, wounds

HISTORY OF ALLERGIC REACTIONS none

HEMOPHILIA **CHRONIC ALCOHOLISM** **DRUG ABUSE**

DETAILS psychotrophic drugs incl Haldol, Thorazine, Sinequan et al. Have been ineffective in trtmnt of antisocial, aggressive acts. Drugs such as sod. Pent., Amytal, the paradyzines et al ineffective (hypnosis therapy: See notes re Alpha Group II.)

FUNCTIONAL IMPAIRMENT nonapplicable/morbid obesity

MENTAL DYSFUNCTION schizophrenia, paranoia

EMOTIONAL DISORDER psychoses not resp. to med. trtmnt.

DETAILS see rider

note that patient is graded Level 7/Violent

CURRENT PROBLEM UNDER EVALUATION require brain implant of loc. device

SERVICE Neurosurgery—Walter Reed

CLINICAL RECOMMENDATIONS AND FINDINGS

require implant be undetectable by patient

NOT FOR DISCLOSURE TO INMATE

CHIEF MEDICAL ADMINISTRATOR AUTHORIZATION Norman

PRIMARY CARE PHYSICIAN same

RECOMMENDED PATIENT STATUS (CHECK) ☐ OUTPATIENT ☐ INPATIENT

NATIONAL SECURITY RIDER

The following is SECRET AND SENSITIVE and is not to be disclosed, divulged, copied, or disseminated:

A prefrontal lobotomy is not indicated although patient cannot be controlled by drugs, due to field requirements. Patient is rendered submissive and potentially nonaggressive by IV admin. of ALPHA GROUP II. A locator implant (laser) is needed.

See attached X RAYS, LAB WORK, CULTURES, CHILDHOOD

PATIENT HISTORY, SPECIAL EQUIPMENT REPORT (on implant device)

DISCLOSURE OF ANY OR ALL PARTS OF THIS DOCUMENT IS STRICTLY PROHIBITED BY THE NATIONAL SECURITY ACT OF THE UNITED STATES OF AMERICA.

5

Waterworks Hill

All afternoon it had looked like it was going to rain, and Royce Hawthorne was not about to sit in his tiny, cramped cabin like some victim, hung and blasted and hurting. He was lurching out the door, still half-ripped, but the shock waves of reality had him moving up the hill paths in the direction of The Rockhouse, as soon as he remembered the impending deal.

He'd slept until nearly 1:00 P.M., coming awake, in search of Darvon. His head was a swamp. There were too many gators and snakes loose in there. He downed two Darvon capsules, washing them down with warmish Olympia Light. By the time he popped the top on his fourth Oly, the Darvon had kicked in and he thought he might live after all.

The stash was empty. There was nothing in the pantry. He put on the shirt he'd worn the night before and extracted a small vial, which was nearly empty. He tapped coke out, straightened it into a line, and did it, rubbing his gums with residue and licking his finger.

That's when he suddenly remembered the deal, and the pressure of it snapped him into action. He had fourteen dollars in his greasy blue jeans. He found a crisp hundred in the dictionary (ĭ-MUR-jen-see: Noun. An unforeseen set of circumstances. A pressing need). When he realized that in the entire world he owned the cabin, a half acre of worthless hill, and the awesome sum of $114, he realized what a world of trouble he was in and lurched out into the depressingly wet day.

October spruce trees stood alongside the pathway up Waterworks Hill, boughs heavy with moisture. Hillside milo, russet and golden, seemingly untended, fought to stand tall in fields of rampant blotches of relentless weeds.

Gray clouds the size of aircraft carriers trailed damp tendrils over the upturned face of the Missouri countryside that flanked the hill above the small town waterworks.

Royce Hawthorne had a guy who wanted weight. David Drexel—money in *el banco*. Drexel was so frightened of copping burn, he'd come to Royce for the connect. Homeboy Royce with a rep for dealing and using, emphasis on the latter. Drexel had not blinked at the tab.

Royce could buy weight from Happy. Keep a piece of the rock for recreational usage, turn the balance for a solid profit. Free enterprise in microcosm—right? On the surface it was too cool.

Never mind that it put Royce-baby in a world of shit. That it might hang him up by his num-nums. Why quibble over the little details?

Happy said he would do the thing, but Royce "better not be jerking his chain." No way, Royce promised. You get it—I buy it. How had he let himself get squeezed into this nasty jackpot?

Today Mr. Happy was coming with the Right Stuff. Three thousand down. He'd carry Royce for the balance due. If Royce pulled a hundred-dollar bill out of his pants, he might as well pull his cock out too, and piss all over Happy's $550 kicks.

Happy would have his goon break Royce's knees, stand him in a fifty-five-gallon Treflan drum full of Sakrete, and drop him into the deepest part of Bluehole Trench. That is—if Happy was in a good mood. The man had all the forgiving warmth of a napalm strike.

"The thing"—as he often thought of it—hovered over him, even while he slept. Within minutes of waking he'd always be slammed back to reality by the dangerous game he'd been coerced into playing. What had it taken to pressure him into becoming a secret player, this guy approaching the big three-zero whose sum total of accomplishments was the shack of a cabin, cool enough in summer but freezing in winter, and a funky cocaine jones the size of a big fat dog? It hadn't been easy to bollix and jumble up so many parts of a life that had once been brimming with potential, as his parents, teachers, friends, lovers, and employers had often said. It had taken an iron will, a steely resolve, and the flinty maturity of a nine-year-old whacked out on LePage's Model Airplane Glue. It had taken a mutha of a jam-up.

"Yo, Royce," Vandella the bartender said. "You up early."

"Ten-four," Hawthorne said, shedding his raincoat and tossing it carelessly in the direction of a Rockhouse coat hanger, holding his fingers apart so Vandella could start pouring.

"Hee ya go." He wiped the bar around the shot glass. "Beer back?" He asked.

"Yeah." Royce tilted it back, almost gagging on the taste. Not swallowing the whole shot. The dirty version of "Louie, Lou-eye" blasted from the juke, a three-thousand-dollar Rockola. He gratefully grabbed the cold Oly in his left hand, tilting it and sucking on it, then downing the rest of the shot and washing it down with beer.

"Again?" Vandella jittered behind the bar, singing, "Stick my finger in the hole of love," as he cleaned a glass.

Royce nodded.

"Happy been in?"

"Not since I been here."

"How long you been here?"

"All fuckin' day." They both smiled. They had a routine. Royce drank another shot of tequila. Cuervo in the right, Oly Light in the left, a two-handed drinker he was. None of that lime and salt and ritual, just put down four or five Mex-Tex boilers and get some hair on the bear.

He carried the next pair over to the open blackjack table when he saw who was filling the card shoe. Only one dealer had come in to work so far, the older woman everybody called Tia.

"What's your pleasure, sir?" she asked, professionally. Then she looked up, and his presence registered in her eyes.

She had lots of wrinkles. A bad dye job. White blouse and string tie. Long, Mandarinesque fingernails. But she was his secret ace, and he hoped she was every bit as good as the Feds had promised him.

He got two-dollar chips and bucked heads with the house for half an hour. Making it look good. Getting half-tanked; the Darvon and the tequila and the brewskis all floating around now in the Feelreal Goodzone while he got his balls up.

"Double down." He had twenty against a bust. Let it ride, and was suddenly sitting with 180 bucks, without help, and feeling the power.

He pushed two hundred out. Caught a pair of face cards and edged Tia by a point. Four hundred and change.

Got chicken and slowed down for about an hour. Eased back on the booze, letting Vandella kick a free Oly over now and again. Nursing six bills.

He lost eight hands in a row. Bet a ten and stood on fourteen and she took it.

Bet ninety and was down one eighty and change. Bet the one eighty. Changed his mind and swept it all back but a dime. Lost.

Pushed it all out again and caught eighteen. She hit seventeen and caught a ten. He won. Ended up with eight hundred bucks.

Bet it all and about crapped when Tia turned over a bright red king. He was sitting there with a nine and a seven, and he put his stack of chips on it and stood. She flipped the hole card, and it was a six. She tapped it and broke her back, and Royce had to go wee-wee real bad. He pocketed his sixteen hundred-dollar chips, toked Tia half his change, and excused himself.

When he came out of the room with "Trouser Snakes" on the door, there was Happy and his bonebreaker, Luis. Luis was a big, dumb goon. He'd been a pro fighter, and the word was he liked to spar with kids and hurt them. He had a face that resembled the bad side of a heavily cratered planet, and fists like cast-iron doorstops.

"*¿Que pasa, amigo?*" Happy called to him jovially.

"*Nada.*"

"My man," he told Vandella, who carefully poured tequilas, "whatever my amigo wants."

"Less sit," Happy said, smiling only with his mouth. "So." He drank. Licked his lips. Nodded. Said "So" again.

"So." Royce smiled.

"I think a cold one would go down real slick," Happy said, pulling the fourth chair out and putting his cowboy boots up on it, getting mud on the chair seat.

"Yeah."

"*Cervezas, por favor,*" he told Vandella without raising his voice, as if he knew the bartender would hear it. Then, in the same tone, as if he didn't care who heard what, he asked Royce, "You gonna take the weight or what, amigo?"

"Sure!" It caught him off guard. "What you think, Happy?"

"Hmm?"

"Don't I always?" Big smiles all around. Big buds having a pleasant drink together.

"Hub?" Happy suddenly had appeared to have lost his hearing altogether. Very hard to talk to. Luis looming at his side.

"Don't I always?"

"Yeah, bro, but you an ounce-pouncer, senõr. No offense. I wanna know you gonna take the weight for true now." Still the fake smile through Columbian tan and expensive teeth.

"No problemo."

"Okey dokey." He laughed his loud bray. Looking at Luis. "I like that: no prob-lem-o." The ferocious-looking dummy beside him tried to look like he was smiling too.

"This is King of Peru now, right?" Royce was going to play it out straight to the end. He even sounded concerned.

"Zorro-d'Oro. El Primo-dreamo. You wanna leetle taste up front?"

"Oh—" he spread hands "—not nec-essary." Getting into it. "Satisfaction gay-ron-fucking-teed, amigo." A hand reached into inner recesses, came out, slid across, and laid something in Hawthorne's palm. "Horn some of this li'l girl up your snout."

"Excuse me for a minute?" Royce pushed the chair back and started for the "Trouser Snakes" sign.

"Be my guest," Happy Ruiz called to him in a loud voice as he headed for the john. Jack Eigen from the beautiful Chez Paree—"Be my guest."

Royce turned with a pinched grin on his face. "Be right back."

"Muy bien."

He went into the men's room again and did some of the blow. It knifed through him, getting his head right for the first time since he'd opened his blinkers. He rubbed his nose, came out, and walked over to the table where Tia was about to deal a customer. He threw his pocketful of chips down on the felt twenty-one layout.

"Let's ride that. You want to?" he asked, those being the magic words. For whatever reason, she wasn't with it. The woman began counting, stacking fifteen chips with 100 stamped on each one in green and yellow. Her eyebrows, painted an inch above where they had originally grown, arched another half an inch as she dealt him in automatically, flipping pasteboards to the three of them.

"You got it, sir," she said. Half a beat late. The encoded response, all right, but clearly she was just registering what had happened. The end of her first shift, probably. The woman was tired. She was human. What the hell.

He stared at seventeen, really starting to sweat. Maybe that stuff about the unknown capabilities of the human brain has some basis in scientific fact—he felt as if he'd known she was turning up an ace for herself the second she began to turn the card, giving herself a blackjack and him a death sentence all in one move. If she turned up an ace, she might as well break out a tarot deck and deal him a death card and be done with it.

It hit him like a lightning bolt as he visualized her raking chips. He'd say—what? Can I go shy? She would have to tell him no—sorry. Rules of the house.

He could feel Happy and Luis staring holes in his back. Wanted to whisper *What are you doing, honey? You're gonna kill me* in the loudest stage whisper in history. Watched her color a little as she snapped back into gear, vanishing the ace and taking another card as smooth and cold as ice—right under the other customer's nose.

Her little red five was like a 10:59 reprieve from the warden. The other guy stood pat. He stacked fifteen hundred dollars on his sorry seventeen. Watched her clobber her fifteen with two taps, the retrieved ace and a natural ten.

"That busts the house, gentlemen, nice going." He breathed again, raking the chips over and filling his pockets.

He toked her, willing his hands not to shake, and strolled back to the table.

"I thought you was changing your mind. You didn't like my stuff and was gonna play cards for a while." Happy was not happy.

"Shit no, bro. That was outray—! Hey! What chew talkin' about?"Royce was now happy enough for the pair of them. "You want some now—" he made the money sign with first finger and thumb—"or what?" he asked in an innocent tone.

"Whatever makes everybody happy," Happy said, as Royce Hawthorne reached for the three thousand in Rockhouse money. All according to somebody's master plan, right? Right.

6

Waterton

Mary Perkins, only half-awake, first wondered if it had all been a bad dream, hoping that it had and she'd be able to shake herself out of this darkly imagined history. But the knowledge that it was real, Sam being missing, came and enveloped her in its cold arms, and she shivered, reluctantly getting out of bed, and struggling into her housecoat.

It was not cold enough to turn the heat on yet, but the October night air had turned chilly, and she went to the bathroom, peed, looked at her badly tousled reflection, and drew the bedroom curtains open. She was still in their house at South Main and Park, and her husband was still gone.

Her reflection in the bathroom mirror had been no help. Normally Mary Perkins was an extremely attractive woman, but at that moment, in her eyes she closely resembled the Bride of Frankenstein. Her hair was standing straight up, as if shocked by a mad scientist, and sans makeup, she looked wan in the rude light. The rumpled sheet she'd clung to in the night had impressed deep sleep lines into her face, and they crisscrossed the right side of her cheek and forehead like ancient knife scars.

One morning—it would be a week tomorrow—Sam had taken a shower, dressed in his charcoal suit and red and black rep silk tie, eaten a nonbreakfast of half a glazed donut, a juice glass of OJ, four cups of coffee—black—and, suitably caffeine-wired, had kissed her and headed out the door. Presumably for work.

That was last Friday morning at roughly seven twenty-five A.M. He was invariably the first one there. Myrna Hyams, the elderly receptionist-secretary, was always on time at eight-thirty, when the office would officially open for business.

Sam was successful as only you can be when you're the "real estate man" for a small agri-community. His was, in fact, one of only two local agencies, and he'd just finished putting together an incredible deal for several of the local farmers. He was a great provider, well liked by all, and his health had been generally excellent.

But the preceding Friday morning he'd left the house, driving down Main, northbound, turning left on Maple Avenue and going around behind the block of buildings in which Perkins Realty was situated between Ed's Gulf Station and P.J. Thatcher's State Farm office, and parked their car. Somewhere between the time he'd locked the car door and started to unlock the back door of his office, Sam had disappeared.

She'd called the office, worried, when he hadn't returned home that evening, and got the standard recording. She went over and asked Owen Riley's wife, Alberta, would she mind running her down to see if Sam was working, late and had forgotten to call? She saw the office dark, assumed he'd become involved in a deal somewhere, and had Alberta run her back home. But when he hadn't shown up by ten-thirty, she was on the telephone calling the police and every hospital within fifty miles.

A guy out East she didn't know, someone named Lenny who'd gone to school with Sam, had phoned and left word for him to return the call. She didn't tell the caller anything.

She phoned the Waterton chief of police, Marty Kerns, at home. Tried the regional highway patrol unit out at Satellite J. Called all over town, phoning everybody she could think of. Nobody had seen Sam that day.

Around midnight Myrna Hyams's party line cleared up and Mary learned that Sam had never made it in to work.

"Myrna, how is it you never called the house to ask if he was ill?" she'd asked, rather more pointedly than she'd intended.

"I just assumed he was out showing properties or something. And then when he hadn't shown up by late afternoon, I did try to phone, but your line didn't answer."

"I'm sorry, Myrna. I went to get groceries about three-thirty."

"So I just assumed maybe he'd had to run you somewhere or something. I guess I did wrong. I should have called—"

"No. That's perfectly—"

"I should have called back. Did you call the hospitals?"

"It was the first thing I thought of. He's probably okay. I better get off the line in case he'd try to phone. I'll let you know if I hear anything. You do the same, okay?"

"Sure, Mary. I will. Call me when you find out something. Please?"

"Course I will. Sorry to phone so late. I'll let you know."

The women hung up. Neither of them had thought to mention—was Sam's car out in the parking lot? Later Myrna would admit that she'd stayed so busy with paperwork, she never thought to look around for his vehicle. In the morning the police noticed his car, and it became an official investigation.

Saturday and Sunday Mary Perkins had stayed close to the phone. But when he was still missing on Monday, she started reaching for straws: phoning the FBI for one thing, and then getting in the car and starting her own hunt.

By midweek she'd been everywhere she could think of, asking around, asking friends, casual acquaintances, Sam's beer-drinking buddies of old, anyone she could think of who might have remembered seeing Sam on Friday morning. She stopped in every merchant's on North Main: First Bank of Waterton, O'Connor Motors, the doctor's office, Judy's Cafe. She went back down South Main to Wilma's and Joe Threadgill's and Dale's Tires. Nobody had seen Sam.

Mary had worn out her welcome with the local cops, and she could tell Marty Kerns hadn't learned a thing. The FBI had blown her off, and everybody else sort of shrugged and said—"We're doing everything we can. He's gone up in smoke and we can't figure out what happened to him."

After six days of it, she was very tired and very worried. She'd slept "like the dead," as her deceased mother used to say, and yet she felt as if she'd been up for thirty-six hours straight. Exhausted, red-eyed, and sick to her stomach with fear, she picked up the phone and called her old boyfriend.

7

Waterworks Hill

Royce Hawthorne was shaking. It was cold in the tiny hillside cabin, but he didn't feel like building a fire. He was sure it would be warmer outside. The brightness of the day shone through the grimy windows. He threw some clothes on—the same old shirt and greasy pair of jeans—pulled on his scuffed cowboy boots, splashed icy water on his face, grabbed sunglasses, and lurched out the cabin door.

Outside it was summertime! The sun was blazing hot on his face. The sky was as blue as it ever gets, at least over North America, and it was a day for the fast movers: the jet jockeys from Scott AFB, and the T-38 pilots out of Eaker all overflew Waterton regularly. This morning there was a big tick-tack-toe game overhead; a crosshatching of contrails covered the blue. The fresh lines were as bright as white paint, as white as pharmaceutical cocaine. Where they began to dissipate, they had the look of downy cotton pulled out in a long strand.

Hawthorne stood eyeballing the perfectly crossed vectors, their straight-arrow pathways intersecting and then softening, dying, vanishing back into nothing.

He took off his shades and rubbed sleep or whatever it was that was gumming up the corners of his eyes. Still a little groggy and hung over, he needed to brush his teeth. Drink a brewski. His mouth was foul from too many tequila shooters and ghetto gang-bangers.

Royce could scarcely believe his deal had gone south on him. That was supposed to be later. But this business with Drexel was too off the wall for words. He felt that old Rockhouse anxiety attack that he'd experienced at the blackjack layout trying to resurface. He had trouble grasping what had happened. Drexel! Of all people to fuck him over, it's Mr. Straight. That preppie hippy dippy yuppy wimpy pimpy prince. Folding on him. Then with the melons not to take his calls.

He'd phoned maybe a dozen times, each time getting the two rings and that suck-face recorded message that he was "unable to come to the phone right now, but if you'll leave your name and number when you hear the tone—" It had tested all his willpower not to leave a screaming threat on his machine, but fortunately he wasn't quite that stupid or that high.

He tried to analyze what it meant. He couldn't. The guy had been golden. *Golden.* Where did this leave him? It left him between the hardscrabble and a rock crusher was where it left him: high and dry and broke and owing and holding serious weight. A whole mothering load of that Peruvian flake. Happy was right. He was an ounce-pouncer, señor. He should have stuck to twenty-one. He'd stepped into the deep end of the pool, this tadpole.

What in hell was he going to do? Call the cops? *Sue* Drexel? He couldn't move that kind of weight for that kind of dough. And giving it back to Happy was out. There had to be a way to save the deal. He blinked his glazed eyes, massaged his aching temples, ran his fingers through his long, stringy hair, and put his shades back on.

The edge of Waterton Cemetery was visible from where he stood. Just the extreme northeast fringe, where they buried the paupers. Unlike its manicured, golf-course green sister burial ground to the southwest, this edge was over-grown with weeds, and covered in a carpeting of dead grass and rotting mulch. There was a thick tree line to the right.

Looking down at the pauper's field, he was suddenly conscious of his aloneness. The empty mud of the hillside baking in the hot sun, the desolate fields below—flat from tree line to horizon—the look of the forgotten burial place, all hit him. He thought of his family's grave concerns, pun intended, their unanswered prayers, the countless families like his own whose forgotten histories were etched in dated stone.

Just as he put his sunglasses back on, he saw the movement. It had taken a couple of heartbeats to register. He caught a fleeting glimpse of something—a man in motion coming through the tree line? Brown clothing, so he wasn't a hunter. Not a game hunter, anyway. Although, Royce told his paranoia, some of these idiots around here were dumb enough to go out in the woods in their macho camouflage gear. "He didn't have no orange on, Your Honor" was a manslaughter defense around these parts.

Royce's sinuses hurt. He felt like he might be coming down with a cold. Well, that could be fixed. Coke paranoia pulled his mind back off the lines and he concentrated on the tree line. He saw him clearly. He was conscious of the fact that his firearms were all in the pawn shop.

He'd taken to wearing a little Legionnaire Boot Knife in a sheath tucked down in his boot. It was inside, naturally. He went in and got it and rolled his left sleeve up and quickly duct-taped a small black leather sheath to the inside of his left arm. He taped it very tight, but a hard pull and seven inches of razor-sharp 440-Stainless, Made in Japan, would be in his hand. He rolled the left sleeve back down, left it loose, and eased back into the doorway. He'd lost the man.

He stood and watched, feeling like Lionel Hampton was pounding out "Flyin' Home" on his face, and just about dirtied his britches when the man came out of the wisteria fifty yards down the hill from him.

"Howdy," he called to him.

"Hi." It was a kid. Maybe twenty, nineteen—empty-handed. But he reached inside his jacket when he was twenty feet away. Mentally, Royce was planning the dive to the deck, figuring how he'd time the throw. The kid pulled a square of paper out. "Mr. Hawthorne?"

"Yeah?"

"Um—Mrs. Perkins is tryin' to reach you on the telephone. She called Daddy when she couldn't find your number. He told me to give you the message." He took the smudged paper. A country hand had printed, "Mary Perkins. Reel important," and the number. "Daddy said bring it up here." He shrugged and turned, moving away.

"Oh, hey. Thanks. Uh—don't I know you? Aren't you Beaudelle Hicks's boy?"

"Yes, sir."

"Well, would you please tell Beaudelle I really appreciate it?"

"Okay."

"Thanks for making the climb."

The kid nodded and disappeared in the wisteria vines. The kid could walk. Beaudelle lived on King's Road, in the field next to the cemetery. Hawthorne didn't have a listed number because, in fact, he didn't have a phone.

Mary Perkins. "Reel" important. He went inside to get his keys, wondering if somebody they'd gone to school with had died.

8

"The Hole"/ Cell Ten Marion, Illinois

In a hard pool of saffron light, locked within the bowels of the "Max," bound, chained, shackled, tethered, and restrained, the beast sits. Waiting.

Deep inside D Seg, Disciplinary Segregation Solitary Confinement—called "the hole"—America's only level seven inmate sits in heavy chains; silent and unmoving.

Huge. Beyond anything you can imagine. Arms and legs like steel tree trunks. Butt, belly, and upper torso heavy and ugly with great rubbery tires of hard fat over the body muscle. Scarred, dimpled face partially covered with a mouth restraint, a "biter," the head appears to sit directly on the torso. The gigantic boulder of a neck is not visible. That part of the face that shows is not unlike a mound of wrinkled dough, but for the eyes—which are tiny, hard, black, and unblinking. There is no life in the eyes of the beast. They are unmistakably a killer's eyes. But these eyes see nothing.

He is far away, inside the nightmare of his strange and amazing mind. Deep within his head he is lost, as free and unbound as a wild dog running through the hills. Several levels of the beast-man's complex brain are at work.

His first books were encountered while he was in a foster home. He learned something that gave him an edge, and the book, which happened to be an adult instruction manual and not meant for the eyes of children, discussed in clinical detail certain vulnerabilities of the human body. He seized on this scrap of information as if it were the Rosetta Stone, using it to decode one of the mysteries about death. He saw that books and other printed matter, when applied to actual experimentation, could further enhance one's ability to destroy an enemy. He began reading for self-defense.

Where are books kept? In public libraries. Logically then, that was the next step: to penetrate the libraries and obtain all the relevant information he could lay hands on. Already adept at swiping toys, comics, candy bars—kid stuff—he graduated to library books. He preferred stealing them to checking them out, on principle, and so Daniel began his lifelong affair with the library system.

Reform schools and adult jails did not offer the wealth of literature one could find in Kansas City's public libraries, but there one could attend impromptu classes taught by street professors of B & E, armed robbery, escape and evasion, identity change, disguise, unarmed combat (from street-fighting to sophisticated martial skills), demolition, and a thousand other nasty subjects from con stings to murder modes.

He would use this information to get better data, since he was aware that these were failed exponents of their respective spheres of expertise, but in many cases their experiences could point the way for him. He soaked up information like an immense sponge, always seeking more.

By the time he'd done his second bit in prison, he had probably ingested (sometimes literally!) twenty-five thousand stolen library books. He once computed his total of overdue fines, and it was in seven figures. He'd swiped everything—from elegant, rare, quarto-size volumes of arcane subject matter to massive coffee-table books which he smuggled out under voluminous shirts and overcoats. He left many a little old lady gasping at the sudden downdraft of noxious sewer stench as he clomped loudly through dusty reference rooms in his gigantic 15EEEEE combat boots.

What did he do with the books? Think of a huge, wrinkled desert that stretches across the mindscape of the imagination. This is the monster's brain. For thirty years or so he's used this desert as his private dumping ground for information.

Every wrinkle is deep, like a chasm; a dangerous, deadly repository filled with stolen library books. He reads the books, sometimes eats pages that he particularly likes—one of his weird and inexplicable habits—chewing the corners, sucking the foulness out of them, devouring special passages that somehow imprint themselves on his remarkable memory.

His memory banks are not the same as yours and mine. At the heart of his brain there is something akin to a mental computer, and it is this oddly efficacious organ that retains data for him.

His is no "photographic memory," which he knows to be a misnomer, but is a freak of nature known as eidetic recall. Perhaps a part of the gift of physical precognition is the essence of this ability: to retrieve those shreds of seemingly forgotten knowledge that become input relevant to specific situational confluences.

At the moment he is reading from the pages of a scientific quarterly he once scanned for pleasure: "Massim Matrilineal Reincorporation and Kula Ring Rituals." He is reading, mentally, about his favorite subject. Rereading and savoring the bizarre anthropological studies of Massim mortuary practices. Considering, with the greatest pleasure and fascination, the cultural implications of eating the dead.

But his mind does not work the way an ordinary man's does. As he mentally screens the retained word groups, graphs, sometimes entire pages at a time, he brings to the reading greater focus, concentration, and specificity. When most of us read, it is a passive act, but in the beast's labyrinthian brain recesses, his computer searches for stored data. Searching his spectacular knowledge of the clinical disciplines and general sciences, he probes for hidden gold: some piece of information that, when retrieved and applied to the subject matter at hand, will give him—once again—that sharp and lovely edge.

A remembered and reread phrase has triggered a flow of images, and he scans them, letting them flow through his subconscious as he reads the now familiar word blocks: he senses blood pouring from extremities, secondary anatomical targets, superior vena cava, pathology of death fetishes, inferior vena cava, theoretical fluid mechanics and applications of Cartesian and general tensors, right auricle, hydrastatic wave-effect stress in surface flow, right ventricle, molecular symmetry in abiogenetics, pulmonary artery, aliphatic open-chain structures.

And as the subconscious triggers *open-chain structures,* yet another level of his brain considers the chain—his "flexible killing club"—and the chains that bind. Considers tension, specificity of heavy-metal laws, kinematics of motion, vector algebra, angular momentum theory, quasi-conformal variationals in isometrics, self-mastery practiced as a physical or engineering science, elliptical intuition, aura-manipulation and wish-fulfillment application to the loosening of bindings, essentials of quantitative prediction and advanced muscular control. These assert themselves. Test the bonds. File automatic situation reports.

The beast is aware of these intrusive thought associations only in the most subliminal way as he senses severing of pulmonary artery, raw umbles, mucoprotein absorption, human and animal spoor, application of nonmetric affine geometry to the healing arts, pulmonary veins, geodesist survival vaults, left auricle, fundamentals of vertebrate rhythmic contraction of life-support pumps, sevenfold man in phylogenetic transition, left ventricle, involuntary organ donations, oracles and auricles, dimensional space and karmic mythologizing of physical nonspace, the human aorta, images that flow by as he scans and senses related possibilities.

Good enough, the beast thinks, mentally reading those words, the closest he comes to telling himself a joke, letting his thoughts run free in lost wordplay through the mortal ritualistic eating of the dead on an island that bears the name. A pun—for someone else. For him it is a fantasy trigger, and he thinks of a heart he took, fantasizing, as he has ten thousand times before, about the boundless pleasures he recalls from the consumption of his enemy's life force.

The beast makes an involuntary noise under the facial restraint, coughing loudly into the biter. A harsh and frightening sound like the attempted ignition of a cold engine. The sound of an outboard motor's initial cough as the starter lanyard is pulled. The barking, metallic noise of a recalcitrant lawn mower. It is the sound of "occupant" laughing.

Does the sudden sound jar him or is it something else? Whatever early-warning system protects this strange, anomalous creature suddenly shuts down all his thought processes. He no longer reads, puns, fantasizes, or scans the bloodied, inexplicable darkness of his mind. He is back in the now, physically and mentally in Cell Ten of the hole, in Marion Federal Pen, and inside his head he pours blackness into his mind until it is absolutely empty and black as night.

Slammed down tight in solitary confinement of one sort or another, beyond the fringe of sanity, Daniel Edward Flowers Bunkowski has become master of his own inner wellspring. Calling on deep paranormal reserves, forcing himself through the walls of normalcy, he has learned to control his vital signs: to slow and still his breathing and the beating of his strong heart, and to freeze his mind into a state of perfect calm.

The beast-man has almost stopped breathing. This human who can hold his breath for four minutes, this monster who can bring his own powerful pulse-beat almost to a standstill—he closes his mind to the absolute blackness, imagining a black balloon dropped into an ocean of ink.

Imagine the balloon floating in the dark, inky sea. Now prick a tiny hole in the top of the balloon, and as it sinks, pour into it a stream of white milk. White pouring down into black, sinking, pouring, falling, the thump of his heartbeat now virtually stilled. His mind filling with bright, white milky essence. White as purest snow. Blank paper. And on the blankness of his receptor screen his presentient warning system keys a single word.

It prints a word across the blankness of his thoughts, bright red neon letters on dazzling white:

WATCHER

He feels the surveillance in the way that a hunter's prey will sometimes intuit another presence, perceiving intangible cross hairs of a silent gun. The awareness, the survival instinct, causes the hairs on the back of his massive neck and head to stand straight up. His hard, cold eyes blink open, and he looks in the direction of the observation window above. Where he senses human eyes watching.

Dr. Norman and the team from Walter Reed hover around an immense prone form, as they monitor the deep drugged state of the subject. One more time—after the brief recuperation period and final interview session—Alpha Group II will be employed as the insertion phase is accomplished.

"He's ready." An anesthesiologist checks vital signs as they make certain the life-support units are functioning perfectly. It is warm in the maximum-security OR. The chief surgeon asks for a wipe, and a nurse mops perspiration from the man's brow below his surgical cap.

"What I want to know is how it managed to swim this far inland." An explosion of laughter. Norman's cheek muscles clench under his mask, but be has been forewarned. All great surgeons have their own style. This one indulges his flair for operating-room comedy. But he is the top man in the ultrahigh-tech field of laser implant work.

No blood from a cranial saw will paint Jackson Pollock—like artwork across the surgical gowns. The subject may not even discover that an incision has been made. Only the tiniest portion of the head is shaved, and care will be exercised that this will not be visible to the subject.

The small patch of bare skull is washed. Anointed with alcohol and other mysterious solutions. Meticulously dried.

The senior cutter examines the results, nods his approval, and holds out his gloved hand for the marking device. Takes it. Makes marks. Drops the object in a tray. The laser is in readiness.

"Let me see that X ray for a second." He looks through it, makes a show of holding it to the light. "Yes. Just as I thought. This mammal has anthrax!" They all break up again. Dr. Norman grits his teeth.

"Okay." Without further jocularity he burns his way in through the skull. "Jeezus!" he says. The stench is overpowering. Even through the tiny "window," the subject's brain stinks.

Driven hard by a powerful wind, a loose bank of vapory clouds scuds swiftly across the sky of his mind. He feels his face in a gust of wind, misty rain, spray driven by the wind, and inside the beast's mind, his eyes open.

A row of corpses stiff as window mannequins, eyeless store-window dummies, their waxy faces liquefied and melting. Blue, Catch, Hardname, and Pluck, eyeless corpse mannequins, faces dripping, sit up and begin a centuries-old ritual, the ballet of pain.

Something alien courses through him.

Melting dummies jerk in the frenzied spasm of the devil dancers, tapping call to nightmare, epileptic seizure of the snake people, deathdance of the voodoo drums.

He has been drugged, he realizes.

The clouds churn and scumble, tossing into a cold, thick, white mist that keeps moving faster and faster, as window mannequins, time-compression film of dizzying sky.

The pull of the drug is strong.

Mortuary ritual and kinship in Bwaidoka, obesity as promiscuity viewed by therapeutic-statist praxeologists, Sudest Island Death Rites, themes that harden into book titles. Data retrieval. Wordstream.

A stream of vapor clouds his thought processes momentarily, as the voice cuts through the icy mist of drugs:

"—am your friend. You will be—" Identification of the voice. It is Dr. Norman, head of the program. Sodium Pentothal? Perhaps the new one he's been experimenting with; the one he calls Alpha Group II. An ice mass splinters, showering its shards through his mind.

"Daniel, it is Dr. Norman."

Daniel. Dr. Norman. Names. The name is filed. Dr. Norman has spared him discomfort.

Dr. Norman is retrieved through the haze of drug-induced confusion. The Physical Precognate: Stimuli and Response Beyond Self. Other titles.

The voice has been identified.

Inside his mind he sees the doctor saying, "I recommend a thyroid function test for Mr. Bunkowski to see if he needs some thyroid replacement medication." The nurse makes a joke, and the doctor sharply rebukes him. He sees Dr. Norman telling the suits about him. Saying a word he does not know.

"Daniel, it is Dr. Norman. Your friend. I have good news for you, Daniel. Can you hear me?"

A lion coughs, and he hears it through the blocks of ice that are freezing around his brain.

"Good. Very good. Daniel, soon you will be free again. The program is a success. Soon you will be free, as I promised. You will be free to do the things you like, my friend. The things you are so good at."

He retrieves the alien word: Algolagnia. *Sees the doctor telling an audience, "Occupant is algolagnic." He knows now that this means he takes pleasure in inflicting pain.*

"You must stay within the boundaries where you are safe. Daniel, you will be free to do the things you like. But for your own safety you must stay within twenty-five miles of the town where you will be set free. So long as you remain within a twenty-five-mile radius of the town, your actions will be protected. No outside harm will come to you. Do you understand?"

Wind blows over a mass grave. It is otherwise still in his mind.

The doctor. Another supervisor. Six correctional officers. Shackles. Cuffs with the security boxes over them. He listens for jailhouse noise. The slam of cell doors.

"You will also—"

Dead bodies wired inside sunken junkers.

"—want to exterminate—"

Bloated inhuman faces under the surface of a shallow stream.

"—particular subjects—"

A cat growling in the blackness of a jungle night.

"—as well as targets of opportunity—"

Haze. Loss of balance.

"—that you encounter."

A prisoner buried under the heart of an icy monolith.

"A dossier has been prepared that will introduce you to—"

A sense of deep perspectives.

"—these targets."

Blurring now as the powerful drugs hose him under.

"Daniel, you will—"

Going to black.

"—of interest. You can study—"

Dissolving on the words of Dr. Norman as he completes the ritual of repetition and reassurance.

The brain implant appears to have been successful, but Dr. Norman wonders how things will go with Daniel. His affection for the beast is deep. He wonders if Daniel has bonded to him as well. Yes. Surely he has.

The dossier has been prepared by him. When Daniel wakens he will be shown the electronic display. General content, purview, presentation, and tone have all been carefully shaped. He knows precisely what it will take to engage that mind, pull him out of repose, enrage and motivate him into the cold kill fury that will allow him to function.

He has studied it himself innumerable times, and can quote content verbatim: "Police removed nine pit bulls from an establishment on Willow River Road, following a series of complaints regarding organized pit bull dogfights. Authorities said animals had been abused . . . were being kept for so-called death matches . . . Humane/society . . . put the dogs to sleep . . . Allegations of other animal cruelties . . . Sutter family."

Norman could see the photos of the dogs. Then the ads of the animal auction and the pictures they had to go with it. "The Genneret Gun Show and Exotic Animal Auction . . . dog 'bunchers' . . . Virgil Watlow . . . left strays that the lab wouldn't take . . . Seventeen were found tied to a tree, starved to death."

It built like a hot romance novel heading for a breathless climax, or a symphony building to a timpani-filled crescendo. There was a certain undeniable aesthetic to it. He could imagine the rage that would flood Daniel's mind when it reached the report about "The Mutilator . . . John Wayne Vodrey . . . private collection of cat tails, paws, and other anatomical mementos." Dr. Norman shuddered as he imagined the retribution in store for the targets of the dossier.

They wanted a "handle" on "occupant." They used the word "control" again and again. They were the ultimate control freaks. He recognized it and played to it.

No, he was frank to tell them. There is no control for occupant. There is only understanding. Understanding and manipulation. But Dr. Norman had found the secret control handle.

Most towns have their share of animal abusers, but this one—simply by luck of the draw—had some of the most flagrant and heinous cases one could find. It had been a simple matter to investigate these, magnify them, and prepare an illustrated presentation designed to engage, enrage, manipulate, and motivate the occupant of D Seg's infamous Cell Ten. One more terrible coincidence with an upside.

"Can you hear me all right?" No response. Nothing. "Daniel, it's Dr. Norman. I won't let any harm come to you. You know you can trust me. I'm your friend." One more time. The briefing period would mark his last hours of incarceration. Then Alpha Group II would work its magic and the subject would be inserted into the observation zone. "Can you hear me?" The lion coughed.

"Good. Just relax. Dr. Norman is your friend. Anything that I do is for your protection. Always remember that, Daniel."

The power of the experimental wonder drug had left its mark on the beast's face.

"You must remain within twenty-five miles of the killing zone. That is for your safety, my friend. As long as you stay there, you will have your freedom. Your old weapons are restored to operational condition and will be turned over to you. I got your weapons for you, Daniel. Your tools. After all, would we ask a master carpenter to build a house for us without his favorite tools? Everything is exactly as it was when you . . . were returned to us three years ago." The beast had been in Marion for two years and ten months.

"Do you understand what I'm telling you, Daniel?" There was a slackness to the features that reminded Dr. Norman of the face of a retarded child. But deep under the drugs, the lion managed another growl. "Your own beloved tools, Daniel! Think of that. Everything will be as you left it, your clothing, your special equipment—just the way you assembled it. We've even upgraded the things that had gone bad over time: you'll have new ammunition." He glanced at his notes. "The explosives—the munitions—all brand-new."

"They didn't like that part, my dear friend. But I made them give you hand grenades and mines. They said, 'Let him resupply himself in the field,' but I reminded them that there were no armories or munitions stockpiles within a twenty-five-mile radius of your operating zone. We couldn't have you wasting valuable time accumulating tools, could we?" The look on the slack features was that of a brain-damaged baby, smiling.

"One last thing before the targets are presented to you. As I've told you, and this is important for you to always remember: Everything I've done has been in your best interests. The drugs are extremely powerful. But even though you cannot respond, you will register and retain this information. Do not be confused by the odd feelings you may experience when you come back to a state of what seems like full consciousness.

"It's likely that the chemicals in your system will have a secondary effect, and there will be a period in which you feel much the same as you ordinarily do, but perhaps your actions will be somewhat erratic or—" he purposely did not use the word "normal"—"unusually low-key. For example, you may find yourself interacting with others in odd ways, or you may notice other behavioristic . . . lapses. Do not be alarmed. Because of your great strength, a particularly strong dosage of the drug must be used, but in time you'll be back to your old self. A day or two, at most." The doctor shrugged. "There will be no further need for such drugs, so you'll soon find yourself completely restored and refreshed. Do you understand?" There was no response. Dr. Norman drew near the huge, bound figure.

"I'll miss you, Daniel. I shall genuinely miss you." He reached out and touched the rock-hard muscle of a tree-trunk leg. "Will you miss your friend Dr. Norman?"

The slack-jawed look of the autistic child's empty smile was unchanged, but deep inside came a low, rumbling animal sound.

9

Waterton, Missouri

"Aw—," he said, the moment she came to the door.

"Hi," she said, almost before she got the door open, and they were in each other's arms, hugging on the porch. "Thanks for coming," she said gratefully, into his shoulder and neck. "Come in." Her voice was softer as they broke the clench and moved inside the house.

"I must have sounded like an idiot when you phoned."

"No."

"You threw me. It doesn't take much," she told him. When she answered the phone, he had said—"Does the name Quasimodo ring a bell?" Part of their old banter. He'd told her she was supposed to reply, "I can't place the face, but I still remember the bad hump." One of their old faves. But the strange voice and wacky opening line had thrown her into abject silence. He'd had to pry conversation out of her.

"I had no idea—you know—about Sam."

"That floors me, Royce. A town like Waterton. I was so sure everybody would know by now."

"I might as well have been on another planet." He gestured in the vague direction of Waterworks Hill. "I'm up there in my own little world. I haven't read a paper or heard any news for three or four weeks. I wouldn't know if war had been declared."

"I don't know what to do. I'm not sure why I'm picking on *you*, but—"

"That's okay. I'm glad you did. I don't know what I can do, but if you need some help—you know—um . . ." He spread his hands.

"I just thought maybe you'd have some ideas. Something we hadn't thought of. I can't sit here doing nothing. I've talked to everybody. Marty Kerns says nobody saw Sam. He just . . . disappeared." Royce nodded grimly.

"Hmm. Wow," he said, and made a humming noise of condolence and befuddlement. He had no idea what to say to her.

For her part, she was instantly sorry she'd called him. He seemed irritated that she'd bothered him with her problem after all these years—and he seemed rather . . . dirty. Or perhaps she'd built him up in her mind. Royce had been a big jock in school, but he'd gone down the junk road. She was wary of him, and he could read it on her face.

"I'm really glad you thought to call, Mary." He felt scuzzy and in need of personal grooming. God—he hadn't thought of being "well groomed" in a long time. She was looking at his roughshod appearance, and he knew he wasn't measuring up.

"It's just that I'd heard something—" she looked down "—some gossip about you doing detective work or something. You know—when you were away from town those years. Sam said you had joined the CIA . . ." She trailed off.

"No!" He smiled, coldly, instantly on guard. "I heard that bullshit too. CIA. Jeezus!" He laughed humorlessly. "Not me, kid."

"So that was why, you know, I thought about calling you . . ." She let it drop. It felt like it was pointless for them to waste any more of each other's time. She looked tired, but Royce's maleness reacted to her, as he always had. She was a lovely woman, even without makeup, and she was clearly out of it.

"I'll help any way I can, Mary. I thought when I got the note that Bobby was gone." They were now uncomfortable as strangers.

"Bobby?" She had no idea what he was talking about.

"Bobby Bartel. Didn't you know he has cancer?"

"You're kidding," she said, dumbly.

"Uh-uh. Heard it a couple months ago from Lyle Garner. You remember Lyle?"

"Sure." She nodded. Sam and Mary had been married for nearly fifteen years, and it had been sixteen years since she'd been involved with any part of Royce Hawthorne's world.

When Sam Perkins left Waterton to go to college out East, he'd made a new set of friends and locked on to the business track. When he returned, the kids who'd stayed around their hometown were still involved with one another's lives, the Waterton-Maysburg sports rivalry, and Friday night brew parties. Sam told her early in the resumption of their dating that he'd left all of that behind. He didn't mean it in an unkind way; it was merely a fact of maturing. Mary agreed, and had been pleased to grow along with her childhood beau.

Royce typified the kids they'd hung out with in high school. He hadn't changed much: a rugged Marlboro man sort of party guy. He'd been stuck back in his Waterton letter-sweater days, memorizing Coach John's playbook, and pretending he was going to be drafted by the Cowboys.

"JoAnne James is dead, you know?" she heard him say, and she shook her head.

"My God. I hadn't heard."

"She and her husband and two or three kids, living down in Florida. I believe she was shot and they never solved the case." They sat quietly for a moment. "Do you know about Hal Stahly?" he asked, after a bit. She looked blank. "He's in Vegas. Struck it rich in the auto parts business. Gale Strickland told me he'd lost about a hundred pounds and was married to Helen Swoboda. Used to be a cheerleader at Maysburg."

She smiled and listened to him run down the catalog of their onetime classmates. Royce was tall, rangy, his looks spoiled by a nose that had run up against a number of hard objects over the years. He still had all his hair (though it needed washing), and a jock's flat stomach, but his eyes were cloudy, squinting against the light, and he seemed to have acquired a few nervous habits, like he had a dozen itches at once and couldn't decide which to scratch first.

He was something of a shock to her system after so many years. One of the strange components at work was the strong attraction she'd always felt when she was in Royce's company. Who can explain these things? Her subconscious gave her a guilty nudge as she recalled their silly nicknames for each other. She called him "Buns," and he called her "L.D.," for Legs Diamond.

The notion that she might in some way even identify those kinds of feelings was such anathema to her that Mary felt a momentary stab of irritation as it drifted through to the surface of her awareness. She pushed it away, concentrating on Sam, and trying to decide what she should do next in searching for him.

Sam and Mary had grown up in the same block, one of the classic next-door romances that blossomed at puberty, and there'd never been any question that one day they'd be married. They were steadies from eighth grade through senior high, and would have wed then, but Mary stayed in Waterton when Sam was attending the University of Maryland.

While Sam was away getting his B.A., she and Royce had become close.

He was spontaneous, carefree, funny—and in some off-the-wall ways he was tremendously appealing. Women probably wanted to mother him, or thought they could change his ways. Men, of course, considered Royce the ideal buddy. She knew that he was a great deal more complex than he appeared to be. But that was old news.

Sam Perkins had become more than a husband to Mary—as their marriage became, perhaps, overly comfortable. He'd become like a brother. Royce, bless his damn heart, had made her take a subconscious glance at that.

"What's the deal?" he asked her, in his most serious and quiet tone. She remembered how he could be.

"How do you mean?"

"I mean Sam. Was there trouble between you?"

"No."

"No money problems? Health problems?"

"Absolutely none. He was very happy." She was suddenly defensive. "Good health. We both worked at it. He was great. His business was wonderful."

"You guys weren't having, you know, personal problems?"

"Uh-uh." She was surprised he'd even ask her.

"From what you say, he just ceased to exist one Friday morning, Mary. People don't vanish like that—the parked car and all. Unless he was kidnapped—and who'd want to do that? Or . . . he decided to leave."

"I would have known. Something happened to him."

"Okay."

"He parked the car at the office—in back. When he got out, somebody probably pulled up beside him or honked at him. That's what I think. He got in the car with them. And then something happened to him. That's the way he disappeared."

"Mm."

"The one who kidnapped him might be waiting for some reason before they ask for money. Waiting to see if the police or FBI can . . . you know, uncover their tracks."

"So you think he was kidnapped?"

"That's the way it looks to me."

"Pretty soon you'll get a demand for ransom money if that's what happened."

"Right." It had been a big mistake to call him. "That's what the cops and FBI think, too."

"You called the Feds?"

She nodded. "Yeah."

"Well—" He wanted to tell her about himself and that he was one of the good guys. At that moment he felt very sad for her, and without thinking, he took one of her hands and held it in his. He had big, rough hands. Laborer's fingers. But he was no laborer, sitting there at the kitchen table in his beat-up leather bomber's jacket and faded jeans, looking as if no time at all had gone by. She took her hand away and got up to put coffee water on, wondering if he'd done lines. "So—if the FBI is on the case, that's good. Right?" He was trying to reassure her, she supposed.

"I guess. They didn't act very interested. These two guys came to town and talked to me here at the house, and they tape-recorded me and asked a bunch of stuff. The same things I'd told Marty Kerns. They said, 'We'll be in touch,' and that was the last I heard from them. I've called a couple of times since. The last time I had to call back three times to get an agent on the phone, that's how they returned my calls."

He just looked at her. She supposed he'd had to get half-stoned to come talk to her. She thought of Sam's name for him. "The Junkie," he'd always called Royce if his name came up, and not unkindly. Now here he sat: her old junkie lover of once upon a time.

Mary Perkins awoke frightened, off kilter, out of synch like a worn film or a badly dubbed Japanese monster movie, and she had to work to fight back the edge of whatever it was that felt so intensely like desperation, shouting herself awake with a loud, unladylike curse of frustration.

Her shout was like an echo in this house without Sam Perkins. The weight of worry for her missing husband came and rested on her, reinserting itself into her consciousness, prodded by Royce's perfectly natural questions about the state of their marriage.

Half of her mind continued to sort options, stack and measure possibilities; size up the paucity of solid information she'd been able to gather about the why of his disappearance. The other half worked to nag her with worst-case scenarios, in which fictional mistresses and torturous plots nudged the dark convolutions of her thoughts.

It was the most obvious of the possibilities if you could look at their childless and increasingly platonic marriage objectively—which she couldn't. Never mind that it had been Sam, not Mary, who'd been adamant about concentrating on career, not kids, in the early years of their marriage, and then sunk himself deeper into his work. Or that it had been Sam who'd found romance too much of a bother.

The picture of this man, successful—no, make that suddenly rich—but stuck with a boring and prosaic existence, kept poking her in the imagination. Suppose this man decides to vanish? It happens. He creates another identity, building up a new persona to help cover his tracks. Maybe his is the sort of profession where his work takes him frequently to neighboring towns, and in one of these, far enough from home that he is sure to be unknown there, he becomes John Jones.

He wears a wig. A mustache. Obtains a birth certificate and carefully builds a life that will leave no paper trail. John Jones buys on credit. His wallet begins to fill with plastic rectangles that give his fictitious life identity. He buys a car, which he keeps secreted in the garage of a rental house. He's a salesman on the road for an out-of-town company, so his neighbors seldom see him. But John Jones keeps his lawn mowed, his sidewalks shoveled, his leaves raked—and the people who maintain his life for him always get their money up front. Cash, perhaps, or maybe John opens a small bank account. If he wants to make the effort, he can even take a driver's test and get a driver's license under the new identity. He does everything but pay his taxes, this fellow, but John Jones will cover his tracks so that even the IRS will lose the trail.

Perhaps the house John rents is only a temporary shelter. His intermediate link, a safehouse, his hiding place. This will be the place he runs to when he appears to vanish from the face of the earth. The rent is paid, the lawn is going to seed, the larder is stocked. He has only to settle down and stay out of sight for a few months. Watch a lot of TV. Read. Exercise. Count his money. When the trail is cold, John Jones's neighbors will learn that his company is transferring him, and this persona will now also disappear.

Maybe he has the cosmetic surgery next. Flies to the Cayman Islands, or wherever his offshore bank is. And there, in time, a new and untraceable identity is built.

When you start this kind of stuff, every newly imagined step of the plot feeds on distorted reality. You recall statements out of context, twist meanings, analyze preoccupations and idiosyncracies with a jaundiced perspective. You can get crazy with it.

Mary Perkins realized this kind of thinking was stupid and nonproductive, but alone in the sunny house, she'd found that she'd built a wall of such scenarios, and at the moment all she could do was sit in the middle of it and look out.

She felt her husband's name shudder through her like a cold chill. Sam.

Royce Hawthorne was driving down North Main, the main drag of their little village, heading northwest in the direction of the river. The street ended where Willow River Road and North Main and the busy Market Road all converged at the floodgates.

It never failed to amaze him, how a burg of six hundred and some souls could always have busy traffic on its main streets, but half of the population farmed, and farmers run the road. A lot of the tiny agri-communities also came into town on their way across the river to Maysburg, or on the way back home.

He found his access blocked by a work crew that stretched from the sidewalk in front of the State Farm agency over to General Discount's front door. He could see a line of trucks and cars and RVs of every description lined up on Market, and he knew where they were all going. Market became Jefferson Street there at the three corners, and everybody was angling around to get at the bank's drive-up window.

A fellow party-hearty he knew slightly flashed a big smile at him, and pretended to subtly masturbate the handle of his shovel. One more layabout easing through the workday on those nice hefty county wages.

He wheeled into Dr. Willoughby's parking lot and hung a left on Cotton Avenue, cutting back around the block to edge his way into the line of traffic. When his turn came, he eased across Jefferson, pulling into the large lot that faced the small cluster of overpriced office space that called itself Riverfront Park. He'd always loved that. There were a dozen or so expensive "suites" and "executive spaces," the big parking lot that the bank and Waterton Drug used for their customers, and a little manicured circle of fescue and Bermuda grass with a couple of concrete bench-and-table setups. All within .22 range of the river, hence Riverfront Park.

He nursed an Oly Light, paper propped on the wheel in front of him, back to the offices, and angled the rearview so he could watch the door of Drexel Commodity Futures.

For once his timing was okay, and after about forty minutes he saw Dave in the doorway speaking to someone, and he was out of the car and moving.

"Yo."

"Hey, Royce. I was just about to get back to you, babe. Sorry!" Big lying smile on his face.

"Yeah. Uh-huh. Dave. We got to talk, hoss."

"Oh, um—wow!" He glanced furtively at his wrist. "I've got to see this guy, babe. Let me call you tonight."

"What the fuck you pulling on me, man?" He couldn't help it. He was totally torqued. "We've got a deal."

"Absolutely. Not here," he begged him with his tone and eyes, pleading Royce to go away. "Not the time or place."

"How many times I gotta phone?"

"You don't understand, Royce."

"That's right." His throat felt so dry.

"I'm in a helluva bind." Drexel spoke quietly. "I can't come up with it. I just got hosed."

"*You* the one don't understand. You don't do that. You don't fuck this kind of a deal over. You *got* to come up with it!"

"I'm into other people, too. Royce. I'm in a world of trouble. I . . . I got in over my head."

"How dare you tell me that shit. You let me stick my dick into something this heavy and you tell me you're over your head? What the fuck is wrong with you?" He was trying to whisper, and it was coming out like a whine. He could see the deal dead in Drexel's yuppie eyes. "Sell your fucking house, and cars. You got to get me out from under this."

"It's gone. I've already mortgaged my house. I'm down the tubes, Royce. I just got in too deep. Listen—I'll call you tonight. I'll explain—"

"You can't explain shit. You can't explain your way out of something like this, bud. Get real."

"Well, it ain't happening," he said, in mock tough guy. Hawthorne wanted to throw him up against the wall of the building. It ain't happening. Drexel turned, starting off. No good-bye.

"You got some set of balls on you for a fucking wimpy, no-dick *pussy!*" He was out of control. Fuck it.

He shrugged with his body and his face. "I'm—"

"Yeah. I know. You're sorry. You're that, all right. Fuck." He didn't know what to do next. Go in the bank and try to move the weight in there? First Bank of Waterton was notoriously loose in their SBLs, and after all—wasn't he a small businessman? It wouldn't be like he didn't have the collateral.

He watched David Drexel get into his big car. Money in the bank. It couldn't have gone south like this. Jeezus—how much bad luck does somebody have to have?

He turned the corner of the bank, walking, nodding hello to people he'd known all his life. Would P. J. Thatcher, the State Farm man, come to his funeral when Happy and Luis finished with him? he wondered as he passed the insurance office. He needed somebody who had some serious bucks to get him temporarily off this dangerous tenterhook.

He saw Myrna Hyams at a desk and opened the door to Perkins Realty.

"Hi." She'd been with Sam for a long time and wore her concern on her face.

"Hi, Myrna. I don't guess you've heard anything new?"

"Not a word."

"Does everybody in town know he's disappeared, do you suppose?"

"They will tomorrow. I gave Jake at the *Weekly Dispatch* the details just a while ago. They put the paper out tomorrow." The *Weekly Dispatch* was printed in Maysburg, and this would be big news—a pillar of the community missing.

"Did you get those telephone bills ready?" Mary had told Myrna that he was "helping the family" look for Sam.

"Yes, sir," she said, glumly. "I couldn't think of anything I haven't already said. I just can't imagine what has happened to Mr. Sam."

He couldn't think what to say, so he just shook his head by way of commiseration. Royce wondered who'd look for him if he disappeared.

Mary Perkins was working her way back down North Main with the handbills. She went in Judy's, the town's most popular cafe, and spotted a woman she knew.

"Hi, Francie."

"Howdy, Mary," a heavyset woman said from behind the cash register, a look of condolence immediately wrinkling her plump, friendly features with concern. "It's awful about Sam. Have you heard any news?"

"No." Mary showed the woman a stack of pages she'd just run off across the street at the bank. "Would you all mind handing these out for me?" They were reward announcements that showed Sam's photograph, followed by a photocopy of the account of his disappearance that had run in the *Weekly Dispatch* that morning.

"Of course not. I'll make sure they get handed out myself," Francie assured her, glad to help. "I sure hope Sam's okay." She had clearly written him off.

Mary thanked her and left, working her way on down North Main. She, too, had a very bad feeling now. She'd already caught herself several times as she spoke of her husband in the past tense. Too much time had gone by.

She worked her way down the block, leaving more of the reward handbills at General Discount, the doctor's office, and O'Connor GMC Motors. She'd parked their car on Maple, and she went back to rest a minute and regroup. The plan was to get more posters and work her way on out South Main. She unlocked the car, got in, and looked at Sam's likeness from a recent photo.

REWARD

A substantial cash reward will be paid to anyone with information regarding the whereabouts of Sam Perkins, 33, of 911 South Main in Waterton, who has been missing since the morning of Friday, October 5, when he was believed to have been abducted from the parking lot of Perkins Realty.

Anyone having information as to his disappearance or his present whereabouts should contact Martin W. Kerns, Chief of Police, Waterton Office of Public Safety, 555-9191 or 555-3017.

Mary's own number had been added to the newspaper account. She only just now noticed that the pasteup had not been trimmed of all its extraneous information. There was a filler line that the paper had run across the bottom, and she'd left it on. In tiny print at the bottom of the announcement it read:

"Support the Maysburg Eagles!"

Mary forced herself into action and started the car, pulling around the corner and parking halfway down the block. She gathered up a big armful of handbills and went in the first building down at the corner, Wilma's Hair Salon.

Kristi Devere was cutting someone's hair, and there was another lady under a dryer. Mary couldn't place the woman she was working on, but the woman acted like she knew Mary. She asked Kristi if she could leave some of the posters of Sam, and was turning to leave when the woman said, in a well-meaning tone, "I know exactly what you're going through, dear."

"Oh." She had no idea who the woman was. A pleasant-looking bottle blonde of mysterious years, but clearly on the high side of middle age.

"I lost my Stanley and I didn't think I was ever going to get over it. Thirty-five years." Kristi stopped and looked at her customer. "It's terrible to have a husband killed."

"Nobody knows that, Clarisse," Kristi said gently.

"Of course they don't. But you know, if your husband gets Alzheimer's or something, and he's elderly, or in bad health, or he has a stroke—you know—" She needed to talk about it.

"Sure." Mary wanted to get moving. Clarisse? Not Clarisse Pendleton? Must be. She vaguely remembered her husband had been killed in a car accident. A drunk driver.

"We had our kids grown and out of the house. Doing well. Our grandchildren were healthy. We had our financial situation—you know—comfortable. I mean, we weren't wealthy . . ." Huge diamonds flashed on an expressive, wrinkled hand.

"Mm-hm."

"I couldn't go in a room in the house without seeing something of Stanley's. I finally had to just box up everything and have Goodwill get it. All his beautiful suits. I couldn't stand it. I cried every time I came in the house. I couldn't fix a meal. I'd open the refrigerator and just break down. I'd find some little note or something in one of my purses. My heart broke ten times a day. You know—you lose someone to cancer, it's awful. But everyone loses loved ones to heart disease, cancer, things like that. To have something like this—"

"Bye bye, Mary," Kristi said. "Good luck, hon." Giving her a chance to thank them both and quickly start out the door.

"Holidays are the worst—" she could hear the woman call out to her back as the door mercifully closed.

10

North of Waterton, Missouri

"Magic Silo. Crossing plowed ground to barnyard. Repeat. Magic Silo. Crossing plowed ground to barnyard." The words register deep in the lion's brain salad. A radio spits noise.

"That's a rog, Charlie Charlie November. Magic Silo out." Trying to fight his way out of the haze of tranqs. Wordscreen wrestles for information. Sorts through call signs: Wicked Trade. Mad Rover. Mud Puppy. Magic Silo does not connect.

Sees the steel. Chains. Feels the cold. Senses loss of equilibrium. Turbulence of some kind. Perhaps he is in Vietnam, on the way to an unknown LZ with the call sign Magic Silo. A bumpy ride, in this UH-1. The slick shudders in a loud eggbeater machine-gun flatulence of turbine whomp. But if this is a bird, where is the cocky pilot? The absentee door gunner? The copilot? No arrogant crew chief speaks. He replays a night insertion: unmarked skinships approaching LZ Quebec-Tulsa, filed as LZ: field expedient.

His body shrugs through layers of fog. Tests the chains reflexively. He is immobilized, but he can hear a radio and a single voice. If the pilot is tantalizingly alone, this is golden data—a neck snaps like rotten wood in his memory and he wants to smile, but the huge face is frozen.

There is the ruck. He realizes he must be hallucinating. His duffel and weapons case! A rush of joy surges through his bloodstream.

The presence of something else washes over him and he is back at Quebec-Tulsa, drag man on a squad-strength spike team. Grabbing ass through the sawgrass. Ten ground-pounders double-timing into the bad bush: trip flares, mines, frags, ammo, det gear, web gear, warm bods sheep-dipped (sanitized), night-fightered in camouflage, every jingly thing taped down.

Daniel Bunkowski is loaded for bear. A backbreaking ruck, X'ed bandoliers of ammo, det cord, wire, and assorted gear for his precious "pies," streaming blast-furnace sweat and killer karma, death out the bazonga.

"Chaingang" he is called—out of earshot—existing nowhere on paper, core name-taker for USMACVSAUCOG, a ghost unit created in the pages of an NSC "action memorandum" to the Joint Chiefs, a "NONSKID JACKS" in jargonspeak: the verbalization of *N*ational *S*ecurity *C*ouncil *D*irective to the *J*oint *C*hiefs of Staff.

It was sanctioned by a few words found amid the verbiage of the National Security Act, which mandated an outfit of its type to perform "such functions and duties affecting the national security as the National Security Council may direct."

The benign-sounding tongue twister of an acronym was said to stand for the *U*nited *S*tates *M*ilitary *A*ssistance *C*ommand *V*ietnam/*S*pecial *A*dvisory *U*nit of the *C*ombined *O*perations *G*roup.

No Army 201. No MOS. No unit clearance. No name, rank, serial number on file. Not even the tradecraft lie of a civilian cover or private sector gig for a legend. Just this huge loose and evil cannon to pull pitch and plow any time the mood strikes.

Dr. Norman's Alpha Group II has frozen his brain. He is back in the Nam, and deep inside his own madness:

Life drips. It drips down through the tertiary foliage of the triple canopy, nourishing, feeding the teeming green. Day slowly comes with time's passage, and yesterday's heat, still trapped down in this leafy, hot world, rises to a boil as the plant life radiates intense warmth out through the stink of rotting vegetation. More warmth builds inside the moist, living greenhouse, catches, builds, cools with the coming night, but never cooling enough, layering heat upon itself, baking again, feeding, dripping, nourishing. Nightfall again, coming soon.

The spike team enters this blast furnace of green heat, moving carefully through the alien world. It reeks with rotting plants, sweltering jungle, an oppressive and stifling humidity index that cannot be described, and a thousand and one organic perils. Heat prostration and deadly dehydration are among the more benign life-threatening dangers.

They eyeball pathways and cart trails and streams, busting jungle, working their way up-country.

"Beaucoup VC," the point man whispers. The man who walks his slack moves his index finger closer to the oily trigger of his piece, whispering to the man behind him.

"Victor Charles." This man turns to the RTO and warns him as he points. The radioman looks.

"Charlie."

The word filters back through the spike team, but they do not tell the drag man. He is far behind, busting jungle at his own pace. Stopping now beside a cart trail where the smell of the little people fills him with thrilling anticipation. He starts moving backward, waddling away from the trail, his huge body atingle with excitement as he covers his tracks, backing into seemingly impenetrable jungle.

Invisible now, motionless, he stands and begins the slowing, stilling of his vital signs. Breathing in the killer heat like some enormous jungle plant, thriving on the suffocating humidity, drinking it in as he shifts down into an almost subhuman stillness, a wide and frightening parody of a grin distorting his features as he listens to the noisy bumblers move farther away.

The spike team breaks through the triple-canopied green, following the cart trail through truck gardens and a ruined villa, moving toward a rubber tree wood line.

"Yo, Rodriguez."

"Say?" Rodriguez is the last man.

"What happened to Chaingang?"

"Fucked if I know, Sarge." He shrugs. "He's back there somewhere. Back in the jungle."

"Fuck," the team leader says with disgust, spitting his chaw into the nearby foliage. They drive on.

With his vital signs slowed to a crawl, slowly he fills his immense body with teeming jungle air, holds it, wills his life support system to chill him out. Listens to the sounds of the deep green coming back to life now that the bumblers are gone. Birds. Animals. Insects. Slithery, slimy things. Creepy crawlers. The thud-bump, thud-bump of his strong heart roaring in his ears.

He is relieved they are gone. Hates their cloying, maddening proximity. Knows they will meet their doom up ahead and thinks it, precognates it in just those words, relishing the phrase: they will meet their doom. It is a pleasant thought that entertains him as he slows his vital signs in preparation for readying his ambush.

He thinks of himself as Death. Death, very still, tired and favoring his weak ankle from the insertion (but happy), lets himself envision the little people who he knows will come. With a massive effort he wills his body to move, his strange brain directing the opening of the "pie box," which is how he thinks of his mines.

Vaguely pie-cut shaped, at least in his mind, there are six to a container, which weighs nearly twenty-two pounds. He carries a full load of claymores the way one might carry a carton of cigarettes. Each one of the three-and-a-half-pound mines, roughly the size of a curved shoe box, is marked M-18A1 ANTIPERSONNEL, *and these are but part of his mobile arsenal.*

Death is a walking hunter-killer machine: M-26s with the four-second and shortened one-second fuses, M-15 Willie Peters, 25A2s with CS, and an MK-26 Model O Haversack for his "wet work,"—part of the arsenal that supplants his primary killing tool, the M-60.

Death senses something now. It jars his mental gyro and he freezes. Sees men—moving—silhouetted against the night, speaking, a flurry of hands and arms, and he snaps out of the haze as he feels his massive bulk being pushed down a slide of some kind.

He hears their voices clearly now. Grunting. Laughing. Swearing men who struggle to move his enfettered dead weight. They strain, and he is moving again.

Sliding from the chopper?

No! He is being offloaded from the back of a truck. Huddled in chains and restraints.

"Go! Take off. Go!" the man in charge shouts, and the truck starts moving. Chaingang's thoughts are clear. He is being freed for some reason. Even though he sees the truck, he wonders why they did not insert him by Huey, then he realizes the Nam thing was hallucinated. Dr. Norman did this to him—for that one instant he feels the hot red desire to rip the sissy doctor's body apart—then he remembers he is about to get free and he's too excited to think of anything else.

There is a horizon of dark tree line. Beyond it he senses a river, and the wordscreen feeds "disembogue": to flow or come forth as from a waterway or channel that empties into a stream. He is near a river and some kind of a canal or waterway, he intuits, then the beast's mind reminds him he heard a distant barge.

He is not in a watery paddy marked LZ Quebec-Tulsa, but he smells truck crops and goat heads. Early bean stalks cut. Cockleburs. Goldenrod, creeper vine, thistle, dog fennel. Poison ivy. Assessment: a desolate piece of farm ground.

Norman's admonition replays: "You will be safe." His mental sensors do not warn him otherwise. One of the monkey men speaks in harsh tones from out of a moving jigsaw.

"Map." He throws a plastic case at the huge bata-boots. "You hear me all right?" Chaingang listens. "Equipment. Everything's in the two cases. Compass." He drops something on the map.

"Everybody mounted up?" There is a shouted reply. The scent of freedom and that of running blood mixed with vengeance is like the loam of the richest bottomland, an earthy, alluvial perfume, fueling what only base feeding will appease.

"Hey!" he shouts, unnecessarily. "Keys!" It obviously frightens the man to say this as he throws them. They hit in the dirt beside the huge bulk of the bound beast, and the man is running before they strike the ground. The trucks disappear into the darkness.

Is it a trick? Possibly. But what would justify the effort? He files the possibility and tries to scoot his body closer. It is not as easy as he thought.

He is able to finally get close enough to snag the keys. Huge paws carefully test each key in the two main chain shackles, first the cuffs, then the leg chains.

By luck he hits the handcuff key on the third try with the tinier keys, but it takes a lot longer than he wants it to before the proper key unlocks the leg shackles.

Chaingang crawls to the massive duffel bag and finds a flashlight and tries it. Batteries are strong. Paws through till he finds his big fighting bowie.

The dreaded biter and the other restraints are sliced and he is standing. Armed. Free.

He knows not to linger in this field. Swooping up the heavy duffel, the two cases—also extremely heavy—and having pocketed the compass and map, he begins a fast waddling trot in the direction of the deepest darkness.

There is some moonlight, but rain-cloud night blankets him. The gigantic beast moves surefooted as a huge, fat cat, the proximity of human beings acting as his biocatalyst, activating and accelerating the mysterious processes that have always protected and guided him.

Instinctively he moves in the direction of isolation and concealment, away from humanity for the moment, away from danger, his mind a seething maelstrom of hatred, relief, and kill-hunger.

There is no one in the darkened field to witness the sight as Chaingang Bunkowski's immense, doughy face stretches wide into its broadest approximation of a smile, and the coughing noise that is his imitation of human laughter is swallowed by the night.

It seems to take him forever to reach the safety of the tree line. He drops his heavy load and rests, reflecting on his lack of stamina. His brain supplies dates of confinement and reminds him of his astounding recuperative powers. He has a dull headache and rubs the back of his head, which is very sore. Perhaps he was struck while unconscious, or hit his head being transported to and from the truck. He arches his big head back and gingerly feels the wrinkles at the back of his muscled rock of a neck. What are those ridges? Fat, he supposes. He massages the back of his head gently, then forces himself back into action.

Chaingang lifts the duffel and the cases, and starts out across the field, again at a fast waddle. He notices he is favoring his leg and promises his weak right ankle that it won't be long.

He hates being weak like this, and his irritation pushes him faster. The load weighs a ton—even for him. He cannot understand this lack of strength and finds it maddening. He'd like to destroy someone before he goes to sleep, but he knows he must rest.

Finally—into another pitch-black tree line. Sees an opening. Starts toward it and almost blacks out.

The drugs slam into him for a second, and their power nearly knocks him off his feet. He knows he must find a place to hunker down for the night.

With a mighty will of effort he shrugs off the mental haze and keeps moving slightly downhill—apparently the tree line is on an embankment.

He must go a few more meters. He wills himself not to drop the cases, fights the fog that threatens to seize his brain again, pushes himself forward, one foot after another. He knows he will be all right now.

He drops heavily into the nearby opening in the thick tree line, seeing now that it is a deep slough, waddling quickly down the embankment. In dark shadow a huge drainage culvert, overgrown with weeds, beckons.

The strangness of his mind tells him many things at once, reminding him that there is also a transitive form of disembogue, that it means "to pour out," and that this slough with its wet and muddy bottom has not held enough rain to flow, come forth, empty into, or pour out into the culvert. The bottom of the culvert will be relatively clean and dry.

Reptiles are not a factor. This culvert will be teeming with its share of arachnidan life, but he is at home with spidery anthropods, mites, ticks, scorpions, and the lesser creepies. The mental computer registers the presence of larvae silent in their silken cases, of the phyllophagous insects that feed on the leaves, the leaves of leguminous trees, the dicotyledonous, angiospermous plants, and the insectivorous creatures that hunt in them. He is fully at home in this swampy, dank world.

The culvert's floor is cool and damp, but contains only that terrigenous sediment formed by the erosive action of time and tide, and the residue of whatever elongated segmented invertebrates and related annelidan forms may have burrowed into it. To some the putrescence of this decaying organic matter would be an unbearably foul stench, but to him it is merely reassuring.

But because he knows, he also knows that larvae hatch. Vermiform feeders and mutant flies, gnats, mosquitoes, nameless winged things, will buzz and swarm and come to life; headless, eyeless, legless flying minimonsters of the order Deptera will mutate and metamorphose out of the ultraslime. And in the early morning he will be gone.

Massive vehicle tarp and poncho spread out to cover the culvert floor. He uses the last ebbing reserves of strength to pull out his weapons, LURP dinners—"Long Rats"—canteen, spoon, netting. The cammoed mosquito netting he pulls over him for a roof, pouring what could be doped water into his freeze-dried spaghetti and meatballs packet, and devouring it cold.

It goes against his grain to sleep without setting up a rudimentary nighttime defensive perimeter of some kind, but before he can consider it, he collapses, falling instantly into deep sleep.

Inside the strangeness of his mind the computer continues to function: counting seconds, minutes, hours on his flawless inner clock; measuring temperature, humidity, wind velocity, other externals; auditing and carefully analyzing the sounds of the night for the presence of possible threat. In the absence of significant changes, it appreciates.

(SLOUGH: noun, meaning ditch. Deep mud. Mire. Swamp. Backwater area. River inlet. Tidal basin ditch. Tide flat. Marsh creek. State of moral decline or spiritual dejection. Cast-off snakeskin. Dead tissue mass. Extreme depression literally or figuratively. Deep bog. Marshy place. Muddy creek bed.) His mind flashes itself a picture of the RSSZ, picturing his image of a slough where he hid in the Rung Sat.

There, too, he was betrayed by those who used him as an executioner. There, also, his masters would have placed him in the gravest peril, telling him he was free to take his pleasures against humans, and—but for his gifts and skills—they would have allowed him to perform their bidding and then exterminate him.

For the first time since the drugs were administered to him in the penitentiary, he appreciates the possibilities, and the body of the beast makes an involuntary coughing noise in its slumber.

Early morning. Daniel is awake in a buzz that is partially caused by the teeming culvert that is a breeding ground for insects, and in part by a massive headache—a throbbing, pulsating thing that robs him of his powers of concentration.

He gathers up duffel and weapons cases and clomps away from this place, the radio call sign "Magic Silo" echoing as he passes a pair of Butler Grain Silos, then three more, standing like a kind of mini-Stonehenge at the edge of an adjacent field. He would ordinarily just flash a mental picture of them and file it in the computer, but does not trust himself in this addled state, and he takes time to dig out his Boorum and Pease Accounts Receivable Ledger that has been with him since his last prison bit. He calls it UTILITY ESCAPES, and it is nearly filled with maps, plans, charts, meticulously rendered drawings of safehouse structures and traps—his idea book which he treasures as one draws comfort from a family Bible.

Long ago he memorized all the material in it, but he derives sustenance and inspiration from it—it is The Word. He reads it for solace, for pleasure, for renewed power, for positive reinforcement; he has faith in it.

He finds a felt-tipped pen, obviously brand-new, removes the cap, and with a reasonably firm, steady hand adds the appropriate landmarks to his ledger, marking them on map as well. The silos are of interest. It is very lonesome here in the boonies, and there are truck and tractor marks, but nothing else since the last rain, he sees. The galvanized sheet metal tells its own story. From these signs he sees safety. One of the doors begs him to bust its easy lock, step up, squeeze in, and pull that door to. Magic silos? Maybe so. An emergency home away from home.

The deep slough where he'd hunkered down in the culvert for the night bisected thick woods, and in the center of it, not fifty meters from the overgrown, leafy ditch banks, a pond of stinking mud and stagnant rainwater hid like a surprise. It was also added to both the scale map and the ledger page.

He looked on field expedient burial sites as presents.

Fifty meters. Let's see—what was that in feet? He tried to recall the key from a military map. Was there one on the map he'd just looked at and folded up incorrectly? He unfolded it and refolded it slowly, weaving back and forth a little. His huge feet looked very far away for a second and he felt light-headed. He rubbed at his eyes, shook his head, tried to shake the cobwebs loose. He poured water from his canteen, splashing it in his face.

That was better. He walked a few steps and decided he'd better sit down a moment and dropped to the ground heavily, as puzzled as he was angry. Bees and hornets and wasps and mud daubbers built nests in his head.

He forced himself to think. His entire life had been a triumph of will over matter, and he would think his way out of these . . . horse latitudes that would render him impotent.

Fifty meters: ten meters, a decameter, would be 32.81 times 5, or 164.05. Was that feet or yards? Feet. Divide by 3: 54.68333333. Half a hectometer? Fifty meters—109.3666, the number of the great beast. The inside of his head felt like a honeycomb. He pushed himself to his feet.

By afternoon he had reached the large body of water that encroached from the western edge of the map they'd given him, and he was in a bad way. Something was wrong. Maybe it was the drugs, maybe something else. He fought to think and to keep moving.

The blue features each had a number. This one was numbered thirty-one. He knew it was the river long before he saw the fast-moving current.

He froze at the embankment and saw the man. He looked like one of the little people, waiting down in a tunnel, a cleverly designed hidey-hole. One of the ghost warriors. He waited.

If you could have ridden by on a log at that moment, letting the river current pull you, you'd have seen quite a sight up there on the bank. There was a little bite-size chunk, a gouge, in the bank, and sitting squarely in that hole was an old man. An old man in faded work clothes, who had a couple of lines out, bank-fishing for cat.

But above him and to the right as you floated by, you would have seen a huge, grinning fat man, carrying a massive load of some kind, looking down at the old man who was contentedly fishing.

The giant was not jolly, but he was green—part of him. He wore green-and-brown jungle fatigue pants—big as a wall flag—and down where they bloused out of gigantic, custom-made 15EEEEE boots, the trousers were duct-taped into the boots, sealed against leeches. (Old habits die hard.)

He had on a voluminous jacket of some kind, which was open, and a T-shirt underneath, and in his right hand, which was the size of a frying pan, he now held three feet or so of heavyweight tractor-strength chain. The cases and large duffel bag were on the ground.

Each big, hardball-size link had been carefully wrapped in black friction tape, as was the case with all his equipment, and it had been rendered as operationally silent as he could make it.

He would chain-snap this one, he thought, silently easing closer to his enemy.

Their underground was an incredible, vast spiderweb of interlocking tunnels and served as command and control, medevac triage, R & R center, whatever was needed by way of supply /resupply. It was all down there in the tiny tunnels where the little people hid by day, sometimes in groups as large as battalion strength, subsisting on diets of rice and a bit of rat meat, fish, and nuoc mam; tough, wiry, hard-core team players—man, woman, and child. Ghost warriors.

It pleasured him to watch them near the blue features where he found their bidey-holes; tiny ratholes he couldn't begin to get a massive tree trunk leg down in. He'd wait silently, watching for the ones who would come after nightfall, either to leave or enter from the tunnel mouth.

Many times he'd been given treats this way, a small, dark figure popping out of the hole beside the blue feature, gasping for air perhaps after an underwater swim. They liked to dig a shallow chamber first, below the water table, and this flooded chamber then acted as a protective perimeter float. But if you knew where the inner entrance was, you could hold your breath, dive, and pull yourself through the inner opening into breathable air, and you'd be safely inside the tunnel complex.

He liked to kill them when they first emerged from the water, quick and dark little people whom he frankly admired—as much as he could admire any human, admiring them for their tenacity and singular meanness of spirit.

The secondary effect of the drugs smashed him and he dropped the chain, stumbling and falling like a felled tree.

The old man heard a loud noise and turned, startled to see a huge figure on the ground up on the bank behind him. He scampered back to give a hand.

"You hurt yourself?" Chaingang looked up into the face of an old man who *had his hands on him*. Where was his fucking chain? "You took a heckuva spill there, feller. I was busy fishin', and I didn't even hear you a-comin', you know? I hear this loud crash—you really took a fall! Can ya' get to your feet?"

"Nn." Chaingang found he could not speak. It occurred to him he had not used his voice in some time. The lion coughed. It sounded far away inside his head. He fumbled around and got the canteen off his belt and took a swig.

The old man stayed next to him *petting him like he was a huge dog.*

"I'm worried about you, son. You ought to go to the hospital and let 'em take a look at you. You might have something broken."

Chaingang wanted to tell this idiot he was going to have his fucking *neck broken if he didn't get his hands off him*. He hated to be touched.

The old man continued to peer into his face. He had a dark stain from a chaw of tobacco that dribbled from one corner of his mouth. Daniel Edward Flowers Bunkowski, mass murderer, had never itched to destroy someone so much in his life. But when he started looking to see where he'd dropped his chain, it occurred to him that such an act would be wrong.

The old man watched him running his hands over his face. After a moment the immense figure managed to get back to his feet, and the old man stood. The giant towered over him by a couple of feet and probably outweighed him by over three hundred pounds. He stared up at the vision for a moment, shook his head in amazement, shrugged, and ambled on back to his hole, leaving Chaingang gaping after him.

"Guess you're okay." The old man smiled. "Come on down here, big 'un, and set a spell." He patted the ground beside him and turned his back on Chaingang, who started down the bank. He'd fucking choke him to death and be done with it.

But when he got to the edge of the hole, he just stood there, looking down at the swiftly moving river.

"Hop on down here, big 'un. There's plenty of room. I'll move over a little." He did so, and Chaingang found himself sitting beside this fool, his brain feeling as if it had been encased in ice.

"What's your name, son? I'm John Oscar." He was holding out his hand to shake hands. Chaingang blinked. The old man was not the least put off, he'd been around the retarded all his life. It wasn't a problem. They was just like anybody else. He patted the big leg of the giant wedged next to him. It was the second time a man had put hands on him like that in recent memory. The next time it happened, that offender would lose those digits.

"I don't know my own name sometimes, son. It's my age. I don't know for sure how old I am, but I'm old enough I can recall riding the rods in the Great Depression. You have no i-dee what I'm talking about, do ya, boy?" Daniel blinked again. Swallowed. Finally managed a monosyllabic grunt. "Don't worry none."

"You ever fish below here? Slabtown? I use rank liver on big ol' game-fish test. And look here, son. Homemade sinkers. You know what I make 'em out of?" The big feller didn't seem to be interested, so he reached for his other pole. "Here." He jabbed it at Chaingang. "Take this. Go on. Don't be afraid. Take holt of it real good."

Daniel opened a fist, and his big fingers swallowed the end of the bamboo pole.

"That's it, big 'un. Now, keep that end of the pole pointed up more," he scolded. "That's right. Soon as that pulls, you hold on real tight and we'll catch us some fish. How's that sound?"

Daniel Edward Flowers Bunkowski, his mind in icy pieces, sat quietly, obediently, on the edge of Blue Feature Thirty-One, fishing with John Oscar. Happy as two peas in a pod.

11

Waterton

Hawthorne's funky ride, a superannuated-looking Ranchero that appeared to have seen about twenty better years, was parked on an out-of-the-way side street off Waterworks Road. Half a block away, near a small convenience store, he whispered hoarsely into a pay phone.

"Thank you," he said, hanging up the receiver. The phone rang shrilly and he snatched it off the cradle, but a female voice instructed him to deposit money. He'd forgotten about the operator. He dropped coins and listened to the pinging routine. Shortly thereafter Southwestern Bell delivered him into the waiting arms of AT&T.

Someone spoke into his ear from two hundred miles away, and he said what he hoped were the magic words: "I'd like to speak with someone about buying some insurance." The connection was noisy and the man's voice sounded far away.

"Who's calling please?"

"This is a man who's insurance—" Jesus in Heaven! Suddenly his mind had gone completely blank. A hundred times they'd gone over this. The stupid fucking routine. "This is a man who's—" What? An insurance fraud? Insurance policy? Insurance *poor*! "—insurance *poor!*" he blurted out, as if he'd just won the bonus question on a game show.

"Number?"

His number. What in the hell was wrong with him? He'd forgotten everything over this Drexel deal.

He finally snapped out of it and whispered the number. The man's voice requested corroboration of the pay telephone number, asking it in a certain way so that Hawthorne could clue them if he was "under severe and immediate threat."

He hung up, and it was a few moments this time before the telephone rang again. He grabbed at it.

"What?" The daddy rabbit's voice was one he had no trouble remembering.

"The guy I had set to make the initial buy . . . he fell apart on me."

"Yeah? So?"

"I need some money, man! I need five grand."

"Go get it. You're the big drug pusher."

"Funny." The fucking prick. "I don't have anybody else to take that kinda weight around Waterton fucking Missouri, you dig? I need you to cut me a huss, ya know?"

"You're jeopardizing this by even using this number. Now, you solve *your* problem, mister!" the voice growled in his ear. "And don't use this number again unless it's important." Click.

God almighty. He just stood there with the thing in his hand, a noisy nothing in his ear. He swallowed and his ears popped like he was depressurizing. He had to do some sniff and get his shit together.

Those fucking pricks.

Royce Hawthorne had called her, sounding so funny over the phone that she assumed he might have learned something. He was on his way over to talk with her.

She was still dressed up from making the rounds with the reward handbills, and was glad she hadn't had time to undress before the telephone rang. She answered the door wearing her fancy black gabardine suit jacket, with a straight short skirt, and Royce made a show about her being dressed up.

"Wow!" he said. "You look sensational, Mary." She was the Mary he remembered. More beautiful, in fact, than he remembered seeing her.

"I bet," she said. She'd washed her hair and put on makeup, but she felt tired to the bone, and she figured it must show.

"I mean it," he said, obviously sincere.

"Thanks." She asked him to sit down, wanting him to tell her what he'd learned. He made small talk, and she started getting the nagging feeling it was something bad.

"Royce, have you learned something about Sam having a mistress or something?"

"Huh?" He was genuinely thrown. He had no idea what she was talking about.

"Obviously you're building up to something you don't really want to say—I know you, remember? You tried to tell me it was possible the other day, and I didn't want to hear it, talking about how he might have wanted a new life and all. Have you heard something? Is it another woman?"

"For God's sake, Mary, I didn't mean to create that impression at all. No. It's got nothing to do with Sam. First, have you got a mirror, lady? You're one terrific-lookin' woman. No. Uh-uh. No way. You misunderstood. I was talking about all the money he'd been making in real estate. That humongous deal he'd put together and all. I guess it occurred to me it would be worth looking at the possibility of him wanting to set something up and vanish. But the more you told me about him, I could see that wasn't the way he'd go. That money he made—the way he put every dime into something that would provide for you one day—those aren't the actions of a married guy who wants to escape."

"If it isn't that—"

"*I'm* in some money trouble, keed. That's why I wanted to talk to you—no, I haven't heard a thing about Sam. In fact, I went over your phone calls here at the house and his monthly bills at the office, and I've got some questions. But what I wanted to ask—and if I'm completely out of line, just say so—I'm in a bit of a squeeze. Is there any way, and I know I've got some guts asking, but could I borrow some money—just for a couple of days?"

"Sure. How much do you need?" She thought he was wanting a loan of a couple hundred dollars.

"Five thousand dollars. I know it's a lot—"

"Five thousand?" She couldn't believe it.

"I'm sorry, babe. I will have it back to you right away, with interest. Just a matter of paying a debt I owe until money that's on its way to me comes in." He gave her some more double-talk, reddening at his own lack of scruples.

"Okay," she said, in a tone that conveyed how totally not okay it was. "If you're certain you can repay me, Royce. I'll have to cash a bond or something."

"I'll make it up to you. I'll certainly repay the penalty too, Mary. So you won't lose anything. I'd be very grateful." He didn't know what else to say.

"You want to go get it now?"

"If we could—?" He felt skanky, unclean, and remarkably relieved.

"Sure." She got her purse and they left in his ride. She decided it would be easier just to get him the money out of the passbook Sam kept for the office. There was nearly eight thousand in it. On the way down to the bank he asked her about the phone bills. There was no way she could do anything other than help Royce, she realized.

"There were a couple of phone numbers someone had dialed three times at the office, and Myrna said it wasn't her that did it. And once from the house. Alexandria, Virginia. It wasn't on the list you made for me."

"I don't know who that could be." He dug out some papers when they pulled up to the bank, and showed her the bills.

"No idea from the dates who that might be?"

"I never heard him mention anybody in Virginia." She felt a cold chill at the presence of something unknown entering her equation about Sam's disappearance.

"Alexandria is next to Washington, D.C."

"Oh! I know who that probably is. That was Mr. Sinclair, who helped organize the deal I told you about—where an out-of-state buyer bought up all this high-priced farmland."

"He was the buyer of the land, this Sinclair?"

"I think he represented the buyer. He was . . . something to do with the environment . . . I don't know. Anyway, he worked out of Washington, I remember." She started to get out and go get Royce his loan, and he stopped her before she pushed the door shut.

"Mary, is that the big construction site north of town?"

"I don't know."

"There's a lot of work going on out there. I know a guy who got a job driving a cat or a backhoe or something. Lots of heavy equipment in there. It's this side of the old rock quarry."

"I hadn't heard about any work. I suppose it could be. You can look at the papers and stuff if you like . . ." she trailed off, and headed into the bank.

In a few minutes she was back, the envelope of fifty hundreds nesting in her purse. She got in and looked at Royce. It was one thing to say, "Sure, you can have a five-thousand-dollar loan," and it was quite another to hand the money over.

"Royce. Will you answer a question, if I ask? A personal question?"

"Yeah. Of course."

"Don't be offended."

"No chance."

"This money. It isn't for drugs, is it?"

"No." He smiled. "It's a gambling debt."

"Well, that's a relief. At least it's for a good cause." My God. She sighed and handed the money over.

"I'll have it back to you day after tomorrow." The check is in the mail. I won't come in your mouth.

She was exhausted, dead tired, but Mary Perkins was not about to give up.

She wondered about the wives of the MIAs. How many months and years of wondering go by before a part of you tunes out? It all depended on the woman, or the man, she supposed. How does a person cope when his or her mate vanishes from the face of the earth? How long can you sit and wait for the word that never comes? Others couldn't begin to know the strain and the anguish until it happened to them.

Only a few weeks had gone by, and Mary was already tired of the weight of worry. Tired of wallowing in what she perceived as disgusting self-pity. Tired of not knowing.

Tired of the nice people who kept saying things to her that made her flinch, cringe, shudder, or weep. Tired of the limelight already. Even in a town of less than seven hundred, there were nuts who'd call—one in particular phoned every afternoon with a hang-up.

There were sickos out there. She'd opened up a handwritten envelope with one of the reward announcements folded up inside. Some wit had written, "Sam Perkins is now a forward with the Lakers." She'd had to get Royce to explain the thing to her, assuring her that it was some cretin's idea of a joke.

She was tired of shocks and surprises. Tired of opening the top drawer of his dresser and finding all those white shirts stacked up so neat and clean, the shirts done the way he always preferred them, the collars just so. The second drawer with his button-down oxfords. The bottom drawer containing Sam's cashmeres. The sweaters he loved to wear on Saturday, soft and cuddly to the touch, folded and waiting.

His clothing smelled so sweet and clean. She had opened his closets and examined all his suits, ties, and shoes. Tried to remember exactly what he'd been wearing that Friday. Tried to think if anything else was missing. Shamed herself as she hunted for luggage pieces and shaving gear and airport carry-alls from old trips.

She was tired of knowing less than she imagined, of wondering what to fix that evening and then realizing it didn't matter, of remembering the look of his square-trimmed fingernails, of hearing his voice inside her head.

Tired of asking the same question: *Where the hell are you, Sam?*

It was beautiful. God, it was something. Perfect. The sky was bright blue and full of cottony clouds, the sun was shining, it was warm, fragrant, spectacular, and Royce Hawthorne was in the salty darkness of the beer joint, sitting in the stall of the men's room, breathing disinfectant and tooting flake. He did another hit and put his coke spoon away. His sinuses felt frozen.

He was so cool, his jones was frozen. His johnson was asleep. His brain, however, was going eighty-four thousand miles a second. He tipped back the can of Oly Light he'd brought into the john with him, and tossed it unerringly into the corner basket, his over-the-stall-top blind free throw, made from lots of practice.

Get it done, chump, he said to his legs, and he got up and walked into the main room of The Rockhouse.

"Yo, Royce." Vandella said.

"Gimme a shooter."

The bartender gave him his drink and started wiping glasses. The day was fabulous, but by ten-thirty the place would be lousy with boozers, dopers, and bust-out degenerate gamblers. Hawthorne took his tequila and moved away from the bar, settling down in the first-base chair of the open twenty-one table.

"Morning, sir," the dealer said. Crisp. Young. Very quick, and cold as the thermometer in an L.A. anchorwoman's poot-chute. He had a name tag that read "Doug."

"Morning, Doug. Wanna play some blackjack?" The man shuffled and made a show of putting a new shoe together. There were maybe six decks in there at the moment, as if The Rockhouse had to worry about a card counter cleaning them.

Doug-baby was all business. Very good, in fact. He took three or four hundred off Royce before he had time to pull the wedgie out of his crotch.

He asked for a pile of quarters and dimes and played push with Doug for the rest of his shift, pushing twenty-five-and ten-dollar chips back and forth.

Dougie finally took his crisp white shirt and string tie out of Royce's face about forty-five minutes later, with a heavy early lunch shot starting to pack the bar. Tia came in on Doug's break, and he was more than a little pleased to see her—wrinkles, artistic brows, and all.

"Hi, doll."

"Good morning, sir." She smiled professionally, flipping in a new shuffle with her Dracula fingernails and long, slim fingers. Her hair was the color of anthracite coal, the Shadow Blue Coal.

"Rock and roll," he told her, feeling a rush through the nasal passages, feeling the tequila earn its keep.

She dealt him a succession of dime-ante bust-out losers, and he pulled everything in his pocket out onto the felt. James Brown was on the juke and he felt good, y'all. Royce's heart was keeping time with the Rockola. He bet it all.

"Let's ride that—you want to?" This time he imagined he could see it register in that pale, expressionless face.

"You got it, sir," she said. She dealt him a straight ace-queen, stood on nineteen, and paid the gambler. He walked out of The Rockhouse with more money than he'd been near in a long time. He got in his ride, put Mary's five away for safety, and headed down the hill to find his main man. They were still pricks, but he understood why they had to be. If they'd made it too easy for him to lay hands on the dough, it would have put both himself and the thing they were building at risk.

Now everybody was covered. The business with Drexel, the five-K loan from a straight citizen, these had not been pieces of stage business—they were real—and they'd stand up to quiet inquiries by interested parties, parties such as Happy Ruiz and the men he worked for.

Royce caught himself singing Sam and Dave's "Soul Man," tapping time on the wheel as he drove. Feelin' good, y'all. It's so easy when the slide is greasy. He hadn't felt so unburdened in years.

In tempo with the driving beat he could imagine the voice of a sportscaster whose name was lost to childhood memory, broadcasting over the roar of the excited home-team crowd:

"An *amazing* catch by seventy-four! This could prove to be the most important play in the game; with Waterton trailing Maysburg by a field goal, an incredible third down dive by sticky-fingered, lightning-quick varsity wide receiver Royce Hawthorne, makes it first and ten, goal to go! Hawthorne is sure to be all-city, all-state, all-conference, all-pro, all-star, and all-hero! Yes, fans, it's Royce Hawthorne, the alllllllll-American boy!"

For the first time in a long while he remembered the way it used to be—when his only worries in life had been scoring, and kicking the Eagles' collective ass.

12 Slabtown

The beast was very hungry. He felt clearheaded for the first time since he'd been given his freedom, really strong, coming awake with a roaring hunger. He wanted real food. Then he wanted a heart.

He tried to sort out the hazy details of the preceding day. The drugs had simply neutered him. He remembered sitting beside the river, suddenly aware that he was holding a bamboo fishing pole in his hand. He angrily tossed it aside, and heard an old man telling him to "—come on down here. I think they're bitin'." He looked down and saw the old bum sitting on some drifted logs in a small eddy that had bitten into the riverbank, fishing. Why hadn't he just buried this geek?

He could have dropped down the bank and nudged this pitiful skin-sack of nothing into the river with no effort, and the corpse might float a good distance before some fisherman would gag on his Budweiser and notify the authorities. He patted the big canvas pocket for his chain and recalled that it was somewhere on the bank behind him.

Perhaps it would be better to bring the body back up the embankment and just stuff him down in this hole where he was now sitting. He could tamp in the sides of the hole, and find some broken pieces of slab to drop on the impromptu grave.

Cottonwoods, ash, and willows grew out of the riverbank. Backwater marks of tide, slime, and flotsam had written history in the bark of the mighty trees. He could select one of the younger trees and fell it with his big fighting bowie. He could see himself bringing down a small tree with a few angry chops, swinging a steel-muscled arm that wielded a blade sharp enough to sever hanging one-inch hemp. He'd checked the blade when he first got loose, and it had been recently honed. It was razor-sharp. They'd not only given him his old survival tools and weapons, they'd upgraded his munitions. Why? He didn't buy any of Dr. Norman's explanation for a moment. Why had the monkey people set him free with weapons?

He stood up and was grateful not to feel any dizziness, but suddenly the old man wasn't worth planting. He had the strangest sensation as he went back up the bank to retrieve his chain: There was a sense of something touching him—a thing he could not begin to isolate, much less identify. He only knew that the idea of killing the old bum was not one that gave him pleasure. He gathered up his load and departed, but as he made his way through the slabs, keeping to the river, being careful not to leave an obvious trail, he thought about the old geezer, remembering the way he'd been kind to him. He found it all decidedly uncomfortable.

By dark he'd found another suitable spot and, after stuffing himself on freeze-dried rations, had slept soundly and uneventfully, sleeping for ten hours. When he woke up he was starving for something he could sink his teeth into, but except for slight soreness, he felt his powers returning.

He resumed his journey along the edge of the river slabs, heading in the direction of the waterfront place called Butchie's. It was the nearest point of interest according to the map. His duffel and weapons cases felt comparatively light—which was a good sign.

Dr. Norman's dossier played inside his head:

"Police removed nine pit bulls from an establishment on Willow River Road . . . animals had been *abused*." There was a lot more, but he allowed his mind to shut his systems down as he walked. He would turn it back on when he reached Butchie Sutter's, letting it enrage him and course through his system in the manner of poison.

The rage would wash over him like a hot red tide, and he would *abuse* Butchie Sutter, he thought, smiling ferociously. One of his big boots stepped over a pile of drift at the edge of the field he had just crossed, and he visualized the face of the man in the dossier as he stepped down into pulpy, squishy-soft log fungus, crushing it the way he would crush a face. He stomped the log into wood slime, and it glowed under his boots with the potency of poisonous mushrooms.

He read an image in the wet slime, much the same as one would read an omen. Butchie, for his dog crimes, would be left with less than sickly phosphorescence for a human face.

Chaingang Bunkowski was already a veteran of juvey incarceration when he entered the prison system for the first time as an adult. At 475 pounds, over six feet seven, the look of him alone was unique. But then—to look inside the mind of Daniel Edward Flowers Bunkowski was to look into the frightening darkness of a creature who was both man and monster.

Dr. Norman had chanced upon his workup sheets, drawn by the outsize statistics and his own clinical needs of the moment. He spoon-fed his special computers the results of the quotient and behavior tests, profiles of biochemical and psychological reactions, the measurements of the unique appetites and weird metabolics, and gathered in the results like golden treasure.

Although it was marginally possible that the power of this man's mind was such he was able to pretend to be in a drugged, hypnotic state, there was a sufficient body of evidence from repeated interviews, interrogations, debriefings, examinations, and drug-and-hypnosis sessions that confirmed Daniel had killed more persons than any other living human being.

His own best guess had been "over four hundred, maybe," a rumbled estimate from the heart of a Pentothal-induced chat, which had given rise to the grapevine legend that he'd taken a life for every pound of his weight.

Oh, if only Dr. Norman could have had Daniel for study for, say, ten years without interruption. Imagine the possibility of serious breakthroughs! Daniel was the ultimate lab animal.

Aspects of the individual's behavioristics begged to be probed. How, for just one example, had he consistently evaded authorities for such an extended period, murdering wantonly and—at first glance—randomly, without thought of being captured?

What were the keys to Daniel's presentience? Was he, as the doctor postulated, a physical precognate whose childhood horrors had produced the ultimate death-dealing machine?

There was little question, after drug-induced hypnosis sessions, that the insatiable hunger that compelled him to commit the most vile acts of mutilation and murder had been fed and nurtured by his childhood and adolescence.

Daniel feared and hated his vicious "stepfather," who left him locked in pitch-black closets for days at a time, who chained him into a suffocatingly hot punishment box, bringing the little boy out only to feed, water, or abuse him, beating him with fists, electrical cord, rubber hose, torturing him with matches, wire hangers, a soldering iron, anything that would inflict sudden and excruciating pain. These were the things that had given birth to Chaingang Bunkowski.

The will to survive had been another formative element. Most abused children, when faced with such a degree of relentless abuse, might wish that they were dead. But something in Daniel's makeup made him fight to survive. Dr. Norman thought it was raw hatred mixed with terror. Locked in total darkness, fearing for his life and for the life of his puppy imprisoned beside him in that stinking, urine-filled closet, the boy had stepped out of this imminent danger and into another room.

The door was inside the room of his imagination, where he had so often gone to fantasize, but there had been another door inside *this* room, and somehow he had learned—in a moment of screaming terror—how to unlock it.

Inside this room within a room, all things were possible: the slowing and stilling of the vital signs, the breath of death, will over matter, eidetic recall, mental photography, the acceptance and knowing of premonitions, the pathway to superhuman strength.

But in this secret room he'd also learned brutal things: how to plumb the depths of abject hatred, and to feed on unspeakable desires that had shaped the thing they called Chaingang.

The beast—bigger, stronger, smarter than any adversary—still had the mental and emotional equilibrium of a child. He was a child who could only trust another animal "like him." A dog, in fact, had been the only thing that had ever shown him love.

If you should abuse a dog, or a cat, or any animal, and he sees you—this towering behemoth of hatred and madness—God help you. You are dead. The only question is—how slow will be your dying. How much screaming will he want to hear as he pays his childhood torturer back, again and again? What grand opera of pain will satisfy him this time?

From where he is hidden in the trees, his first glimpse of the river shack called Butchie's registers an immediate prickling, tingling feeling on the back of his hairy, steel-muscled forearms and shoulders. That initial vision calls up the dossier photograph again, and the momentary feeling he experiences, which he knows is called paresthesia, a creeping sensation felt on the skin that has no objective cause, is often the precursor to his most extreme violence triggers.

He hears a barking dog and wills it back down, to sit and burble on hold, feeling the ambience of the place as the bad vibes wash over him.

Graceful cypress boughs, river oak, and huge cottonwood trees bend their leaves out over the water in the direction of the morning sun.

If Daniel Bunkowski stepped into the tree line, it is another thing that steps out now, moving in a brisk and purposeful waddle in the direction of the back door of the shack. This back-door man smells richly of open fields, and sweat, and something else. An ordurous thing that will resist identification.

He sees the watchdog and lets the red tide pour through his senses. A starving, badly mangled pit bull, short-chained to the corner of the shack, barks at him. He will deal with it later. He doesn't let himself look at it. He has his syringe kit in the duffel bag. If the monkeys have run true to form, they will have replaced the animal tranquilizers he always carried prior to his incarceration. He drops his load a few feet from the building, and a fist like the business end of a huge sledgehammer pounds on the back door.

Cursing inside.

"We're closed till eleven," a voice screeches from inside. Again. Hammer time.

Curses. Movement. Slam of door. A woman, hair wild, face a snarl of anger and disarray.

". . . closed, goddammit! Don't you fuckin' speak English?" Daring him to offend her.

He tries to speak. To do what he normally does in such instances, which is to manipulate with his voice and speech. He is a master of the mumbled nonsense phrase, the double-talk aside that buys an extra moment of time from the unsuspecting.

He opens his mouth, but nothing comes out. The drugs, perhaps, or the long time in the hole—over two years since he was in the field like this. All these elements, combined with his rage, render him speechless. All he can do is roar and growl and it explodes right there and he is carefully chain-slamming her and waddling past her moving into the shack, moving quicker than anyone alive has ever seen him move, silently, a deadly killer who only wants one thing—to destroy! He opens a door ready to strike.

Another starving dog! This one is muzzled. Their house pet, no doubt. These fucks. His rage is a blinding thing, and behind him a voice snarls, *"Who the fuck are—"* But this serious threat is negated as the bearded gutter face is split open, a yard of tractor-strength chain links smashing down at it, upside Butchie Sutter's ugliness. Nice 'n' easy, by Chaingang's standards.

He goes through the shack. No more human filth. No more pit bulls. He turns. Goes back the way he came, getting his bag from beside the door, getting leather gloves, this and that. Dragging the woman into the main area of the barroom beside her employer.

He finds identification. Connie Vizard is her name, William Sutter the oaf's handle. He binds the man's wrists in a wet bar towel, searching for things, people, goodies. He turns up a length of stout clotheline, tests its tensile strength, binds Butchie with a vengeance, stuffing another wet rag in the man's mouth.

Gets bottles from behind the bar. The gasoline container from the back room. Pours, soaking Butchie and assorted rags, papers, flammable stuff. He wants Butchie awake when he lights him up.

Examines both pit bulls again. Should he feed them? Then what? He checks his kit—he has the tranquilizer. He could knock them out, leave them at a vet's with money and a note. Both dogs look beyond help. He destroys them quickly, as humanely as he can.

It angers him to do so, and he puts his silenced firearm back in the duffel and returns to the woman. Grabs her hair, pulls her face close to his. She is groggy but conscious when he tenses from the diaphragm and hauls up a monstrous regurgitation of foulness, belching residue of freeze-dried Long Rats, halitosis, and the clump of hot wild garlic he munched on the way to Butchie's, into the face of Ms. Vizard. She gags on the breath of death and he snaps her neck while Butchie struggles, showing them his disdain for them as he takes them out.

He trails the last few droplets of gasoline to the door. Leaves. Outside he lights the matches and tosses them into the nearest trail of dripped gasoline, holding the door open to watch the fast tongue of flame shoot into the house toward the pile of burnables. The papers, rags, paint buckets, curtains, Butchie—the mound of soaked shit catches fire with an angry *thwomp!*

He could be anywhere now as he moves away from the burning shack. The leaky rowboat and tippy dinghy at the crude pier could as easily be junks or sampans. Just another Zippoed hootch.

Heading down through the waterfront woods that border Willow River Road, moving away from Slabtown, Daniel's face is a ferocious, crinkled smile. The air is crisp. The day is sunny. It is pleasant listening to the crackle of the flames. A good day to be alive.

13

Waterton

Royce Hawthorne felt like a ten-ton weight had been at least partially lifted from his shoulders. A weight in keys, actually, but it could have gone ten tons worth of bad.

The special unit would have been proud. It was so typical of their ways. As he drove in search of Happy, the memories of the two nightmare years he'd spent "away from home" played in his head like bad dreams.

Mary wondered if he'd been doing "detective work of some kind." Sam telling her he'd joined the CIA. How could he tell anybody about what he'd been through? A world as far removed from the covert ops planners and need-to-know poli-sci majors of Langley as one could get. Yet, oddly, such a similar world, where case officers and informants and blackmail and twisted motives were a way of life.

He shrugged off the thoughts. Nothing would spoil his mood. The "Package" was now wrapped. In the care of the United States postal system and—presumably—safe and sound. His sinuses were aching and he pulled over and did some snort. So good. Good for me. Good for you. Umm good. Feel good. Real good.

Royce pulled off Quarry Road, northbound, and followed a dirt-bike trail for about half a mile. The roadhouse had been built to resemble a saloon in an old B-western: hitching posts, covered step-up porch, extended front wall, swinging doors—now permanently nailed open against the outer wall—and more bullet holes than a county road sign.

Called "2 Daze 3 Knights," this place had begun life as a gay bar for rough trade, drawing patrons from as far away as Memphis. But the isolated location and access made it the perfect biker bar, and the guys on the two-wheelers promptly took it away from the gays. Now it was where the people of color hung. Jamaicans, Cubans, Colombians—mostly Latinos frequented the roadhouse now, with an occasional black of two in their company. The original cutesy name had long since been deep-sixed, and the only name now was a large painted CANTINA over the entranceway.

Royce made sure that Mary's dough was well hidden in the stash and he locked his ride, feeling very pale as he entered the bar with all those greenbacks in his pocket.

Happy and Luis were at a table in the corner with two other men, in a heated discussion. Royce went to the end of the bar and nursed a tequila until Happy made eye contact. Royce nodded. The man got up, Luis beside him, and sauntered over to the bar, leaving the other two at the table.

Happy, a.k.a. Fabio Ruiz, was twenty-something going on a hundred. Five feet one, but on a good day, Cuban heels with lifts brought him up to maybe five four. Long hair in a choppy, little-boy haircut that covered his forehead and most of his ears. Sulky mouth and cokey nose. A real hard-on.

"Yo, homes. Ju a long way from Wallyworld." They all laughed.

"I hear ya."

"So. Ju wanna cold one?" Happy's accent had thickened perceptibly.

"I'm good. I brought something. You want it in here?"

"Less see—whatchew brought me." Luis Londoño was on the other side, and real close—Royce realized. If he came out with something in his hand they didn't like . . .

"Here ya go." He slid a thick package out of his pocket and into Happy's hand. Royce was surprised to see him casually open it right there. The guy behind the bar was making a show out of not looking anywhere near them.

"Nnn-hm." The man made a little two-note humming sound of satisfaction.

"Happy?" Royce said in a quiet, hoarse voice, lowering it more and whispering, "I got a dude—really moving for me, mano."

"Uh-huh."

"You know I'm for real now, huh?" He felt like everybody in the bar was looking at his back.

"What's not to love?" it sounded like he said.

"I can move serious weight, if you can set me up."

"Whatchew call serious, amigo?"

Royce whispered a number in the crow's wing of oily hair over his left ear. He could see the kilos tumble into place like cherries on a one-armed bandit.

Happy made a little whistling sound. "Thass—"

"Same quality."

"—no prob-lemo."

"How much you nail me for?"

Happy did some mental math and whispered a figure in his ear. They haggled a little. Happy redid his math. Royce nodded, watching himself sell it in the mirror of the back-bar.

"Let's do it, then," he said.

"Whatever makes everybody happy."

"How soon?"

"Whatever, bro. I set it up ASAP. Whatever it takes. All right?"

"Hey, Happy," he said, pushing it a little behind the cocaine, "I ain't no ounce-pouncer now, am I, señor?"

"Chit no, *jefe*," Happy laughed. "Ju drivin' the heavy Chevy."

They said their good-byes, slap-dapped, and Royce patted Luis on the back and left. It was like patting a large tombstone.

"Hi, Royce. Come on in," Mary told him, turning away when she saw who was at the door.

"Thanks, hon. I owe you big," he told her, handing her the envelope of cash.

"Oh, sure," she said, absentmindedly, but pleased to have her five thousand back. She glanced inside the envelope but didn't check it. "Any time." She appeared to have no further curiosity about his bizarre loan.

"I put a couple hundred in—you know—for interest or whatever. If you're penalized more than that, let me know."

"No. Take that back. It wasn't hardly anything."

"That's yours. I came out great. It's for the inconvenience. Don't give it back—I'll only waste it."

She didn't even hassle him about taking the two hundred back, so he knew she wasn't with it.

They sat at the kitchen table and he asked the usual question. She shook her head, telling him that Marty Kerns had called. Telling him the details of their conversation. As she did so, her pretty face registered worry, great anxiety, doubt, and suspicion—an assortment of quick despairs that blew across her attractive features like a chilling breeze.

Marty Kerns. There were three salient features about the good chief of public safety, or chief of police, as everybody in the town still called the office. He was tough, corrupt, and stupid. Royce decided he'd start trying to really help this woman—whom he'd just taken advantage of without a thought to any possible consequences.

"Marty Kerns isn't doing anything, Mary. Whatever gets done from here on, we're going to have to do—or some other law enforcement agency like the county or the Feds will have to do. Kerns couldn't find his fat ass without help."

There was a moment like the old times that flashed between them in that heartbeat of candor, and he read an unspoken question in her eyes. He imagined that she was asking him—you think something bad has happened to Sam, don't you? And he tried to answer her on the same wavelength.

"Listen," he began, "let's start with what we know. Take it from the top. What was the biggest thing in Sam's life besides you? It was the land deal. Since the first time you told me about it, the thing has bugged me. Something doesn't play. Something wrong. I think that if we follow what Sam did in putting the land sale together, we might get some clue as to what happened."

"I . . . uh . . . don't have any better ideas," she said, shrugging. Telling him that she thought it was useless.

"Go back to the beginning. When was the first time he mentioned the deal to you? Who was this guy—this Sinclair whatshisname? How did he get in touch? Let's start by calling the phone number in Virginia that Sam called."

She took him through the whole thing, step by step. The walk-in who called out of the blue one day about wanting to purchase rural properties, not sounding like he was anybody who would actually follow through. Then showing up a week later and meeting her husband at a restaurant in Maysburg. Describing Christopher Sinclair later to Mary as having "pink skin the color of a baby's tush." The big cash offers that whoever he represented intended to make to ten local landowners. Whoever he was fronting for had done their homework. They knew how to make offers that would be extremely tough to decline out of hand. Something that no outsider should have been able to do without spending a lot of time in research, Sam emphasized.

There was supposedly going to be a major ecological research and development center located on this three- or four-hundred-acre circle out in the middle of nowhere. There were already rumors flying around the town about what the piece of ground was going to be used for.

She told Royce about the big cashier's check that the man gave Sam to present to Cullen Alberson at that initial meeting.

"Take me through the offers, Mary. How was it handled?"

"Well, Cullen was first. Sam took the money out to him that evening and got a done deal, as he called it. Got Cullen to sign his piece of ground over right then and there. All it took was a look at the numbers on the check."

"How much was the check for?"

"Fifty thousand dollars!"

"I shouldn't wonder. That's ten times what it's worth. My God!"

"Sam said it was way out of line. But that's how he knew Mr. Sinclair was a legitimate businessman, when that first cashier's check went through without any problems. Anybody with that kind of serious money, you know, they have a way of getting your attention.

"Next was Weldon Lawley. They sent a payment direct in the mail to him. I don't recall exactly—but it's all in the office papers. A few days later they deposited money here in town and had Sam finalize the deal with the Poindexters. And it went on like that until they had all the ground."

"I want to get all the contracts, copies of abstracts, deeds—everything that Sam kept on this deal, okay?"

"Sure." They dug out the Alexandria, Virginia, phone number, and Royce dialed it. An intercept clicked on. It was no longer a working number. Directory assistance had no such party in any of the Alexandria or D.C. listings.

"I think we should go to all these people and talk to them personally."

"I already have—some of them."

"I know. But let's start from square one and try to put this deal together just as it happened. See if anything holds up a red flag, y' know?"

"Okay. I want to put this money back. Let's go down to the office, if you want to, and we'll get all the stuff."

"Fine."

"Royce . . . you don't need to waste any more of your time with this. I can ask around. I should never have got you involved. I'm sure you've got your work . . ."

"I have nothing but time. Come on," he said, and they left the Perkins house. After the bank, they got the papers, then Royce dropped off Mary at home and took everything back to study overnight.

He wanted this to immerse himself in tonight. He did not want to have to be alone with the Royce Hawthorne who knew him so well, who knew what he'd become and what he'd chosen to do. He wanted no part of his own self-centered thoughts, and the last thing he wanted was time for any self-analysis. Tonight was not the night to look into his own soul. He would occupy his mind fully. So that he'd not accidentally look into himself and see the bottomless black hole that had once been a conscience.

14

Berthalou Irby's Property Near Waterton

Chaingang was tired, hungry, cold, angry, and irritants he could not yet precisely identify were tugging at him. He sensed three things simultaneously—none of them strong vibes—tingles, really, and hardly enough to evoke serious disquietude in the beast's gyro. Yet—anything that stayed at the edges of his mind continued to irritate him until his powerful awareness could pull it into focus.

There was the fire upriver. He'd waddled down through the nearby wood line, covering his tracks from habit, and set traps for any searchers who might follow him. None came.

That was number one. The second thing was the time factor—the hick fire department wailed onto the scene when the blaze had all but gutted Butchie's. Whatever postfire investigation had taken place was ludicrously cursory, and suspiciously inept.

He heard Dr. Norman's admonition "You will be protected . . . twenty-five mile radius of—" again, and these things triggered the sense of a hidden pair of eyes. He waited for the word to nudge him.

W A T C H E R came back into focus. Only the suggestion of something: surveillance, an eye on high, an unseen manipulater. That was it—

he was sensing their manipulation. It angered him this morning, to find himself doing a suit's bidding. It enraged him to think they considered him so easy to control. He would show them what control was, before this was over. He would feed their control to them, tear it from them with steel sawteeth, fill their orifices with it. Small wonder they gave him weapons. *He was being watched!*

He had spent the night in a place the map indicated was Willow River Slough. It had turned surprisingly cold. At first light, wrapped in everything he owned that wasn't a tool, food item, or weapon, he waddled back half a klick or so and took down his cop-traps. During the night he'd amused himself watching a two-story frame house. It had caught his eye because it appeared empty of humanity.

Chaingang returned to the site where he'd hunkered down for the night, repacked his gear in weapons cases and duffel, and continued to surveil the lonely home until the sun went under. He killed time by rigging a crude mantrap which he would leave as a parting gift—a surprise for whoever might chance to blunder along. The house continued to appear devoid of people.

As he stood waiting in the last rays of the setting sun, cold and pissed, one of the things that had been pulling at him finally inched into view. There was something in the thick growth of wild honeysuckle beside him. Gingerly he reached a huge paw in and found the soft mass of rags and twigs. Until he pulled it out, he thought it might be an odd bird's nest of some kind, but he saw in his hand a mass of wriggling newborn mice. It had been the tiny heartbeats he'd sensed.

His bloodlust had grown to such proportions that he almost choked on his own saliva flow as he popped one of the rodents into his mouth, chomping it in two and crunching it as if it were a piece of popcorn. It tasted foul and he spat it out, wiping his mouth with the back of his hand, and flinging the murid hors d'oeuvres away from him.

Why would he—this lover of animals—try to eat a baby mouse? Because he was so *fucking hungry*, is why. It was a fierce thing that tickled his throat and made him slightly faint.

The early darkness settled around him. He took a deep breath and gathered up his belongings, waddling up out of the slough toward the isolated house.

He knocked at the door forcefully. Rang a silent doorbell. No reaction. In the distance a dog barked, but it was across the field from him. He penetrated the flimsy lock and closed the door behind him.

His powerful flashlight's beam stabbed into the blackness, illuminating a room full of genuine American antiques. Chaingang, whose disinterest in monetary values—not to mention aesthetics—was organic and complete, registered the possessions in his computer.

Swiftly he moved through the house, first determining the downstairs was empty, then negotiating the stairs in measured, surprisingly quiet footsteps as he eased his massive bulk up to the second floor of the old home. Nobody home, as he'd surmised.

He began with the upstairs bedrooms, working his way through the closets, bureaus, and trunks, looking for those things that always piqued his interest. By the time he'd made his way back downstairs, he knew a bit about the house and who occupied it.

Berthalou Irby, 67, female Cauc, widow of farmer Everette Irby, lived here with their only child, a retarded forty-one-year-old daughter named Imogene. Mrs. Irby had kinfolk across the river in Tennessee, and a sister in Bella Latierre, Louisiana, where they had gone to visit. He gathered they would not be coming back within the week.

Counting insurance, farm proceeds after sharecropper deductions, Social Security payments, medical disbursements, certificates of deposit, bonds, and other income sources, Berthalou Irby was getting by on somewhere between sixty-five and seventy-five thousand dollars income per year, one tenth of which she tithed to the Holy Trinity Church of Waterton.

The heat had been turned down and the house was like a tomb. He kicked it up to roasting and removed his clothing, careful not to track excessive dirt on the fine antique rugs. He'd already decided not to trash the house, his usual MO, for a variety of reasons—all of them self-serving.

Nude, he took his massive fighting bowie, and went in and took a steaming hot shower.

Once, during a period in which he was institutionalized, he'd heard a conversation about a motion picture in which somebody is stabbed while taking a shower. He was not a stupid man, and a thought tried to enter his head to the extent that such a scene was now ready to be played in reverse should an intruder enter this bathroom. But the thought was too close to normalcy and he rejected it as superfluous.

He realized this house had pleased him, bringing him from a bad to good mood almost instantly.

Nude but for his bata-boots, the heat feeling wonderful on his body, he ventured down into the basement to find the best treat of all—Mrs. Irby's food pantry! The larder was incredible. This woman liked to eat.

The canned goods alone dumbfounded him. He stood, awestruck, trembling with pleasure at the gold mine of edibles.

One wall of the large cellar was wall-to-wall, floor-to-ceiling Ball mason jars of canned foods, every jar with a neatly printed label. No art lover walking through the MOMA or the Tate or the Louvre ever thrilled at the beauty of a masterpiece the way the beast filled with appreciation at the colors and textures of such a display of food. No cocksman ever eyed an eighteen-year-old starlet with more unbridled desire than Chaingang felt as he lusted for munchies.

The beauty and diversity, the symmetry and promise of pleasure, the sheer size of such a display—it was beyond anything in his experience.

What a picture it would have made, the gigantic fat slob of a killer, mother-naked except for his combat booties, standing in front of the rows of waiting food: baked apples and applesauce, stewed tomatoes and potatoes, green peppers and green beans, corned beef and beef roast, chow-chow relish and piccalilli, cabbage and cauliflower, lima beans and pinto beans, baked beans and black bean soup, ham and pork sausage, grape jelly and apple butter, blackberries and peaches, pears and juice, peas and carrots, asparagus and broccoli, okra and squash and turnips and corn—everything cannable from chopped beef in gravy to Mrs. Irby's chili!

He selected his dinner with the confidence of a gourmet, his mind taking each item through chopper, blender, pressure cooker, jar lifter, funnel, ladle, food mill, water-bath canner, strainer or colander, into those beautiful capped and dome-lid jars.

Back upstairs, still nude, he cooked everything in a huge metal pot, black beans and beef stew, brussels sprouts, corned beef and cabbage—all simmered together, filling the kitchen with smells so rich, he almost fainted. He found a container of whipped cream in the freezer and ate a jar of baked apples with topping as he waited for dinner to cook.

Folding his tarp into a huge napkin and hotplate, he ate directly from the big cooking pot, ladling great slurps of food into his maw and swallowing it down without seeming to chew it. Devouring it—inhaling it—absorbing the food directly into his life-support system.

Afterward, belching expansively, he searched for beer or whiskey. Found cooking wine and tried some but spit it out. It was bitter. Baby mouse wine. Finally he located and prepared a rich cup of coffee, making it with three heaping spoons of Maxwell House and a preposterous amount of sugar.

After double-checking his security, he turned two of the smaller lamps on in the house, ones that would not change the dark exterior appearance of the home, and he flipped through a couple of magazines, yawned, went into the downstairs bathroom and defecated. Tried the old woman's bed. Didn't care for it. Went in and plopped down on the retarded daughter's bed and was sound asleep within thirty seconds, snoring like a pair of chainsaws.

In his untroubled slumber a three-headed dog named Cerberus came and stood guard, watching over him while he slept. Man's best friend at the Gates of Hell.

The sturdy old home had been built back in a time when carpenters were artisans who took great pride in their craftsmanship, and in what they did for a living, rather than simply working to earn a living. The home was relatively soundproof, so he did not hear the light patting of raindrops on the roof over the second floor. But as the curtain of heavy rain drew nearer, the beast came awake just as thunder crashed in the field beside the farmhouse.

Pleased he was not sleeping out in the thunderstorm, he immediately fell back into deep sleep, waking up two hours later, at early dawn with the rain still falling. There was no way he was going to leave this warm house. He went back to sleep again, and slept until midmorning.

It was a gray, rainy day, and he was enormously pleased to remain where he was for the time being. He spent the day lolling about nude, giving the house and its contents a thorough investigation. From time to time he would go down into the basement to bring up more mason jars of canned food, and fix himself snacks. By afternoon the kitchen was filled with empty jars everywhere one looked, and he busied himself for a time washing out the jars and packing them away in cartons he'd found in the basement. When he left, he would rearrange the shelved goods so that things would not appear to have been tampered with.

He spent a few minutes gazing out the windows at the wet, heavy sky and the muddy fields. There was no traffic whatsoever. His huge belly full, his body rested, he turned on the television set with the sound off, and became tumescent while watching a young actress on one of the soap operas. He started to masturbate, but it seemed like too much trouble and he stopped, realizing that he was going to have to have a woman very soon.

After a while he turned the sound up on an obviously rigged game show, thinking what enjoyment it would give him to rip the host's heart from his fatuous body. The monkeys jumped up and down and squealed with excitement, and he shook his huge head in amazement.

He was not a fan of movies or television, but on occassion he would watch TV, invariably transfixed by the spectacle of the monkey people and the small, strange window through which so many of them experienced the world.

Was this really what they did each night in those cozy, snug homes in the suburbs? He was perpetually fascinated by the monkeys . . . by their lifestyles and Weed Eaters and miniature golf courses and county fairs. They were as remote a species to him as he was to the normal man, and he could drive through their clusters of tract homes at night and be vastly entertained just trying to imagine what their tax-paying, lawn-tending lives were like behind those ornate front doors.

He had no frame of reference for "family." No sense of common bond. No remembered childhood pleasures of the hearth and home. To his mind these gibbering, monkeylike fools were as alien as visiting other-worlders. He'd sometimes drive stolen vehicles through the suburbs of whatever city he was in, captivated by the warmth of the lights in those darkened homes.

Often he would see a family watching the box, perhaps visible through their open curtains, and the sight never failed to mesmerize him.

"—a way you can earn up to a million dollars a year just by letting your friends and neighbors in on the secret. And best of all—"

"—order before midnight tonight and you'll not only get those wonderful steak knives, but you'll also get, absolutely free, and at no charge, this marvelous potato peeler as well—"

"—remarkable low price of only twenty-nine ninety-nine. With these spectacular new miracle wipers, you will never again have the problem of—"

"—earn while you learn this richly lucrative business from the ground up. In a moment we'll introduce you to the man who pioneered the dynamic no-money-down method of purchasing—"

"—Gabe, I want you to go ahead and rub it all over the hood. That's right. Just rub in anywhere on there. Now, Margo, you rub your side. There you go. Start in anywhere and cover those hoods with wax. We're going to let both coats set under the hot lights, and in a few minutes we'll come back and take a look at—"

"—lost over a hundred pounds with this amazing new product. There was never any between-meal hunger because of the—"

"—many who wished they could play but didn't have time to study the piano. Now you can start in playing songs right away! It only takes—"

One scam after another. Political scams. Snake oil scams. Art scams. Music scams. Costume jewelry scams. Every greed-targeted con job, bogus shuck, and jive sting that had ever been conceived of was right there on that weird tube.

The monkey people scammed each other all day, scammed themselves all night, and in between they watched people scamming one another on a little box. They were idiots!

He turned the channels. Puzzled somewhat, as always, by the obvious insincerity of the hair-care hucksters and car salesmen and televangelists whom he perceived as parts of the same great network of con games:

"God says we must wage *war* against Satan! We must *take back* what the devil has stolen. Our ministry must spread to the far corners of the world." The strange, extremely earnest-looking evangelist spoke with a voice that rose and fell like ocean waves, but now he hardened his pitch and spoke in no-nonsense tones. "Here is what it will take to reach out and take back what belongs to the Lord. It will take . . . fifty-two million dollars!"

He switched to another channel where a beautiful dancer moved across the small screen to a driving hard-rock audio track. An incredible montage of graphic images blinked above and behind her. The combination of the music and the imagery was intensely compelling and he turned the volume up. It was sensual, somehow, the way the pulsing rock pounded in tempo with his own strong heartbeat, and without thinking, it brought him to his feet and he was aping the movements of the dancer—Chaingang Bunkowski was dancing to MTV! Almost five hundred pounds of lard and muscle bouncing and boogieing across Mrs. Irby's floor. Another first! Daniel Edward Flowers Bunkowski rocking out stark naked. What a sight!

He didn't like the next video and he switched channels again and got a man extolling the virtues of B-12 spray packets, switched again and a woman, an actress on one of the daytime soaps, sat sobbing for the camera's eye.

Chaingang had all the actor's gifts, among them observation and memory, talents that he had in enormous abundance. An actor prepares by observing, for example, and his powers of observation were unequaled, but he hated those humans who were the object of observation—yet he found them fascinating. Even when he was not incarcerated, he preferred to spend most of his time alone, having little stomach for personal interaction—and yet so closely had he observed his fellow humans, and so painstakingly had he filed away the memory of their behavior patterns, that he could mimic them precisely—and on cue!

The soap opera actress wept, and Daniel Bunkowski allowed himself to remember the sadness of his past, contorting his fat, rubbery mask of a face in a mocking parody of the close-up on the screen, holding his huge head as she held hers, shaking with sobs the way she was, as he opened the fawcett on a waterworks of weeping. He killed the audio of the television set, and the sound of his crying filled the Irby home.

It was strangely pleasant and he gave in to the emotion, milking it at first as an actor would, enjoying the fact that his dimpled cheeks were covered in real tears and not glycerine. He soon realized that this thing he had never done in his entire adult life, this inarticulate expression of pain or distress known as crying, whether ridiculous or not, was tinged with genuine sadness that such an act was a rare outpouring from all that remained of his humanity.

At precisely 0600, almost to the sweep of the second hand, Daniel Edward Flowers Bunkowski was up like a shot, charged with electrical energy, moving, quickly waddling through the Irby house doing his cleanup chores. The kitchen spotless, the empty mason jars cleaned and stored out of sight, the shelves re-dressed and rearranged, the house restored to its pristine state, his clothing cleaned and dried, he shaved meticulously, showered luxuriously, and—having made a last top-to-bottom sweep of the house—was out of there by 0800.

The dancing clown bear made its way across the road without incident and deposited his heavy gear in the same patch of wild honeysuckle where the baby mice once lived. He watched the road for a while, halfway hoping to see a vulnerable motorist chug by in a nondescript pickup. Watching the house where he'd taken such a pleasant R & R.

The Bunkowski one-man family picnic had stored fuel away the way a camel stores water for the desert: and it was all he could do to tear himself away from the basement. Mrs. Irby's boned chicken and dumplings, baked beans swimming in brown sugar, barbecued spare ribs in hot sauce, corned beef and cabbage—he didn't need a vehicle, he probably had enough gas to fart his way to his destination. What a feast!

By noon he was well around the long curve of Willow River Road, and nearing Waterton's city limits. The blue feature was marked "Jefferson Sandbar."

After the preceding day's heavy rains, the new day had turned bright, and although the weather was cool, the sun felt good. By midday the breeze had abated. He could see the sandbar now. The river was still as a flat desert of brown glass. Voices carried from around the curve.

He kept moving through the trees, parallel to the blue, taking his time, keeping the brown-colored blue to his right, the road to his left, walking softly and carrying a big stick.

The chain would not come out to play today. Today he had other needs. Other priorities.

There were three of them, and he could see them now. Their voices were clearly audible.

"—wanna go with John when we run 'em?"

"I don't know. Where y'all a goin'?"

"Jes' goin' out to the levee. Nothing to it, ya know? Jes' turn 'em loose up there on the top of the levee."

"Mel goin' with you?" a third voice asked.

"Yeah."

"Okay. I reckon so. When you wanna go?"

"Oh, I dunno—"

He had the SKS out of his duffel. Four magazines, each with about a three-quarter load. This wasn't the Swiss job, but a crude Chinese copy, and he'd had some trouble with the springs in the magazines. But the SKS was light, and he knew the piece. He knew precisely what the 7.62s would do and what the range was. He knew the trigger pull. The recoil. The way it had to be held a hair high and to the left.

Twisting the suppressor onto the threadings, tightening it down with a grip that liked to close the prison shower handles so tight, the washers would split in half. Closer now. Hearing the monkey men discuss their dogs.

"He goes off down the road and that's when Red got hit. I thought I was going to have to horsewhip the hardheaded sum'bitch."

"Elgin's got him two of them blue ticks. Man—they make a fine dog if you—" Easing the bolt back. A boltface that he'd personally baffled down with felt and milk-base glue first, then, when that didn't work, fixing it right with Iron Glue. One monkey-shooter up the spout now.

"—wouldn't have one of them gol-danged beagles. You couldn't give me—"

Trigger pressure now coming out of the woods. What did they think—whoever saw the beast first? This . . . apparition stepping out of the woods holding a machine gun, the thing looking like a toy in its huge paws.

Only the terrain was changed. Only the color of the river dirt. There it was red and green, here it was brown and gold. The same sky, sometimes. Two hundred lightly oiled and wiped rounds for the pig, carried in X-crossed Pancho Villa-style bandoliers. *Snake One to Mad Rover. Rough Trade to Magic Silo. Green Giant, this is Heavy Brother. Nitro One, what is my call sign? Quiet Cruiser, this is Jolly Roger Two, do you copy? Read you, Lima Charlie, Magic Silo.* Fondly remembered kill zones.

Another magazine facing correctly, cartridges away, held in the left fist which cradles the SKS. He'd been here a hundred times.

Snake One, this is Mike Papa. Sitrep: LZ is hot.

BATBATBAT.

BATABATABATA.

BATBAT. Loud metal clatter against felt-covered boltface. Not wasting a round with the first mag. Dropping two of them in beautifully synched two- and three-round groupings. Taking the third bass-ackwards with the next magazine, in a long quick-trigger burst of semiauto fire. Three greased monkey men down.

He'd done an arsenal job years ago. They were dangerous and tricky, but he'd ended up with all the munitions and small arms he needed. He'd made off with an Uzi, which was all the rage as the most popular SMG. But the grip safety didn't suit him and he'd finally picked up a semiautomatic Chinese knockoff, doing the conversion himself to keep it street-legal. He trusted it, and was pleased Dr. Norman and his superiors had not forced him to scrounge up a piece.

For a few seconds he considered picking up the brass. But he opted on leaving it, stomping as many shell casings as he could see into the mud, kicking some into the river, leaving some.

The wallets first. The first two. The one he'd back-shot had a money clip but no wallet or ID. A nonperson. Keys next. Checking hands for unusual jewelry. Feeling for hidden holsters, stashes, money belts. Moving them quickly and easily to the vehicle that would act as their temporary sarcophagous. An aging orange-brown Toyota with a camper on the back. Perfect.

Textbook ambush. Almost. Almost . . . He was a perfectionist. All that spoiled it were the unseen watchers. He really spent some careful time checking it all out, trying to scope out the hidden eyes. They were out there somewhere. Maybe following him through high-tech binocs from the far hills across the road. Perhaps they were out across the water. Wherever they were, they were keeping their distance. But he was almost certain of their presence.

Some suit was filming him with a telescopic lens, maybe sound-on-film, capturing the suppressor clatter of the SKS with a state-of-the-art government parabolic.

But it was of no consequence. After all, taking someone's game and running it back down their throats was what he did. His hobby, you could say. He was a collector. He collected payback.

15

Waterton City Limits

There were ten tracts of land, each a complex negotiation in itself, where dual abstracts had been drawn up by both parties, and the contractual boilerplate was mind-boggling to Royce Hawthorne. He promptly became lost in a cloud of easements, adjacencies, parcels, and legalspeak; adrift in a choppy sea of restrictions and covenants.

The tracts were far from equal in size—the smallest being a four-acre divot at the edge of Luther Lloyd's river ground, the largest being the entire Weldon Lawley farm.

Lloyd's was simplest, too, regarding paperwork. Perkins Realty had a slim folder on the deal consisting of map coordinates and title search, general warranty deed with statutory acknowledgments, dual abstract updates, letter of freedom of incumbrances, copy of clerks reply, the bill of sale, the canceled cashier's check, and a couple of pages of notes on the negotiation and purchase.

Each time he'd begin reading, something would throw him. The first sale was a "lot, tract, or parcel of land lying north of County Road '598' and being situated in the NE$^{1}/_{4}$ of the NE$^{1}/_{4}$ of Section 9: T915N; R174E of the Third Principal Meridian, Waterton County, Missouri, more fully described by metes and bounds: beginning at a point in the center line of County Road '598' therein distant east 347.83 feet from the northeast corner of Section 11-71-T915N; thence . . ."

At approximately the fifth "thence," he would start to fog up.

All of the general warranty deed documents were signed with the formal "TO HAVE AND TO HOLD the premises aforesaid, with all and singular the rights, privileges, appurtenances, and immunities thereto belonging or in anywise appertaining unto the said parties of the second part, and unto their heirs and assigns forever, the said

[Cullen Alberson and Regina Alberson, his wife]

hereby covenanting that they are lawfully seized of an indefeasible estate in fee in the premises herein conveyed; that they have good right to convey the same; that they will Warrant and Defend against the lawful claims and demands of all persons whomsoever. IN WITNESS WHEREOF, the said parties of the first part have hereunto set their hands and seals this the day and year first above written.

(Signed) [Cullen Dale Alberson] (SEAL),

[Regina Louise Alberson] (SEAL)."

A notary public had stamped her stamp in testimony whereof, a copy of the thing had been microfilmed, the instrument had been filed for record in the recorder's office by the clerk of the circuit court and ex officio recorder of Waterton, one Elizabeth Smythe.

On all of these documents the party of the second part was a very well heeled and anonymous buyer calling itself the Community Communications Company, headquartered in Alexandria, Virginia.

He drove to the nearest isolated pay phone and punched in money and the 703 area code for Alexandria, Virginia.

"Jean, what city please?"

"Alexandria."

"Yes?"

"May I have the number of the Community Communications Company, please?"

"One moment . . . Hold for the number." A recorded voice dropped the digits into the long lines:

He hung up and dialed direct. An operator asked for money. He complied and the line rang.

"Communications Company."

"Yes. My name is Royce Hawthorne and I'm phoning long distance about a piece of property your company has purchased. I need to speak with your general manager or president, or whoever acts as chief executive officer for the company. Who would that be, please?"

"You want Guy Kelber. Would you like me to connect you with his secretary?" Royce said yes, and when a female voice identified it as being Mr.

Kelber's office, he repeated his message. After a wait of nearly a minute, she came back on the phone.

"Who did you say you were with?"

"I didn't say, but I'm representing a law enforcement agency in regard to the disappearance of a man who had dealings with your company. It's vital I speak to Mr. Kelber." He kept a hard edge to his tone. He waited, hoping the "law enforcement" bit wouldn't come back to kick his ass.

"Hello. This is Guy Kelber."

He went through the routine again. Kelber had never heard of the land deal or Sam Perkins. Nor had he ever talked with a Sinclair.

"This is the Community Communications Company of Alexandria, Virginia, isn't it?"

"This is the Communications Company, Mr. Hawthorne. You apparently have the wrong firm. Sorry." Royce apologized and rang off.

He redialed directory assistance. Went through his request from the top.

"Sorry, sir. We don't show a Community Communications Company in Alexandria."

"Do you show a Community Communications Company in Washington, D.C., or is that a different area code?" Knowing.

"That would be two-oh-two, sir." He thanked her. Dialed. Ran it by another operator.

"We show a Community Communicators in Bethesda. And there is a Communications Company in Alexandria and Arlington, Virginia. But we do not show a Community Communications Company. Would you like to try one of these other numbers?"

He told her yes, he'd try them all. He wrote down the three numbers, including the one he'd just dialed. The Bethesda, Maryland, number proved to be for a school that taught teachers who specialized in learning-impaired students. The Arlington number was a separate listing for the first place he'd called. They were in the broadcasting business. Had no land holdings. Yes. Mr. Kelber was chairman of the board. No, he'd never heard of a Community Communications Company of Alexandria.

Royce Hawthorne's adult life, much of it, had been lived on phones, or through events and transactions that had transpired or gone down with the aid of that instrument. He knew people who were very much "into phones." It was one of those persons he called next, leaving a terse message on a recording, and hanging up.

If there was a more nagging brand of angst than doper paranoia, it had to be "phoneman" disease, a uniquely lethal strain that apparently spawned in the invisible energy bogs that surrounded high-voltage transformers, microwave transmitters, and Lord knows what else, and that headed—like iron to a magnet—for the nastiest dope burns it could find. Telephones and junk—what a combination!

Royce felt it prod him like a hard jab to the kidneys, and he suddenly visualized Happy and a couple of cartel wire-tappers: alligator clips, recorders, headset all in place, tapping into *Jefe* Hawthorne as he set them up for double-digit bits in the slamarooney. They would not be amused. Happy would not be happy.

Royce's hand was slick with sweat as he reached for the pay phone again, stopped in midair by a frightening apparition, a sight that froze him in the warm noonday sun of Willow River Road. He saw someone or some*thing* coming out of the woods.

Shades of Beaudelle Hicks's kid appearing from out of nowhere, but my God—this was the most frightening-looking man Royce had ever laid eyes on, just gigantic, a hulking behemoth moving through the trees, carrying what looked like a couple of large wooden cases under one arm, and a thing like a heavy punching bag slung over one shoulder. It came through the trees, and Royce saw the behemoth look at him just as he saw the huge man moving out of the woods.

This fearsome giant, bigger than anything imaginable, looked at Royce with the most venomous stare he'd ever seen, and it chilled him to the bone.

There was just a beat when it looked like the man was stopping in his tracks, trying to make up his mind whether to come over and kick Royce's ass for the fun of it, but he turned and kept going, moving across the road and disappearing into the brush again.

Who the fuck was he? Royce had never seen him before, and for a few seconds he got mixed into the dope equation—he sure as hell could have passed for a stone killer—but then he regained control and realized how he was letting his imagination screw him around. He took a very deep breath, hopped back in his ride, and headed out Cotton Avenue to talk with Cullen Alberson, if he could find him, visions of "Bigfoot" still stomping around in his head.

Royce Hawthorne had spent the better part of two days calling and visiting and calling again. He'd come nearly full circle, and only managed to actually interview—if that's the word—two persons who'd sold ground to the mysterious Community Communications Company of Alexandria, Virginia. Weldon and Cullen, the first two guys he'd tried to reach, had both been open and accessible. But as luck would have it, he'd spun his wheels the rest of the next day trying to make contact with the other eight property owners.

He was now around to the tenth seller, Bill Wise, who owned, among many other holdings, Bill Wise Industrial Park, a precariously prosperous gamble that had once held great promise for Waterton. Wise, who'd made a fortune in used office furniture down in Nashville, had moved to Waterton thinking it was virgin investment territory. He'd set up a used office furniture outlet in Maysburg, which had done well, and purchased large pieces of ground in both Maysburg and Waterton, calling them—optimistically—industrial parks, and landscaping them for the flood of industry that would someday push out from Paducah, and Memphis, and St. Louis, looking for low-rent settings for plants, factories, offices, and other building sites. When the industrial parks had withered on the vine, Wise had filled them himself: with office furniture showrooms, warehouses, and sprawling flea markets that always seemed on the verge of going under.

Bucky Hite, another drinking/smoking/snorting buddy of Royce's, was one of a dozen men working in the corner of Wise's northeast property, on the piece being developed by Community Communications Company.

There were several cats and backhoes at work, and some heavy equipment Royce wasn't familiar with, and he was parked at the edge of the field waiting for Bucky, who was busy being harangued by a man who appeared to be the foreman on the job. He looked at his notes that summarized what he'd learned on Mary's behalf during the last couple of frustrating days:

1. CULLEN ALBERSON—He had been presented a "killer offer," his words, fifty thou, so much money he hadn't even talked it over with the missus—he just signed the deal then and there. He'd had no further contact after the deal was consummated with Sam Perkins, and no dealings with any Mr. Sinclair or the buyer.

2. WELDON LAWLEY—Sam had done the initial leg-work, and Lawley had looked at the contract. Said okay. The company sent him a bank draft. (It had taken a visit by Mary to pry the info out of First Bank of Waterton's office manager, Lester Peebles.) The draft came via a New York bank, Chase Manhattan. Another hour of LD calls had netted the information that the draft had been purchased by Merchant's Bank in Washington, D.C. They had no information, or were not able or willing to find out, about the initiation of the large cash draft.

3. GILL POINDEXTER—Sam had finalized the deal, and they had again deposited money. This time First Bank was unable to help. The family was apparently out of town, and neither Royce nor Mary had been able to get hold of Gill or Betty Poindexter.

4. RUSSELL HERKEBAUER—He and his sons were on a hunting trip out West. Would be gone for a couple of weeks. Mrs. Herkebauer did not know the details of the deal, or she wasn't talking without her husband's okay.

5. DOYLE GENNERET—Gone on a business trip. His foreman, Dean Seabaugh, was busy with the animal auction and didn't have time to talk. Royce had tried to get him to open up, telling him a man had disappeared and that if Seabaugh didn't talk to him, he'd eventually have to talk to the cops. This had really frightened Seabaugh, who had said, "Big fucking deal,"

and slammed the door on him.

6. LUTHER LLOYD—Gone. Mrs. Lloyd said he was "running around somewhere" and didn't know when he'd be back. "Probably late." Royce left word. When nobody called back that evening, he dialed the Lloyds' and nobody answered.

7. RUSTY ELLIS—Gone. Nobody had seen him around the farm in a while. Royce had driven out to the farmhouse and found some papers in the driveway. He peeked into the mailbox and saw a collection of junk mail.

8. CELIA and LETITIA BARNES—Out-of-town owners. He had not been able to reach either of them by telephone. Their sharecroppers knew nothing about the land deal.

9. AUGUST GROJEAN—Just about took his head off when he called. "I ain't saying nothing about nothing without my lawyer." He'd just been through extensive legal battles over his ground, and he refused to listen to reason. He had given Royce his Memphis lawyer's number for a telephone contact, and so far he'd been unable to reach the lawyer by phone.

10. BILL WISE—Last on the list. He had just missed Wise, somebody said at the flea market, and was waiting for a word with Bucky, whose voice carried across the field.

"They do that to everybody. They do it every damn time. I don't see how the crooked sum'bitch stays in business."

"I called him," the foreman shouted from his truck. "I told him, 'You short me two yards every time you pour out here, goddammit, and I ain't taking that shit off you people again. If you short me again, I'll buy from fuckin' Flat River if I have to, but I won't use you again.' I told him."

"What did he say to that?"

"'Oh, I never shorted you no two yards,' he says. Well, I know better." Another comment was drowned out by the equipment noises.

"He's nothing but a fuckin' crook."

"I'm going."

"All right."

The truck pulled out across the bumpy field, and soon Bucky Hite made his way to where Royce was waiting.

"Sorry about that. The boss had a bug up his butt."

"Sounded that way."

"Fuckin' Jerome Thomas crooked us outta some more concrete. Nothing new there." He frowned.

"So I've heard."

"Got anything?" Hite asked.

"Say what?"

"You holding?"

"I got a joint."

"No. I mean blow."

"Not right with me," Royce said.

"Oh well, no biggie."

"I wanted to ask you about this deal. What's cooking with all this?"

"Some big company, man. Outta D.C., I hear. Going to make a big park like Six Flags. That's confidential. Going to mean a shitload of new jobs." He raised his eyebrows. "You know—some of us got to have them things."

"Fuck you." They laughed. "Six Flags? Out here? Bullshit."

"No—really. That's what I heard. Foreman says in a few days they going to pour footings, and man, it's going to be big. You trying to get a gig?"

"Not so's you'd notice. I'm just asking for a friend." He decided he'd tell Bucky. If anybody in Waterton hadn't heard about the disappearance, this would take care of it. "Sam Perkins? I don't know if you heard yet, but he's missing. I'm a friend of the family. Just, you know, asking around."

"Yeah. I heard. Cops asked everybody already. They got hold of some dude that he was doing business with, and he told the cops he didn't know anything. So I heard." This guy driving a backhoe knew more than the man's wife, Royce thought.

"What dude? Somebody Sam was dealing with?"

"Yeah."

"Was it a guy named Sinclair?"

"Beats the shit out of me." He shrugged. "Ask the cops, man."

"Me and the cops aren't on the best of terms."

"Yeah, I hear that," Bucky said.

"Where'd you hear that anyway?"

"Foreman. No . . . shit, I don't remember. Maybe it was some guy at Judy's. Hell, I can't remember."

"Try."

"We were eatin' at Judy's. Seems like—oh, I know who it was. Kelly McCauley's husband."

"Who's Kelly McCauley's husband?" He was getting very tired of this. He wanted to go back to the cabin and do some tootski and get his shit together.

"Jeezus. Kelly's the chick with the big guacamoles that works in Kerns's office. She overheard him talking about this guy who'd been doing business with the real estate dude, okay? He told 'em he didn't know anything. They had two or three missing people, and they all had some mutual connection with the project." He pointed at the construction work behind him. "It turned out to be nothing. Just coinci—"

"Hold it, Bucky. What people? I never heard anything about any two or three missing people. Who were they?"

"Beats my ass." He shrugged again. "You wanna know—go ask Kelly

McCauley. Don't she live over near you?"

"I don't know her."

"Kelly McCauley," he repeated, cupping his hands in front of his chest. "Lives over there by Waterworks Hill next to Diane's."

"Oh. Wait a minute." Royce's mind finally slipped back into gear. "She lives in that trailer next to Diane's Hairquarters."

"That's the lady."

"I know who she is. Yeah—I'd seen them around, I just didn't know the last name. Where does he work, do you know?"

"Uh-uh."

"Okay. Thanks, man. Hey—if you hear anything about Sam Perkins, or hear anything else about these missing people . . . do me a favor? Call me. If I'm not there, just leave word, 'kay?" He got out a pen and wrote Mary's phone number on a scrap of paper.

"Okay. No problem."

"What the hell would somebody wanna put a Six Flags way the crap out here for?"

"Not a real Six Flags, man. Some kind of . . . um . . . you know, like Expo deal, where they do scientific shit and people take tours through it. Hey—how the fuck do I know? Just don't knock it, I'm draggin' double time and a half!"

"Lotta new hands around?" Royce glanced around.

"Some."

"What's that big fucker do? You know who I mean—about the size of two refrigerators?" Royce held his hands apart as wide as he could. But Bucky just looked at it, obviously having no idea who he was referring to.

"What big fucker?"

"You'll recognize him if you see him, dude." Royce laughed. "He blots out the sun." He thanked the man and they said good-bye. Hite went back to work, and Royce started driving back to town. He was surprised the big boy wasn't one of the new construction guys.

As soon as Royce was out of sight, Bucky Hite crumpled up the phone number and threw it into the dirt.

Fuck it.

Waterworks Road was a short piece of well-traveled blacktop that ran from Cotton Avenue, at the base of Waterworks Hill, to the boonies beyond Waterton's remote water treatment plant and reservoir.

The low-rent housing started about fifty yards off the road on some corner pastureland where an old single-wide was visible behind a thicket of weeds. Royce thought about knocking. Asking his questions real friendly.

Next to the broken mailbox a piece of rubber tire lay coiled like a dead blacksnake. He'd seen Kelly McCauley before. A slightly heavy young woman with a child's hands, big, bouncy breasts, and a provocative if rather porcine look around the eyes and nose. She lived there—in the trailer—and the look of the place stopped him.

Maybe he thought her old man would hassle him, coming up to the crib to rap with little Mama. Everybody was always sniffing around Kelly. Checking out those big, soft handfuls of love. Hanging around the city administration building, where the jail was, trying to get a look down those low-cut things she wore to work sometimes. Maybe Kelly had a little problem, too.

Or maybe he could imagine her slamming that door in his face when he started asking questions about what she overheard her boss, Chief Kerns, say about this and that. That's striking pretty close to the lunch bucket. If Kelly had half a brain, she'd clam up. Next thing—Marty Kerns would be bringing him down to the jail for a little talk and a late night swim in the fish tank.

Whatever brought him to his senses in time stopped him dead and turned him around, sent him back to his ride, and headed him on down Waterworks past Diane's Hairquarters and around the corner.

One of his fave pay phones was located in front of a ma-'n'-pa grocery. He stopped. Got out. Dropped change and dialed the McCauley residence. Three rings.

"Hello."

"Is this Mrs. Kelly McCauley?" he asked, putting as much hard twang in it as he could muster.

"Yes."

"Mrs. McCauley, this is Sheriff Guthrie. Are you the lady works for Marty Kerns over in Waterton?" Tough and coarse, with most of the resonance coming right out of the nasal passages. A rumble he could almost feel in his face.

"Yes, sir." A little question mark in her tone now. The voice she used when Marty got pissed at her. Her deferential kissy-ass voice.

"Ma'am, I understand that you have been overheard making some statements that several persons are being sought in missing-persons cases in Waterton. Do you know you could get in serious trouble repeating what you heard there on the job? That's privileged law enforcement information."

"I don't know what you're talking about."

"Don't bother denying it, ma'am. Marty Kerns has already heard the tape, and so have I. You were recorded in a surveillance of another investigation, and you were taped at a place of business called Judy's Cafe, Mrs. McCauley. Your voice has been ID'd as being the one who divulged information about an ongoing case. Don't you know that's punishable under three different Missouri statutes?" He was really getting into it. In the pause for air he could almost hear her brain going a mile a minute. Trying to remember what she might have said. He pushed it. "Now, why did you tell Mr. McCauley that all these other persons were missing?"

"I didn't say that," she blurted. "I just was telling him about the one Perkins case. And, you know, I might have said that Rusty Ellis and them Poindexters was missing, too. That's all I told him, honest. It was just them three cases, and they wasn't related at all. And what I say to my husband don't go any further." She was starting to get hot about it.

"Chief Kerns is not pleased about you talking like that in public where anybody can hear you. You know better than to be discussing cases like that."

"I'm sorry." She put a little whine back in her tone.

"What else did you hear about the Poindexters or Rusty Ellis or Sam Perkins? Did you overhear other things about the case?" He knew the second he said it, he'd lost her, but he was patting his pockets looking for notes, a pen, something to write on, trying to keep his voice in character, and he knew as he uttered it that it didn't sound official enough.

"Who the hell is this, anyway?" She was smarter than she appeared. He mumbled something about being in touch with her later and hung up. Back in the car and hooking back to Cotton and down King's Road in the direction of the Perkins house. More cocaine paranoia with claws perched on his shoulder, ready to go for the throat.

"Hi." She was surprised to see him at her door.

"I—" He choked up and coughed, so full of information, he couldn't pull it all together. She knew it was something bad.

"Come in and sit down, Royce. You're so pale you look like you're about to pass out."

"Something's wrong, babe. I don't know what the hell's happening here, but . . ." He shook his head, not believing the thoughts bouncing around inside it. "Sam isn't the only person missing." He took a deep breath.

"I've been asking everybody who was part of the land deal, that I could find. Some don't want to talk. Some don't know anything, or they're damn good actors. Others—they've vanished or they've gone into hiding or been abducted or . . . whatever. I know this guy, I see him around the bars and stuff. He's got a job out there at the big construction site. He let it slip that he'd overheard Kelly McCauley, Marty Kerns's secretary, talking about others being missing. Mr. and Mrs. Poindexter. Rusty Ellis. Sam. All parties to the big land deal. And Sinclair or somebody else Sam had been dealing with has been in touch with the cops or they've found him." For the first time he was consciously aware he'd neglected to ask the McCauley girl about who that was.

"I acted like I was a sheriff and called her. Confirmed the business about Gill and Betty Poindexter and Ellis being missing. But I forgot to ask about the cops having had contact with the firm Sam was representing. She probably wouldn't have known much. Marty Kerns knows a lot of information that he's been keeping from you."

"Son of a—" She was beet red with anger. Getting up to get her purse and car keys. "I'll get an answer from him, and it had better be a good one or—"

"Keep your cool if you can, Mary. You might need him before this is over."

"I'll keep my cool, all right." She was raging. This was no surprise. She'd known that Kerns had information he wasn't giving her. "Come on, if you want to go with me."

"I probably would just make it worse. He'll be more likely to talk if I'm not there. We don't get along."

"Stay here, Royce. I'll come back as soon as I talk to him."

"Okay."

"Thanks." She looked at him with deep feelings, wanting to say more, but too full of this news to articulate it. He nodded and smiled, and she was gone.

At first Marty Kerns was cool, and tried to play it close to his vest, but when she started screaming she was going to the paper, calling her state senators, and suing the town—among other things—he opened up and told her about the case for the first time.

"It's something that looks a lot worse than it really is, Mary; that's part of the reason you weren't brought up to speed about the others that are missing. We're pretty certain it is just coincidence, and the last thing you want to do is start rumors in a little town like Waterton. That's the other aspect of it. If some of these folks got the idea people were vanishing or somethin', you'd have a panic on your hands in no time. People would be spotting UFOs, and serial killers, and God knows what! The truth is that people turn up missing all the time, even in small towns. The police get routine calls every day from somebody whose wife or husband has been missing for a couple days. Ninety-five percent of the time it's a . . . uh . . . domestic problem or something. Not like your situation with Mr. Sam. You get older folks vanish all the time, Mary. They wonder off and get lost or lose track of what time it is—things like that. Usually it's no big deal. It isn't this time either. It just could be blown up outta proportion because a couple of the people happened to have been doing some business in a real estate deal. That's the only reason you weren't told. It wasn't necessarily that relevant."

"Relevant? It seems very relevant to me. And why did you purposely withhold the information that you'd been in touch with somebody who had business dealings on the land sale and had been in contact with Sam? Wasn't that relevant either?"

"I don't know what you mean. We never had contact with any . . . Oh, you mean the guy with CCC? That didn't have a bearing on your husband's disappearance."

"How can that be?"

"He had never been in personal contact with Sam. Only with his representative, who was Mr. Sinclair, the one who had the dealings here in town. He knew nothing about Sam being gone."

"Well, where *is* this Sinclair?"

"He's out of the country, is what Mr. Fisher said."

"Who's Mr. Fisher?"

"He's the man putting together the park out there." He gestured to the north of town. "If you want to talk with him, I'll be glad to set it up for you, but I promise you you'll be wasting your time."

"Please give me his number. I certainly do want to talk to him." She felt like this stupid slob had violated her, lying to her as he had about her husband.

"I understand he'll be in town tomorrow. Why don't you get together with the gentleman if it will ease your mind?"

"Fine."

"I'll take you out to meet him myself, in the morning if you like."

"That's all right," she said. "I've got my own car."

"Fine. I'll call him when he gets in town tonight and tell him you will be coming out sometime in the morning to talk with him. How's that?" She nodded. "He'll be somewhere out there with the construction crew, I imagine. Name is Joseph Fisher. Okay?"

"I'll be there."

"As I say—you won't learn anything about Sam. But feel free. I don't want you talking about the Poindexters and Mr. Ellis being missing, Mary. There's no reason to get people worried more than they are."

"I won't say anything." Her eyes hardened. "At least for a while. But I'm telling the FBI and the sheriff's office about it."

"They already know," he said, letting a smirk show on his face for the first time since she'd gotten on his case. "Speaking of the sheriff, you know this dope fiend you been talking to about the case, this Royce Hawthorne, I want you to tell him it's only out of deference to you that his tail isn't sittin' back in my jail." Mary felt a hard knot in the pit of her stomach. It was bad enough with Sam—she didn't want to cause anybody else problems.

"He's been stickin' his nose everywhere, asking questions where he has no business, and then he has the gall to pose as the county sheriff and interrogate my personal secretary. It took me exactly one minute with his good friend and fellow junkie Mr. Hite to know who had bothered Kelly."

"He was trying to help me find out something. It was more than the police seemed willing to do. You would have never said a word to me, would you?"

"Not until there was some reason to, no. But let me ask you—now that you know what you think you know, are you any more informed? Do you know anything more about Sam's disappearance? No, little lady. You don't really know anything more. It's just upset you, is all it's done."

She wanted to spit in his ugly face. The "little lady" really brought the red back into her cheeks, but she remembered what Royce had said and forced herself to keep her mouth shut.

"Do you know what Mr. Hawthorne is, Mary? This friend you seem so willing to confide in about a police investigation and whatnot?"

"I know him very well."

"He's a dope addict. He's a cocaine dealer, did you know that?"

"No." She shook her head. "He's a friend, is all I know."

"We're watching him very closely. He's going to make a serious mistake one day, and he'll end up in the hoosegow for a long time. I'm telling you for your own good—not to help him. He's not about to change. He's been no good as long as I been knowin' him. You'd be well advised to cut loose of him, Mary."

"Please—" He'd thrown her off with this talk of Royce. She knew that what he was saying now was probably the truth. "Just help me find my husband," she said, quietly. Then she turned and left. Empty and hurting in the hollowness of her stomach. She imagined that Marty Kerns would be pantomiming blowing a kiss to her parting back, and she imagined she could hear the laughter of the other officers.

Royce had brought her a wealth of information. He'd caught the cops in lies—big lies—about a major missing-persons case. She'd thrown all of it in Kerns's face, and somehow it had all bounced off of him. He'd turned it around so that she and Royce had ended up looking like idiots, and he'd come off as the responsible public servant. If the FBI had all this information—and there were four persons gone, all connected in a land deal—what were the implications?

She'd go home and ask her personal adviser, her junkie buddy.

16

Memphis

"Mark, I think we're about ready," the daddy rabbit said in his command voice. The agent named Mark hit the lights.

"Okay." The conversations in the room subsided. "Ladies and gentlemen, as you know only too well, the so-called war on drugs was never a war at all. It was a holding action. Not even that, really. It was a series of dog-and-pony shows." Like this one, he thought.

"The Medellin, Cali, Bogota, North Coast—" his pointer flicked across the background display "—and various other Colombian organizations have operated for years without fear of serious reprisal by law enforcement agencies. It's only in the past year we've been able to mount a real campaign against the active drug cartels.

"As we're all aware, painfully aware, the U.S. government has done what it could to make the smuggling of drugs easy. We tell these Third World countries to give us their tired, their poor, their huddled masses. Give us your dope mules, in other words." There was a murmur of agreement in the conference room.

"From the blue-collar immigrant who loads it, to the ones who mule it in, to the street kids who act as lookout for the peddlers and pushers, our open society and open borders have made it impossible to control the flow—especially in states like Florida and Texas. And—let's give the rats credit: they've been very smart.

"We've known for years there was little point in trying to stop the traffic once it hit the street. Our only hope in staving in the Colombian cartels' machine has been to try to hit the second-level guys. The big boys have been all but untouchable, and the little guys are too numerous to do anything about. It has always been the secondary level where the Colombians have been their most vulnerable.

"The cartels' traffic managers, the bagmen, the bankers, the intermediary distributors, the money launderers—that's where the weaknesses could be found.

"Purchases, transfer of funds, the actual shipment and so forth, these second-level activities—these were the primary areas where we've put our manpower, and it's really paid off.

"Because of limitless funding, they were always able to provide their secondary-level personnel with the best security money could buy. But they made a big mistake. When the state-of-the-art electronics gave them access to DISA codes and such, they couldn't resist the temptation to use it as a communications mode. We were waiting for them.

"How have the Colombian traffic managers communicated with their distribution links? Traditionally it has been by phone. Pay telephones or black boxes. Sometimes, in the more sophisticated operations, they've employed bounce systems and elaborate telephone-relay blinds.

"But when the computer hackers learned how to obtain the security passwords for Direct Inward System Access on private branch exchange numbers, it was a new ball game. They had a way to set up blind two-way phone security, with the added benefit of beating the telephone companies out of the charges.

"They bought the access codes from dumpster divers, or black and blue boxers, or from pirated voice mail bulletin boards, or pay phone taps—a dozen ways. Or used the second dial tone after accessing call-processing features. They'd get in—make their blind call—and get out free. The call would show on some corporate bill—uncheckable at either end and, in theory, as secure as an unscrambled land line could get.

"What our job was here at ELINT was to monitor all the DISA heavyweights in markets with abnormally high rates of DLD fraud. We'd had a 'watch' on the Romero family for a long time, for example. Papa Romero—" his pointer tapped an ugly face "—Midwestern traffic manager for the Medellin.

"His MO has been to set up call pads with his distributors. Then initiate the calls at prearranged times to untraceable units, using DISA passwords.

Even if you tapped the line, the calls were so structured that Papa Romero would never be implicated. The distributors used codes, and everything was by the numbers. Romero did not personally touch either end of transport or delivery—only the money itself—keeping him insulated from the narcotics.

"We used an informant to begin a series of larger and larger buys. Establish his dealer credibility with the distributor. When we knew Romero had just muled in over four hundred keys of cocaine, we had our snitch set up a buy for real weight. Then—when the deal was down—go shy on the deal. It put the distributor, who works out of a small town called Waterton, Missouri, in one helluva bind. He then had to initiate a call for help to Papa Romero.

"We kept tight surveillance on the distributor and put together a package to show sufficient PC for a Romero wiretap. It was a can't-lose deal, you see: Even if he ultimately beat the coke thing, we could go for complicity in a federal telephone scam. Bada bing, bada boom—we had him set to fall two ways. Any questions?"

A DEA man spoke up.

"How did you keep the snitch from getting whacked?"

"Well . . ." the daddy rabbit said, "you know how it is. You got a user who's dealing to support his habit, you don't worry too much about taking him down, you concentrate on turning him. Putting him back to work for our side. And you hate to lose a good informant, but this operation had to look totally kosher every step of the way. We had to leave it up to him to survive.

"Both the distributor and the dealer are still in place, by the way. If our man can stay alive until we get the other guy taken down, then fine. If he gets whacked—" he turned his palms up and shrugged "—then we'll take the distributor down on a homicide as well as a narcotics bust.

"As I said, it's a can't-lose deal."

17

Maysburg

When Chaingang pulled out from Jefferson Sandbar, which is where the local fishermen and boating enthusiasts "put in," the beat-up brownish-yellow-orange Toyota was riding a mite low on the springs. The shocks were probably gone to begin with. And . . . consider the weight load.

He took the bridge across the river, flowing with the traffic about ten miles over the speed limit. In a matter of minutes he'd passed through the center of Maysburg, Tennessee, via its "business route," and was pulling up behind a Big 7 Motel, whose rather spacious parking lot had precisely one vehicle in it.

He parked beside the car, a Buick Regal belonging to one Conway Woodruff, Jr., a salesman out of Decatur, Georgia, who had been in his room for all of fifteen minutes, and was both surprised and annoyed to hear someone banging on his door.

"Yes?"

Inside his massive head Chaingang had his speech ready, and his friendliest shit-eating grin was plastered across his dimpled, beaming countenance. He had his usual line of confusing dialogue prepared. A bit of impromptu nonsense about how flat-out goddamn stupid he was for having left an envelope with some money in it taped to the bottom of the dresser drawer and how crazy it sounded but could he please come in and reezle frammen for a second?

The words would rush out in a storm of hot blasting confusion, startling yet nonthreatening, a fat comic bear's windy rhetoric infused with a kind of topsy-turvy logic, and while the unsuspecting party tries to respond to this intrusion, there is that awful coil of heavy chain snaking out of the huge canvas pocket, and it would all be over in an eye-blink.

The words stuck in his throat. Perhaps the cumulative effect of the powerful drugs had damaged his central nervous system. He'd been struck on the head at some point, because there was a place where his skull was tender to the touch, so perhaps that contributed to his inarticulateness. Or maybe it was just that he hadn't had much to say in the last couple of years.

Whatever the problem, nothing came to his tongue, so he brought up a juicy regurgitation and belched an expulsion of death-breath into poor Mr. Woodruff's face, pushing him back into the room, slamming the door behind him, and chain-snapping him in a blur of quick moves.

His computer was working well, if his speech center was not, and it notified him of the possibility of watchers to his flanks and rear. Tiny black marblelike eyes peered around the curtain. When he was satisfied that no one behind him was a potential threat, he took Mr. Woodruff into the bathroom and undressed both of them as if for intimacy, and—truly—what is more intimate than an organ donation?

Chaingang, naked, took his big fighting bowie and made three deep, precise cuts: the "autopsy Y." Blood was everywhere. Fingers like huge steel cigars reached, ripped and opened Mr. Woodruff. He sliced the steaming heart loose and fed. Finally the scarlet roar of hot desire had abated. The delicacy was unusually sweet and tender. It had been such a long time, he'd almost forgotten the rush.

It didn't take long to exsanguinate the gentleman, and they took a nice shower together while he cleaned them both, pulling the gentleman back together with his all-purpose duct tape until he could get him loaded up for disposal. The bathtub and tile walls were easy to clean since he did not have to worry about traces in the trap.

He got dressed, went out to the Toyota and got plastic sheeting, one of the poncho halves, cord, and his Utility Escapes material.

The bed had not been slept in. He rumpled it, pressing in the indentation of a sleeping man. He wrapped his large bundle, which was somewhat lighter. The donor had given blood, for one thing, and there was the matter of a heart, which weighed approximately three quarters of a pound.

From Mr. Woodruffs clothing he took the driver's license and turned to the pages where his master motor vehicle blanks were tipped in. He selected the appropriate state, double-checking coded prefixes and license style, and removed the one he wanted. Not only had the authorities returned all his survival items, they'd upgraded them in some cases. There were new license blanks with the same small photograph of Daniel Bunkowski already affixed to each coded ID for all the states.

It was almost as if he were an employee of theirs. He expected that kind of arrogance from most monkeys, but not the sissy doctor, who purportedly understood that he had superior competency. What made them think he wasn't going to escape with this material, not to mention the munitions?

His mind sorted possibles: Perhaps they knew that MVB blanks were easily available both from street people and subculture bookstores. They might have realized that mail-order publications and other materials required a shipping time of several weeks. Maybe there was a time consideration attached to whatever motivated them to set him loose.

They'd inserted him into Vietnam in the 1960s, free to hunt and kill. He'd shown them that he could escape their plans to control or terminate him then, so what made them think he was under their thumb now?

He tried to examine, as objectively as possible, his various points of contact with the monkeys, beginning with his first adult jail time; through escape, evasion, revenge, recapture, the period of quasi-mercenary service, the bungled "abortion" by friendly fire, escape and evasion, more retaliation, the hunt by a detective who had become devoted to his destruction—when he was shot and almost killed, his wonderful time of recuperation and vengeance, and the child he'd sired—all the history that had brought him to this moment.

Where was the weak link? Had Dr. Norman learned something about him during their drugged sessions that had led to such arrogance on their part? What made them think that he would follow their agenda?

Daniel chewed it over as he added GM keys and Conway Woodruffs money to his billfold. He loaded up, and without encountering further problems, he and Mr. Woodruff left the Big 7 Motel for the last time.

He'd spotted the fairly deserted river access route on the Maysburg side of the bridge. Driving with tremendous concentration, he returned there next, the low-riding Toyota's camper filled with what appeared to be camping gear. Chaingang had almost no rear visibility, and he could hardly breathe cramped in behind the wheel, which he could barely steer for his huge gut and massive legs.

There were a few trucks and a car or two on the access road, but it looked good to him, as it ran parallel to the blue feature, and was country enough to do the trick.

He stopped and phoned a taxi from the nearest pay telephone, at a small auto repair place near the road. Found his voice and told them when and where to pick him up. Gave the motel as his destination. His name was Conway Woodruff. The salesman's keys and an appropriate ID were in his pocket.

Luck, or the power of evil, led him directly to a suitable bluff. His weapons cases and duffel bag were safely ensconced in the trunk of that big, beautiful Buick back at the Big 7.

He took pliers and wire and made certain the Toyota's crew were in for the duration, battened down the hatches, wiped prints out of force of habit, and ran the vehicle off the low bluff into the river. Nobody but the fish heard it sink.

By the time he waddled back down the road, he saw his taxi about to pull out and stopped it with a shout like a cannon shot, waving at the driver, who started down the road to meet him.

"Howdy, I got to sightseein' out here and—"

"I just about drove off without ya," the driver snarled.

That was all he needed to launch into a tirade about the cheap Detroit garbage the auto industry was cranking off the assembly lines these days, immediately finding a kindred soul. The two of them cussed and fussed, and by the time the cab driver deposited his heavy load back at the motel, they both agreed that the world was going to hell in a handbasket.

When the taxi pulled away, Chaingang unlocked his Buick Regal and went in search of some fast food, and then—secure lodging. He thought about checking in at a motel somewhere. After all, he had enough credit cards in his pocket. They identified him as Gordon Truett, Walter Smith, and Conway Woodruff, none of whom could put up an argument.

In the creek he could see a ribbon of scum along the edge by the nearest bank. Floating in the slime, a white plastic jug, part of a dead perch, and small twigs were discernible. Up on the bank he noticed pieces of rotting tackle and the brightness of expended shotgun shells. He registered these things subconsciously as he flipped through the pages of UTILITY ESCAPES, day-dreaming, glancing back and forth at the map for inspiration.

He'd driven to the bridge, crossed it, followed a small service road on the other side, finally stopping after a few miles near a deep, unmarked creek. He sorted options. Eyes scanning. Registering. Open to the inner sensors that directed his movements much of the time.

Mr. Woodruff, as he'd signed the register, had spent a pleasant night and day in the VACANCY Motorlodge, the only name remaining on the chipped, painted billboard adjacent to the neon sign. The tab was a reasonable $31.90. The real Mr. Woodruff had paid.

There would be a need to dump the vehicle. If he'd gleaned sufficient data about the salesman's itinerary, people would be asking questions about his absence very soon. One option was painting the car. Changing tags. He decided he'd prepare for that contingency and started the car, driving to a nearby hardware store and picking up the necessary items. Rather than shoplift the items—which he ordinarily would have done—he bought a few large spray cans of Krylon acrylic, plenty of masking tape, scissors, and a big roll of brown paper, which he preferred to newsprint. He'd work something out. He wanted to keep those wheels as legal as possible.

He left the store and crossed the bridge to the Missouri side, moving toward Waterton on Maple, right on Park Street, turning back left around the small park, crossing South Main, turning due east on Oak Street. He kept going until he reached the boonies. A small county sign indicated a road number. He turned. Farmland. Another sip: BRIARWOOD.

He saw woods, took a tractor turnrow access road, and cut down off the blacktop, killing the engine.

In his duffel was a compact kerosene space heater and a one-man poncho hootch—but he was not about to spend another night outside on the ground. October had turned frigid.

He sensed a rumbling and watched a big, loaded eighteen-wheeler thunder by, a real blacktop-buster, probably too heavy for the scales and staying on the back roads away from the ICC. Something—the trucker perhaps—galvanized him into action. The access road was not safe. He started the car and pulled back onto the road, heading deeper into the boonies.

In his mind he replayed the look of the gravel road where he stepped down into a ditch and found the dry culvert. The markings of the handy grain silos and the dump sites stirred another vista. He visualized the hidden pond. Reached for the remembered off-kilter hints of unseen observers.

It would be wrong to say that he felt the eyes of watchers the way he had in the hole at Marion. He perceived premonitions with his "sixth sense"; received inexplicable sensations; was attuned to warning vibes. Precognated.

Never had he felt a stronger indication of hidden manipulators. They were everywhere, and yet he could not see them, and he was THE VERY BEST AT SPOTTING WATCHERS. Why hadn't he seen them? They couldn't be present in such numbers and all be that good.

In that flash of understanding, he *knew* why. He *knew*. He floored the accelerator and sped down the blacktop, determined, with every ounce of his powerful mind on full, focused concentration. Inside his head he was analyzing possibilities, painting the Buick, substituting plates with the tags from a junkyard rust-bucket whose plates would allow him a bit of prefix-coded poetic license. Threat assessment and tin snips, evasion techniques and application of masking tape—dozens of disparate thoughts passed through his mind.

He pulled off the blacktop onto another access road, but this time it was near a wooded area that began with a grove of small trees, and became a thick, overgrown tree line. More dense woods appeared to border the back of the field, which was visible in the distance.

From the second he pulled onto the road, he felt safer, and he eased up on the gas pedal. They were up there. That's why he'd not scoped them out—the watchers. A sky eye of some kind. They were probably keeping track of him via aerial photography—he imagined what the state-of-the-art capabilities probably were. They'd known exactly where he was from the moment they shoved him off that truck in a deserted bean field, and they gave him weapons!

He had been placed here for a reason, of course. But what? Would the key be in the ones who had been cruel to animals? Hardly. Was he a lab experiment? They were cold enough. No. What, then? He wished for the presence of his sissy friend, Dr. Norman. Oh, the pleasant time Daniel would have had, extracting the man's knowledge and heart, in that order.

It was of no consequence. First things first, he thought, bringing the sharpness of his mind back to the matters at hand. He must find shelter and concealment.

He swung around the tree line, driving through an overgrown lane of mud ruts, and bounced along through open pasture, going much slower now, as he kept to the extreme right and the overhanging protection of the big trees.

Finally he reached the end of the path. He was almost at the far end of a second field, this one in obvious disuse. He could take the vehicle no farther—not without tearing out the bottom of it. He pulled off the pathway sharply, a ridiculous thing to do, surely, driving into tall weeds at the edge of the woods.

But whatever it was that guided him had served him well again. He stopped the car and got out. He was bracketed on all sides by thick woods, and could see almost no sky overhead because of the limbs of the huge oaks around the car. He'd sensed the one place there was a small opening in the trees and driven through it.

He could hear traffic noises in the distance and knew precisely where he was, as always, in relation to his map and the steps of his journey to this point. He was due east of Waterton, and quite close to Briarwood's main drag, but in woods that were inaccessible from any direction other than the one he'd just come.

Quickly he took an antipersonnel mine and "closed the back door," also stringing some wire and setting out a pair of M49-A1 trip flares, which would illuminate any unwanted sneaker-peekers who chose to attempt penetration of his nighttime defensive perimeter. Cross his turf and fifty-thousand-candlepower illums would spotlight you for the minute or so necessary to dispose of you. A two-pound pressure or a cut of the wire would fire the devices, and you would be very, very sorry you had come to call.

He removed his belongings from the car and covered everything in a car-size cammoed bush-net he would use later, after the car was painted, and—mindful of the dry cold—began to cut sheets of the brown paper to mask off the windows and grillwork. Then he saw the edge of a concrete blockhouse, and the thrill of the find shivered through him.

He chopped his way through the multifloral rose bushes and poison ivy, impervious and invulnerable to either thorn or itch, and accessed a small door. It took him a few moments to realize what he'd found. The sound of a 75-horse outboard starting rumbled from him as a coughing laugh escaped his innards.

The adjacent field, not tillable, had been empty for a purpose. Once upon a time it had been a parking lot for cars. Doubtless there would be a couple of entrance/exit throughways somewhere to the south of him on the other side of the neighboring field.

He was too pleased to fool with the painting. He decided he would postpone that job until the morrow. He unpacked the space heater from his duffel and began cleaning out the inside of the long, thin concrete shelter.

Within the hour Chaingang Bunkowski was eating dinner inside his comfy, cozy new hideout: what had once been the concrete block projection booth for Briarwood's Tinytown Drive-in Theatre.

It is a cold but clear morning and Chaingang is up early, stiff from the night's sleep inside the abandoned projection blockhouse that was by turns suffocatingly hot or freezing cold. The space heater left something to be desired. The stiffness has settled in his lower groin.

Sunrise was a streaked palette of reds, golds, and powder blues. The air was crisp and clear. The birds were singing. He was so horny, he'd fuck a bush if he thought a snake might be in it. Chaingang horny: every woman's worst nightmare come true.

He uncovers the car, still unpainted, camouflages his belongings, checks and resets his perimeter security after having moved the vehicle, and takes off in the direction of Waterton.

His strange mindscreen rushes many things past his awareness: memories of isolation and sleep deprivation, long vigils and torturous fasting, abstinence and celibacy. Silence and hunger. He feels the warmth in his loins. In his computer he watches himself:

A slave candidate, both arms extended, is gripped by the elbows. He steps into his own shadow. Narco-hypnosis. "I am the lamp of darkness. Flame of the Illuminati. "Debilitating fear. An altar built of human skeletons—ah, yes! CRUCIFIX AND AMULET. PUDENDA BOUND IN STRING. Ritualistic pleasures recalled.

He remembers alkaloids and henbane. Symbolism and ceremony. Stimuli and exhortations. The turn-on of a sex slave sacrifice. Sabbath eve at the gate of death. Chaingang's mind sees these things.

His computer prints out the date for him. It is Halloween. All Souls' Day is coming. Dia de los Muertos—Day of the Dead. A closed tribunal of the Imperial Chamber. The Blockula Sabbats. The path of the rose. Night of convocation. Moon of diamonds. Court of the Holy Vehm. It excites him to remember.

In his mind *he drinks from a bowl of blood. Sniffs the overpowering fragrances of myrrh, cinnamon, calamus cassia, olive oil, aloes, storax—the rich incense of sudden death.* Death itself can enjoy a fantasy.

"In the name of the cruciform, I swear to sever all blood bonds . . . Astarot, Beelzebub, Beliar, Bhowani, Baal Ammon of No, Himavati, Kumari, Priestess of Shiva, Kali the black one, Menakshi, Rabbana . . . Benedictus Deus qui dedit nobis signum. Kiss the maiden of iron."

A beautiful woman, head shaved, eyes blindfolded, nude on an altar in a pentagram of flame, bleeding into a bowl. All sustenance derives from water, fire, sap, waste, and odor. "I pollute with my semen." Foreplay. The beast once dabbled in the occult arts.

No wonder he must have a woman. It is Halloween. How the memory of an absurd ancient ritual amuses him, but also hardens his need.

The sky eye is temporarily forgotten. He is rolling down Oak, turning on Jefferson—the main drag of the town Waterton, turning again on Maple and again on Park. He has seen a woman lock her car. She is young. It is broad daylight, but Chaingang cruises her. He waves. She enters a small shop. Waterton Pharmacy.

He parks. Out of the Regal and waddling in after the woman. He sees her now, doing something behind a counter. Long, shiny hair, huge earrings, too much lipstick. But a long neck and wide mouth.

Whatever fog or incapacitation had been rendering him inarticulate appears to completely burn off in the sexual heat of the moment. He is almost back to his old self again.

"G'morning," she says, in a loud, chipper voice.

"Happy Halloween," he says. He moves back in the direction of the long drug counter, where he senses another human presence. Peers into the sanctum sanctorum. A man in a white smock sees him.

"Can I help you?"

"Can I get datura stramonium or metaloides without a prescription?"

"What's that now?" He is nearer. Chaingang's huge hand is on the private door. The pharmacist is used to being in charge. He has never seen this man who is already inside the private area.

"Please—"

"Do you have any almond-wood or essence of tantic Himavati?" He plays with the man and chain-snaps him before he can answer. Turns instantly as the druggist falls in a heap, moving back out the door—which he can barely squeeze through—saying loudly in the direction of the unconscious man, "—appreciate it. I'll be back to get it in a minute."

Smiling. The smile a frightening mask. Waddling up to her.

"Hi." Friendly bear. "Are you going to have a big Halloween?"

"Nope. We're gonna stay home this year." Says something about her daughter.

"I've seen you around town before," he says. "What's your name?" A big smile.

"Trish Clark," she says. Trying to hold her breath so as not to have to inhale any of the foul reek of body odor that is so stingingly strong on the man.

"How much are those, Trish?" he asks politely, as his eyes scan the street for watchers. She turns to see what his big finger is pointing at and sees nothing more. A shower of black, blue, red, and golden stars explodes inside the blindness of her mind, die as they are extinguished in inkiness.

He has her long hair, dragging the inert body back to the back. Dragging her over her employer's form. Now returning to lock the door and turn the OPEN sign to CLOSED.

Checking the register first. Surprised at what he finds. He can dump the Buick and buy a nice used car.

She is very sexy, even in her slack-jawed position, and he pulls her to him to bestow a serpent's kiss with teeth meant only to wrest meat from bone.

"Trick or treat," he says, lowering his bulk onto her.

18

South of Waterton

It took a three-way clearance to get past the guards at the control center: one had to pass visual, palm-print, and spectrographic ID checks, and as the honcho liked to say, "everything from a metal detector to a bullshit detector." There were detection devices visible as one made one's way past the armed guards in the hallway, but neither the visible detectors nor the visible guards were the ones with the real teeth.

The honcho led the VIP civilian into the deadlock between the two nine-and-a-half-inch steel-sheathed doors, a "lock vault" in the jargon, and they stood there for a few long seconds waiting for the duty sergeant to pop the inner door.

"Evening, sir," the duty man said smartly.

The honcho nodded and escorted his guest past a desk where a rather attractive woman sat, staring at them as they strode by. Neither rank nor civilian brass impressed anyone inside the control complex. There were no salutes here. The attractive woman was too busy to salute, for example. In her left ear she was listening for the order to execute, which in this case was a literal order. It would mean that the individual or individuals who had just gained admittance to this highly secret chamber were not to be allowed to leave. There was no such order, and she removed her right trigger finger from the .22-caliber pistol concealed under the desk. She happened to be a world-class handgun champion, and she'd miss her period before she'd miss a head shot at that range.

"Who has him?"

"Red tracker."

"Good." They walked over to the appropriate cubicle where a civilian sat with his hands on a control console and his eyes glued to an electronic display.

"That's the subject. That little blip right there," the honcho explained. "Probably gone nighty-night, but—" he shrugged "—one never knows. We stay on him right around the clock. Change these monitor teams constantly. Helluva lot of manpower, but it pretty much assures us that he doesn't take off. He's in a twenty-five-mile radius of protection—that's his kill zone. And if he sets one big toe outside it . . ."

"You guys pick him up?"

"No, sir. We dust him right there."

"How do you keep an eye on him? It looks like there would be so many places he could go, you know?"

"We've got two hundred people in place. Eyeball surveillance. Every move recorded—sound-on-film. Overflights. Infrared. Satellites—he belongs to us every second. We own Big Boy."

They watched the tiny, glowing pinpoint of light with a mixture of unspoken anxiousness and proprietary pride. There was a kind of pioneering feeling inside the control center, a sense that one was part of a history-making endeavor.

The COMSEC and NEWTON SECURE systems interlinked with the on-line terminals served by OMEGASTAR, the mobile tracker that had been developed to monitor the man who was the core of SAUCOG'S continuing experimental research program.

Inside his weird brain a microscopic servomechanism (one that had cost a millionaire CEO his job when a Japanese firm beat his San Jose chip company to the punch and delivered the goods to Uncle first) happily rested, sending out its perpetual emission to whosoever might receive it.

Whosoever, in this control complex, watched the glowing screens of the Omni DF MEGAplex Secure Tranceiver Auto-lock locator Relay unit and movement-detection monitor.

Every telephonic, radar, infrared, seismic, satellite capability known to engineering science (and whose battery never needed replacing) tuned in, hooked up, plugged in, switched over, clicked on, and down-linked the signal from the eye in the sky—the cyclops that received the continual transmission that emanated from inside Chaingang Bunkowski's head.

Owning "Big Boy" was one thing. But *taming* him—ah, that was an altogether different can of worms.

19

Waterton

According to the official record, the incident report, Officer Harold Schaeffer was "investigating locked premises, gained entrance to Waterton Pharmacy at approximately 10:39 A.M., at which time I found the decedents." But Marty Kerns had the tape where Harry Schaeffer, crying, throwing up, on the job for eighteen months, had stepped into one of the worst multiple homicide scenes in memory, run in flat-out panic, mashed the handset of the two-way, all radio procedures and call signs and codes thrown to the wind, and screamed, "Oh, Jesus, help, Christ, there's two dead people maybe more. Waterton Pharmacy. There's blood everywhere and they're all cut up—Jeezus somebody *help me! Hurry!*" Not exactly "One Adam Twelve requesting backup." And this about a hundred feet away from the chief's office.

Bob Lee, the pharmacist, and Trish Clark. Both corpses mutilated. Huge footprints in the blood. No witnesses. Perpetrator had come in about the time they opened and somehow done the deed without any screams being heard, or passersby observing anything going on. If Mabel Dietz hadn't gone on so about having to get her prescription, and Mrs. Lee saying that her husband had gone down to open up the drugstore "over an hour ago," it might have been noon before the bodies were found.

Waterton Pharmacy. Next door to the jail and the city administration building. That was what really got Marty Kerns going. Kerns sealed off the crime scene best he could. Took a thousand pictures. Measured. Lifted. Dusted. Tried to think like a big-city evidence technician, and remember everything he'd learned from those criminology seminars. He called Doc Willoughby over at the clinic, who served as ME, coroner, undertaker, and lab man.

First thing he learned was "some kind of sex pervert" done the deed. There was sperm in just about every one of Trish's orifices other than her ears. And there was one other small detail that wouldn't require an autopsy: her heart was gone.

He was on the phone screaming to the FBI, both the regional SAC and Washington. They'd send agents in, but go ahead and "shoot us the lab work," they said.

Meanwhile Marty Kerns was sitting on a spate of murders and missing-persons cases and suspicious-looking "accidents," the likes of which he'd never encountered.

Kerns got his gig through patronage. He was an old-time Waterton pol with a half-assed record as a cop. Once upon a time he'd run the local Eagles drinking emporium, where he'd acquired a couple of small scars and a rep for being a tough guy. Paunchy, jowly, corrupt, stupid Chief Kerns was simply not up for this:

Rusty Ellis. Missing.

Butchie Sutter and Connie Vizard. Dead in a suspicious-looking tavern fire. Nobody was crying over them—not even the Sutter bunch. But they were on the list.

Betty and Gill Poindexter—missing.

Luther Lloyd—missing. One of Kerns's only modest successes: so far he'd been able to convince Mrs. Lloyd to keep quiet about his disappearance.

Three dead over in Tennessee. Maysburg PD found 'em along with a fourth John Doe, wired into a car: Gordon Truett, Walter Smith—a fine old boy —and Slug Kelly. Those three shot to shit with some kind of machine gun, it looked like. The John Doe with the heart gone.

Sam Perkins gone.

Now two more for the list. Bob Lee and Trish Clark. Whoever this crazy bastard was, he had the balls to take two people down right next door, and in broad daylight.

That was fourteen dead bodies, maybe. He wasn't sure about the fire at Butchie's, but all the others—he had a real bad feeling. He was certain they were all tied in somehow. What would Mary Perkins have said if he'd told her he knew there were five, not four, missing folks who'd been in the land thing together? He still knew damn well that was pure coincidence. This killer was doing away with people at random.

Why weren't the Feds already moving in, the way they always did on a big serial case like this? Why did they keep blowing him off when he tried to get outside help?

Marty Kerns had learned to trust his big gut. And his gut kept telling him this thing was going to get a lot worse before it got any better.

It hadn't helped that old goofy C. B. Farnum had called, swearing up and down that he'd been driving down Market Road and he'd seen "Bigfoot" heading into the woods. That was all he fucking needed now—a raft of goddamn Sasquatch sightings.

"I'm going to turn the heater off for a little while—you mind?"

"Go ahead." She shook her head absentmindedly, looking out at the bare earth. A vast circular hole in the ground that had once been the center of Weldon Lawley's farm—now the foundation of "THE FUTURE LOCATION OF ECOWORLD," according to the black and white billboard that had been erected the day before.

It was cold. Only ten minutes to seven in the morning, but they wanted to be present when Joseph Fisher made his appearance. He was supposed to be on hand in person, sometime "around seven," they'd heard. He was the ramrod with the elusive CCC, the firm that had paid Sam to set this deal into motion, and—in Mary's as well as Royce's mind—the outfit responsible in some way for his disappearance.

"Let me know when you get too cold and I'll turn it back on."

"Okay," she said in a small voice. There had been more tears last night than all the weeks since Sam had vanished. When she'd returned home yesterday, she'd had a call from her neighbor and friend Alberta Riley, who had asked her if she'd heard about the awful massacre in the drugstore.

When Mary had learned about the killings and told Alberta the latest, and they compared notes, it finally hit her. She was sure that she was not going to find Sam alive. It had shaken her to her core.

Royce had been a big help to her. He'd tried his best to be some comfort, but there wasn't much he could say or do. She knew now that Sam had met a bad end. It was still there, an awful thing in the pit of her stomach that felt like acid eating its way through, as she tried to make some logical sense out of it all.

Both she and Royce were certain that whatever fate Sam had met had been shared by these others, the Poindexters and Rusty Ellis. Now, this morning, they felt as if they had added another name—Luther Lloyd. Royce had insisted they drive out to the Lloyd place at six, to confront the man whom he could never reach on the telephone.

Luther Lloyd, of course, was not home. Mrs. Lloyd confessed that he, too, had vanished. "The police told me not to say anything," she told them.

Mary wanted to call the FBI again, but Royce had asked her—convincingly—if she thought there was any point to it. After the reaction she'd received the day before, she admitted there probably was not. Clearly the law enforcement agencies, for whatever reason, were not letting the spouses of the missing persons know any details of the ongoing investigation. Assuming there *was* an investigation.

"Somebody comin'," Royce said. It was a couple of pickups with some of the early work crew. They continued to wait, watching the heavy-equipment operators begin their day, until nearly seven-thirty, when two vans and a truck pulled in together. Some of the men getting out were in business suits, and Royce started the engine and drove over to where they were.

Mary and Royce got out and talked to the group, introducing themselves, and being introduced in turn to Joseph Fisher. Suave, soft-spoken, a lawyerly type in his late fifties, Fisher seemed solicitous and genuinely concerned about Mary's situation.

"When we couldn't find your company listed, and we couldn't reestablish contact with Mr. Sinclair, we became worried, Mr. Fisher," Royce told him.

"I understand that. It's all rather easily explained. I only wish that this frightening business of Mr. Perkins and others being missing could be explained. I'm extremely concerned about all of this. As far as CCC goes, it's actually just a name on paper for the holding company, World Ecosphere, Inc., which holds stock in and supervises the various companies such as Community Communications. We're located in Washington, D.C., and have been for twenty-one years."

"But why wouldn't Sam have known all this, as the real estate agent responsible for setting up this deal here?" Royce waved his arm in the direction of the great circular hole in the ground.

"Oh, I can assure you he did, Mr. . . . uh. . . .?"

"Hawthorne."

"Mr. Hawthorne. He was given all the background on our company." Fisher motioned to an aide. "Let me have a brochure, Mel." The man smiled pleasantly and removed a thick booklet from his briefcase. "This tells all about World Ecosphere, Inc., Mr. Hawthorne, and Mrs. Perkins." He handed the lavishly printed brochure to Royce. "And you can get some idea of the scope of our project here."

"We couldn't find Mr. Sinclair listed in the phone directory, either, and his number had been disconnected."

"Again—it was just a timing thing. He was working out of that office temporarily. He lives in New York. He goes where the job is. Mr. Perkins would have had all those facts and so on, you see. And I suspect that some of his personal effects must have been lost, because he had a clear and comprehensive understanding of the way our company was set up and how this Ecoworld project would be brought to fruition."

"Where is Mr. Sinclair?"

"In the Orient," Fisher said, easily. He glanced at the expensive-looking watch on his wrist. "Sound asleep, as we speak, I should think. I think there's a real problem here, but we're not part of it."

"What do you mean?" Mary asked.

"Folks, I think we have to face facts: an awful lot of missing persons in a small community, and within a short time, are very suspicious." *Tell us about it*, Royce thought. "We've been in touch with the authorities too, as I'm sure you know by now. When they reached us about Mr. Perkins, and the Poindexter family, we sent our own investigator in, and his report in a nutshell is this: there's the possibility a serial murderer has targeted the Waterton area." For a moment neither Royce nor Mary spoke. Then they both tried to speak at once.

"How—"

"Why—" Royce nodded and said, "Go ahead."

"How do you know that?"

"The murders at your town pharmacy yesterday seem to confirm it. But there are some things you may not know. And I'm in a rather ticklish situation here. I want to help you folks, but I've been asked by the chief of police not to divulge certain information our investigator obtained from another law enforcement agency.

"There is evidence of more than one murder. Near Waterton. And I think we all understand and sympathize with Chief Kerns wanting to keep the lid on what could be a panic-inducing situation, but on the other hand, you folks have a right to the information, it seems to me, because of Mr. Perkins."

He told them a lot more. Voluble, helpful, straightforward, and surprisingly forthcoming, Royce thought. After having obtained Mary's and Royce's word they'd not repeat the information, he shared the corporate investigator's report.

It was typically company-oriented and task-oriented, aimed not so much at determining what happened to the missing persons, but whether or not their absence was going to have an ill effect on the Ecoworld project. The summary was as Fisher had stated: It appeared that a serial murderer was killing and/or abducting random persons from the Waterton/Maysburg area. While the report did not have the data on Rusty Ellis, or the conclusions on the fire at Butchie's, it did contain the "Smith-Truett-Kelly-Doe" murders from Maysburg's police department, which indeed seemed to confirm the existence of a brutal serial murderer on the loose.

For the first time, Royce was not so certain about the land deal having been the focal point that linked the missing persons, Sam in particular. Inarguably, there was a serial killer who was taking lives at random.

"What did you think?" Mary had asked him as soon as they were in the vehicle and homeward bound, Royce behind the wheel, his mind going a mile a minute. He was trying to sort out two parallel worlds, make that three, at once.

"You mean Fisher?"

"Mm."

"Seems like a decent guy. Nice guy." His voice saying something else altogether.

"Something's going on here, right?" Mary was no rocket scientist, but she'd always been proud of her ability to size things up. After all, this was the woman who'd loaned a former junkie lover five thousand dollars. What do the banks call it—unsecured? She trusted her BS detector—always had.

"Yeah."

"Well?"

"I don't know."

"Come on, Royce. Talk to me."

"I don't know, babe. What can I say? It looks bad. It's going to get a lot worse. And it probably is a helluva lot worse than that, but nobody's telling us. There. That pretty well do it?" She just looked at him. "Sorry," he sighed, letting out air. "I—"

"But . . . do you think . . ." she really didn't want to articulate it "Sam is . . ."

"Yeah."

"The idea of a serial killer in Waterton—it's ridiculous. Unthinkable. But why wouldn't we have found Sam if that was it?" The concept of a serial murder case in a town of less than seven hundred people, a town so rinky-dink, it grows 50 percent larger when the migrant workers come through, was absurd!

"Let's just talk about the things we know, Mary. We've got enough to try to sort out without running through hypothetical situations. Sam is missing. He's not dead. We're not sure. Let's remember that." Funny. Him telling her this. As if she didn't know.

"Yeah. But you think he's dead too, don't you? Be honest."

"Yes. I do," he said quietly, after a few seconds. It seemed noisy in the silence of the car. "I have nothing more to base it on than the others being missing. But I think he's gone." He reached over and patted her arm. She felt stiff.

"Yes," was all she said. Yes. That's what I think. That's what I feel. Yes was enough.

"As far as the Ecoworld deal having anything to do with it. I don't know.

Five minutes ago I thought it might. At this second I don't believe that it does. Five minutes from now I may change my mind again. We don't have real facts. We're working from suppositions based on what others are telling us. And we know the legendary Marty Kerns isn't giving us anything. This CCC deal still looks fishy as hell to me, I don't care if there is a serial murderer out there somewhere."

"This thing says that World Ecosphere surveyed 'small towns throughout the middle-American states, from the northern heartland to the South, in search of the perfect community for development.' Jeezus! Royce—I just thought. Sam was supposed to make all this money by buying up surrounding land and what they called 'access properties.' This was supposed to be one of the perks for setting up the deal, see? He'd be in the know and all, and nobody else would know about it, so he could buy land at reasonable prices. Then when the Ecoworld park was promoted nationally, the 'nothing ground' he'd been buying up would have become choice real estate."

"So?"

"First—he was reluctant to wade in and invest. You know, he never totally trusted these guys—it was all so bizarre. And he'd seen some of these pipe dreams fall apart. But what I'm saying is, I just recalled that there was a big flurry of paperwork on it. The company had their access routes that they didn't want him 'muddying up'—I remember that particular phrase. It was fine for him to cash in on surrounding land and whatnot, but there were certain areas he wasn't to mess with. This was when it was all real secretive, and they had a code name and stuff."

"A code name?"

"Yeah. I just remembered that. He wasn't supposed to refer to the Ecoworld project by name in any fax or cable or whatever. There was a mound of telegrams and night letters and stuff—and I know he wasn't carrying all that around in his briefcase. I'll bet all the paperwork is still tucked away—either in the office or at home."

"Think you could find it?"

"I can't imagine where to start looking that I haven't already looked. It probably wouldn't tell us anything we don't already know. Joseph Fisher would probably let us look at their copies if we said something."

"Maybe . . . What was the code word?"

"Oh . . ." She thought for a while. A lot of time had gone by, and her mind didn't seem to want to function. "Rampage? No . . . mm . . . something about the waterworks. *Ramparts!* That was it.

"The idea of a code name—Sam thought it was kind of silly. As if somebody would know what the heck Ecoworld meant. I just finished reading about it and I still don't know."

Mary had turned in the seat, and her skirt pulled up more than she meant it to. He kept his eyes on the road, but that was okay. He knew every sweet dimple and lovely curve. He knew all too well what those beautiful legs looked like.

"I'm sorry, Mary," he told her.

"Hm?"

"You know—" He didn't say it. Just covered her hand with his. "Everything." He let it go.

She thought he seemed different. In school he'd been the least likely guy to end up as some skanky doper. He was more like the Royce she remembered.

"Yeah," she said, and it was as much a whispered prayer as anything else.

Royce took his hand away. Without saying anything, she'd spoken to him in the intimate language of old friends and lovers, and there was no way on God's earth he'd put a move on her. All he wanted to do was start over. Turn the clock back and start acting like a man for a change.

He'd told himself a thousand times he was over her, always knowing that was complete bullshit. You didn't "get over" Mary Perkins, with that soft skin and that mouth and those sweet ways and those legs. You didn't get cured of her. Mary was fatal.

She'd left a part of herself in every place where they'd been together, like a Persian cat shedding small, fluffy balls of itself, insubstantial but real legacies that would catch in the currents of the air like microscopic tumbleweeds, and come back to whisper to you.

Just about the time you'd kicked the Mary habit, you'd chance upon an errant long hair in an unexpected place, and you'd hear that lovely voice, her throaty, warm contralto, or you'd see that natural, sexy, skinny-legged, loose walk of hers in your mind, or you'd smell the fragrance of her memory, and—*wham!* No cure. Jonesin' for Mary. It dawned on him that it had been days since he'd done lines. How weird. His new jones: Mary-wanna. Hey, Mary . . . Wanna?

Mary knew she was feeling something toward Royce that she shouldn't. It was an emotion she'd been fighting.

What was it about some men? There were those certain guys who could get on a woman's wavelength. Her junkie lover of long ago, with the wide, lopsided smile so full of unexpected warmth and tenderness, he'd been one of those. He could send her into a mood swing the way north draws the needle of a compass. Explain it? She couldn't even define it.

All she knew was that they occupied two different worlds—physically, spiritually, and sexually—yet he nudged her at the oddest times in a way that could only be compared to the desire for a guilty pleasure. And it wasn't sex, truly. Sam had been a sensual lover and sufficiently ardent and gentle to keep her content in that department. Mary realized that it was something more than sex or romance, a deep and not insubstantial part of her that was drawn to this man.

That night she dreamed of him, watching herself enter a room where Royce Hawthorne was. She sees herself as a vision, suggesting the best of early Perry Ellis and most inspired Marc Jacobs, the classiest Geoffrey Beene tailored with flashes of striking Armani, the tearoomiest Ralph Lauren with a hint of Ms. Herrera, mixed and matched by the latest kids—the ones with the unpronounceable names—and just a spritz of Fredericks. The vision moves.

His beautiful eyes follow the deep V-cut of the double-breasted black gabardine with the gold buttons, devouring her with his gaze. She feels the heat of his look. The vision at her best, striding through the room in a scented cloud of Opium, Poison, and Serpent's Eve—her special bedroom fragrance that triumphs over Royce's masculine aromas and engulfs the room in heady perfume. Royce, captivated, comes to her.

He offers her his arm and she takes it, seeing his old leather jacket with the worn elbows, imagining his forearms bulging with thick, ropy veins between the ridges of hard muscle, wanting to feel his big hands touch her again.

In the car the vision's tousled hair is the colors of brandy and champagne, streaked with highlights, lips glossy and desirable, and as she turns, the skirt rides up on her legs—which he tells her are "still A-one." She is in the front seat with Royce, in her cognac-colored wool jacket with the stone white poorboy turtleneck, and she watches him not look at her thighs.

Fear-shackled, tragedy-pinioned guilt speaks to her in a familiar man's voice.

"Mary?" She turns and looks for Sam, treading water, doing her best not to drown in the dizzying, unexpected waves of whatever this emotion is.

Royce wanted to open up to Mary. That was a problem. He couldn't. Not right now—the way things were hanging. Too much was going on. There was too much at stake. He was carrying too much baggage.

How could he ever begin to explain it to her—about the dope? He knew that she knew he'd fallen into the cracks, somewhere along the line. Royce could see it in her eyes sometimes, that how-did-you-let-yourself-get-this-way stare. Where does one start trying to explain a life? Your weakness and your vices and your mistakes look so easy to control when one is on the outside looking in.

He'd grown up in Waterton, just as Mary had. Born in 1962, in a hinterlands bump in the road that hadn't changed since the Second World War—Waterton, Missouri, was an American ghost town. The only thing good about it was, a kid could drive across the river to Tennessee and get illegal schooners of cold beer, vodka-laced watermelons, or home-grown reefer that just about everybody tried at one time or another when they were in their teens.

Grass was no big deal. Some kids smoked wacky-tobacky and some drank. Some—like Royce—did both. It was something to do. You fired up a joint, got in somebody's ride with a half dozen close friends, and cruised.

He'd been withering away. He'd have died if he hadn't gotten out of Waterton. He'd wanted all the sex there was, all the high times he could find, and he'd wanted out. Mary'd had a marriage jones that he felt snaking out for him like a hangman's noose. He'd run. Things had happened. He'd met women. Fast-lane types. Big-city junkies who'd taught him how to get his nose open. He'd never been that crazy about weed anyway. One thing had led to another. No biggie—hell, George Washington had been a hemp farmer.

Royce had gotten jammed up in the worst way and had taken the only way out left to him. That's how he'd got himself inserted into this king-shit jackpot. He knew he was going to have to open up to Mary about it soon. She deserved to know. No. That was bullshit. She most certainly did not deserve any part of his act. But he'd already used their friendship—just because she was there, and handy—and he owed it to her to run the whole thing down. He had to make it right.

He locked the car, a study in pensive concentration and gloomy dope-fiend rumination, his mind far away, as he headed for the door of his cabin. He was not alert.

There was a huge presence in the shadows. Hulking. Silent. A man standing very quietly waiting for Royce Hawthorne.

The man was good. Very quiet. As Royce walked by the large trees, the shadows moved. Like a gigantic animal, the watching man stepped out from this hidden nocturnal post, and moved behind Royce.

It was only as the man stepped heavily on a dry twig that Royce realized there was someone behind him. He flashed on the massive apparition he'd seen out on Willow River Road. The presence chilled him and dried his throat. He was frightened to the bone. He'd let all his powers of concentration become lax—what an idiot!

He froze, barely containing himself as he felt fingers of steel grip him from behind.

They say you see your life flash before your eyes. He did not. He only saw huge fingers, a hand, the long arm, squeezing his shoulder and pulling him around. Nearly scaring him to death, as he looked into a frightening scowl. The menacing, bearded face of the ex-boxer, Luis Londoño.

"Hey."

"Jeezus! Man, don't *do* that!"

"Come on." The massive head jerking to the side. Body like a small car standing on end. An immovable object.

"Yeah. Sure." What was he supposed to say—no? I have to take a piano lesson first?

He didn't recognize the car.

"What's Happy been up to?" he said, trying to make conversation. Luis only grunted and drove. Royce was aware of the little toy knife in the holster taped to his leg. He could feel it. He let his knee move slowly, inching his left pant leg back just a bit with the weight of his left hand. No way. First, he would never get it out fast enough, and if he could—what then?

The heavyweight was as tough as nails. He'd picked up both his purple and green wings when he'd been a biker. The green was for having oral sex with a dead woman confirmed as having active gonorrhea at the time of death. Royce had never asked what the purple wings were for. Royce might get his little toad-sticker out and take his shot, and while Luis died, he'd rip his face off and wipe with it.

That had never been the idea. The last thing he was going to do was get into some physical conflict with Happy Ruiz or his goon. The idea was to buy weight. And that was what he would do, or die trying, he thought—humorlessly.

Being summoned by Happy was somewhere on the pleasure scale between eating road kill and struggling with a bad yeast infection, but he had to put the danger completely out of his mind. He wanted to look anxious to talk with Happy when he got wherever they were going. And there'd be no reason for him to be apprehensive—after all, wasn't he the man's business partner? He calmed his mind as they bumped along in the direction, presumably, of The Rockhouse.

He remembered parking in front of the bikers' "cantina" where Happy and the guys like to hang. Standing between them. Reaching for the money. Louis, again, on his left.

He tried to recall the signs over the back-bar. Carnes Finas—something like that. Some kind of beaner faro game or whatever going on in the corner. Remembering him telling old Fabio he was for real, and getting the *jefe* treatment. Walking on very thin ice again. This time with megaserious weight in the balance. Killer weight.

They stopped. Got out. He went in first. Vandella not at the bar. The place "after hours" now. Closed sign out front. Junkies and dealers and degenerate gamblers—the clientele.

Once upon a time nookie and sports had been his whole life, and not in that order. He wished it could be like that again, that he could turn back the clock and live it over with the advantage of that twenty-twenty hindsight.

Right now he was going to have to summon up his wits and dazzle Happy with some real fancy broken-field running.

"Yo. Where the fuck you been, amigo?" Happy was decidedly unhappy.

"Hey, dude. I was gonna ask *you*. We gonna do a thing or what?" Bluffing like a bandit. See if those head fakes still worked.

Brown. Slot. Motion. Two. Jet. On One.

No pain, no gain. No first and ten—no win.

Gut up, Burt, and play through the hurt. Pray for those key blockers.

"Who the fuck are you to ask me if we gonna do a thing?" Happy had his lapel in hand, and he was whispering his burrito breath in Royce's face. "I already told you twice we had it set. You said go ahead and do it. I do it with my people. I overextend based on your word. The word of a trusted amigo. You gonna carry the big time, you say. I got to come looking for you for my money now? What is this bullshit?"

"Hey, dude—cop some Valium or something. I never stiffed you five dollars five seconds. Can you dig that? Who the fuck are you to come muscling me, man?! All you gotta do is *ask* and I'm here, Happy!" Letting himself get very righteous and loud. Selling it. It either flies or it doesn't.

"All I gotta do is ax. Okay, *jefe*. I'm axin' you. You got it?"

"Of course I got it! I got my shit covered, mano."

"Uh-huh. Well, where is it?"

"I'll bring it to you in the morning. Will that get it?"

"In the morning." The serious black eyes stared at him from under the oily Presley-colored hair. He met the gaze, letting his eyebrows come up a little as if to say—yeah? Any problem? A long couple of seconds ticked by.

"Whatever makes everybody happy," Happy said, smiling. "Let's catch a buzz." He turned away, and Royce tried not to take a deep breath.

Brown Slot Motion Two Jet had looked a little raggedy from the sidelines, but this time the big guy was ruling it a completion.

20

Jackson's Grove

The night brought a hard, cold blanket of rain. From where he stood, in a copse of trees at the edge of Jackson's Grove some fifteen miles to the east of Waterton, the tiny farmhouses in the distance looked like frightened survivors huddled against the weather, and whatever else might be lurking out there in the cold rain. He smiled his parody of a huge grin at the thought, thinking of himself as the "whatever else." It always amused him that the worst thing out in the darkness, or the fog, or the great unknown—was him.

Distant fires smoldered on open hearths in sharecropper shacks and small frame, tar-papered rural dwellings. The monkey people were at their most vulnerable at night, but on a morning such as this, he always thought of them as a stupid, terrorized herd, absurdly easy to manipulate and destroy.

The curtain of rain enveloped everything in a stinking veil of wormy fish odor that he did not find unpleasant. The wet stench and the smell of his own scent in his nostrils accentuated the desolate look of these flatlands, broken only by occasional clots of woods and turnrow tree lines, and the little Monopoly-board houses of potential victims. It was his kind of morning.

Near the distant river there were rocks, willows, and a long ribbon of blacktop that fringed the man-made river levee. He thought about the woman and hardened, breathing slowly, savoring the memory of her look. He would have to get a live one next time. That was how he thought of it—a live one. Somewhere at the end of the blacktop, perhaps, she waited for the taking.

The rain increased in intensity, painting the landscape in a misty silver haze, and he gathered the huge tarp around his face and stomped out of the woods to the used Oldsmobile.

Chaingang Bunkowski could not waddle in off the street, reeking of subterranean sewers and dank drainage culverts, and ask to test-drive a new Peugot. He could, but it would be to create an unforgettable and altogether remarkable image. Nor could he wander into his friendly neighborhood BMW dealer's showroom without arousing considerable suspicions. So that was always the initial consideration when he interfaced with the monkeys: his predetermination of which places might allow him to effectively "blend in" and operate in the persona of a more or less "normal" consumer.

The buying of a used car was typical of such acts, and needed to be handled in the most surreptitious manner, with special care toward the selection of dealers. Williams Auto Mart, a lonesome strip of previously owned chrome, iron, and fiberglass just inside the twenty-five-mile barrier reef of so-called safety, looked appropriate.

Handling the prelims via telephone, delineating parameters, testing resistance quotients, probing the acceptable behavior tolerances, assessing risk factors, preselecting product possibilities, he further narrowed his field of choices.

There was a 1982 Cutlass, an "extremely clean" four-door Buick Century. The salesman, Mr. Williams, thought it was a '79. And there was the '81 Delta, which he ended up taking for pocket change. It didn't look like much, but it ran just fine.

The pink slip and appropriate DMV paperwork, replete with sanitized history and photo-correct laminated rectangle to match his tags (almost certain not to jar any wants-and-warrants priors) all made him as close to street-legal as he could reasonably get.

These formalities additionally paved the way for certain creature comforts like a place of inexpensive lodging, even a rental property, and—if he wanted to push it—financial respectability at the thrift institution of his choice.

It was, to be sure, a world of cars. Cars, trucks, RVs, and bikes were the core of civilized society. If you had a driver's license and a paid-for pink slip, you couldn't be all bad, so the inference seemed to be. And with that magic talisman, matching registration papers, and an engine block with original numbers—you had what it took to earn the Man's theoretical blessing.

Open the correct door, say the secret words, and you could then open checking accounts, apply for credit cards, hold your head up high, and walk tall and straight as any other lawful taxpayer.

"C. Woodruff" was a GM man, by golly, and he'd drive this old Delta till the bottom rusted out of it. And if Chaingang Bunkowski slammed his nearly 500 pounds into it too many times, the process might be accelerated, but it made a convenient and affordable throwaway.

The car ran quite well, he thought, although he immediately detected bad brakes, and his sensors filled him with an abiding distrust of the master cylinder.

Such thoughts were far from the top level of his perception as he slowly negotiated the pothole-laden blacktop, the faulty wipers producing a rather pleasing background noise. He was somewhere else at the moment, far from Waterton and Jackson's Grove, Missouri, collating and reassessing tables, lists, logs, balance sheets, and graphs. Analyzing deceits, misstatements, distortions, inventions, falsifications, and an entirely counterfeit spectrum of lies imposed by Uncle's hidden agenda.

The physical Chaingang, a well-oiled dispenser of final solutions, trained to kill with machinelike precision and efficiency, was controlled by his mental computer. That computer, in turn, reacted to a variety of triggers, some of them as inexplicable as the influences and confluences of earth, wind, sky, and water.

This morning it had come to him as cold rain, and the thing—whatever it was—had triggered the computer as the beast slept. He came awake with a violent jolt, full power of concentration locked in, packing his belongings with a vengeance, leaving his apparently safe hideaway in Tinytown for the last time.

With the blanketing rain had come a mysterious honing of the discriminatory faculties, a deepening of the sensory capacities, a sharpening of the perspectives—real-time and historical—an enhancement of creative thought and intuitive analysis, and whatever it was that Dr. Norman defined as "physical precognition."

This data-base-directed logic bomb, this cold-hearted heart-taker, idiot savant killer, mindless monster without redeeming humanity, saw the reality with eyes that few of us are even permitted to open.

He drove, driving on automatic pilot, the sky eyes forgotten, because he knew—understood the larger game. He saw the invisible wires. Comprehended, for the first time, the real plan, of which he was only a disposable extra. Stopped. Stood, hiding in rain-drenched woods, listening and sensing the busy, invisible world around him:

Under his 15EEEEE feet, ciliated protozoans, minute infusorian organisms, decomposed. Slow-moving tardi-grades, microscopic eight-wheelers, came from their watersheds and mossbanks. His computer sorted assertions, theses, conjecture, hypotheticals, ipse dixits; chose the most likely unproved dictum. Scanned.

And just as the four pairs of microlegs moved the tardi-grades in the direction of the decomposing protozoans, the thing that no one could explain pulled him in the direction of the least resistance.

Who understands—in an earthly sense—the mysteries of faith? There are those phenomena that are unknowable, but made conceivable to reason by one's spiritual soul.

Those who believe in God are in very real touch with the supernatural, mystical, yet incontrovertible truth of a holy divinity. The Lord's invisible but certain presence churns out of the believer's heart, appealing to the noble aesthetic sense that is the sum total of one's inner reality.

For Daniel Bunkowski the inner essence is altogether different. Where someone else has the Immaculate Conception, for example, he has this—the thing that lets him see.

This is the truth of what Chaingang believes: that an unseen, unknown watcher clicks a hidden field cam loaded with Ektachrome 400 stock, shooting with one one-hundredth-second shutter speed at f11, using 200-mm telephoto, and he is going to take those fingers that hold that camera and RIP THEM FROM THE ARMS AND THEN RIP THE ARMS FROM THE HANDS AND THEN RIP THE HANDS FROM THE MONKEY SOCKETS and that is what he truly believes in the madness of this cold, wet dawn.

There is a prison term for a con who has an ability to work himself free from handcuffs—even when "black-boxed." The phrase sits on Chaingang's mental shoulder and smiles: *monkey pawed*, such an inmate is called. For a souvenir he will take a pair of these monkey paws. That is Daniel Edward Flowers Bunkowski's inner reality.

He was passing through Briarwood on his way toward Tennessee. He'd decided he'd shag a motel, maybe give some thought to an appropriately déclassé rental of some kind—there were ways to remain away from the transaction, but these ways all required elaborate setups and time. He liked the looks of the isolated phone and stopped the Delta, heaved his bulk out from the groaning seat, and splashed through a deep puddle toward a bank of vending machines and telephones.

He stopped in front of a large soft-drink unit, almost blocking it from view as he spread his massive poncho even further, reaching in as if to get coins. He was reaching in for his tubular pick. Great for coin ops like commercial washers and soda dispensers. He carefully inserted the business end, adjusting the tension with the knurled collar as neoprene O-rings held the feeler picks in place. He was a superior locksmith, among his other talents, and could penetrate a simple center-spaced TL with his mind on autopilot. He swung out the coin tray and helped himself. Took a bottle of cold soda and closed the machine, going to the nearby wall phone to dial.

"East Coast Big and Tall," the woman's voice announced after a few rings.

"Howdy, could I speak to a salesperson, please?"

"Surely. One moment."

"Yes?"

Chaingang placed an order with the salesman who answered. Referring to a catalog number in his head. Charging it to Mr. W. W. Conway, who had just rented a tiny mail drawer. His order would be shipped via general delivery, Briarwood, which would be routed from the nearest small town USPS office.

Mr. Conway had been referred by a longtime satisfied customer of the eastern company that specialized in clothing for very tall or very stout males. He assured the nice man that his remittance would be immediately forthcoming. Thanked him. Hung up, and went into the store.

The place with the handy machines outside was called a Mini-Mart. He waddled inside to shoplift, more out of habit and meanness than need. The beast always carried a substantial sum of money tucked away for emergency usage, and true to form, Dr. Norman had seen to it that his duffel bag's money stash had been replenished. But Chaingang shoplifted out of principle.

Had he been born with a taste for money or material goods, rather than blood and vengeance, he would have been a master burglar or armed robber. He was a superbly talented "natural" thief, and an awesome shoplifter.

"Hi-dee, Kenny hep you?" it sounded like the clerk said, eyeing this stinking giant from behind the counter.

Chaingang ignored him. No, Mr. Monkey Man, you cannot *hep me*. Kenny hep yourself? He examined the prices of things he didn't want, eyes immediately clocking the surveillance mirror, and positioning himself so that one of his hands was blocked by his bulk.

The master of playacting and misdirection held up a can of ravioli with his left hand, swiping chili with his right.

None of this stuff looked particularly edible. Berthalou Irby had spoiled him for these lesser culinary offerings. He wanted to go back to the Irby house, bag Mrs. Irby, shag the retard, and eat the rest of the stuff in the basement. It was a very real and strong pull, the kind that sometimes went over the line and nagged him into enacting a particularly attractive fantasy.

He picked up a package of American cheese, knowing Kenny Hepyou was watching his actions very closely, enjoying himself thoroughly as he dropped a packet of smoked ham into his voluminous chain pocket.

"You got any trella crane?" he rumbled.

"Beg pardon."

"Trella scrate. Where do you keep it?"

"Cellophane? You mean like Handi-Wrap?"

"Heinie wipe." He opened a jelly jar and forced the top back at a tilt.

"It's over yonder. First aisle."

"Somebody done opened this here grape jelly, 'n' stuck their dick innit or whatever, 'n' screwed the top back on against the threads." He was moving down the aisle toward the clerk. Feeling dangerous and lucky.

"What's that now?"

"Somebody dicked in your jelly back there yonder. Top looks like it's got trella scration all over it. Thought you'd like to know." He shrugged, ever the helpful patron.

The clerk went back and saw the jelly.

"Kids come in here. They probably done it."

"Yids? Uh-huh." Chaingang hadn't had this much fun in a long time. Not without actually hurting someone.

"Did you find the Handi-Wrap?"

"Why would I want to do that?" Chaingang asked, genuinely appearing to be puzzled, having just shoved two stroke books up under his jacket.

"I thought you said you was wanting some Handi-Wrap and—"

It was too much for him. He made a coughing noise and the huge tractor-strength steel snake uncoiled and put the clerk out of his misery.

Instantly, the second he saw the poor man fall into the potato chip bags, he was irritated with himself. He had forgotten, uncharacteristically, that he was driving a semilegal Delta '88 he'd gone to a great deal of trouble to acquire. Now he'd just put his ride, his hide, and his clean tags at risk so he could hurt Kenny. Not smart.

He hit NO SALE and cleaned out the big stuff, pulling the tray up and seeing checks and—surprisingly—a gold coin. He was always finding interesting treats. He tucked the small gold piece away as a lucky charm, went around and checked Kenny's wallet, and felt a tiny surge of pleasure seeing that it contained nearly six hundred dollars.

Moving with a burst of speed, he chugged out the door and hurled his quarter ton of weight into the poor front seat of the old car, grinding the ignition to life, and pulling out into the northbound lane. There were no witnesses. No traffic to speak of. But of course, the sky eye man would be duly recording his moves. Of no consequence.

He'd ordered, and within a few minutes, paid for, his little going-away present to himself. Later, when he'd had his fill of this community, he'd have a nice, fresh get-out-of-town ensemble all ready and waiting for him.

At the next roadside phone that presented itself, a Mr. Conway dialed—strictly by coincidence—Perkins Real Estate, calling from the Tinytown phone book chained to the wall. Asking about rental properties.

"I'm sorry," an elderly woman's voice informed him. "This office is not presently open for business." She referred him to a realtor in Maysburg and he called there, "hoping to rent a small trailer or farmhouse."

"We've got something about ten miles north of here. It's a two-bedroom. But it's not in very good condition right at the moment, I'm afraid," a man's voice told him.

"That's all right. I'm not real fussy. I could even hep fix it up before the wife and kids get here. How much is it and—" He started to use the phrase "take occupancy," edited his choice of words, and said, "Would I be able to move in right away?"

"It's only fifty a month, sir. The owners just want to keep it rented so the house doesn't deteriorate any faster than it has. And you know, you can't get insurance on a dwelling unless it's occupied—so that's why it's available. But it's really rough, I won't kid you about that."

"It sounds just fine." It sounds like a fine shithole. "Could I look at it right now?"

"Yeah." The voice paused. "Let's see—what time is it? Uh—where are you now?"

"Just over yonder a ways from your office." Chaingang was really having fun with the monkeys. "I'm over by trella scrate's, and I could be over there in a few minutes. I could meet ya at the farmhouse or—"

"Nah, you better meet me here at the office and follow me out there. It's pretty hard to find—way out on an old gravel road in the country. I doubt if you could find it by yourself."

"Okay. I'll be there in a few minutes."

"Fine. And your name, sir?"

"Conway."

"Is that first or last?"

"Uh-huh," Chaingang said, his face contorted by the rictus of a snaggle-toothed grin. "See ya in a minute." He hung up the phone and flung himself back into the car. Kenny Hepyou had turned it into a good day after all. The fun was just starting.

Disturbed in his slumber by ever-watchful sensors, the beast shakes his bulk loose from the folds of deep sleep, belches an eight-inch naval salvo of gas, scratches, yawns expansively as he pulls himself to his feet.

Infested repose gave this gargantuan monster physical rest, but it was a restless dormancy. He is awake in two filmy eye-blinks, and as the sleeping behemoth emerges from the swamp of nocturnal hybernation, he is aware of a vague layering of intelligence and trivia.

He scans the dossier page on Virgil Watlow, and the phrase "dog buncher," the name for the scum who act as procurers for laboratories, tears a fingernail off inside his mind. In this dormant period some part of his brain has been relishing the memory of a woman at his second murder trial, and his mindscreen catches a fragment of her courtroom shrieking, the termagant's shrill "—and then and there, Daniel Bunkowski did proceed to strangle, bludgeon, and mutilate—" He savors the verbs, trying to taste her in his head.

But the sensors override all of this pleasurable trivia with the unmistakable urgings that he has learned to interpret as warnings. They came during his steep. Mental printout lighting the lip of his pocket of slumber with opaque, filtered rays of illumination. The beast, snoring away down in the shadowy hole at the bottom of his awareness, is somehow touched by this unexplainable phenomenon. It reaches down into his mysterious inner trench, and his subconscious moves him, trailing slime and mutant poisons, as he is nudged toward the light source. He is moving, on automatic pilot. Dressing. Not bothering to curse the bad luck that refuses to let him rest for a few days in his own rental home. Especially when he went to so much trouble to get the car, interface with the monkeys, play the game, talk the tall. But he would rather be safe than lazy. He can be lazy later, when Mr. Watlow has had a full manicure, pedicure, Chaingang cure. When all those bad teeth have been extracted. He wants to take his time with the *dog buncher* oh by Christ in Holy Heaven how he wants to RIP EVERY NAIL, TOOTH, HAIR, STRIP OF SKIN FROM THE DOGIE MAN.

Idly, to occupy his mind as he packs, he unscrews fuses, takes down trip wires; sorts the intelligence his mindscreen provided. Somewhere in all the analyses of meetings with realtors and dead convenience-store clerks, he will see the red flag. An unacceptable risk factor that has come to alert him in the night. Something he missed, that his sensors caught. And perhaps by then he will be long gone from this temporary haven.

In the car. Moving. He gives himself over to the vibes once again. That strange, powerful mind clicks, purrs; assessing, collating, accepting or rejecting what the eyes see and what the brain transmits.

His mindscreen searches for remote haunts where the ambience is just so. This plowed ground is too obviously arable, that chunk of bush insufficient protection in the wintry nights that will come. He registers a rusting metal sign: REELECT BUBBER (something) as he drives past eighty acres of early morning smoke and corn field stubble.

Rusty corn pickers. Hollow catalpa large enough to inhabit. Looming, twisted walnut trees stand by a decrepit tractor shed, against which eight giant tractor tires have slowly disintegrated. All of this flags his concentration. Across the road ten or twelve acres of tulip poplar, maple, and sycamore slowly inch their way up. The word NURSERY registers. He keeps moving. Searching. Hating.

He was in a funk. Parked. Irritated. The vibes were stubborn. His computer wasn't down so much as it was operating on the wrong level at the moment. He felt frustrated by his own warning devices.

Chaingang's equilibrium, a wild thing at best, was maintained by a bizarre system of interlocking defensive mechanisms that were the emotional equivalent of a surge suppressor.

Just as there were those dangerous sights, smells, and tactile sensations that could send him off into a boiling fury, there were sounds that grated on his psyche worse than the vilest curse: a hallway scream, a certain footfall, the cry of an animal in pain, a ripping sound of masking tape, a taut guy wire struck by a hammer just so—any number of noises could push him over the edge.

Banging noise. Loud, harsh voices. Guffaws. Rednecks in the field. The abrasive sounds reached out for him. Something moved beneath his vision arc. He looked down as the grasshopper jumped. The next time it moved, he was over it, and the insect was captured in a hand that was roughly the diameter and density of a bowling ball. The fingers, like steel cigars, held the thing, its hind legs scissoring for traction.

Squoosh! It was much the same with that first cut that exposed the internal human organs. The ritual itself gave pleasure, pleasing him the same way a child is pleased and riveted by the pulling apart of a grasshopper, and the gooey, gross-out look and feel of its exposed ventriculus.

Again the loud hammer strike on steel and the grating human voices. The eyes scan large walnut trees, searching hungrily for nutmeats, walnuts, squirrel sign, dog tracks, deer prints. He retrieves a long-distance killing tool from his duffel. Moves off in the direction of the voices, carefully threading the noise suppressor in place. That is his idea of a pun—this is a noise suppressor that he is about to utilize. A field-expedient noise suppressor.

The monster's computer does not react to the noise that carries, or the snatches of conversation and laughter.

"Nitrate." The jarring sound of the hammer.

"—got two tanks of beans over at the other place."

His mind sees two magic Butler grain silos, but the computer ignores this vision. He is memorizing mnemonics and equations for the computation of induction and capacitance. Trying to tap into himself—see the thing that is so jarringly off kilter.

"—it's gone up, too. I just don't know what—"

Capacitance:

"—damn girl run away with him, and we got the boy to look after, so—"

The property of an electrical nonconductor that permits the storage of energy as a result of electrical displacement when opposite surfaces of the nonconductor are maintained at a difference of potential. He tries to scan.

"It's getting too tough out there to cut."

IFPEC is his induction mnemonic. He cannot think for the noise of the hammering on metal. This monkey man will pay for intruding on his concentration, he thinks, recognizing his petulant mood and not caring.

"You oughta see what (something) got docked for moisture. I mean—"

The bolt moves in between a huge index finger and thumb. One up the pipe.

"I don't like throwin' em out the back."

"Never seen anything like this year."

Safety off. Finger in the trigger housing.

"I put down potash and phosphorus on that ground over by the other place, ya know?"

"Yeah."

"That fertilizer is up seventy a ton. I was gonna put wheat in behind it."

"Fuel cost me fourteen hundred dollars more this year," the man pounding on something behind the combine said, "and two days later I swear if it don't drop nine cents."

Both in view now. This is what they mean by targets of opportunity. He keeps moving, stepping out where they can see him clearly. The one with the hammer turns.

"Hey," he snarls, in a cautionary warning tone. Trigger pressure.

BAM.

BAMABAMABAMABAM.

BAM.

BAMBAMABAM.

Nobody near us to see us or hear us, he whistles, waddling across to the bodies.

The hammer of justice. His face is contorted in a maniac's parody of a smile. The hammer is dwarfed by his fist.

Italians have a joke they sometimes tell in restaurants and at the dinner table. Ever eat any *Sicilian chicken*? No? It's the same as regular chicken, but all the bones are broken.

21

Waterton

Royce Hawthorne had kept his bargain with the phonemen who were supposedly watching over him. It was time to call in the cavalry. He'd done his part. It was their turn now.

Sitting across from his old girlfriend, he felt a lot of different things tugging at him in several directions at once: He knew he was changing. He already felt like a different man from the one who was looking to pack his nostrils a few days ago. There was one upside to being scared shitless all the time—you didn't have time to worry about staying high.

The thing that cocaine does is, it tricks the brain. The great rushes of fear that Royce had been experiencing had acted as a kind of neural blocker to his addiction, and his system was working overtime to rebuild the bridges he'd burned with the seductive white lady. He felt like he wouldn't go that route again, if he could just stay alive.

The skanky, strung-out, self-centered burnout was history. For the first time in a long while he had something better to set his sights on, and the lady was here right now, looking delectable without trying. What he really wanted was to touch her; to stroke Mary's beautiful hair, cup her lovely face in his hands and kiss her, and tell her this bad stuff was all going to go away.

"I got hold of the law again," she told him.

"Kerns?"

"No," she said, "that FBI bozo. You know something? They don't pretend to take what I say to them seriously."

"You can forget the Feds."

"I can't forget them," she said, misunderstanding him.

"I mean if we're going to find out anything, it has to be us that does it. For whatever reason, the law is not giving out any information it doesn't have to. I'm not even all that sure they're trying very hard to investigate the missing-persons cases—much less the murders."

"But that makes no sense."

"Yeah. Right. But we have to run with the ball now." *And I do mean run*, he thought.

"What can we do without the cops? We don't even know anything." He could see how tired she was.

"There's actually quite a lot we can do—but it won't be easy. And you should realize—I think you have to assume you're in danger. Don't ask me why I feel this way. Part of the feeling is just gut instinct. Doll, I think we've got to start being very careful. I think we need to get you out of here—maybe to a motel or something, for, you know, just a few days till we see which way this is going. And I may do the same." She cocked her head at him. "I mean get my own motel room. I don't think we should be too easy to find for a while. I'll explain it more later, but right now I want to know if you really feel like pursuing this thing. No matter where it leads?"

"Sure I do. I just don't see—"

"Look. There's a time element involved now, and I'll explain that, too. But here's what I think you should do: Start packing. Pack enough that you don't have to come back here for four or five days."

"That's out of the question, Royce." She thought it was a ridiculous idea. Where would she be safer than in her home? "I might get calls here about Sam or something—I've got to—"

"I've already got that covered, babe." He explained to her about the answering service, and how they could call in from pay telephones to get any messages.

"Oh." She sighed, "I don't know . . . I don't see why it's necessary." But she knew him well enough that she recognized something altogether different in his face, and it frightened her. "Do you really feel like it's that important?"

"I really do. Come on," he said, taking her hand, "let's get to work." And without letting her really sort options, he had her filling a suitcase before she knew it, and making notes of whom to inform.

He didn't even want to tell the authorities. He told her he'd explain more about it as they got moving, and he did, telling her of some of the things he suspected, of his massive "professional paranoia" about the newest innovations in electronic surveillance, and how easy it was to put an ear into a home or business.

"I don't think we should go to a motel. Do you know of anywhere we might go? Relatives or friends in a nearby town—anything like that?" He was deadly serious.

"No."

"My cabin is being watched. I think your house will be, if it isn't already. The phone may be bugged. You don't know who we're dealing with. There's no point in going to some motel. If somebody wanted to find either one of us, it would make their job too easy."

"But why would they want to? I don't—"

"Just trust me for now. Keep trusting me—okay?"

"Okay."

"Don't give up on me yet."

"I'm not giving up on you for a second, you nut case. I'd like to know what suddenly made you like this, though."

"I'll tell you. But first things first. We need a place to kind of hang out for a while. Think."

"We've got a little place at Whitetail. It's just a shack. No running water. We couldn't stay there—"

"Sure we could. It would be perfect. I didn't know you guys had a place out there."

"Sam bought it the second year we were married. As a little place to get away on the weekends. We ended up taking a couple of vacations there, we enjoyed it so much."

Mary felt absurdly vulnerable and uncharacteristically malleable. She realized that for years now she'd let Sam make so many decisions for their mutual welfare, trusting him to shield her, to make her world safe. Suddenly she was plunged into something that had torn that world apart, and her knight in shining armor had been replaced by a man she didn't really know. "A cocaine dealer," Marty Kerns had called him.

"I hope you know what you're getting us into," she said to Royce, smiling to take the barbs out of it. Her teeth were small, well formed, and the front teeth were as prettily white as an actor's cap job. Royce wanted to put his arm around and lean over and stick his tongue in her mouth, and he knew the second he touched her, she'd be out of the ride and walking back home, and any chance they'd ever have would be over from that second.

"I hope so, too," he said, thinking that it was pretty damn late to start worrying about little details like that now.

"Phew! Gross!" Mary screamed, fanning the air and opening wooden shutters.

"Home away from home."

"I told you it was just a shack."

"You think this is a shack . . ." he laughed, ". . . you should see my place." Maybe we will sometime.

"We need to talk about something." She pointed to the bed, and he read her mind, or thought he did.

"No sweat. We can hang a sheet or something. I'll put my sleeping bag over there. We'll build a fire. It'll work out fine."

"Okay," she said, very unsure and more so all the time. Here they were cut off from the world. No running water. No stove. Worse yet—no telephone anywhere around for miles.

"As soon as you get your stuff unpacked, we need to get to work on our overall plan," he told her. He'd decided she was about to fall apart on him, and he wanted to keep her game as tight as he could. "We're going to need each other now, Mary. I won't kid you. This may get hairy."

"All right," she sighed. But she finished getting her things put away, and after lugging some firewood in, he made a mark on the crude wooden trestle table in the center of the room.

"Here we are. There's the rock quarry. Okay? Here—" he swept his arm in a half circle "—is the back edge of what's supposed to be Ecoworld. Right? That's where we're going tonight."

"Why?"

"Recon. Take a nice quiet look-see. Something's wrong with that deal. The first thing we're going to do is find out what the hell's going on. Are you game?"

"I'm game, aw'right," she said. "I just don't understand."

"Right." So far he was doing one great job keeping her out of any danger. The first thing they were going to do was break into a construction site.

"I want you to look at my notes. I'm not sure they prove a damn thing," he said. "But I don't have any better starting places, and no matter how many times I run World Ecosphere, Inc., through my head, I set off some kind of buzzer. It stinks. The whole deal."

"I'll admit it never made a lot of sense. Even when Sam was so excited about the fortune we were making on it."

"Who are the people involved with the land deal? What are their links, if any, to the other missing or murdered persons in this area?" He pointed to a hand-lettered list of names, the names connected with curving arrows.

"Who is investigating each of these cases of missing men and women, and who is investigating the violent deaths? Look at the jurisdictional breakdowns. The amount of known follow-up within our community. We're a town of six hundred and change—okay? We know when the heat is shining us on.

"What are the suspicious elements that keep pointing back to a possible involvement by the Ecoworld guys?" He pointed to a two-page summary he'd put together. "Read it."

She started reading it, and he said, "Read it out loud," wanting to hear his thoughts played back to him. Maybe he'd think of something they'd overlooked. She began reading slowly:

"* Adult men and women—disappearing. Links? Geography. Land deal.

* Adult men and women—murdered. Links? None known.

* Adult men and women—violent deaths. Murders? Links? None known. No proof of crime.

* Jurisdiction: Waterton. Attempt to cover up murders. Stated reason: to control possible panic situation.

* Jurisdiction: Maysburg. No further follow-up known by Tennessee authorities after liaison with federal and Missouri authorities.

* Jurisdiction: county (Missouri)—No further follow-up.

* Jurisdiction: federal—FBI agents investigate two crime scenes. Request other lab work. No follow-up known.

* Suspicious element: initial approach by Christopher Sinclair for mysterious holding company's nonexistent front.

* Suspicious element: ecological research & development center/theme park building in remote Missouri small town. (Reasons such as 'underdeveloped real estate within easy driving distance of several major population centers, ready regional pool of inexpensive skilled/unskilled blue-collar labor force, acceptable climate factors, etc., not convincing.) What is reason for location?

1. Mineral rights? Oil? Gold? Other?

2. Low density of population: toxic waste dump? Missile silo? Nuclear power plant? Other?

3. Cover for government-sponsored production or manufacturing of some type?

* Suspicious element: the lack of available information on violent mutilation murders—a multijurisdictional ongoing investigation of deaths and perhaps related disappearances in a community of less than seven hundred persons has generated only gossip and street rumors. Yet World Ecosphere, Inc., was able to investigate privately and conclude that a serial murderer was operating in the Waterton- Maysburg area. 'Has targeted the Waterton area' were Joseph Fisher's exact words. Slip of the tongue or did he have reason not to say 'Maysburg-Waterton area'? Same conversation: Fisher said he wanted to help us, 'but I've been asked by the chief of police not to divulge certain information our investigator obtained from another law enforcement agency.' Is this the Maysburg police department or a federal agency such as the FBI? *Why does the chief executive officer for a Washington-based* (or *New York-based*) *compa-*

ny know more about a possible serial murder/ missing-persons case in the Midwest than the immediate families of victims?

Conclusions: Based on the known facts, it appears that 'World Ecosphere, Inc.' and their hush-hush land development project could be responsible in some way for at least elements of Sam's disappearance, such as the subsequent cover-up of related information. The big question is—what is their motive?

Best guesses as to possible motives:

(a) They have learned about the serial killer and are afraid that adverse publicity about such a widespread spate of (unsolved) murders might have an unfavorable effect on public's acceptance of the proposed theme park.

(b) They have learned about the killings and abductions and fear a possible adverse effect on whatever is really behind the land deal, such as creation of a nuclear dump, strip mine, or whatever (possibly a government-funded. project).

(c) They themselves are directly responsible for the disappearances and/or deaths. The least likely possibility.

Bottom line: the project itself must be investigated further. We need to know if Ecoworld is what the company purports it to be."

She went over and sat down on the dusty bed, suddenly quite cold.

On the way to town, they were both in their own world. Royce was concentrating on playing detective, telling himself he was paying Mary back—for a lot of things—and Mary was trying to sort out her weird emotions.

Her world was upside down, yanked inside out. She was hiding—from what, she wasn't completely sure, a serial murderer, she supposed, trying not to second-guess the man beside her—sequestered in the Perkins vacation cabin at Whitetail. It was all too strange, and a no-win cruise for all hands aboard. Nothing good could come out of this mess.

Royce had spoken with Cullen Alberson, and they were going to see him today. The man had been open and seemingly unguarded, which was more than one could say of most of those involved even peripherally in the land deal. They'd gone by the Alberson house and he'd left for town already, and Royce had used their phone to call the hardware store and left word for Cullen to wait for them there.

Horvath's, one of the town's thriving all-purpose "general stores," was located under the Waterton water tower, a distinctive silver and green onion standing tall above the north edge of the city limits. They pulled in to the parking lot and saw Cullen standing near the bed of his pickup, in animated conversation with another farmer. They waited until the other man walked away. Then they got out and said hello.

"Thanks for letting us pick your brain about this, Cullen," Royce said.

"Sure 'nuff. Still no word about Mr. Sam?" He looked at Mary and she shook her head, making a face of sadness. What would everyone say when they heard she'd been hiding out with Royce Hawthorne in the family's cabin? That would give the town plenty to talk about. It was the least of her troubles—what people thought of her.

"I know you've already answered a bunch of questions and so forth, but I was talking about the deal Sam had been working on—talking to Mary, you know?—and we wondered if we could ask you, in confidence, when the contract was signed, were there any riders or changes to this contract? This is the copy from Sam's files." Royce handed a photocopied sheaf of legal-size papers to Cullen Alberson, opened to the page where it told what the "Community Communications Company" was getting for its money.

Alberson, a man close to retirement age, took his spectacles out and started reading, holding the document rather far from him and squinting, even with his bifocals on.

"We noticed that you didn't sell off any mineral rights, at least in the contract we saw," Royce said.

"Oh, no. I wasn't about to sell no mineral rights. That was the first thing me and the wife talked about when Mr. Sam told me about the offer. I figured a—whaddyacallem?—geologist . . . somebody'd done some testing and found something valuable. I made that clear from the start. He said no—I could retain all mineral rights. They just wanted that little bite out of my corner ground. At the time, I never could understand why they'd throw that kind of money on the table—but, hey, I wasn't going to look no gift horse in the mouth neither." He shook his head, chuckled, and looked at the contract some more.

"But you never got a direct explanation out of them why they were paying so much for a small piece of farm property?"

"Yeah." He looked up. "I felt like they were honest enough about what they wanted it for. You know how these big corporations are, they got more money than sense. They take it in their heads they want to do something, it's got to be the way they want it. Somebody out East drew a circle on a map, and I was just lucky enough to be part of the circle." He smiled and handed the copy back. "Who'd turn down money like I was offered?"

"Not me. We just thought maybe—like you said—they'd found something like a rich gold ore deposit, or oil, or whatever. And when I couldn't find anything about you selling the rights—"

"It was the same with Lawley, ya know?" He meant his next-door neighbor to the east, Weldon Lawley, who'd sold his entire farm to CCC and the parent holding company. "He said—'Shoot, I'd gladly sold them mineral rights for reasonable money, if that's all they wanted.' It was part of his package deal, but they didn't seem 'specially interested in that. According to what he said to me."

The three of them talked some more, and Royce and Mary left, checking in with Mary's answering service from a pay telephone. She phoned Alberta Riley, and they made a couple of other calls, including one to Luther Lloyd's home, trying to see if anything had changed with respect to the missing persons. Mrs. Lloyd was no longer stonewalling it for the cops. Mary spoke with her, at Royce's suggestion, and the woman confided in her.

"They tol' me not to say anything about Luther being gone and such—said I'd just be making folks panic. They're all in a panic now any which away. There was more killed yesterday—Kenneth Roebeck and Dub Olin and a feller that worked for him. Shot down in the middle of—" She caught herself, and Mary thought she'd decided she was overstepping her place to say these things. But she was weeping. Soft, muted snuffles into the telephone.

"It's all right, now. It's okay there." She didn't know how to comfort the woman. "I've done plenty of crying, too. It's a terrible feeling—not to know." This only made it worse, and the floodgates opened. Royce watched Mary. She teared up a little herself. Finally Mrs. Lloyd was able to get back under control.

"We don't have to talk anymore if you don't want to, Mrs. Lloyd."

"No. It's okay. I don't mind."

"Have you ever felt like there was something wrong with the deal they made to buy your ground? I wouldn't repeat what you say to me."

"I don't care if you do repeat it. Of *course* I've felt like there was something wrong with the thing. Luther would a never sold that piece of ground. It was slicked offa him some which away. I don't care how much money they give us, he loved the farm. It was no-account river ground that had just about been farmed out, and we could barely scratch a living off it, but by gols, his gran'-daddy give him this ground."

"But yet . . ." She wanted to be careful how she worded it. "The contract and all . . . That was Mr. Lloyd's signature on it, wasn't it?"

"I reckon so. But I went to the lawyer over in Maysburg, and he said that, aw, you know—if we wanted to try to go to court an' that we might be able to prove that it wasn't done under the right conditions and so forth—"

"Or that he was under pressure of some kind to make him sell—something like that maybe?"

"Yeah. I forget all the things he said. I tol' him go ahead and do it and I'd pay him best I could. And then he called up later on and said he didn't think he could recommend it on my behalf anymore. That I'd just spend all my money for nothing. He said he'd still take them to court if I insisted, but he was purty sure I'd lose."

"Why was that?"

"He thought they were too big. Some big company that had dealings with the U.S. government, he said. And they'd tie it up in court for years. I told him finally if he thought we'd best drop it, then drop it. If Luther was here and it was him and me, it might be different; he'd want to fight it. But I can't deal with all that and him gone too."

"I understand." They traded wishes of sympathy, Mary thanked her and wished her well, and rang off.

She filled Royce in on the other side of the conversation, and he voiced the question that had occurred to her as well:

"It would be very interesting to know what Mrs. Lloyd's lawyer found out, and who told him. I wonder how difficult it would be to get any information out of him."

"You know lawyers." She shrugged.

"Right. But what if we had Mrs. Lloyd call her lawyer and ask him where he got his information. Just have her hint around. You know—she wants to know so she can decide whether or not to pursue the thing against the company for maybe forcing him to sell the farm under duress or whatever?"

"Do you know Mrs. Lloyd?"

"Umm. Yeah. I see what you mean. She's good people, but I can't really see her bringing that off either. What if you were to go to him—as a friend of the family considering the same kind of lawsuit? Think that could work?"

"I'd be willing to try."

"Tell you what, Mary, let's see if we can find out any more information by poking around out there at the construction site. We'll see what we can find out this evening. Maybe we can learn something that will point us in the right direction. Tomorrow—if nothing's changed—we can go rattle the bars on Mrs. Lloyd's lawyer's cage. Okay?"

"Yes. What do you think we'll find out there?"

"I don't have a clue. But all that traffic and massive concrete work and whatnot—there have got to be some plans around, maybe in a trailer or something. Surely we can get a better idea of what they're doing out there in the middle of the boonies."

"Won't it be guarded?"

"Typically a job site like that might have a guard—a retired cop glued to his TV, or a kid sitting around in the trailer getting high. They don't even make builders get construction permits on unzoned county ground—and if they do have a construction guard, he won't be any big thing." He'd have good cause to reconsider the wisdom he'd just dispensed.

The first thought that occurred to Royce had been that they were building some sort of military airfield in the middle of nowhere—there was such a vast expanse of concrete. Poured concrete had covered much of the construction project, from the center of what had been the Lawley farm to the northernmost edge of Bill Wise Industrial Park. The great span of concrete reminded one of several airstrips viewed side by side.

But this was no airfield. The concrete formed a sublevel, a gigantic flooring and walls. A shallow-walled fortress? Some kind of NORAD deal maybe? A defense command to be housed in this immense subterranean bunker? For what purpose? The North American Defense Command was buried under the heart of Cheyenne Mountain, and impervious to nuclear strike. This one was only a few feet down—too vulnerable.

He tried to imagine a Disneyland for adults. What would it resemble? A fanciful landscape of spiraling turrets and minarets and geodesic domes as drawn by Alex Raymond? Perhaps this was the beginning of an environmental theme park, a showcase for earth-sensitive projects of research and development just as World Ecosphere, Inc., claimed. Maybe they'd had the misfortune to concoct a land deal at the worst possible time and place, coincidentally picking a small town targeted by a serial killer.

Royce turned to Mary, bundled up in sweaters and a heavy coat, and whispered, "Let's get closer." She whispered okay and they moved as quietly as they could, going over the top of the embankment where they were parked, and down the fairly steep hillside that was adjacent to Russell Herkebauer's drainage ditch, and Lawley's northern ground.

There was a wood line at the base of the hill, and they stopped there, hiding in the trees.

"That's the place where we want to go, I think." He pointed to a rectangular-shaped building about the size of a trailer-truck bed. "I think that's the office trailer." There was a similar-size affair without side doors, which he knew was a place where tools were locked up at night.

He was starting to get up, almost ready to reach for Mary and tell her they were going to check out the trailer, when the first guard came out of the trees beside them. Royce grabbed Mary, shushing her and pulling her down all in one move, and only luck kept her from making a noise.

"Jeezus! I didn't see him at all," he whispered, when the man and his dog were well away from the trees. Mary was frozen in terror, literally speechless. She tried to swallow. Realized, suddenly, she needed to take a breath.

"That was close," she said, gasping.

An armed man, carrying what appeared to be, by its silhouette, a rifle, with a leashed guard dog, had been in or very near the wood line at the base of the hillside, not fifty feet from where they'd just come down the embankment.

"Right. Just stay chilly." In a couple of minutes, scanning the dark shapes, he spotted a second man. This one carrying what was unmistakably a small machine gun of some kind. No dog.

"Come on," he whispered after a bit, "we're going back." In the vehicle he told her.

"That cinches it. You don't put guards with silent attack dogs and machine guns on an environmental research park. No way."

"What is this all about?"

"I don't know . . . I know one thing." She looked at him quizzically. "If the wind had been coming from the other way and that guard dog had picked up our scent—we'd have been in a world of bad news."

"Is that what happened to Sam, you think? He found out what they were up to?"

"Maybe so. We've got to get some help. Whatever this deal is, it's a lot bigger than you and yours truly can do anything about. And Marty Kerns—forget it!"

"If this is something to do with the government, maybe the FBI is in on it somehow. That would explain why they haven't done more about the missing people."

"Yeah. Let's get out of here." He started the engine and they headed for the county highway that would take them over to Market Road, and eventually across the bridge into Tennessee.

"I got a bad feeling," Royce said. "And I've got you in over your head, too. I've turned out to be some friend to you."

"You've been a good friend," she said softly, touching the back of his hand. "I'm the one who got *you* in this mess, remember?"

Little did she know. Little did they both know. Royce had nothing to go by but his vibes and a lot of experience running games on folks, and having games run back on him, but one thing he knew: They were in deep shit. And everything he did, every new fact he gleaned, seemed to leave them in a more precarious situation, and knowing less than they knew before.

22

North Quarry Bayou

The beast crosses an open field of wild pastureland, keeping close by the protective thicket that divides the piece of ground, a dense border of interwoven bushes, thorn-studded trees, and commingled vines. Moves in the direction of swampy bayou, dark glade, secret hollows made for hiding, killing, and burying.

From the distance you see a huge waddling clown man, fatso bear, limping a bit—if you look closely—favoring the tired right ankle that supports its share of the quarter ton, but begins weakening when the beast grows tired.

If you have the bad luck to view him from closer range, you will see he is not the grinning simpleton the stereotype suggests. Mean, hard, unforgiving intelligence flashes in the strange, doughy face. Eyes as cold as graveyard stones flicker constantly, registering every sign and movement of life. His breath mists in the cold air as his sensors scan for the presence of humanity.

Should he see your footprints or your recent tire tracks amid the Hereford cattle and water moccasin sign, he will lock on to your heartbeat and find you. His present mood gives new meaning to "obsessed." Killing and torture have become a relentless and insistent need.

Last night he slept in a frigid box of a cramped automobile, and tonight he will spend it in a warm house—if he has to leave Mommy, Daddy, Bubba, and Sissy with RIPPED ABDOMENS, TORN KIDNEYS, BLEEDING HEARTS, AND PILES OF STEAMING DOG SHIT to do it. He sleeps inside tonight.

As he scans he thinks of BELLY BILE, GUT JUICE, VENTRICLES, VISCERA, OFFAL, FAT, SMILE, BLOOD, GUTS, GORE, GRUE, GOOP, CHITLINS, SHIT TUBES, RIPPED RENDERED DEAD FUCKING MONKEY PEOPLE.

The field is crossed and he is in dark woods. It is colder here. Cow flop. Snakeskins. Wet, green clumps of shadowed moss thriving in the rankness of deep, canopied murk. His sensors pick up his own sewer-main stench, the fragrance of pastureland manure, compost, humus rich with a mulch that he imagines as decomposed flesh—what a superior burial site!

Out of the cold shadows now he tops a ditch bank over a bayou. A viscous green scum lies across the surface of the water. He leaves his deep 15EEEEE indentations along the top of the bank. Follows a cattle path. Skirts the bayou. Reaches the edge of the world.

Chaingang peers over the side of the cliff. He is looking down into what appears to be a bottomless pit, an old marble quarry, fathomless, deep beyond measure, going down beyond visibility into the darkest, blackest core of the earth. He throws a rock in and listens, but does not hear it strike bottom.

No stairs or steps or paths lead down into the quarry. How has the rock been retrieved? He idly speculates on this oddity, initiating a query about the queer quarry, smiling broadly at the potential of this gaping, grand invitation. What a mass monkey grave this would make!

By nightfall he is on the other side of the black hole, snug and warm in Frank and Lucille Stahly's farmhouse. He has the heat cranked up, a big bowl of chips and Mrs. West's Party Dip in his lap, and his muddy boots rest on Lucille's coffee table, waiting for them to return home.

* * *

He'd slipped the cheap lock in about eight seconds, found the small farmhouse empty, dirty dishes in the sink and on the breakfast table, and the bed unmade. Within a half hour or so he knew what there was to know about the people who lived here, and was waiting patiently for the party to get under way.

Darkness had fallen early and he'd enjoyed his quiet vigil, eating the entire contents of the Stahly's fridge, drinking some wine he'd found, and resting his bones. He amused himself reading, in his mind, "Eating One's Dead: Susu and the Southern Massim."

It was nearly seven-thirty when he heard the pickup truck crunch along the gravel driveway. He was on his feet, moving through the darkened house, standing against the wall behind the kitchen door and away from the windows, frozen motionless, willing his vital signs to a halt, his killing chain dangling from his right hand. Waiting silently.

"They pulled three truckloads out when melons were going for nine cents, and then, see, the early winter set 'em back—and so they started givin' 'em away by the truckful, and trying to wholesale 'em out to these roadside vendors."

"If everybody had knowed about it, they would have come out and got some. They shoulda' told the folks in town." A woman's loud voice.

"John said he was (something) that'd been shipped too early to turn sweet."

"That's right."

The sound of the door unlocking.

"He asked me if we wanted a bag of broccoli. They had about ten bags that was damaged coming off a truck from Mem—" He took the man down with the first chain-snap, catching him across the left temple and forehead, killing him instantly, reluctantly almost. He could listen to monkey talk for hours sometimes, fascinated as he was by the extremely prosaic nature of their endless blabbing about melons and broccoli and damaged veggies. He hated them for their ways but was intrigued by their mundane, weak lives and superficial thought patterns, because, deep down, he was one of them.

The man was ordinary in appearance. The woman, ample-bosomed and rather big-boned, was an attractive lady in her fifties. She immediately began to fight him, and he was surprised and amused, a barking cough of laughter escaping as he subdued her as gently as he could, opting to knock her out with his frying-pan-size fist.

"Stop!" the woman screamed, regaining consciousness, feeling great weight on her, the nakedness and stench of her attacker adding to the blind horror. A stocking bit into her mouth.

"Now, now, Lucille," a deep basso profundo rumbled hotly in her ear, "it's going to be all right." She felt as if her back were breaking. The monster was in her and she almost passed out trying to fight him. Her wrists and ankles were bound to objects she could not see, blindfolded as she was and spread on the living room floor, tethered to the stove and other pieces of heavy furniture.

The heaviest furniture of all was on top of her, on her back, one hand cupping her breast, another squeezing her right hip, stabbing into her from behind.

"Oh, Lucille," he rumbled, as she gagged with nausea and fear, "You're a live one."

23

South of Waterton

"What time did Big Boy check into this location?" the civilian at the monitor screen asked. Big Boy was their in-house name for Chaingang Bunkowski.

"Just a second. Let me get the log." The warrant officer took a clipboard down and read it for a few moments, then read the time to the man in front of the screen. "Seventeen twenty-two thirty. Yesterday."

"Occupants arrived when . . .?"

"Nineteen twenty-eight."

"Jesus. The bastard's still in there with 'em." He made a note on a manifest in front of him and keyed a switch on his console. Then cut the switch and double-checked his code-pad. Big Boy was "Friendly" on the one-time voice pad. He opened his microphone again and gave the radio call sign for the disposal team:

"White Tracker to Natural Athlete, you copy?"

"Read you, White Tracker. Over."

"Friendly's got an overnighter in North Sector Four. Check your directory under four hundred and eleven Yankee. Please confirm. Over." There was a pause while Natural Athlete asked White Tracker to wait one, and they looked up the skinny on a location in North Sector Four, and then ran down the "grids" in the Yankee quadrant. Their directory confirmed the location of the residential listing under the name Stahly, Frank, at four-one-one Yankee.

"Natural Athlete calling White Tracker. We confirm—that is a rog."

"Okay. We'll let you know when Friendly is outta there, and you guys can be standing by with the meat wagon, you copy? Over."

"We copy. Over."

"Ten-four. Y'all have fun now. This is White Tracker out." Christ. He wouldn't have their job for anything. Uncle Sugar didn't have that much money.

The man who was occasionally Christopher Sinclair sat behind a metal desk in his office within the Control Center. Names meant nothing in his line of work. He was one thing in the Clandestine Services interagency directory, another thing where he got his personal mail. His own name—that had been buried long ago. The names he used were worknames. Part of the business he was in. They meant about as much as did titles. His happened to be "chief of section," which—in this situation—meant chief scapegoat.

The project had begun for him during the COUNTRYSAFE operation, which had been, in his view as well as his boss's, an unmitigated disaster. That had been far away in another time and place, and his name had been Robert Newman back in those halcyon Vietnam days.

There were forces within the service as well as within the embassy that conspired to mitigate, not to mention distort, the failure that was to be officially perceived as a success. He'd been called upon to draft a CYA memo, a cover-your-ass document that would—in carefully drafted and oblique language—present the debacle's best face.

"We are not the KGB," he had written, contending that while we could mount a small commando mission, call in a well-placed air strike, bring a carrier into the South China Sea, or mine the Gulf of Tonkin, we could obtain from neither the military or private sector "expendable assets who have proven to be highly adept at sensitive assassinations."

When push came to shove, we had no expertise at hiring cold-blooded killers who excelled at their special craft. "Uncle Sam is not," he was pleased to observe, "in the murder business."

There were those operations that demanded the services of such monstrous horrors as the legendary Chaingang Bunkowski, around whom the COUNTRYDAY operation had been structured. Serious and vital hits, among them being the most delicate and important missions entrusted to the Action Unit, demanded pro-level wet work of the highest degree of skill. The elite military units and the usual roster of "cowboys" simply would not do.

But COUNTRYSAFE, a different (but related) ill-conceived, covertly mounted op originating in the secret swamps of the intelligence community, had not lived up to its name. If anything, it had put the country in the gravest peril.

During the blizzard of cables and CYA memoranda in the wake of the op, a man doing R & D in one of the service's Midwest shops, a Dr. Norman, happened to access certain correspondence from workname Robert Newman, née Christopher Sinclair, to his superiors. Norman knew a like mind when he encountered it, and an alliance was formed during those Southeast Asian War years that would stand the test of time. Both of them, to be sure, were Chaingang Bunkowski believers.

Someday they knew there would be a chance to restructure the unit in a domestic setting. To create, perhaps, a hard-core cadre capable of sensitive wet work: counter-terror, spike teams, orchestrated assassinations, either state-side or wherever covert missions were set into place. With Mr. Bunkowski at its center, such an ultrasecret unit was potentially capable of the most terrifying efficiency.

But planning for these things and implementing them would prove to be an all-consuming challenge that would become a kind of awful obsession. The initial problem was in the emerging technologies: They had the level of weapons development that was required even back in the sixties, but there was (1) the matter of finding drugs or some other reliable, scientific means of controlling their "assets," and (2) the problem of monitoring the operations. One could not just turn a Chaingang, Bunkowski loose—however great the temptation—because although he could perform the mission, there was too much danger he could evade his keepers.

By the time the technologies finally caught up with their lifelong dream, in the early nineties, the problems had shifted. Now there was the matter of Chaingang's weight and his advancing age.

No accurate birth records survived, but Dr. Norman was sure he'd been born in late 1949 or early 1950. He was middle-aged. Could he physically perform as he had when he was eighteen? The answer to that was clearly yes. It had taken a small army to capture him some two and a half years ago.

The weight was the primary concern. He'd lost all the excess weight once, in the 1980s, when he'd hoped to completely alter his appearance, but had promptly regained a the original poundage and more. At five hundred pounds—give or take—how many years were left to him?

The problem was therefore to train other Chaingangs who could take his place. This was the time to begin the comprehensive on-the-job film and tape record of the most prolific mass murderer in history, to observe him at work, record his every technique, amass a visual catalog that chronicled his every MO, so that others could learn his extraordinary "art."

These were among the exigent needs demanding action when Dr. Norman convinced his colleague to move on the project. When the computers found Waterton, Norman convinced like-minded associates that they had the implant, the tracking system, the "overview"—his word for their trump card—and a sufficiently obscured control mechanism that would allow the plan to work. Even Chaingang Bunkowski, presentient though he was, would have difficulty seeing through the superficial elements that hid their few agenda.

Now it was happening. The service was now in the motion picture business, busily creating documentary footage of a mass killer filmed in the act! If anything went wrong, he knew how much hell there would be to pay. The one critical aspect, the overriding one, was that this thing could never go public. The American body politic would never buy any part of this one.

Because he was a thirty-year veteran at CYA, that's what he did now; he began his version of the op in case the thing misfired—his spin on the project, close to the truth but never all the truth—what he would tell the hierarchy when he was summoned on high to do his word-dance when this mutha' went out of control.

He sat at his rented desk, took a piece of blank paper, took pen in hand, and in a neat, medium back-slant, wrote across the top of the page:

What to say if we fuck up.

The silver-haired man stared at the piece of paper for a long while—maybe ten minutes. Then he laughed out loud, crumpled up the paper, and tossed it into the bag marked INCINERATE.

24

Near North Quarry Road

Daniel Bunkowski awoke precisely one hour before dawn, yawned, stretched, and heaved his quarter ton from the rumpled bed, urinating carelessly onto the bedroom carpeting.

He waddled across the carpet, stepping over the inert bodies of Frank and Lucille Stahly, entering the bathroom and taking a long, steaming shower, preparing for a good day by availing himself of the Stahly conveniences, making a big breakfast, eggs and canned ham, and eating it where he could watch Lucille's face while he swallowed. Lucille had been a treat. Lively, and then—when he was spent—quite delicious. Who would have guessed that she'd have been so rich?

A quarter hour after first light he was crossing the road and moving into the field, feeling bright-eyed and bushy-tailed, and pleasantly surprised by the warmth of the early dawn. It was going to warm up.

By nine o'clock, according to both his inner clock and the position of the sun in the sky, he had almost reached the turnoff to Whitetail Road, which led to the pond and the conservation area beyond the North Quarry.

The odd weather pleased him: a near-freezing November one day, tropical heat the next. He registered the field in his mental computer, noting that there were eats to be had here. In season he could gather and devour a found meal of mouse-ear, pokeweed, lamb's quarters, wild mustard, and assorted "soul greens."

He stepped down into a thick scrub of staghorn sumac, wild carrot, black locust shrubs, butterfly weed, horse nettle, common mullein, and a rampant Mother Nature lode of weeds and edibles even he could not identify.

He crossed a mud-and-sand-filled ditch, weapons cases and duffel sinking those huge pawprints even farther down into the soil, and he clambered up on a rock road. Quickly moved across it, over heavy chunks of broken machinery, a tap and bolt the size of a golf ball, and—on the adjacent ditch—turtle tracks left in the mud like the marks of a bike tire.

Something prodded him and he moved into the protective arms of the overgrown road ditch, trampling bright red careless weed, the bloom like sumac, the stalk scarlet to bloodred, and his scanners were on full alert. He registered everything that moved, that lived, that pulsated: a row of barn swallows lined up and evenly spaced along an overhead power line; a mockingbird that sat on a rusting advertisement for Northrup King Corn; yellow butterflies. He moved cautiously through the overgrowth, up over another bank, and saw the ditch forty feet below.

The ditch contained moving muddy water that appeared, variously, as olive drab, khaki, brownish green, and black. Wind and the current rippled the water and left it looking like a wrinkled, moving sheet.

The ditch almost stopped at a point near a fallen tree that had dropped across some mud flats that extended to nearly meet and touch in the center of the dirty stream. He could jump across there. The mud was dark black in the shadows, gray in the light.

A table leg stuck up out of the water. It could have been part of someone's trot line or fish-box. Gnarled tree roots grew down into the ditch from the centuries-old oak and sycamore that blanketed the other side. He saw the old bridge.

The bridge was made from mighty planks the size of railroad ties. He stepped across deep cracks in the parched earthen pathway and walked out onto the bridge.

It is a railless bridge, and forty feet up one gets a sense of vertigo, a high anxiety that attacks not in the head but in the feet, and he feels himself swaying a bit, losing his balance. It enrages him for no reason other than it fucks with his head. Daniel Edward Flowers Bunkowski is tired of people fucking with his head and no more Mr. Nice Guy, so to punish himself for this offense, he grasps his own hands together and squeezes as hard as he can, really bearing down on his own hands, squeezing until he almost passes out. There. *Maybe that will teach you*, he thinks.

Pushing his limits is an old hobby. He forces himself to stare down between the two-inch cracks of the bridge planks until he gives himself a queasy acrophobic feeling of disorientation. He sees fishing line caught in a nest of vines and tree roots under some overgrown limbs. Feels that nauseating, swaying feeling in his huge feet again and immediately clasps his hands together to dish out more punishment to his obstreperous brain, but something pulls him off the bridge.

First it is the two diving dragonflies, their wings beating maniacally as they swoop and soar across his field of vision like a pair of Cobra gunships in an aerial dogfight. Does he see the dragonflies or hear them first, or does he hear the distant chopper noise and free-associate the Huey slick comin' for to carry him home? He makes a dive for the underbrush nearby.

The bird is coming closer and is audible to the human ear now, with the water giving it an intermittant turbine sound, and the dragonflies adding to his misperception, but the helicopter turns out to be a loaded eighteen-wheeler rumbling around the corner and over the bridge.

OUT
OF
NOWHERE
THE
RED
TIDE
IS
ON
HIM
AND
HE
WANTS
TO
TEAR
SOMETHING
APART!

He can hardly focus for the scarlet roar in his head and he grasps his huge, meaty hands again—frustrated and enraged—squeezing with a grip that can make the FUCKING ACID OOZE FROM A FLASHLIGHT BATTERY—squeezing with all his might, and then the worst of it passes. How did he get in such a foul mood? He tries to remember Lucille, the live one, who reminded him in some way of the girl who once bore his child. He cannot think of them now. He realizes it is the monkey presence that has brought about this black mood.

Even here, on the dark side of the booniemoon, there is traffic. It never ceases to amaze him—the busy business of the monkey people. They are always in such a hurry, populating every isolated, distant corner of the planet, dropping their unwanted frogs hither, thither, and yon, hurrying to copulate again, to impregnate, to bring to term, to propagate once more, to make more screaming and unwanted monkeys. Daddy must drive his eighteen-wheeler seven days a week to make more money so he and Mommy and Buddy and Sis can buy a poorly constructed, overpriced home in the burbs, and drop more frogs, who will someday drive their own eighteen-wheelers and so on. If *he* was mad, what were the monkey men?

How he hated them with their credit-card vacations to Yellowstone, and their squalid romantic interludes, and their tireless, remorseless quests for fur coats and tax shelters. If there were a nuclear button that would wipe their millions off the face of the globe in a series of all-kill mushroom clouds, he would push it in an instant.

His unbounded loathing and murderous desire act as his flexible chain mail, the lust and the killing, linking themselves together to form a kind of neurological protection from normalcy—or so his mindscreen suggests, as he thinks of the chain reaction of mushroom blasts, and he moves across the bridge, into the next field, and sees a rust red, discarded refrigerator with a heavy chain around it. His life has been a chain of violent events.

Enters woods, surefooted now, pulled by his homing mechanism. Finds the old shack. Rectangular blocks of scorched steps, with bent iron pipe and broken conduits and reinforcement rods protruding. Charred timbers, combat-assault concrete, battlefield brick, exploded masonry, mortar fragments, and twisted firefight wreckage—this site suggests.

Half the shack is gone. A fire consumed it, seemingly in one big black bite of hungry flame, then it was extinguished. What remains is half a shack, roof and walls more or less intact, one side open, and a square of burnt earth where the rest of the shack stood, bordered by what was left of the stove and the blocks the house sat on.

A sharecropper's place, perhaps, tucked into this little woodsy grove of trees and shrubs, not a hundred feet from the rock road, but hidden and safe from prying eyes.

With one level of his mind he is rebuilding a temporary wall, sealing off his newly acquired snuggery from the elements. With another he is thinking about the sign he's seen for the last half a klick, remembering the abandoned end of a railroad spur now far fields away, and the assorted tracks and messages he has duly recorded.

His entire life, both institutionalized and—for wont of a better word—free, has been spent in close proximity to riffraff, robbers, rascals, ruffians, scamps, scoundrels, scoff-laws, scumbags, burglers, buggers, brutes, bangers, deadbeats, derelicts, desperadoes, degenerates, criminals, cutpurses, cracksmen, crooks, tramps, tricksters, thieves, thugs, fakers, freeloaders, fugitives, felons, freebooters, footpads, fag-bashers, and fruit-rollers of every type, size, shape, creed, kind, and color of the rainbow's dirtiest oil slick.

He is—therefore—multilingual and fluent in street guinea, gypsy, carny, cowboy, bum, drifter, grifter, and the assorted dialects of homeboy, gangster, and juju man. He reads hobo chalk-talk easily, and watches—with no small degree of amusement—the crossbar variations advertising free medical aid, handouts of clothing, food, and the quid pro quo expected of the recipient in the way of work, con, or fast moves.

He puts no store in such childishness, but it pleases him to watch for the intersecting circles, stick-figure-and-triangle art, and the slashes that speak only to the brethren of the boxcar and the denizens of the drunk tank about such monkey dangers as hobo-haters and men with guns nearby.

His doughy baby face is distorted by a beaming, dimpled ear-to-ear grin when he sees the ticktacktoe scratches on the side of the foundation cornerstone nearest the front door, that is, nearest to where the door would have been before the fire.

But only if you speak hobo do you realize it is five lines and not four. It is a serious, adult signal, not a child's game. It reads, to the initiated:

EXTREME DANGER! A CRIME WAS COMMITTED AROUND HERE, AND THIS IS A BAD PLACE FOR STRANGERS.

Night takes its time, this day, but it does eventually come and erupts layers of liquid black lava over Tinytown, slough, dump site, and reservoir. Light is gone from this remote and moonless spot, and the fortresslike factory brick is gone, the ramparts of the old water treatment plant, the tree-line silhouettes and false horizons, and the look of country, town, warehouse, walkway, railing, and water all blend into darkness.

Death waits here in ticking readiness, tremor-sensitive, vital signs stilled to a near-motionless flutter-crawl, in absolute menacing silence, waiting and hating, precognating and gestating, alembic poisons refining, transmuting, distilling the venomous loathing into its most lethal essense. The beast lets it build, boil, bubble over into the red-hot tidal thing that will sweep over humanity in a murderous mutilating frenzy of destruction.

This hatred, which has a life of its own, has changed, mutated, and—hypertrophied and swollen like a tumorous membrane—it will sicken him if he does not expunge it. It wells up inside him now.

He knows that he has been extrinsically controlled by this, even partially manipulated into position by suits who play his fierce, deep loathing like a finely tuned instrument of mayhem, and this only worsens the hating, amplifies his hunger, deepens the thing that lives on the hate essence, forcing him to kill. Death is troubled by the unseen hands that set him in place. And he uses this, too.

Arising from his temporary den near the reservoir, concealing his burrow with twigs and boughs, he inhales deeply, light-headed by the musk of bloodlust, awash in his own sewer fumes, faintly nauseated by the sudden purity of pine, spruce, and the sweet scents of fern and earth.

The man is in the small cottage, and dogs bark inside, fueling the beast's madness. His mental computer takes over now:

VIRGIL WATLOW, he screens.

LEFT PROFILE. Grainy shot of an unshaven man. Late twenties. Close-cropped black hair. Unimportant history. Irrelevant statistics.

DOSSIER: He hits DOG BUNCHER, skips the details. His anger is already beyond the manageable stage.

He is at the door, having deposited duffel nearby. No weapons. No chain. This is hands-on work, and if he has the bowie, he will waste this **BUNCHER**. And that would be wrong.

"Yeah?"

"Mr. Watlow," he says, in a mincing sissy voice, "I'm Kenny Harman, from the clinic?" Kenny hep you?

"Eh?"

"I'm buying dogs for the clinic." He foists a huge pawful of documentation at the man, who dumbly stares at the papers. "We were told you'll sell direct. We'll take all you have." The papers have the local clinic's imprimatur, along with trash from drug companies that he's rescued from local trash bins. "What do you charge per dog."

"Aw . . . that depends . . . uh . . ." Barking is a constant accompaniment to their dialogue.

"Would you mind terribly if I came in? I think we should keep our transaction private, don't you?" Chaingang as a simpering homosexual is something that must be witnessed to be believed. He has the actor's naturalness.

"Yeah. Aw' right." Virgil Watlow moves back into the living room of the home which stinks of urine and feces and animal smells. A woman, surprisingly, comes out of the next room, looking at Chaingang as if he were a float in a parade. Mouth agape.

"Could I see what you have?"

"Get the dogs," the man says, and his significant other sulks off, returning with the weight of a file drawer.

"Uunn." She drops the drawer.

Chaingang sees movement in the drawer under a wire screen. Noise. Hears the man say something.

"—only got four right now. I'll have some more next week and—"

There is a blur of movement. Daniel Edward Flowers Bunkowski's hand-to-eye coordination is extraordinary. He would have quick hands if he were an NFL wide receiver. But on a human blimp they are always a surprise.

He bops the woman on the head with a hammer-fist, a bottom-fist blow that sounds like a bolt gun taking a cow down in the abattoir, and she snaps that dirty whore-hole of a mouth shut when he pops her head, dying even as she goes down for the count, and the elbow is across and striking, focused beyond the back of Virgil Watlow's head, smashing between his eyes just to stun—not to kill.

Bop. Pop. That fast. Both down.

He secures Mr. Watlow and begins work on the drawer. Gets the screen off. Tries not to look into the stinking thing. Dumps the four live ones and the dead one onto the filthy kitchen floor. Proceeds to open every can, jar, dish, and container in the Watlow refrigerator and kitchen shelves. The small dogs feed. There is more barking out in back of the house, he now realizes, and he will tend to the others later.

He opens drawers and finds a kitchen knife of just the right sharpness. It must be just sharp enough, but he does not want a scalpel edge—this needs to be painful and just a tad blunt. The cuts must require a certain degree of pressure.

He has pedicured Mr. Watlow and is beginning the manicure when the man comes around for the second time. But he passes out on the first cut, so Chaingang gets smelling salts from his duffel, and returns. Revives him yet again. Saws at the next knucklebone and—bang! Mr. Watlow passes away.

Sad at this tragic and untimely loss, the beast cleans up and frees the dogs, preparing to leave. There were twenty-one digits that required attention, and—unfortunately—he only got to twelve of them. Tenderly he opens the woman's mouth and inserts the parts from Mr. Watlow's extremities, placing the tips of the toes and fingers in, so that the mouth will remain agape. He wants to leave her just as he found her. More or less.

He realizes some of the dogs may not be able to fend for themselves, and that it may indeed be cruel to turn them loose. He fights the impulse to stuff a couple down in his shirt for pets. Perhaps they will survive—the hardier ones. He observes, not for the first time, that life is cruel.

25

Maysburg

Seth Pisckovik did not seem to be particularly whelmed by Mary's and Royce's inquiry, much less overwhelmed. The second or junior member of the firm of Pisckovik and Pisckovik, pronounced Puh-SHO-vick, was neither better nor worse than the average small-town attorney-at-law. His reputation varied to both ends of the spectrum, depending on whom one asked.

A brusque, middle-aged man with dark, poorly complected skin and a widow's peak, he greeted them the moment they arrived for Mary's appointment, showed them to seats in his office, and spent nearly five minutes with paperwork and a phone call before he managed to finally speak to them again.

"I apologize. A matter that couldn't wait. Now—how can I help you?" Mary explained. Told him about her husband's disappearance.

"My husband and I were friends with the Luther Lloyd family. Both Mrs. Lloyd and I had the same reaction, that something wasn't quite right about the large-scale land sale involving the World Ecosphere company. She told me in conversation that you'd advised her there might be a way to prove that the land deal wasn't completely on the up and up—that it had been done when Mr. Lloyd was under duress, perhaps."

"I mentioned that as one theoretical possibility, not as a serious suggestion."

"But you suggested Mrs. Lloyd should not pursue any legal action, is that correct?" Mary hadn't liked his curt tone, and her own took on a sharp, inquisitive edge. He fielded it easily.

"True." So?

"I ask because I was considering retaining an attorney to pursue a similar matter on my—and on my husband's—behalf. And Mrs. Lloyd gave us the impression you thought World Ecosphere was too big. And that they were involved with the government and could tie any litigation up for years and years."

"Are you asking me to represent you in a legal matter, Mrs. Perkins?" he said, rather frostily.

"I want to know if you think . . . such an inquiry, you know . . . could be . . ." It was getting too much for her, Royce sensed, and he jumped in.

"We wondered if they're actually involved with the U.S. government. If so, in what way? Obviously Mrs. Perkins can't sue the government." He figured the lawyer would ask what his part was in this, but he didn't. Instead he simply finessed him.

"I haven't any notion, offhand, not having studied what Mrs. Perkins's particular situation is. As I understand it—" he waved a beringed hand in the air "—Mr. Perkins was an intermediary, representing the purchasing agent—so to speak—and I don't see what possible relation that would have to Mrs. Lloyd's situation. She thought her husband would have said no to the offer, which—again, I'm just guessing here, but—which your husband tendered. Is that about the way it was?"

"Yes."

"As I say, there's no relation, other than the fact that each of you has had a tragic thing occur—but that has no provable basis for an action against the land developers. None that I see, anyway."

"Are they a U.S. government-related company? Could you tell us if you have any knowledge about that?" Royce wasn't letting go.

"I have no knowledge, other than my own casual surmises which I made to Mrs. Lloyd. They're dealing in a massive amount of development on behalf of a holding company, and as I understand the project in question, it's some sort of environmental center, which, of course, suggests at least a working relationship with . . ." He droned on in a lawyerly, boring tone, and Royce let his mind relax. They were learning nothing here.

"A case with contingency fees . . . limited when you're taking on the government . . . twenty-five percent recovery . . . lots of property work around this area . . . trust lawyer . . . be glad to recommend someone with a better . . ." Slick mumbo-jumbo legalese.

As soon as they could, they thanked him and left the law offices, once again going forward three paces and going back four.

"The more we learn about this thing, the less we know," Royce said.

"You're not just realizing that, are you?" They laughed mirthlessly. "Let's hear some good ideas."

Royce shook his head. "Um . . ."

"Me too." They went to a phone and did their thing. Mary was first. It seemed to Royce as if she'd been on the telephone for a very long time, and most of it was listening.

"Listen," she began, as soon as they were back in his vehicle, "you know Jimmie and Lurene Gallagher, don't you?"

"Uh-uh."

"She's with the welfare office here, and Jimmie works on the county road crews. They live out by the land project. Alberta Riley heard that they had a run-in with the Ecoworld people. Jimmie Gallagher's dog was rolling around in some garbage they dumped out by the construction site, and the dog died. They got all crazy about it because they were afraid Jimmie's little boy might have played with the dog and got some of it on him."

"What kind of stuff—something radioactive?"

"Pardon?"

"What kind of garbage?"

"Oh! I don't know—poisons, I think. Anyway, they went to Marty Kerns, and he said he couldn't do anything—naturally. They were supposed to go to the EPA about it. And they had an inspector come look at it, but he wouldn't do anything either. He said it was the Gallaghers' fault for letting their dog run loose. Apparently the little boy is okay, but they're really mad about it."

"Where was this garbage?"

"It was at the edge of the Poindexter farm—just over the property line on Ecoworld's ground. They're throwing chemicals and stuff out there, I guess."

"Let's go look at it."

"Okay. We could try. If it's still there. I don't know what we'd learn that the EPA guy doesn't already know, but—"

"Where did Alberta hear all this stuff, did she say?"

"Her hairdresser."

"That figures." In a small town the local hairdresser is the rough equivalent of "60 Minutes." He should have known.

"Royce, wouldn't we have a chance of finding out a lot more by concentrating on getting inside that office out there? Couldn't we create some kind of a diversion and try to get it while—"

"Mary, those guys aren't doughnut-gobbling rent-a-cops we saw. I recognized the weapons they were carrying. The riflelike thing is called a Steyr AUG. It's a specialized assault weapon. This one was silenced and had a night-action scope on it. That's the sort of modification they use on a countersniper rifle. The other guy had what looked like a Heckler & Koch MP 5. This is serious, major-league armament. They've probably got another team asleep nearby—maybe in the office or the tool trailer. Two on, two off—revolving shifts, maybe—so they don't get tired. Working 'em four out of eight hours and then a new set of teams comes in.

"We could create a diversion. Let's say we'd rent the services of a crop duster and he'd make believe like he was strafing the office—okay? Make a whole gang of noise. The guy with the Steyr would pop a 40-mm MECAR rifle grenade attachment over the muzzle, and if that didn't work, they've probably got a Stinger missile in the office. It'd be a diversion, all right."

"What are we gonna do?" she asked in helpless tone.

"Whatever we can. Come on, kid. Let's go see if we can figure out what Jimmie Gallagher's dog got into." He turned the ignition key and they headed across the river, behind an old clunker with "UT" and "Go Vols!" stickers on the bumper, replete with a fake license plate in the rear window reading, "I M 1. R U 1 2? O, I C, U 1 2 B 1!"

Royce realized it had been a good while since he'd packed his sinuses with nose candy. He passed the UT car on the Missouri side, getting in back of a dirty truck whose mud flaps warned about his wide turns. On the back of the filthy truck the moving finger had writ: "FUQ IRAQ." Everywhere you looked, there was a joker waiting.

The vista was bleak and cold, with wintry tendrils of cirrocumulus woven through the pale gray sky. Intermittently clinquant glitters of sunlight flashed on the grimy windshield. There was corn stubble to the left, remnants of milo stalks to the right, and a muddy brown stretch of tractor and combine turnrow between.

They saw the garbage dump and the newly erected concrete construction work at about the same time. The concrete foundations were now complete over the three-hundred-acre building site, and many walls were already up. Near the southeastern edge of the property there were areas that already wore thick ceilings of reinforced concrete. The interiors of these sections appeared to have had their doors and passage entrances boarded up. A pair of guards could be seen in the distance.

Here, far away from the new construction, impedimenta and refuse from Ecoworld had been dumped unceremoniously into a kind of landfill hole, and hastily covered with earth. Here, it seemed, a pack of dogs had decided to dig for buried treasure, and Jimmie Gallagher's dog had been one of them. He'd been one dumb pup to wallow here.

Royce parked and they walked to the center of the unearthed garbage and trash pit, shaking their heads the minute they got out of the vehicle. The smell was incredible.

"My God!" Mary whispered.

"Yeah." The guards could not see them where they'd parked, and the landfill was below the slope of a bordering tree line. "You know what I keep thinking?" he said to her, sotto voce.

"Hnn?"

"Jeezus!" He saw the first of the containers. A group of colorful outer shells giving a tessellated, almost coherent pattern to the mosaic of industrial trash.

"What is it?"

"Hazardous materials—see?" He swallowed. Everything he saw only confirmed what he'd been about to say to her.

"I—" She was fighting to make sense out of this. The lettering was government-style yellow stenciling.

"When I said toxic waste—" It stuck in his throat. His mind was racing. Hydriodic acid. Potassium compounds. Sulfuric acid.

"Come on. Let's go." He had to pull her away from the landfill.

"Toxic waste. You mean radioactive stuff? Plutonium and—" She had partially shut down. Too much information. Sam. Ecoworld. Poisons. Her system had reached Data Overload.

"Come on, Mary, *move*," he said, in a voice that was several decibels louder than he meant it to be.

He was more scared than the night Happy had braced him, just easing into the ride, not slamming the door, waiting for Mary to get in, waiting for the dude to come around the nearest trees with his Steyr AUG, waiting to learn what the first 5.56-mm round would do when it tore through the door, the bullet tumbling from the expanding gasses and the punch through metal. He had a shotgun in the pawnshop—talk about being prepared! The car sounded as loud as a jet engine when he started it, and no time was wasted getting in the wind.

"What?" She demanded.

"It's a fucking drug lab!"

"Why—what makes you think that?"

"Believe me. I know. That's what those bastards are doing out here in Nowheresville—they're fixing to cook up ice."

She was trying to re-join the conscious. She felt as if her brain had fallen asleep.

"Schmeck. Crank. Crack. Ice. Something very potent, maybe." He shook his head as he drove. "I could never figure it out. I could never see it. It's a fucking lab! Probably the biggest ever built. Imagine—the scale of the thing. And they've brought in all the chemicals and stuff and walled it in, see, so later there's no problem starting to cook the junk. You've got guys unloading tools, pouring concrete, taking supplies off trucks every day—who's going to suspect anything if you go ahead and fill your lab? No wonder they've got armed guards."

"But who would do it? . . . What would be the point?"

"The point. What's the point every time? Money, of course."

"I don't—"

"Mafia maybe, or the Latino families or—hell, what's the difference who? Somebody got a few business guys to front for 'em. Found this pure virgin—" he meant the town "—carved a place out in the middle of the boonies—with nobody around to know from bupkes. Very fucking smart."

"Why come out here?"

"Cause the people are stupid around here. Because it's a damn ghost town full of greedy business pricks and farmers. Because crank is a smelly, dangerous mess to cook—and so's some of the other stuff. Because—they came, they saw, they built. Now they can cook all the dope they want and call it chemical research and development. Probably charge tickets to watch them wash the by-products down into the water table. *Jeezus fucking shit I should have known!*"

"What should we do, Royce?"

"Listen. Listen to me: There's a lot I haven't told you. But this is too much. We're in too deep. You have to know. I got jammed up on a drug thing. I'll tell you the details later, when we have time. I promise. They . . . the assholes I was involved with—they turned me. I had to set up a guy who was a big drug dealer, act like I was the same thing. Engineer a deal to bring down a major supplier—you follow?"

"No. I haven't followed any of this since we saw the chemicals. And what kind of drug people bury their incriminating—you know—containers in their own backyard?"

"The kind who don't really give a shit. The kind who have so much clout and such ironclad protection, they can thumb their nose at local law, for one thing."

"But, Royce—I don't get this. You say you were setting up a drug dealer. Kerns said they were watching *you*—that you were a drug dealer and—"

"That fat shit doesn't know *dick*, okay? I'm a half-assed undercover narc, a former fuck-up who's getting over a bad cocaine dependency, and finally seeing a way to pull himself clear from a terrible situation. Just help me, baby, and don't bail. I need you. The people I work for—they gotta know about this. We got to tell them about it and get serious outside help. This could be so big—" He fell silent. Literally speechless. He began again.

"This Fisher guy—whatever his name is. Sinclair—the famous and elusive Christopher Sinclair. Fisher said he was in the Orient. What if the Japanese are behind this? Some megazillion Godzilla Megilla Gorilla consortium, backed by the Yakuza or somebody?"

"I don't see how you can know this is going to be a drug thing from finding some cans and things. Are you sure you—"

"It's what I do. This is what I do, dig?! I'm a fucking—" He could not quite bring himself to put a name on the sign he was wearing around his neck. He stopped and got coins and dialed a Memphis number.

"I'd like to talk with somebody about buying insurance please," he whispered into the phone.

"Who's calling, sir?" A voice resonated into the other end of the line.

"A man who's insurance-poor." He waited for the beep and gave his work number and read the dial tone off into the recording unit, hanging up. Within thirty seconds it pinged and he picked it up.

"I need to talk to Wilcox."

"This is an insecure line, sir. Please use proper procedure," the agent on the phones scolded him.

"I don't give a rat fuck how insecure this line is," he seethed, "put that prick on the phone." His poison threatened to melt the phone.

"Problems?" A familiar voice crackled in his ear.

"You'd better pray not. You got the makings of a three-hundred-acre processing lab in Waterton, Missouri. Don't say anything yet. Just get this down. Ecoworld, they call it. A construction project supposedly funded by a D.C.-area or New York-based company called World Ecosphere, Inc. Guy named Joseph Fisher. Probably bullshit front guy. Major money behind it. There's all kind of PC to bring in the Feds, a CLET and a HAMR unit—the whole works. Armed guards with H&Ks and silenced Steyrs, missing people, dead people—they—"

"Whoa. *Whoa*. Hold it! Take it easy. Slow down. What's this about missing people?"

Royce forced himself to slow down and run it down—every last nasty tidbit that he could remember, from the setup with Sam Perkins to the rumored serial killer.

"What about Happy and his biker pukes?" Royce asked.

"All under control."

"You got Papa then?"

"Nailed and mailed, man. You did great."

"What the hell was he doing with a scumball like Happy? I could never see how this punk got a rating."

"Ruiz? He and the old man did a bit together in the joint. Happy did some chump time in ATC and Booneville, little felony-assault priors and crap—coupla voluntaries that got pled down and whatnot, and he fell on a technicality and ended up in the bucket again. Just a puke, but him and Papa became big buds, and the man set the little weenie up with some bikers. He's nothing. He's shit."

"But have you busted him yet? He's gonna be jazzed to get me, man.

What's the story?"

"I'll get right back to you on that, but I gotta go get on this. We'll send a team in—you say it's that righteous. You're gonna be out from under the brown blanket." The daddy rabbit broke the connection.

"But . . ." Yeah. That's what it was gonna be, all right. *Butt!*

26
Near Whitetail Pond

They drove back the long way around, so as not to have to get near the Waterworks Road area, or the more-traveled Cotton Avenue. Royce went down the county gravel to Farm-to-Market, and cut through Bill Wise's place to Market Road, driving all the way out past Slabtown on North Market. He was fighting serious seizures of fear. They'd written him off.

He tried a dozen times to begin telling Mary, who was visibly confused and frightened.

"Are you gonna talk to me?" she finally asked.

"Yeah," he said, forcing a smile. "I'm gonna talk to you." They passed a pizza joint and he slowed down. "You hungry?"

"No."

He pulled up and stopped in front of a small packaged goods store. "I'll be right back." She didn't say anything. He went in and bought some chilled wine and snack foods. He had to have something in there to help soak up the acid that was threatening to eat its way through the lining of his stomach.

"Okay," he said with a sigh, getting back in the vehicle and starting the motor, putting the sack behind the seat and pulling out onto the blacktop.

"I'll start at the beginning. It's a long story."

"I've got lots of time, Royce," she said. It was all he could do not to say, "I hope so."

"You know what it's like here. Not exactly your cosmopolitan big city. Two Jews and one black guy, and they don't like to admit it. Nothing to do but get high and gossip. I hated this place then. Remember?" He meant when they broke up. She remembered only too well.

"There wasn't an ounce of sophistication or excitement here. You were the only thing good about it, and you wanted to be married so desperately, it was your entire focus. You were in love with the idea of settling down. It was like a—" he edited himself and didn't say the words bear trap "—thing I couldn't come to terms with. I thought we'd get stuck in the marriage, like so many others had, and we'd both come to hate each other." He looked over. She was listening, without any expression.

"Right or wrong, that's the way I felt. But all the marriage talk had me ripe for a relationship exactly like the one we had. You made me want constancy, a stable thing with a sexy lady, all the trappings of marriage without the reality." Without the trap. "And the next girl I met hit me between the eyes.

"She was just like me. It's funny now. Actually a laugh riot. I really thought this beautiful dope fiend had chosen me to fall for because I was such a stone hunk, see. I really fucking loved myself back then." Mary laughed. "I was a goddamn fool.

"We got onto the fastest lane there is—really heavy into junk. Then she let me find out who she was. She was an undercover narc. I just couldn't handle it. I went deeper over the dope edge. That was when I was given my option. I could do hard time—they had me on 'possession with intent,' which carried a stiff mandatory rap, real serious time in the can—or I could help her make this case."

"The case turned out to be a caseload. And they kept pulling me deeper and deeper into the jam. I stayed with this—I stayed with her. That's what's so impossible to understand now. Why I didn't just do the time, I'll never be able to explain even to myself. I did end up doing more time inside my skull. They trapped me. Of course, they had a lot of help. The thing about undercover work is—you got all that nice junk right there at your fingertips. You're not much different than a plain junkie—your life is centered around scoring—it's just that narcs are also trying to bust their fellow junkies. Other than that, we were the same as any other doper."

Mary watched him as he talked about it. His hands were moving all the time: rubbing his eye, scratching his arm, touching his face, tapping time on the steering wheel. She read the fear in his body language, and it made her even more afraid.

"Eventually you get pulled into things you couldn't imagine doing before.

Hell, I was straight compared to what I'd become when she got through getting me into the scene. It's amazing how easy it is to slide from doing a little social blow to having a big-time jones. Or to slide from a couple of hits at a party to doing eight balls or slamming or basing. You just slide in. That's the problem. Your head keeps telling you how great it is."

"But you knew right from wrong, Royce. How did you ever—" She cut herself off. "I just don't see how you could believe that drugs wouldn't take you down. You're not that stupid."

"I still don't say all drugs are bad for all people. Hash . . . weed . . . there are some things that some individuals can handle, and they get a nice high and that's it. It's like boozers—some people can drink some things. Moderation. That's the thing. But if you've got an addictive personality, you shouldn't be doing these things. Cocaine, that's another matter altogether. Nobody handles it. Everybody thinks they can. It's so insidious. It's 'not addictive.' Everybody and his brother is blowin' snow. Suddenly you've got a second mortgage on the house and you're talking kilos, dealing, and you just keep sliding."

He told her all the details of the operation against the punk Happy Ruiz, how they were going to use his vulnerability to get a big trafficker, one of the top executives for the Colombian cartel. The details of the setup:

"I was perfect for it, since this was my turf. I was a homeboy. I was a known stoner. I would start using, become this punk's good customer. Then I do some small-change dealing, supposedly. Keep buying more coke, and finally—set up a deal where I could contract for serious weight, getting our boy into as much of a bind as possible. Time it to coincide with a big shipment so they'd be anxious to move a large amount, play to their greed; only, when the punk set it up, I'd vanish into the woodwork. He'd have to use his emergency line of communication to contact the boss man."

He explained about the phone scam and how ELINT, the phonemen, could nail the otherwise invulnerable dope trafficker by the local pusher initiating an emergency contact. Everybody would fall, and Royce Hawthorne would be cut loose in the bargain.

They reached Whitetail and got out and went in the Perkins cabin. Royce built a big fire in the stone fireplace and they sat in front of it, sipping cheap wine and munching cheese.

"For whatever reason, they've decided to let me twist slowly in the wind. The thing about that is—you're in trouble, too. You're with me, and they know you're the one I—cared about. That we've been seen together a lot since Sam's been gone. They'll try to hurt you, too. I was an imbecile and a jerk to get you involved. I just didn't think.

"Now—I call 'em at the regional office with a tip on the biggest drug lab in the history of the Western world and they like blow me off!"

"What do you mean?"

"They're not about to do anything. The head guy just goes—oh, yeah, that's very interesting. Three hundred acres of—uh-huh. Armed guards and dogs. Yeah. Okay. Cool. We'll get right on that."

"Maybe that's just his way."

"You don't get it. Look: If you're mounting a big-scale, expensive operation against an underground lab, you've got to coordinate your Clandestine Laboratory Enforcement Team; it's a major-league-type SWAT operation. You've got what they call a 'hammer'; a HAMR is a Hazardous Materials Response, and it involves special vehicles, personnel, weapons, tactics. You don't just say, 'Oh, yeah—what's that address again? Twenty-fourth and Plowed Ground? Okay—we'll see you next Tuesday. Take care.' It doesn't work that way." He took a large gulp of wine.

"What does all this mean?"

"It means that for whatever reason, they've written me off. And that means you're in great danger. Happy and his biker goons are still running around loose. For all I know, this so-called serial killer they keep talking about is part of this whole mess. I have nobody I can go to. The FBI doesn't appear to give a shit. It's as if this were a U.S. government operation of some kind. It's got like a security umbrella over it—almost as if a the bad guys had diplomatic immunity."

What he didn't say would have just frightened Mary more, and for no point. He rubbed his ankle where the sheath knife was itching. He didn't even have any weapons to protect them with. His shotgun was in the pawnshop, and didn't work too well to begin with. He'd had a Saturday night special he'd sold to buy coke one night. She had no idea what a bodyguard he was. He looked up at the fireplace, noticing the pegs in the stone, as if an old musket might have hung there once. Even it was gone.

"Did you have a gun up there once?" He hoped it was still around.

"Yeah," she said, "it was broken—didn't shoot." Her mind was on other things. She was thinking about that money he'd borrowed. About what Marty Kerns had told her. "Something was broken off it. It was an old antique. It'd been Sam's grandfather's. I think he decided it would get ripped off and he put it in our cold storage box. I haven't seen it for a long time.

"I want to ask you something. When you borrowed that five thousand dollars . . . it was for cocaine, wasn't it?"

"It was for gambling. I was supposed to scurry about and act like a junkie dealer would act. Trying to get his investment money together. It was all planned. But I had to make it look real. You were convenient, and I knew there was no risk—I wasn't going to lose."

"How did you know that?"

"There was a dealer at this place—The Rockhouse—where all the stoners hung. This one dealer, she was one of us. She'd been put in place just to make sure I'd win my seed money."

"So I was just a—somebody to be used, to you."

"You have to understand, babe, when you think like that all the time, it becomes an unshakable habit. I'm a user. It's my nature. Did you ever see that movie with Charlie Chaplin—*Modern Times?* Remember the scene in the factory where Chaplin is caught between the gears? That's the way it is—the way it was—for me. You reach out for whoever or whatever is at hand, you know?"

"Yeah." She knew.

27

North of Waterton

Doyle Genneret, the belligerent, rich, and ruthless "cattle rancher" who was the owner of the "World-famous Genneret Ranch and Exotic Animal Farm," was in the main office with a bookkeeper, Sally Peebles, and his hirsute foreman, Dean Seabaugh.

Genneret's background had been in livestock and farm machinery. He'd made a killing in the market and sensed an undeveloped category of stock sales: "exotics." Giraffes, camels, lions, tigers, bears, kangaroos. "Lordee!" he was fond of saying. "If you don't see it here, it don't shit."

His main customers were farm boys who wanted to show off for a good year in wheat, or play one-up against the neighbors, something for the grand-kids to ooh and ah over. He was aware that a lot of these old boys were turning around and selling exotics themselves, some of them were in the breeding game. But he didn't mind—he knew what the market could stand, and it was fat and juicy. You could turn on the radio or the TV and hear what hogs was a-bringing', but they didn't have a quote on leopards or honey bears. He knew where the roof was on the prices—there flat wasn't one.

The primary cash producer was the Genneret auction, a monthly "Exotic Animal, Livestock, Gun Show and Auction."

They'd had a few problems with some of them humane society dingbats, but nothing to worry over. He didn't even call 'em animals, he called 'em his "stuff." He kept his stuff in a series of twenty-three overcrowded barns and corrals which required a staff of nearly two dozen hands. More when he went on the road with an exhibit.

His rule of thumb for hiring was simple: you got to be smarter than the stuff. Dean Seabaugh, his foreman was a like mind. He was infamous, even on the ranch, for having whipped a lion to death. He has a slight temper. He shared the boss's view that if them animal rights assholes want to worry about something, "let 'em go take a tour through the freakin' slaughterhouse. Whey do they think them streaks, 'n' belts, 'n' shoes 'n' crap come from?"

Magic Silo had come to the edge of the Genneret property line and flashed on a tubular opening in the thick, junglelike wooded area. His storehouse retained the images of masses of gigantic verticillate leaves, looped and whorled like huge fingerprints, that papered the walls of the jungle conduits similar to this one.

He looked closely. Something nudged him. Déjà vu? The floor bore the signs of trail. He'd seen incredible "hardballs" inside natural tubes such as this one, ceilings with precisely carpentered dink bamboo. He touched a great leaf with a midrib like the rigid blade of an epee and saw his sign.

Saw the man-tracks the way he'd spotted trip wires and traps and deadfalls—saw the sign, felt the presence of some human intrusion. He, Daniel, was the grandmaster of concealment. Nobody could track a human being like him. He read sign in bright moonlight—but how?

He froze. Chilled those vital signs. Waited. Listening. Reaching out for the enemy who was somewhere near. Would the Genneret outfit have a security unit? At night? Working the woods?

He remained very still for a long period—motionless—barely breathing. He heard something and his face broke into a wide and dangerous grin. Slowly he eased into the pipeline, with the focused concentration that had kept him alive so long, moving through the shadows.

The Genneret outfit was forgotten the instant he saw the watcher and identified him. The farm and the cruel men would have provided him with a smorgasbord of wildly delicious opportunities. Another time—perhaps.

When he saw the movement in deep shadow, he froze again. The huge links of the yard-long, friction-taped killing chain dangled at arm's length.

Now he knew what the sound of the human voice he'd heard represented; it was a watcher whispering into some kind of microphone. A headset thing, maybe, with a transparent tube-type mouthpiece and connected earplug.

"Negative," he heard the shadowman whisper, "Blue Leader, I do not have a visual." Chaingang moved forward as the man spoke into his tiny plastic mike, the powerful right arm in motion as he moved, the massive tractor-strength chain moving through the air, propelled by a wrist and forearm and upper bicep of steel, a blur of snaking chain whirling into the deep shadow and connecting.

The chain made more noise crashing into the bushes than the man did falling. Only a hard splat, an *oof* of air, a relatively quiet clump of dead weight—two hundred pounds plus machine gun—falling in a crumpled heap, marked the kill. It was a far more merciful extermination than Bunkowski would have been preferred, but this was no auction house security guard. This was one of them—the invisible eyes. If they were this close, and in the numbers that they would have to be, logic dictated that he expedite his plan's final stages.

He checked the fallen man for life signs. Quickly searched for ID and found neither vital signs nor identification. The weapon was ID enough. That and the commo gear. He was very still again, listening, his sensors scanning for the presence of a partner.

Satisfied after several moments, he eased his great bulk down to the ground beside the man, carefully inserting the earpiece, which he'd found near the watcher's bloodied head. The umbilical cord that connected the headset to the guts of the radio apparatus was too short to facilitate much slack, but with his head beside the inert man's, he was able to insert the earplug.

There was nothing. He waited. As the seconds ticked by, he wondered if they had decided to move in and take him. Were they though with him now? Had he fulfilled his function? Was this experiment or operation now to be aborted with extreme prejudice?

"Blue Leader to Blue Tracker Five—do you read, over?" He grinned into the dark silence, stifling a coughing explosion of mirth. He could utter words now, and the watchers would hear him. What of it?

"Blue Leader, this is Blue Tracker, did Five confirm a visual on Side Show?" The other voice was less clear, but he could hear it.

"Uh—Negative, Blue Tracker, stand by one. Blue Tracker Five, do you copy this transmission? Over."

Chaingang removed the small earpiece and took the high-impact microphone between his thumb and index finger and squeezed. Crunch!

He silently backtracked his way through the pipeline to his vehicle, fighting to keep a damper on his rage, but boiling with irritation at having his plans for Mr. Genneret so rudely interrupted.

Chaingang was gone. Inside the office of the show and auction company, mean Dean Seabaugh, Sally Peebles, and Doyle Genneret shuffled papers and talked of a workaday things, oblivious to their luck. They should have run to their wheels, driven to the nearest airport, and chartered the first thing that would fly them to Vegas.

Lady luck was smiling on them this night. They'd come this close to riding the Genneret Exotic Animal, Livestock, Gun Show and Auction on the midnight red-eye straight to hell.

There are those to whom solitary confinement, isolation, and the horrors of restricted movement would be a nightmare. Others, perhaps, might find solace in the heart of private darkness. If it is all you have known, your escape can be a kind of exquisite pleasure—even the severe challenge of the biter.

He is wonderfully alone now, and the night is chill, but he relishes the feel of it on his enormous body and stands—nude and gigantic—the cold breeze somehow pleasant as it cools his skin. He thinks about monkeys. The lights in the distance twinkle and beckon, as his mindscreen scans poisons and toxic drugs in preparation for John Wayne Vodrey, the amputator of children's pets.

What care he will manifest in his application of extended pain to Mr. Vodrey. Curare, Pavulon, Succinycholine, and Venticol all cross his field of thought. Paralysis, respiratory malfunction, pain enhancement, each widen the travesty of a smile that distorts his doughy face.

Who is this strange, poor, genius, idiot, clown, killer, animal lover, people hater? Is he Lucifer, Gilles de Rais, Iago, or Frankenstein's monster? Whoever he is—he can hate. God on high, how can he hate! To him you are less than a microscopic mote, less than the smallest, slimiest elongate, less than a whiff of puke-stink, less than frog-spit on stagnant water, less than the sum of your parts which he will cheerfully render into blobs, clots, gouts, of bloody clabber and gure-dreck. So imagine, if you will, how much he feel about Mr. Vodrey?

No evil will suffice. No screaming, splatter-drenched revenge will begin to palliate, abate, or atone. He cannot show Jones Wayne Vodrey the blunt chain-kiss of his great disdain or the Poe-fear of premature burial (paralyzed by rare poison and made insane by drug-enhanced awareness of pain) and the awful anticipation of the unknown. But he will come up with something.

Having identified the problem, his unique mind will collate and assess the product stored, produce a working hypothesis, test and reassess, forming in the anomaly that is his cerebral cortex a procedure and course of action.

Even now as he examines data retrieval, something tingles on his skin. Perhaps it is only the cool of the November night on his vast nakedness. As always, he does not ignore the pinpricks that have touched him.

He shivers as a leisurely lizardly slithery leathery feathery thing causes him to shudder in the darkness, while he watches the Tinytown lights across the flat field.

From the road one can see nothing, but from behind the ruins of the sharecropper shack—from the empty field—one would see the bright stab of light in the mouth of the thing, and know that a hot fire burned in the belly of the beast. It scared his innards with the unexpected intensity of the sensation that something, a factor out of his grasp and beyond his field of vision, was wrong.

Travel down Whitetail Road far enough in a meandering northwesterly direction, circling around the pond and through the surrounding cotton fields to the northwest, and you come to 771, a county blacktop that runs back toward the river. Right before you hit Market Road there's a little job to the right, nothing more than a gravel run, and it will take you through a pit stop known locally as Finch Hollow.

There's a café and general store that doubles as the post office drawer for the thirty or so inhabitants of the tiny farm community, a gas station, a feed-and-seed operation, and an out-of-the-way pay phone located over by an MFA oil sign.

The same phone had been used the day before by a "Mr. Norman of General Discount Stores, calling from Scottsville, Kentucky." He had reserved a room at the Tennessee Motor Courts of Maysburg, for their sales manager, "Mr. Conway." They thought he would be checking in within the next couple of days. They'd call and cancel if he was going to be late. "He'll bill it to his Visa or MasterCard," the sissified voice of Mr. Norman proclaims to the motel clerk. The line rang.

"Tennessee Motor Courts, Good Evening."

"Good Evening. This is Mr. Conway. I believe my company made a reservation for me—General Discount in Scottsville, Kentucky?" The rumbling basso profundo resonated in the motel clerk's ears.

"One moment, sir. Yes. We have your reservation."

"Well, I'm sorry. I'm not going to be able to get there for a couple of days. I'd like to change my reservation accordingly. May I do so?"

"You certainly may. Any how long will you be staying with us?"

"Just one evening, the way it looks now. Say, listen, I've got a package that I've had forwarded to me there at your motel. And I'm afraid it's going to get there before I will. Is that going to cause a problem?"

"No, I don't think so. I'll make sure the other clerks on duty know that a package will be coming for you, and we'll just hold it at the front desk for you. Okay?"

"I appreciate that. Thanks. That'll be a big help."

"The package is coming addressed to you here?"

"Yes. It's from a clothing store out East, East Coast Big and Tall. And I also have a fellow sending over some petty cash, which I would like the front desk to hold for me—the reason I'm doing that, the package is being delivered by taxi cab, and I want the clerk to pay the driver out of my cash envelope. Can that be arranged?"

"Well..." The clerk was suddenly on his guard. They'd never had to do anything like this before, and he wasn't sure. "I'd have to ask my manager."

"Listen—that's fine—but there's no problem. It's very simple. You'll be getting an envelope in tomorrow's mail, and I'll check back by phone to make sure the cash is on hand. It has fifty dollars inside—in cash. I doubt if the cab driver will charge more than twenty dollars, and I want to give him a least twenty dollars for a tip..." the deep voice rumbled on, confusing the clerk with a stream of details. The clerk had to break away twice to answer calls and deal with the desk traffic.

During the telephone call the name Conway and General Discount Stores became identifiable in the clerk's mind. When they finally saw the envelope with the return address "Mr. W. Conway, Scottsville, Kentucky," with the big red GDS logo, it would all be an official paid-for transaction. Nothing solves problems like crisp new ten-dollar bills and corporate names. The motel would "sell" the transaction, in turn, to a taxi driver who would be asked to pick up ad deliver a package that had arrived in care of general deliver.

The cab driver would already have his cash in hand. If he was asked to leave a package atop a certain pay telephone kiosk or booth, he might think it weird, but he would be likely to comply. Mr. Conway was going to be born again—born out of the box—and no one would see the delivery.

Mr. Conway, who would materialize at some far-flung location, might or might not remember to cancel his reservation at the Tennessee Motor Courts of Maysburg. And the busy clerks would never think it a bit odd that the envelope containing fifty dollars cash had been postmarked "Finch Hollow, Missouri."

Nor would they know that the corporate envelope was one of several that had been retrieved from the bottom of a company dumpster.

28

Whitetail

Somebody was always uttering succinct aphorisms that stayed in the back of the mind and cooked. When you needed a profound thought, and you reached back in too far, you'd grab one of those all-purpose maxims instead. "Vigilance is the price of liberty." Who said that?

The price of vigilance—that was something else. That price was up there in the stratosphere. It could cost you. The price of one's thrills could get up there, also. You do pay for your big chills—no question about it. There was another adage to live by.

Royce sipped at his wine, but it had gone bad. It was bitter. Nothing tastes so strong as raw truth, taken straight.

"World Ecosphere, Inc., presents ECOWORLD," he read from the glossy brochure, "with a commitment to research for a better tomorrow." Awkward. For a megabuck outfit, the copy sure was stilted, almost as if it had been translated into English from Cantonese or Taiwanese or Korean. That's what it was. Their hype read like the instructions on an imported battery-operated toy.

"Cleaning the air we breathe, greening the land we inhabit, and gleaning the sea's harvest" were among the parent company's prime concerns. "Development of fossil fuels, solar power, and other low-cost energy sources for home and industry . . ." The thing had the feel of one of the old documentaries they used to show in school during civics and social studies class.

"The public will be a part of ECOWORLD, participating in a vast and innovative recycling complex based on new scientific principles that could literally change the world's face!" This read like VCR instructions translated from Japanese.

He took his pen and wrote the word "Japanese," followed by a question mark. Then wrote another paragraph and stopped, reading the whole thing back to himself. What if they made copies of an "investigative report to the people of southeast Missouri" and circulated it everywhere? Not just media and law enforcement, but had it printed as a leaflet and dropped over the town.

"Hey," he said to Mary, who was in bed, thinking. "You asleep?"

"Uh-uh."

"What if we . . . uh . . ." His voice faded away.

"I'm awake. I'm listening. Go ahead."

"What if we had leaflets made. Who's the guy that drops those—the pilot?"

"Huh? Oh! The guy in Cape."

"Yeah." He tuned out on whatever he was going to ask her, and resumed reading his notes. She was miles away, a few feet from him, with an old sheet clothespinned to a rope across the width of the cabin, for propriety, she supposed. She was in the bed but with her eyes wide open. Royce was at the trestle table. He reread the notes.

"The supposed 'Community Communications Company' that is building Ecoworld is not what it appears. The company exists only on paper, a front for something called World Ecosphere, Inc., a mysterious, well-funded corporation operating in Washington, D.C. and New York as a holding company. But the company—again—is more than it appears to be, just as Ecoworld is not what they claim it is. *We have hard evidence that indicates Ecoworld may be a sophisticated cover operation for the largest clandestine drug laboratory ever built in North America!"*

He read the details of their find—the itemized list of toxic and hazardous chemicals found on the property subsequent to the construction of the first concrete structures—a list that read like a recipe for cooking *killer ice,* the street name for the most deadly strain of freebase cocaine ever manufactured. How it might be possible for the people behind Ecoworld to distribute worldwide from their drug lab, under the noses—no pun intended—of the townfolk of Waterton. The amusement park aspect, with displays, tour participation, even circus-type rides tied to ecological themes, would work both as a physical cover and a money-laundering conduit. Even the foul stench of cooking narcotics down in the concrete bastion covering the central excavation might be explained by the research-and-development theme. They could be experimenting with toxic waste eradication, or pollution control—any number of plausible possibilities to choose from. It was the beginning of a perfect drug operation that could prove to be all but impenetrable.

Royce further posited that World Ecosphere was the start of a paper trail that would end in South America or Japan. The bad guys would prove to be "a consortium of politicians, drug enforcement officers, and top-level narcotics kingpins." Perhaps an even more nefarious foreign power was providing the financial backing—who could say for certain?

The notes would be signed by Mary Perkins and Royce (whose signature would be less than worthless), and they would obtain other witnesses as soon as possible. Credible townspeople like Mary's friends and neighbors who would attest to what they'd seen at the Ecoworld constructions site. This would be augmented with a couple of clear photos, all of which would be legally documented and notarized. They'd run the thing off at some quickie printer and drop fifty thousand of the leaflets on Waterton, Maysburg, and the surrounding agri-community.

He wasn't pleased with the presentation. He tried to begin with the line about how all it takes for evil to triumph is for good men to do nothing. He started over:

"What is going on here?" he wrote. He liked that better. It was catchy.

A killer or killers wantonly murdering our families, friends, and neighbors? People vanishing without a trace? Yes! These are not just small-town rumors you've heard—Waterton, Missouri, is in serious trouble, and the law is doing nothing! Ask yourself, *why?*

We have hard evidence to indicate that "ECOWORLD" may be a sophisticated cover for *the largest clandestine drug laboratory ever built in North America*—and neither the police nor the Federal Bureau of Investigation is lifting a finger to stop it! These findings speak for themselves:

[WITNESSED, NOTARIZED PICTURES
AND DOCUMENTATION]

These are hazardous chemicals used in the manufacture of a powerful and deadly type of "freebase" cocaine. World Ecosphere, Inc., is a front for a richly funded drug cartel, perhaps even a consortium in league with a foreign power. *We believe that the murders occurring in this community may be directly linked to the clandestine drug lab's construction.*

WE MUST ACT AS A COMMUNITY TO BRING THESE KILLERS AND DRUG PEOPLE TO JUSTICE. CONTACT YOUR SENATORS AND REPRESENTATIVES, THE DRUG ENFORCEMENT ADMINISTRATIVE, THE JUSTICE DEPARTMENT, YOUR COUNTY SHERIFF, OR ANYONE ELSE IN A POSITION OF AUTHORITY AND SEE THAT THIS INFORMATION IS ACTED UPON NOW—WHILE THERE'S STILL TIME!

Just awful. But he was too tired to work on it anymore. This would do. He read it to Mary and asked her what she thought.

"It's real good, Royce, but do you think people will *do* anything after they read it and see the pictures of the chemicals? Remember, this project has already made a lot of money for the town. They say old Gabe Augustine and his family are millionaires now from the concrete they've poured. And it's brought a lot of jobs just in construction work. What about all the money that they say will be coming into the area in tourism? Won't people around here just figure the chemicals deal is some kind of smear campaign, and choose to ignore it?"

"Maybe." He shrugged.

"And if they did get up in arms about it and called Marty Kerns, imagine what would come of it. He'd give them some soft soap and pat them on the head, and that would be that. What can we realistically hope to accomplish? I'm not putting down the idea, I'm just asking."

"I don't know, hon. You may be right. But it's our shot—the way I see it. And it might even give us a bit of protection. You, anyway. Perhaps they'd realize it would make them look bad if anything were to happen to the person who accused them of being drug manufacturers. Also—I know sometimes you can have a lot of heat and no light, but maybe this will produce a little light along with the heat. Maybe some newspaper will get interested, or one of the TV channels, and—who knows—somebody who sees the leaflet might have some clout with a U.S. senator or the governor or—" He didn't really believe what he was saying. "Let's sleep on it," he finally said, and collapsed into his sleeping bag in front of the fire.

"There's one thing in our favor," he said, yawning. "Waterton! We're in a town where they actually report UFO sightings. There's people here buy those papers at the supermarket and will swear to you that Elvis is still alive. There's been how many Bigfoot sightings recently? I mean, we are talking Small Town America, right?"

"You'd better believe it," Mary said. "Woman's place is in the home, and we pay wages to prove it."

"Exactly."

"The ERA wasn't even a rumor here."

"So you take my point. This is Redneckville. Hayseed, U.S.A. An NRA stronghold. Used to be a Klan stronghold not so long ago. If you ain't white and Christian, you know—like the song says, red, white, and Pabst Blue Ribbon—we don't want you. That's Waterton. Maybe the people around here won't be too thrilled about Japs buying up three hundred acres for their underground drug lab." She ignored his heavy-handed irony.

"But you don't know that the Japanese are behind Ecoworld."

"You don't know they aren't, do you?" She just laughed in response. "The point is—whoever's behind it, Colombians, Little Green Saucer People, or—God forbid—the damn Democrats—they ain't one of us."

Mary smiled when she heard him lightly snore. He was so tired, but he'd done his best. She'd have to watch him when they had the handbill printed in the morning, she thought, or he'd have them out at the Ecoworld dump site searching for "Made in Japan" on the chemical containers.

Mary tried to go to sleep, but she was wide-eyed. There were feelings inside her that were growing stronger by the day, part of what she thought of as her "dark side." She felt them coming to the surface.

The thoughts she was thinking were forbidden thoughts, and that made them all the more exciting. It was almost a turn-on to be near this man for whom she had such steamy feelings, like a kind of taboo sex act. He wanted her. She knew that. This was not the time or the place, of course. And that made it even more taboo, and even more of a turn-on.

She tried to isolate the title of a faintly recalled book or dimly recollected film in which the couple had just returned from a funeral, and there's a hot, raunchy bedroom scene. What was it that was so strong and undeniable that linked the death, or the metaphorical loss of someone close to you, with the act of making life?

The dark side of death-and-sex lust was yet another area Mary would have identified as thoroughly alien to her, yet here it was, running its fingers up and down her nude flesh, trying hard to get her attention, and succeeding in a big way.

Royce Hawthorne stirred, bones cracking, from the sleeping bag on the hard floor of the Perkins vacation abode. He'd "painted the ceiling" twice—once in his sleep, and again since first awakening—mulling over the many facets of the day ahead. He'd been up since before dawn, and was now readying Mary for the rigors of the morning.

"I've decided I definitely should not sign the thing," he said. "It'd only give Kerns or the sheriff something to use to counter the statements we put forth in the circular. They could say—a known drug guy blah blah was part of it. It wouldn't stick as a charge, but the point is, it would take away from the impact of our documentation. Agree?"

"Sure," Mary said through a yawn. "If you think so." Whatever. *Just do it and wake me when it's all over* was the way she felt. She was not a morning person, and she wanted coffee and silence, not necessarily in that sequence.

Royce kept talking, going over ideas, content, where they could go to get their circular printed, details of the leaflet drop—all very real in his mind. He was acting, differently now, she thought. She knew he couldn't have done drugs in a while, and wondered how difficult it would be for him to stay clean.

"If we do all this," she said, "and it doesn't work . . . you know . . . we can't let it throw us. We'll have taken our best shot, as you said." He knew she meant *him*, not *we*, but he nodded—taking her meaning.

Mary talked about who she thought might accompany them as signatories to the documentation.

"Alberta and Owen will go with us—I know." She was referring to her next-door neighbors. "Terry Considine, Faye, Mr. and Mrs. Dale, Kristi and Wilma, maybe—uh—Joe Threadgill . . ." She was making a list and checking it twice.

"One thing you have to stress, Mary, is the possible danger to anyone who goes out there. I—don't know how to handle it. We don't dare go to the cops. If we take any kind of guns, it might even be worse if something would happen. I think what you have to do is tell the folks the truth about there being armed guards, that we'll be careful as we can and—you know—take a surreptitious look at the evidence and leave quickly. But they need to know it is a potentially very dangerous thing we're asking of them."

She agreed, naturally. But as it turned out, the dangerous part wasn't the problem at all. In theory, everybody they spoke with was itching to go the moment they told them about chemicals, and the possible cover-up by the authorities. But if you ever want to find out what citizens are more afraid of than armed guards, just drop words like "witness," "deposition," or "affidavit." They all ran like scared rabbits.

By midmorning, with a photographer meeting them, they had lined up a grand total of four persons, one of whom—Mrs. Lloyd—sounded so ill, Mary hated asking her to do it.

"Better have her go, hon," Royce urged. "Everybody who sees the evidence gives that much more credence to what we say."

They left for the Ecoworld property, driving out the back way and down the road that edged the Poindexter property, all of it now in World Ecosphere's corporate claws. Royce realized, but didn't voice, the fact that in such a small town, the grapevine would have spread their comments about the incriminating chemical containers by the time they hung the phones up. Would the parent company be tapped into such a pipeline—perhaps through Marty Kerns? For that matter, would they care?

They met the photographer at a prearranged spot, and he followed them to the place where everyone agreed to meet. They waited till Mrs. Lloyd and the Rileys arrived, and Royce took them to where the containers were.

He was relieved, yet frightened at the same time, to find everything as before.

"I don't understand why they'd leave this stuff to be found," the photographer said. "Talk about stupid." He was taking some pictures with a flash attachment, some without. Every time the shutter clicked, Royce felt like he was having a small heart attack.

"Apparently a pack of wild dogs thought something smelled like buried bones and started digging. This is just the way Mary and I found it."

The Rileys and Mrs. Lloyd signed the statement that had been prepared, but when they were told that they needed them to go to Maysburg with Mary and Royce, and be present when the thing was notarized, Owen Riley said he didn't think it was a good idea.

"If they've got the gumption to do this, we've got the gumption to go with them," Alberta Riley scolded him. He got a sort of caged animal look in his eyes, but to his credit, he went along.

There would be two sets of photos—35-mm shots, which would need developing, and the set of Polaroids they'd use for the notarizing and as a safety copy. The photographer would do them ASAP, and they'd pick them up after they went to the bank.

The caravan went on its way immediately, sans Mrs. Lloyd, and once again there was no problem getting the papers and photos notarized and witnessed, this time in front of bank personnel. They had to wait around for an hour before they could get the shots, and took the Rileys to lunch, Royce feeling like brown shoes with a tux the entire time.

Fifty miles and two hours later they were at PRINT-WHILE-U-WAIT, and they were doing as the sign said—they were waiting. Royce, meanwhile, was back on the phone, having his dream dashed by a crop duster pilot.

"I couldn't allow somebody in my two-seater like that. It's against the law." Royce had never known what a richly lucrative profession crop dusting was until he started getting prices.

"Well, could *you* drop the leaflets?"

"Nope." Eventually he found a man who owned an ancient Piper Cub that he kept tethered at the Charleston Emergency Airfield.

"I understand you drop leaflets?" Royce asked of the man.

"Sometimes. I have a time or two. What you want dropped?" Royce told him about the circulars.

"Do you have your license?"

"License?" Royce asked, and learned about an entirely new aspect of the circular-dropping biz. Apparently you had to get a license from the city. Where did one go to get it?

Marty Kerns's office. Couldn't they "work something out?" Royce wondered.

"This baby is a J5—one of the rarest Cubs in private hands, my friend. My father won it from 'Wings of Destiny' in 1940! It was Grand Champion Antique three years running at the aeroplane show. I could never do anything that might jeopardize—"

"I understand." Royce said, thanking him. Royce's picture of himself dumping leaflets from two thousand feet, his white scarf streaming over the side of the cockpit, was in tatters.

By early evening, the ink barely drying on the print job, they were no longer trying to get the circular dropped, but were still shopping around for a way to get it into the Waterton homes. The Maysburg *Weekly Dispatch* was out. The *Jackson Grove Star* was out. There was one way they could get it into area homes tomorrow morning, and that was to give a great deal of cash to one Fred Finch, who put out something called the *Tri-State Shopper*. They would be an "insert," sandwiched in between coupons for discounts on rump roast (USDA choice boneless: $1.99 a pound) and hog jowls (SPECIAL! Only 59À a pound!).

Fifty thousand leaflets, Mr. Finch assured them, would be tucked into his two-page, two-color throwaway.

"I ain't never done this for nobody before! Hope I ain't making no mistake," he said. Not at these prices, he wasn't.

Royce was a worrier. He worried that Mr. Finch might just dump the leaflets, which he swore would be "tucked by high-speed insertion machine into each and every *Tri-State Shopper*" that went into the mailboxes. Who would be the wiser? Mary was even more worried than he was.

"This whole idea was lunacy, Royce," she raged, using his name like a knife blade. "We didn't use our heads. I'm going to be sued from one end of the country to the other—we didn't think about that. I can't believe I've been such an idiot!" Wisely, he kept still and let it pour until she wound down.

After shed calmed down considerably, she picked up their mail.

"You got these," she said, handing him a stack of envelopes, bills and junk mail. There was something with a Memphis postmark. He felt a surge of excitement as he ripped the envelope open and read the communication.

A clerk without a name, a faceless nonentity seated in his/her workspace area in front of a flickering green screen, had processed the number search he'd requested, and the search, trace, transfer procedure had imprinted the results, sending the data back to Memphis.

Another faceless bod at the Tennessee end of ELINT's daisy chain had punched up Hawthorne's code number, got an active clearance, retrieved his mail drop particulars when they couldn't find a telephone contact number, and the printout had been forwarded, in an unmarked (except for franking stamps) government envelope to Waterton, where it had in turn been forwarded to Mary Perkins's post office box in Maysburg. A no-no. Something that was never done without prior consent by the case handler. An error that could have put somebody's tit firmly in the wringer. But it hadn't.

The communication had come the day after Royce stopped near Waterworks Hill and called the phonemen to ID that frequently dialed D.C.-area disconnect showing on Sam Perkins's telephone bill.

The printout listed the number. Gave its status as having reverted to Intercept. The official user: North American Medical Research Consultants. ELINT's probe identified it as "Control cover for military counterintelligence operational unit. Parentheses CLASSIFIED OPERATIONS slash DOMESTIC end parentheses.

"What is it?" Mary asked, reading something in his face and long silence.

"I'm not—hell, I don't know. Who did Sam know in a military counterintelligence operational unit?"

"Nobody." Her pretty face was blank of expression for a second, then began to appear more thoughtful. "Unless . . . no. Nobody. Not that I ever heard about. Why?"

He showed her.

"It was probably Christopher Sinclair. Does this mean he was in a military counterintelligence unit?"

"This wasn't Christopher Sinclair. Those calls were to New York—remember? We figured those out. This was someone else. Somebody Sam had a lot of contact with."

"Mmm." She shook her head. "I don't have a clue."

"If it was World Ecosphere, Inc., one of their dummy phone fronts, we're in a dilly of a mess. That would mean that Ecoworld is a U.S. government drug lab. Which makes no sense whatsoever."

"But it would explain one thing: why the FBI and the local cops haven't done anything. It would mean there was a government curtain of protection around it. As you said—it makes no sense."

The next morning Mary checked in with her neighbor Alberta, who informed her she'd already had calls from her sister, a friend of her son's, and two women she and Owen churched with—all of whom had seen her name on a certain "ad," as her sister referred to it. The circulars had indeed been delivered. The rest of the day was as uneventful as Mary and Royce could keep it.

The following morning, Friday, the Maysburg *Weekly Dispatch* was delivered, and they were a tiny footnote to the big news—which was a story about area drug arrests.

"We have to buy a paper," Mary said excitedly, coming out to the car after touching base with the Rileys.

"Yeah?"

"There was a big raid on drug dealers."

"You mean—"

"I don't know. Alberta said she hadn't had time to digest it all—something about a bunch of people arrested for dealing drugs yesterday—but the story mentions our circular by name."

"Does it mention you by name?"

"She said it didn't name any of us, but it told what 'CRAC' stood for." CRAC was a name they'd made up to give them an official sound—Mary, Mrs. Lloyd, and her neighbors were the Coalition Rallying Against the Conspiracy. Royce thought "Coalition" sounded serious.

"I hope this isn't a game somebody's running on us. If the names Fabio Ruiz and Luis Londoño are in that story, I'll breathe a lot easier." They spotted a newspaper dispenser, and he pulled over and jumped out, getting two papers. They perused them in silence.

Royce read the story twice, fuming. He knew some of the people arrested. Nobodies. People chipping. Happy, of course, was not among those under arrest. He read the words a third time:

MASSIVE DRUG BUST NETS 16

Maysburg—A major drug raid Thursday netted 16 arrests on nearly 50 counts of trafficking in illegal substances, according to authorities.

The raid was coordinated by the Tennessee Narcotics Task Force and utilized 12 law enforcement agencies operating on the municipal, state, and county levels, as well as supervisory personnel from federal agencies.

According to a statement issued by the task force director, Gene L. Niswonger, the massive raid was the "end result of a long and continuing investigation into area drug dealers." He described the raid as "a major success. It just shows you how many different agencies can work well together when everyone coordinates their efforts."

Niswonger stated that property seized totaled in excess of thirty-five thousand dollars, and that the task force would use a "substantial portion" of the income derived from the sale of the property to help fund other drug-related operations.

The 16 defendants were arraigned in Maysburg Thursday afternoon. Those arrested were:

Beryl Crites, 27, three counts of sale of cocaine; Jimmy Frye, 31, two counts sale of methamphetamine; Thedra Jones, 24, four counts sale of cocaine, Bobby Tatum, 33, four counts manufacture of a controlled substance; Donny Ray Wagner, 29, two counts sale of marijuana . . ."

Royce skipped down to the last paragraph of the newspaper article.

Niswonger said the drug sweep was unrelated to rumors of a possible clandestine narcotics laboratory allegedly under construction in the Maysburg-Waterton area. "The idea that this community is the victim of some kind of a conspiracy is just plain ridiculous. It shows how people can act unwisely when they don't have any expertise and try to take the law into their own hands," he stated, referring to leaflets which were mailed to homes throughout the Waterton area by a group calling itself CRAC, the Coalition Rallying Against the Conspiracy. The leaflets, sent inside supermarket shopping circulars, claimed that the group had found evidence of chemicals used in drug manufacture at a local construction site.

"Those lying fucking pricks!" He wadded the paper and flung it into the backseat. "It's all a big shuck. They have this kind of thing ready to go at any second. Anytime they think they're going to get any heat—they've always got X numbers of small-timers they can round up." He shook his head, gritting his teeth in disgust. "This is their way of defusing the stuff about Ecoworld—see? The War on Drugs, Chapter 763. It's bullshit."

"What now?"

"You tell me." He started the car and began driving aimlessly. Mary felt as lost as she'd been since Sam had vanished. She reached across and squeezed Royce's hand for comfort, and he caught hers and held it.

"Your hand is like ice," he said. "Do you have any blood circulating in your body? You are ice cold."

There were a dozen reasons why she shouldn't put her head on his shoulder:

1. Men borrow money.
2. Men are trouble.
3. Men get jealous.
4. Men take drugs, and drink, and gamble, and get sick, and die, and sometimes they just up and disappear.
5. Men don't always smell good, and sometimes they have bad breath.
6. Men will tell you that they love you when they don't.
7. Men tell you they respect you when they don't.
8. Men promise they'll be true and sometimes they won't.
9. Men can be overcritical, ungrateful, sloppy, and mean.
10. Men interrupt you when you're talking, don't like your friends, leave their dirty socks on the floor, tell you you're gaining weight, and make a mess in the bathroom.
11. Men complain when you eat in bed.
12. Men don't take you out enough.

A dozen? There were a thousand reasons why she shouldn't put her head on his shoulder.

But she was too tired to think of them, and she *was* ice cold.

29

Waterton

John Wayne Vodrey lived catercorner from Mathis Cotton Gin. He had him a nice little place with a sweet soundproofed living quarters so he wouldn't have to listen to them big ol' reefer trucks rattle while he tried to get hisself some shut-eye. He drank a bit now and again. He was taking forty winks in his nicely soundproofed cottage when he awoke, drenched in a nightmare litany:

"Gommle-grabber, gommle-grabber, gooble-gobble, gooble-gobble," repeated over and over, spoken very fast, the name of a strange cat toy he'd once had, a gommle-grabber, it was called—a chase ball this one kitty cat had liked.

He was a cutter and a slicer and a castrator. He had a mean streak wide as a four-lane highway, and he hated four-legged things of all kinds. The nonsense inside his fucked-up head inserted itself into his booze dreams, and suddenly he'd be soundlessly repeating gommle-grabber, gooble-gobble, like in *Freaks*, you know? The ratcheting of train wheels and the noise of the cars over the amputator's night sweats.

"Pachyderma-dromadery pachyderma-dromadery, gooble-gobble,

gooble-gobble," Oh, my land's sakes, he was going to die from this hangover. It had its big fat hand over his nose and snoring mouth while he slept, and suddenly he was choking and being lifted, lifted out of the nightmare by a hand, and he saw the pig eyes burning in the doughy face and smelt human and flailed around for the .45 he kept under the bed, but he was in the air, all 208 hard, mean pounds of John Wayne Vodrey, trying his best to grab, claw, hit, smash, rip, get hold of his night monster, a big fat assailant looked like he might go six or seven hundred pounds stripped out.

Big ol' mean John Wayne tried to holler something, but a hand the shape of a blacksmith's anvil hammered his dirty yap shut.

For some reason Chaingang recalled that official executioners work in groups called execution teams. He chuckled, remembering the look of "Violent C10," the only time he'd got a look at the sign on the outer door beside the one-way glassed viewing port. He recalled with some pleasure the large stenciled word imprinted in black bold font on the institutional beige paint: V I O L E N T, it said, simply.

John Wayne jerked at the sound of the thing that was the beast's laugh. It spoke to him in a deep rumble:

"I am the execution team, Mr. Vodrey."

"I don't—" The blow sent him into blackness. When he came to, he was nude and on his back, and the big fat crazy was over him with a-holt of both his feet. He was in his bathtub, in about three or four inches of water.

"I—" Preemptive pressure.

"No."

"Please, uh—"

"No!" Chaingang said, smiling his most dangerous and evil grin. "Don't open that shithole. You need all your strength." He put pressure on the amputator's ankles, watching him try to muscle his way out of the tub. "Just . . . to . . . survive." Mr. Vodrey was going to commit suicide in his own bathtub. And he was going to take all day to do it.

He would not allow the red tide to flow over his mind. Not this time. This time he would work for his fun—and he planned on spending hours and hours with Mr. Vodrey.

Imagine that you are a large man. Strong. Your hands aren't tied—right? Just reach up, grab the top of the tub, and pull yourself up. Easy—eh?

Try it. Go run three or four inches of water in your tub. Get a four-hundred-pound man—or, if that's not practical, two two-hundred-pound men will suffice. Have him/them grasp your feet firmly by the ankles. Oh, make sure these are men who can lift their own weight, by the way—big, strong men. While they are putting downward pressure on your feet, you pull yourself up out of the water. Eventually, as you grow tired and more tired, you'll begin to realize the plain and nasty truth. You are drowning in four inches of bath water.

It is a rather graphic physics lesson, and Daniel had the entire day to teach it to Mr. John Wayne Vodrey, torturer of dogs, cats, horses, hamsters, gerbils, goats, sheep, mules—God only knows what all—who kept cussin' and fussin' and grabbin' at the slick tub, straining with every ounce of strength in his body.

Finally all the man could do was blow bubbles, and they were coming out of the wrong end. Another accident in the bathroom.

30

Maysburg

Royce felt Mary snuggle against him and put her head on his shoulder. His heart went out to her. He was beat, and he could imagine how she felt. She suddenly seemed cold and vulnerable and very small. Her body shivered, or perhaps he only imagined it.

He'd been driving aimlessly for miles, realized suddenly that he'd crossed the bridge to Waterton. Pulled in to the first paved road that ran parallel to the river, stopped, backed up, turned around, and headed back across the bridge to the Tennessee side.

He's seen the billboard and it registered subconsciously, but he was too tired to say anything or do anything about it at first.

"Let's take a motel room here. Just for the night." She didn't protest, and he pulled in and registered, but when he came back to the car, it was nagging him.

A billboard by the river road, advertising "Inexpensive, safe, year-round cold storage" had gnawed its way through to his brain.

"When we were at the cabin, you said something about putting Sam's grandfather's gun in cold storage."

"Sam did. I didn't."

"Do you have other things in cold storage?" She just sat there looking like she was twelve years old. Blinking in the sunlight. "Anything else that you all stored? You didn't ever mention cold storage when we were talking about Sam's papers and things."

She came alive. "I don't know what else is in there. If you want to look, it's over in that little shopping area near the bank and the drugstore."

"Let's go," he said, and started the car.

Back over the bridge they drove a second time, heading down Jefferson in the direction of North Main, but stopping when they came to the cold storage facility, two doors down from his old buddy at Drexel Commodity Futures.

"I'd like to open 421, please," she told the woman at the counter, who admitted them to a huge, dimly lit room full of locked vaults and screened partitions. Sam had rented one of the partitions. They didn't spend long inside—it was about the temperature of a meat locker—and the old gun, wrapped in a blanket and then fastened with wire, was the solitary occupant of the partition.

Mary teared up a little but made it okay, and they took the long package with them and returned to the motel.

She was sound asleep before Royce had the wire off the blanket. He had to bite his tongue to keep from waking her when he found the roll of paper.

Sam Perkins had taken the Ramparts material and his notes, laid all the correspondence and documentation in a pile, and rolled it into a tight cylinder, with a plastic sheet around the outside of the papers so that it would slide in and out of the old musket.

Royce worked on the papers and the notes for three hours, finally waking Mary about the time it was getting dark. He was scared shitless, and had to talk to her about it. For the first time he had some glimmer of a notion as to just how much trouble they were in.

"Hi," she said, her pretty face wreathed in a silky tangle of hair, still half-asleep. "How long—what time is it?" He told her. "Did you sleep?" she asked.

"No. I found out why . . ." He started over. "I think I know what happened to Sam."

He told her about the roll of papers hidden away inside the big barrel of the old rifle.

"Do you remember someone named Leonard Schuette or Lenny Schuette—someone Sam knew?"

"He went to school with him. Lenny Schuette—I heard him mention the name. He called him 'Lenny the Spook.' He was supposed to be with the State Department or something—a political strategist or, you know, that kind of thing."

"He was the one Sam kept calling. All those calls were to him. He was in military intelligence. They'd been in college together—right?"

"Yeah." Some of the haze cleared. "He . . . uh, called Sam once . . . I forget—"

"Sam apparently had stayed in touch with him, or at least he knew how to track him down. He was suspicious of the deal—the land thing. It was a hush-hush operation with code names and stuff, and he thought there was something very fishy about it. He had Lenny Schuette check it out, and the word was it was a U.S. government training center for covert operations. Schuette said it was supposed to be a school for assassination. Sam wanted to blow the whistle on it, and either he had talked a few of the landowners out of the deal, telling them what their land was going to be used for, or they were people who had not agreed to sell.

"I've tried to put it all together, and my guess is that they had Sam and Luther and the others killed."

"The government did?"

"Not the government, a faction of total crazies within the intelligence community—fanatics who thought having a force of trained killers would protect us against other countries, against terrorists, against traitors—"

"You mean Ecoworld isn't about drugs at all?"

"I don't know. Who the hell knows?"

"Who can we go to about this?"

"I don't know that either."

"My God."

"Yeah. Exactly."

"Could we contact Lenny Schuette—tell him about what happened to Sam?"

"How? The number's a dead end. Who's to say they didn't get that guy as well? Everyone who's stood up to them has vanished. These are people who look at assassination as the logical solution to every problem."

"But those chemicals—" She couldn't sort it all out in her mind, and he wasn't much help.

"For all I know, making drugs was going to be a sideline. I still say it looked like they were putting together a crack lab. But let's say it *is* going to be a training school for government assassins. That implies that the Feds, the DEA, ATF, the CIA, the DIA—the damn Sheriff's Benevolent Society of Greater Podunk—everybody could be part of the cover-up."

Her hands tightened on a piece of paper. One of Sam's notes. He could read the word "Ramparts."

"We'd better go back to the cabin. It's too dangerous to stay here." She nodded numbly, and they got in the old car and started back in the direction of Whitetail.

31

North of Waterton

He hated everything about the monkey people, but one of the things he loathed the most about this alien planet was, there were fewer and fewer places to find true isolation. When one was anywhere near urban centers, it took an increasing amount of effort to find raw chunks of emptiness where one's thoughts and privacy would not be invaded by the loud laughter and grating voices of the imbeciles who populated every corner of the globe.

How he despised their blank faces brimming with confidence and herd instinct. The cleansing of the lonely places invariably renewed him—made him feel whole again.

Their crap, which they dropped everywhere in a nauseating litter of garish billboards, empty beer cans, and discarded TV sets, followed him everywhere, it seemed. Even back of beyond the monkeys came, laughing and chittering and taking one another's pictures.

Chaingang was irritated to begin with, at the prospect of having to go through the enormous effort of relocation, but it was time to go. His sensors felt them closing the net. He knew he was no longer safe. Whatever he'd been a part of was drawing to an end.

This was his dark mood as he waddled to his ride, removed the huge camouflaged bush-net from it, and squeezed his blubber-gut behind the wheel, starting the car and pulling out down the gravel road in a northbound direction.

He had one more small chore to attend to, and then he could be on his way. There was the small matter of misdirection, for which he would now prepare. He would find a safe, isolated spot to hunker down for the night, far away from the sharecropper shack. Take care of the last-minute details tomorrow, then be about his business.

He turned on a country road that looked fetchingly untraveled, and followed it up over a steep embankment where it dead-ended abruptly. The other side of the tall bank was covered in weeds. An abandoned pasture, perhaps?

Turning off the motor, he eased his bulk out from behind the wheel and got out of the car, unzipping his fly and urinating carelessly in the direction of the road behind him. A stinking stream of pee splashed across the gravel, and he noticed, as a few drops of urine fell onto his 15EEEEE combat boots, a detail he'd overlooked. Rather astonishingly, to him, he realized that he had to be bugged in some way.

It was so obvious that it was amusing he hadn't bothered to consider it. Clearly those watching and manipulating him would have taken the precaution of marking him in some discernible way. He thought immediately of the most practical methods, rejecting each as he did so: A marked car was out—he'd switched them; a hidden homing device in his gear was out—too much chance of being discarded. It had to be his clothing.

What would be the most difficult thing for Daniel Bunkowski to replace? His enormous pants, belt, shirt, and custom-made gunboats. He smiled venomously at the thought, walking over to examine a brightly colored object that had caught his eye.

It was a plastic wrapper. Cheap stuff. Day-Glo pink. Wrapped around some sort of food advertisement. His stomach rumbled at the thought of groceries as he idly unwrapped the ads, glancing at the listings of munchies while he considered his next move. If there was a current newspaper here, that meant there'd be a dwelling close at hand, so it wasn't an abandoned pasture after all. No mailbox. Maybe there'd be a cottage tucked away behind those trees. Should he investigate or move along? He took pleasure from reading about food:

Butter and eggs, beans and bacon, cinnamon rolls and chocolate cake. Somewhere between the Velveeta and the hot pepper cheese, the word CONSPIRACY caught his eye.

"WE BELIEVE THAT THE MURDERS OCCURING IN THIS COMMUNITY MAY BE DIRECTLY LINKED TO THE CLANDESTINE DRUG

LAB'S CONSTRUCTION." His coughing bark shook his gigantic stomach like a bowl full of jelly.

Those arrogant fools. The second he fed the words into his computer, he matched it to a newspaper story he'd read about an unlikely construction project, and felt the hot juices dripping through his thoughts. He saw himself in the house where he'd had a live one, reading about a monkey "theme park called Ecoworld." It stretched his face into a fierce mask of hatred when he read about the poisoned dog.

They wanted a scapegoat, it seemed. One who could be put into play to divert attention from whatever lame nonsense they were concocting.

No. He didn't think so. Instead he thought he might go sniff around this construction project and see if he couldn't help them with their problem. If people thought there was a conspiracy afoot, then obviously the monkeys needed a helping hand. Perhaps he could redecorate the thing.

First things first. He unbuckled his belt, a huge thing big as a blacksnake whip, and began taking his custom-made boots and voluminous pants off.

It took him all of three minutes to find the small devices, which he knew must be microbugs, that his benefactors had secreted in his clothing. No wonder they knew exactly where he was at all times. In due course he would eliminate that bothersome problem too.

32

Waterton

If Royce's fears alone had been ruling him, it might have ended differently, but he was bone-weary. He just couldn't go through the long hassle of driving all the way out Market to the back road, taking another twenty minutes of driving to get to Whitetail Pond, especially tonight, with the headlight glare as blinding as he could remember seeing it. Maybe he needed glasses for night driving—or perhaps he was just more tired than he had realized.

He decided to take Cotton to W.W. south, and that was how they picked him up. The car must have come fishtailing all over W.W. when it pulled out, which in fact is how he happened to notice it, headlights all over the highway in his rearview, coming like a bat out of hell, one second two little dots of fishtailing lights, the next second some fool with his high beams right in Royce's eyes.

Then the lights disappeared, but the inside of his ride lit up. They were on top of Royce's car! He swore just as they cracked him hard, reaching out with his right hand to catch Mary, slamming his foot to the gas, swerving left to right as the car stayed with him, dangerously close.

"Get that safety belt on!"

"Who is—"

"Do it!" he screamed, catching a glimpse of the car enough to see what it was as the cars shot past a bright yard light. Not that there was any doubt who was behind them.

"Shit," he said, his foot to the floorboard, "it's Happy." Happy Ruiz, and, for all he knew, a load of bikers. The black LTD. Happy with his foot in the carburetor, both of them with the pedals mashed, Royce's needle crawling in the direction of 110. Then 115 mph as they rocketed down the long, straight stretch of W.W. southbound.

He took the curve before he got to Industrial and careened around the curving road in the direction of Ecoworld, trying his best to shake them. Royce's weird car, a 1970 Ranchero junker, was painted in a charming shade of murrey primer and mismatched paint. A brownish, purple-black sort of rotten mulberry color, with tints of mauve, lilac, purple, and violet were all visible along with the rust. But that was on the outside.

He had one of the last models made with a 351 Cleveland high-performance engine. Once in a rare while a '69 or '70 would surface in a junkyard; an old Ranchero with that original big-block Cleveland in there. Compression ratio like a damn diesel. Four-barrel-carb gas-sucker—and in this case, Royce'd had a guy bore it and cut a high-lift cam to make it step out and pony. They dropped a four-eleven rear end in the lady, and she could flat out strut to the party!

The first shot hit the tailgate as they were almost on the next straightaway, inching toward 120, and you take a round moving that fast, it's like somebody bounced a concrete block off one of the fenders.

There was another bark, and the back window spider-tracked. Whoever was doing the shooting was damn good—too damn good!

"We're going off."

"Jesus!"

"Hold on!"

"You're going too fast! We won't make it!"

"Hang tough!" he shouted, as much for his own courage as anything, praying to God—with both hands clenching the wheel in a death grip—getting ready to reach down and yank the taillight wire.

He'd had it rigged so he could jerk the wire if somebody was right behind him, and in theory you could tap the brake and the car in pursuit would be denied that extra half-second warning before it had to duplicate your sharp, high-speed turn.

All that's well and good in theory, but in actual practice, doing 120 miles per fucking hour down some dark road, in a 1970 Ranchero, with Happy Ruiz on your case—you reach down and jerk something, it's likely to be the ignition wiring or your dick!

It was a two-handed job, just to keep it from rolling as they went fishtailing like a bandit, swerving down onto a stretch of service road leading into Ecoworld, those brights still in his eyes as he zoomed past crop stubble and onto concrete—miraculously, rubber side down.

33

Ecoworld

The beast waited, having parked at the edge of the vast sprawl of construction. He'd spotted an old smokehouse and penetrated it, wrapped himself in cammo tarp and let the darkness close in around him.

He was waiting for his night eyes. It was still very black. Stars were barely visible out there in the measureless void. But he simply shut his internal engines down and relaxed, thinking of a time when he'd waited for a night ambush very far away. He pictured the mist that clung to the jungle floor, watching it swirl through the darkening foliage like a cottony, solid thing, as he waited for the ones he would kill. It was pleasant to fantasize about these things, and the time passed quickly for him.

The moon had come back out, and inside the small, ramshackle smokehouse he watched clouds move across the killer's moon, and remembered the house where Mrs. Irby lived, where he'd filled his tanks and watched dust motes falling like snow imprisoned in an antique paperweight. He was in a fine mood again, and with a massive grunt he lurched to his feet and waddled down toward the nearest concrete, the full weight of his weapons and munitions cases in hand.

There were two guards, and they were both imbeciles. Amateurs. He ignored them and went about his business. Setting timers on HBX haversacks, wiring the satchel charges, moving closer to the guards all the while.

His strange mind computed cone diameters, air cavity physics, jet energy statistics. One of his areas of expertise was improvised shaped charges utilizing high-velocity explosives.

He pulled a 'nade from his voluminous coat and felt the notched spoon. Good. One of the short-fused jobs. He was just starting to fasten it to one of his bomb devices when the car shot by. An old junker of some kind—looked like a Ranchero—kids hot-rodding, he assumed.

The guard closest to the access road opened up with a machine gun, spraying everything in that general direction as the car sped by, and Chaingang flung himself behind the nearest concrete wall, the grenade falling to the ground—fortunately with the pin in place—and rolling.

Just as he started to peer around to see how near the guard was, here came another car, roaring out of nowhere! More gunfire whocked off the surrounding walls. These intrusions were not to be tolerated. Grimly Chaingang reached for the duffel and his long-range killing tool.

They were going too fast, even on the concrete, blasting through the Ecoworld construction project, every separation between the footings feeling like sledgehammers bouncing off the Ranchero's rusting frame. Happy was right on him.

"Oh, fuck!" A wall. It was ending—the fucking thing was dead-ending!

"Stop!"

"Stay down!" There was no room to maneuver or turn around, and Happy would plow right into them. He reached down and yanked the wire—by luck hit the one to the taillights—then mashed the brake, holding Mary and gritting his teeth for the crash. But Ruiz was damn good. He slammed him, but he was on his own brake, and the cars skidded to a halt.

"Run, Mary! Get behind the wall!" It was their one chance.

"I can't. The door's stuck. Oh God!"

"Come on—" He tried to pull her, got her arm but she was at an angle, and it took an instant longer than it should have to get her out on his side. Happy and Luis were on them. Both held MAC-11s. "Wait! She isn't part of—" He was in the middle of a shouted plea when Ruiz and Londoño were stitched in half, literally.

He and Mary were almost dead. They were greased. And suddenly two dudes with guns turn to bloody dead meat, right before their eyes.

Royce forced himself to move. Made himself kick one of the MAC-11 shooters away from the bodies. Picked it up. That's when he saw the giant.

His skin crawled as he looked into the face of "Bigfoot," the Goliath he'd seen on Willow River Road that day. If he thought the dude was big from across a blacktop, he was breathtaking up close. The largest man he'd ever seen, not just tall but big, a giant of a fat man with a weapon of some kind, looking at him with those same hard eyes; he could see them in a reflection of moonlight, and he'd never forget the look on that face as the huge man calmly began loading a magazine into his empty piece.

Daniel Edward Flowers Bunkowski never saw the guard. He was too occupied shooting these monkey intruders. But his warning sensors let him know the nearest guard, the one without the dog, was right in back of him, about to squeeze the trigger, when this other monkey man raised a weapon and fired a magazine off in the guard's direction, saving his life.

Chaingang clicked the next mag into his SKS, but by then the first car of monkeys was pulling away and he concentrated on the other guard. He had to get out of there soon. His inner clock was ticking at him. He saw the dog coming first and squatted down and got something, putting his weapon beside him. He took the dog from a balanced position, but it still nearly knocked him over—such was the power of the dog's spring at the moment of attack.

But puppy met with a terrible surprise. This was Chaingang fucking Bunkowski, heart-eater, doggie. And he caught the dog in his left hand, holding her by the throat, trying not to strangle her until he could work the cork off the hypo and tranq the bitch. Within a few seconds the attack dog's long, pink tongue was lolling out like she was dead.

"Ilsa! Where are you? Here, Ilsa!" Her master's voice.

"Doggie's asleep," a deep basso profundo rumbled from out of the darkness as Chaingang blew the guard's head off his neck. "And so are you."

He grabbed the hundred-pound puppy in a fireman's carry, slinging her over one shoulder as if she were a sack of onions, and waddled off to his wheels.

Up on the service road he heard the monkey man shout something to him as he waved.

"Thanks, pardner!" it sounded like.

Chaingang, had Ilsa safely down the road when the south edge of Ecoworld blew into the cosmos.

Royce braked the second he saw the olive drab sphere at the edge of the concrete drive. He was frightened of it, but he was desperate for a weapon, and the MAC-11 was useless to him without a magazine full of cartridges. No amount of money in Christendom would have sent him back into that exploding hell for ammo. He chucked the thing into the backseat and stopped.

He prayed it wasn't a booby trap. It didn't explode when he picked it up, but he didn't start breathing again until he had it resting on the pile of blankets from the old musket. He made a nest for it, tossing the MAC-11 into the road ditch.

"Is that a hand grenade?" Mary asked quietly. She was afraid of very little now. The worst was behind them.

"Yeah," he told her in a quivering voice. "It's a hand grenade. And I'm scared to death of the damn things."

"Well then . . ." she wanted to know, the way women so often do . . . "why did you pick it up?"

It was a perfectly logical question. It made him lick his lips. He tasted salt.

"What are you going to do with it?"

"God knows," he said.

34

Whitetail Pond

There was a three-man team in the car. There were four cars full of agents on the case, one on his cabin, one on Mary's house, one cruising, and this one at the pond. They'd been parked there since four in the afternoon, and everybody was bored, restless, and coffeed out. The replacement car would be a couple of hours more.

"I gotta take a piss," the man on the passenger side in the front seat said, and cracked the door, walked over to the road ditch, and urinated noisily into the weeds. They were parked on the road overlooking the Perkins cabin.

"Any more jelly doughnuts?" the one in the backseat asked.

"Nope," the driver said, yawning. "Wish these fuckers would show. I'd like to whack *somebody*."

"I can dig it," the one in the backseat said, stretching.

The man who'd had to pee got back in the car, and it was then that Royce came around the bend in the road and saw the flash of light when the car door opened.

"Somebody's up there," he said.

"Where?"

"Above the cabin." He pointed. "I saw a light flash. We've probably got company. They're probably in the cabin, too." He was so calm-sounding, he surprised himself.

"Who do you think it is?"

"The Avon lady?" he said, trying to make a joke and succeeding beyond his wildest dreams. Both of them giggled like schoolkids.

"You're such a zany guy," she said.

"I really am." There were limits to how scared you could get. Apparently they had found theirs, because he drove back around the pond and parked about 150 yards from the top of the hill.

"What are you going to do?" she whispered.

"Probably get my ass killed." Mary just looked at him as he took the wire and the pliers and the grenade and quietly closed the car door. "Stay here. I'll be back."

She didn't say anything. *Be careful* stuck in her throat. He was gone.

Royce came up out of the bushes as silently as he could, very worried about his breath. It was so loud. His breathing sounded like an antique bellows. Thankful that the woods came nearly flush with the edge of the road ditch, he came out of the woods slow and low, trying to keep the left rear corner post of the car between himself and where the driver was sitting. It was pretty dark, and he was counting on luck.

If one of them in the car turned or if the driver looked in one of his mirrors at the wrong moment . . . well, what was the point in worrying? He had to force himself out of the safety of the ditch, hurting his hands and knees on the rocks and finally making it to the car. It occurred to him it would be just about his luck to have them start the engine about that time. He could hear small talk through the open windows of their vehicle.

He got the grenade wedged between the underside of the bumper and the gas tank, feeling his hands sweat as he attached the wire to the ring that pulled the cotter pin out. He'd already put a twist in the thin wire at the other end. Now was the tough part.

He tried to slowly peel some of the duct tape from his arm, where he had the little Legionnaire Boot Knife taped in place. It made way too much noise and he took what he had and secured the wire and the grenade as best he could.

Taking a deep breath and clenching his jaws, he crawled back into the ditch, found a root that he trusted, and fastened the wire around it. Would this work? He had no idea. Maybe he should just throw the thing in the car. Too late for that now.

The hairiest part of all was the four or five feet from the ditch back into the woods. It seemed to take about half an hour, and the whole time he felt the gunshot—imagining what his scream would sound like when the first bullet hit his back.

He made it, though, and he and Mary were going to come out of the thing okay—one way or the other. He promised her that, starting the old Ranchero and heading back toward Maysburg. He didn't want to be around when they decided to move that car up on the hill. He didn't even want to know about it. He'd also found the limits of his curiosity.

35

Maysburg

"Yellow Cab?"

"Hi. This is Mr. Conway over at the Tennessee Motor Courts on Central. Would you send a taxi over please?"

"Okay. What's your room number?"

"Have the driver come to the office please."

"Okay. Will do. Be about ten minutes."

"Fine. Thank you." He put another quarter in and redialed . . .

"Tennessee Motor Courts, good morning."

"Morning! This is Conway with General Discount Stores—I'm going to be checkin' in this afternoon. Say, listen, I've got an envelope there with some cash in it, don't I?"

"One moment, sir."

"Sure."

"Yes, sir. There's an envelope for you."

"Does it have fifty dollars cash in it?"

"I don't know sir. We haven't opened it."

"Do me a favor please. I have a cab driver on his way over there. Would you open that? I'll take the responsibility."

"All right . . . Yes, there's money in here."

Fine. Would you please give the driver—no, I'll tell you what—ask him to pick up a package for me in Waterton. It's addressed to me in care of general delivery. Tell him there'll be a nice tip in it for him if he'll come back to the office with my package—save me a lot of driving around. Okay?"

The clerk agreed. But by the time the cab made it back to the motel with the large box full of clothing and accessories, Daniel Edward Flowers Bunkowski, née Conway, was back on the phone, this time wanting to speak to the driver. By coincidence he'd timed the call just as the man was coming in the office—but it helped that he was dialing from across the road.

This time he wanted the driver to bring the box to him and leave it at Discount Thrift on Central—just down the road from the motel. He instructed the office clerk to give the driver forty dollars "and keep a ten" for a gratuity.

He asked the driver if he knew where Discount Thrift was.

"Sure—couple blocks from here."

"That's it. You know the stone wall to the left of the front door?"

"Yeah?"

"Just toss the box up on the bank there. Okay?"

"If you say so, but don't blame me if it gets ripped off. Don't you want it left inside the door?"

"No. Not necessary. Just throw the box up on the bank to the left of the front door. Keep the forty for your trouble. Fair enough?"

"You got it." People never failed to amaze him, and they kept getting loonier by the day.

The watchers with eyeball surveillance on Chaingang saw him park his car, the same car they'd watched all along, on the gravel service road that ran in back of the busy Maysburg Shopping Center.

As always, the surveillance team leader kept a running account of movements on the battery-powered recorder all the agents carried:

"Blue Tracker Six: subject getting out of vehicle again . . . going over the fence between Taylor Chemical and the shopping center . . . moving on into the wooded area there." The two men in the front seat of the unmarked government car saw the huge man appear to unzip his pants, glance around, and then move behind some trees.

"Looks like he's going to urinate." They joked with each other about him going in the woods for a quick piece of fist. When he hadn't materialized in a couple of minutes, they looked at each other.

"What dya' think?"

"I'll go circle around by the center. You watch the woods on the side by the plant there. Stay with the car. If he comes back and leaves before I get back, I'll catch up with you tonight. 'Kay?"

"Go." The second man opened the door and jogged off around the woods. But Chaingang was long gone. That would be the penultimate observation they would make of him. Daniel Edward Flowers Bunkowski went into the woods, and something went wrong with the monitors—"a bobble in the power," the rural power company told them, apologetically. By the time a salesman by the name of Mr. Conway, resplendent in three-piece vested suit, tie, and wig, came out the other side, melting into the shopping center crowd, "technical difficulties" had developed. It seemed that the battery could die, after all . . . in a manner of speaking.

The lone watcher who monitored his movements only for Dr. Norman reported that the clear glass spectacles were a nice touch.

36

Washington, D.C.

The office was beautifully done. He had been in enough CEO and directorate executive suites and boardrooms to know this one had cost serious crown jewels. Not your run-of-the-penthouse leather-and-chrome Mies van der Roe-buck barcelona knockoffs and fake Manets. There were genuine antiques and real masters on the walls.

The two silent men who flanked him escorted him through the kings' throne room past the most beautifully ornate Wooten desk he'd ever seen, through a plush silk-walled anteroom where a tiny but unmistakable Braque was enshrined under subtle track portrait spots.

He was seated in the presence, across a polished cross section of rare wood approximately the size of a modular Rondesic home, and allowed a moment to gather whatever was left of his wits. A fierce neon by someone he didn't recognize, and a wonderful Larry Rivers, flanked the Man.

"Grant Silberman?" he said, with a question on the end, but it was clearly rhetorical. He tried to look sincere, contrite, studious, and worthy of forgiveness, all without changing anything in his face. "Aka Robert Newman, aka Christopher Sinclair. Chief of Section—" he made it sound like *Chief Dunderhead*—"and survivor of the debacle?"

"Yes, sir," he answered, quietly.

"Matters not." He gestured, and gold winked. "You know the old saying—shoot them all and you'll always get the guilty." The Man smiled, and poison dripped. "Not that it will have any exculpatory value, but just for some semblance of an explanation, how did Clandestine Services ever obtain the responsibility for the creation of anything as *insane* as a domestic-based school for *hit men?*"

He decided—fuck it—he'd just give straight answers and damn the torpedoes. To a point, anyway. The brain implant and their "ace" would remain in-house secrets.

"When the idea of a training program of this sort was first broached a quarter century ago, it was quite natural for it to come under the military intelligence umbrella. We were at war, unofficially, but at war nonetheless, and of course, it was a question of eminent domain. This would be the sphere of operations where such things should rightfully take place, so it was within Clandestine Services that the responsibility for the initial program fell."

"Were the initial stages of the program documented, and if so, in what form?"

"You mean memoranda from on high? Written orders?"

"When options were discussed, when the various beginnings of the program took place, were records kept?"

"Yes. There were many special memoranda, minutes of meetings, and general notes—which in turn would become support documents and position papers. The sensitivity of such documentation was such that many records were limited to only one copy, with a carefully monitored 'subscription' list. The lab people and the R & D people had their own records, naturally, so all we really saw would be the memos—their projections or appreciations of program development and personnel."

"Do you know if such records are still extant, and if so, where?"

"No, sir."

"An educated guess as to where such records might exist?"

"The head of the research and development for the project was a doctor who was working for the government, but I believe he is deceased. I have no idea. Presumably all records were destroyed due to the nature of the matter."

"How could such a program be put into play, given the enormity of horror with which most of us would receive anything along these lines?"

"It's difficult to explain how it all developed—these things develop over time and—"

"To play with human lives as if they were tokens on a game board! How could any of you live with yourselves?"

"I was following orders. In the military and in other—"

"The Nazis said the same thing. How does that excuse the killing you personally sanctioned?"

"I was doing my job. Nothing more. We were responsible to our government to create a team of expert, professional killers. Individuals capable of the most sensitive assassinations. We did not have such men. We had people with martial skills, law enforcement skills, men who could go to war for their country or things of this nature, but we did not have what the Committee for State Security or the SDECE—or for that matter, the Mossad—had. We were mandated to structure a program and get it rolling, and that's what we did. Many of us might have shared your horror at the idea of it, but we did our job. We were good soldiers."

"What made you think you could get away with it? What were the precedents for such a thing?"

"Well, there were precedents. There were parallel programs such as MK ULTRA, and the top secret STAR RACER. Those were programs created by the United States government to create killing machines, robot assassins, whatever you want to call them. But in our case we didn't want robots, we wanted experts. And it was . . . extremely difficult. But as to what made us think we could get away with it—we were building the program around a man who'd done just that for twenty years. He'd killed, again and again, and clearly he'd been able to get away with it. We wanted to learn what he knew, to study him, and to apply what we could learn to similar persons whom the government would employ for that work."

"So you decided to study a mass murderer?"

"Yes, Sir."

"And no one in Clandestine Services demurred? Everybody thought this was perfectly okay, this madness your superiors were proposing?"

"No, sir. There were many who thought it was evil, that it would be an awful disaster. But the program was going to be put in place over the protests of any analyst or tactical adviser or researcher. And when you're in an explosive program and under time constraints, the bureaucracy is even more quick to find scapegoats than usual. The ones who didn't see the program as workable, or who were too critical, they had a way of becoming part of the problem, and suddenly being transferred or demoted. There were only one or two appropriate responses—when you were asked if the thing would work, you said 'yes' or 'can do.'"

"Who was the force behind this program? There must have a guiding maniac who shoved this massacre through the bureaucracy?"

"There were many people who were forces behind the program, both in the military and out of it. Generals. People in intelligence. Admirals. Think-tank people. I'd say the doctor who ran the primary subject was the main person in the civilian sector. Everyone was looking to him to make it work, to establish control parameters and so on."

"Did this doctor, and we presume you mean Dr. Norman, answer to anyone higher up?"

"Yes, sir. He would have answered to the NSC and to the president, and to the director."

"The director of Clandestine Services?"

"Yes, sir."

"But presumably he directed that the subject be freed, and be encouraged to murder civilians, is that correct?"

"Yes."

"As chief of section, you were responsible for carrying out the orders of putting this killer in place, and of restraining his activities within a certain area?"

"Yes, sir."

"What resources were brought into the area to see that those activities would be confined to the specific area of operations?"

"We had over two hundred covert operations officers in place, over a hundred hunter-killer teams armed with silenced M3A1 machine guns, every high-tech air-land-sea surveillance device imaginable, any equipment or communications or transport mode we could wish for."

"And you thought this would be enough to keep a mass murderer within a certain geographical area?" The man asking the questions was incredulous.

"No, sir. We thought that because of the controls involved—the information the subject had been given free access to—that he'd operate in that zone for a minimal time, but when he attempted to escape, that he would be terminated."

"Uh-huh. That's what we're getting at. What made you think you could stop him—just because you had manpower and equipment?"

"We had him tracked every minute of the time the subject was in the killing zone. Overflights, satellite technology, infrared—we had the subject under a microscope . . . It seemed like he could be contained." The temptation to tell this bureaucratic stuffed shirt about the implant was almost overwhelming, but both the need-to-know criteria and the knowledge that he'd have to invent a plausible reason for OMEGASTAR malfunctioning were sufficient incentive to dissemble.

"Let's recap: A doctor working in the prison system convinces you and the rest of your outfit that a known serial killer can be manipulated like a lab experiment. That while he—and let me quote the record here—'and while he cannot be controlled, he can be handled by the manipulation of his hatred for humans, and his strong protective urges for animals.' That this could be achieved by—again I'm quoting—'a presentation of data which would effectively target specific individuals for assassination. Subject would be informed that targets lived in a community which had been carefully zoned for his protection, if he stayed within a twenty-five-mile radius. Subject would be transported to and set free in this area of operation, and his killing techniques would be surveilled and monitored to be studied and analyzed later. This would present the service with a unique opportunity to produce a fully documented clinical study of a mass murderer's behavioristic modes, in a civilian setting, under textbook conditions. Was that about the size of it?"

"Yes. It would be a dual operation, a 'field appraisal' of an actual series of premeditated assassinations, and because there had been some problems in the securing of a location for the assassination school, which had involved the termination with prejudice of certain indigenous personnel, the actions of the subject would serve as cover."

"But what about the killing of innocents? What about the danger to the community?"

"These were deemed acceptable risk factors."

"But . . . even if such a school had to exist, why did it have to be built in this particular country town? Why couldn't it have been located in any suitably desolate locale?"

"There were several sites which were geographically suitable, sufficiently low population density, heartland centrality, that type of thing, quick access to major airports—the various logistical and geographical criteria were met. Then after what we called the "spoon-feeds" were done and we had the communities where a school could be put in place, each one was investigated for prevalence of animal abuses and so on, which were the control factors."

"So you had your location and your mad-dog killer working for you, and all the cameras going, and two hundred people in the bushes with machine guns—and not only do you idiots let a madman slay fifty civilians, you let him get away!"

"Yes, sir."

"But how can that be?"

"We fucked up." He wondered how the wife and kid would like it in Reykyavik.

37

Waterton Two Months later

ROYCE HAWTHORNE was never terminated. ELINT rescinded the contract when SAUCOG'S murderer-at-large hit one of their own surveillance teams. That tore it. If they wanted anybody else hit, they could do it themselves.

MARY PERKINS started studying for her Missouri Real Estate Sales License, got serious about aerobics, and turned Royce on to health foods.

SAM PERKINS'S remains were among those positively identified in the mass grave site uncovered in the explosions that blew apart Ecoworld's concrete footings. Subsequent excavation revealed six males and two females, with predominant cause of death recorded in autopsy findings as "chemically induced pulmonary embolism(s)."

ECOWORLD, what was left of it, was sold to a Maysburg, Tennessee, investor group in search of a quick tax write-off, but development of their "high-concept entertainment mall" was halted.

GRANT SILBERMAN (aka Robert Newman, Christopher Sinclair, etc.), along with his wife and child, were killed in an automobile mishap, while vacationing in the Great Smoky Mountains.

GABRIEL "GABE" AUGUSTINE, whose Ready-Mix company was principal low bidder on the ill-fated Ecoworld job, won one of the largest lien judgments ever awarded in the state of Missouri. He purchased a three-thousand-acre cattle ranch in Montana, and the family estate included a Ready-Mix runway in the shape of a huge concrete letter A.

"MEAN" DEAN SEABAUGH was found dead in one of the Genneret stables. He'd suffered a broken neck, and it is believed he may have been kicked in the head by a horse.

DOYLE GENNERET was blinded when a package he received in the mail exploded in his face. Authorities determined that a "sophisticated letter bomb of the type favored by terrorists" had been sent to him by an unknown individual.

DANIEL EDWARD FLOWERS BUKOWSKI disappeared. He was last seen clean-shaven, sweet-smelling, and wearing a charcoal three-piece suit. "He was a big, heavyset guy with glasses. Mr. Conway, he said, from Marion, Illinois. Seemed like a real nice old boy," a motel desk clerk told police. He was last observed in legal wheels, heading northbound on I-55.

CLANDESTINE SERVICES became "The Fifteen Group," and that became something else. The assassination school was abandoned.

SAUCOG vanished. There is only one official record that the unit ever existed. *A Chronology of U.S. Military Roles in Southeast Asia* (vol. II), published by the Histories and Museums Division of the Tactical Institute of Military Sciences, states:

"For a brief period U.S. Military Assistance Command Vietnam/Special Advisory Unit/Combined Operations Group (USAMACSAUCOG) assumed tactical responsibility for the planning and execution phases of various operations mounted by their Covert Action Team(s).

"Following execution of these missions, USAMACVSAUCOG withdrew all personnel from the TAOR(s) and tactical responsibilities were reassigned to the Vietnamese military in place."

REX MILLER. has had many different jobs and several obsessions. He has been a radio broadcaster and has done voiceovers and announcing for nation-wide radio and television programs. Mr. Miller's obsessions have also proved fruitful, and he is considered one of America's most knowledgeable authorities on popular culture memorabilia and the culture of nostalgia in general. His many novels include SLOB, STONE SHADOW, and THE EICHORD SAGA, which deals with the ongoing battle between Good and Evil.

CPSIA information can be obtained at www.ICGtesting.com
Printed in the USA
BVOW031516020212

282032BV00001B/36/A

9 781585 860791